Who wants an Amish cowboy?

Annie liked a challenge. She thrived in tough situations. Tossing her *kapp* strings behind her shoulders, she plastered on what she hoped was her prettiest smile. "All right. You agree to date a couple of my friends…not at the same time, mind you."

"Of course not," Levi agreed.

"And in return, I won't try and stop you from talking to my family about moving to Texas."

"So now you're a matchmaker?"

"Think of me as a concerned bystander."

"All right. It's a deal." He held out his hand. "But you have to shake on it."

But, just possibly, she'd found a way to keep her life firmly rooted in Goshen, because she had the perfect woman in mind for Levi Lapp and this person would never consider moving away.

All Annie had to do was see to it that the two of them fell in love. It would mean she'd have to live around Levi the rest of her life…but at least she wouldn't have to do so in Texas.

Vannetta Chapman has published over one hundred articles in Christian family magazines and received over two dozen awards from Romance Writers of America chapter groups. She discovered her love for the Amish while researching her grandfather's birthplace of Albion, Pennsylvania. Her first novel, *A Simple Amish Christmas*, quickly became a bestseller. Chapman lives in Texas Hill Country with her husband.

Debby Giusti is an award-winning Christian author who met and married her military husband at Fort Knox, Kentucky. Together they traveled the world, raised three wonderful children and have now settled in Atlanta, Georgia, where Debby spins tales of mystery and suspense that touch the heart and soul. Visit Debby online at debbygiusti.com, blog with her at seekerville.blogspot.com and craftieladiesofromance.blogspot.com and email her at Debby@DebbyGiusti.com.

VANNETTA CHAPMAN

The Amish Christmas Matchmaker

&

DEBBY GIUSTI

Amish Christmas Secrets

LOVE INSPIRED

INSPIRATIONAL ROMANCE

LOVE INSPIRED®
INSPIRATIONAL ROMANCE

Recycling programs
for this product may
not exist in your area.

ISBN-13: 978-1-335-22990-8

The Amish Christmas Matchmaker and Amish Christmas Secrets

Copyright © 2020 by Harlequin Books S.A.

The Amish Christmas Matchmaker
First published in 2019. This edition published in 2020.
Copyright © 2019 by Vannetta Chapman

Amish Christmas Secrets
First published in 2018. This edition published in 2020.
Copyright © 2018 by Deborah W. Giusti

This edition published by arrangement with Harlequin Books S.A.

For questions and comments about the quality of this book, please contact us at CustomerService@Harlequin.com.

Harlequin Enterprises ULC
22 Adelaide St. West, 40th Floor
Toronto, Ontario M5H 4E3, Canada
www.Harlequin.com

Printed in U.S.A.

CONTENTS

THE AMISH
CHRISTMAS MATCHMAKER

Vannetta Chapman

This book is dedicated to Bob, my very own cowboy.

Delight thyself also in the Lord:
and he shall give thee the desires of thine heart.
—*Psalm* 37:4

Thou shalt love thy neighbor as thyself.
There is none other commandment greater.
—*Mark* 12:31

Chapter One

Annie Kauffmann thought she'd just experienced a perfect day—business had gone well, the fall weather was exquisite and each member of her family was happy and healthy. She leaned her bicycle against the tree in the front yard and ran up the porch steps. Her mother was sitting in a rocker, knitting a baby blanket for her next grandchild. She had twelve and counting. If her mother was sitting, she was knitting—blankets, sweaters, caps and mittens.

"*Gut* day?" she asked.

"*Ya.*" Annie sank into a rocker, smoothing her apron over her dress and sinking back with a sigh. "I confirmed two more weddings."

"Your catering business is growing."

"It is. The *gut* thing about these is one is for December…"

"Not many winter weddings, so you must be speaking of Widow Schwartz."

"The same. The other is for later this month."

"You had an opening this month?"

"*Ya*, since you know… Jesse's was cancelled."

"Real shame that Emma changed her mind. I believe she'll regret that."

"Maybe not though, Mamm. Maybe not."

Annie was suddenly aware of voices in the house—her father and another man. She peeked out over the porch railing, wondering whose buggy she had missed, but there wasn't one there.

"Who is Dat talking to?"

"I believe his name is Levi."

"Levi King?"

"*Nein.* Levi Lapp."

"I don't know a Levi Lapp."

"He's new here."

"New?"

"Arrived yesterday."

"Did he walk?"

"I imagine he rode a bus to town, but he walked here today to see your *dat.*"

"Who does he know in Goshen?"

"He's staying with Simon King."

"Is he related to Old Simon?"

"I'm not sure."

Now Annie's curiosity was thoroughly piqued. "I think I need a glass of lemonade. Can I get you anything?"

Mamm smiled, not fooled for a minute. "Of course, dear. I would love that."

Annie stepped into the coolness of the house. Though it was September, the temperatures had remained warm, and the cool living room was a relief after her bike ride from town. Her father and Levi Lapp were in the kitchen, which would work perfectly. She straightened her apron, made sure her *kapp* wasn't askew and walked into the kitchen as if she had no idea she was interrupting.

She aimed for a casual stride but stumbled when she spied the man in a cowboy hat. A cowboy hat? She shook her head as if that would clear up what she was seeing.

"Annie. I'm glad you're home. I want you to meet Levi… Levi Lapp."

"Hello."

Levi tipped the cowboy hat, revealing blond hair that curled at his collar. "Howdy, ma'am."

Howdy, ma'am?

Had she fallen asleep and landed in a Western? "I'm Annie."

"It's nice to meet you."

"And you, as well. I was just fetching two glasses of lemonade. Don't let me interrupt…"

"Levi's from Pennsylvania—the Lancaster Plain community."

"*Ya?* I imagine it's cooler there." She didn't care about the weather in Pennsylvania, but she couldn't exactly ask about the hat.

"It was cooler when I left. Now Texas, where I plan to go, is still much warmer. They have days in the eighties right through November."

"Texas?" Annie had pulled two glasses from the cabinet. At the mention of Texas she turned toward Levi, holding the glasses and trying to remember what she was going to do with them.

He wasn't ugly exactly, only odd looking because of the hat. He seemed to be tall and on the thin side, had a healthy tan and broad shoulders. His blue eyes twinkled as if he understood her confusion and was enjoying it.

Annie raised her chin a fraction higher. "I wasn't aware there were Plain communities in Texas."

"Oh, *ya*. There's one in Beeville, which has been there nearly twenty years. Only a few families, though."

"And you're going there?" It was really none of her business. She placed the glasses on the counter and walked over to the propane-powered refrigerator. Removing the pitcher of lemonade, she held it up, but her *dat* waved her away, and Levi didn't seem to notice. A dreamy expression had come over his face. It was as if he'd been transported to another place. She'd seen that look before—usually on a man who was smitten with a girl.

"Not to Beeville, to Stephenville."

"But you said…"

"There's no community there now, but there was. It's where I grew up."

"You should hear the stories he tells, Annie." Her *dat* leaned back and crossed his arms. "Rolling hills, space for a family to grow, cattle and horses…"

Now she was noticing the starry look in her *dat*'s eyes. She'd seen that before. The last time, it was because he was dreaming of moving to a pig farm in Missouri that he'd read about in *The Budget*.

So that's what this was.

Another one of his daydreams.

Nothing to worry about there. This Levi fellow would probably be gone by the end of the week.

"*Gut* people too," Levi added. "Texans are quite friendly toward Plain folk."

Her *dat* thumped the table. "Sounds *wunderbaar*. Just what I've been thinking of."

Annie didn't answer that. What was the point? This

was the way Dat's crazy ideas went. By next week he'd have moved on to raising exotic animals or trying a new crop. She loved her *dat*, loved everything about him, but she'd learned long ago not to worry about his wild ideas. She had a business to run—a thriving wedding-catering business here in Goshen, Indiana. The last thing she needed to concern herself with was pulling up roots and moving to Texas.

Instead, she poured the lemonade into the glasses, smiled at her *dat* and the Amish cowboy sitting at their table and said, "I'll leave you two to your discussion, then. It was nice to meet you, Levi."

"And you."

He tipped the ridiculous hat again and smiled as if she'd said something witty. Not just a cowboy, but a charming one to boot.

Levi spoke with Alton Kauffmann another fifteen minutes. When his wife, Lily, came in and started making dinner, he knew it was time to go.

She smiled at him as she pulled what looked like the mixings of a ham casserole from the refrigerator. "It's nice meeting you, Levi. I hope you'll come visit again."

"Oh, he will," Alton said. "The bishop has come up with a work schedule for Levi, since he's new to the area. He'll be helping me here two afternoons a week— Wednesdays and Fridays."

"We'll expect you to stay for dinner on those days… if you can."

"*Danki.* I appreciate that."

Alton said something about checking on the horses, so Levi let himself out the front door. Annie was sitting in one of the rockers, writing in a journal. She didn't immediately notice him, and so he was able to study her for a minute.

Young—she couldn't have been over twenty.

Pretty—not that he was interested. He was here to recruit families to move to Texas, not court a woman.

Focused—she still hadn't looked up.

Levi cleared his throat. "Pretty place you have here."

"*Ya*, it is." She finally glanced up. "*Danki.*"

"Reminds me a little of Texas, the way the hills stretch out to the west…"

He could still see it in his mind. He wished he had pictures to show her, but of course being Plain they didn't usually fool around with cameras, even the ones on cell phones. He had a few Texas magazines that he'd brought with him. He'd have to remember to bring one over the next afternoon when he came to help Alton.

"You were awfully intent on what you were doing there." He nodded toward her journal.

"Oh. I have a catering business…for Plain weddings. I keep all my notes and calendar in here."

"That's interesting. I've never met an Amish businesswoman before."

"Really? You've never purchased something from a local bakery?"

"Oh, *ya*. Sure."

"Or bought fresh jam?"

"Peach and strawberry." He moved to the rocking chair beside her, placed the knitting basket that was in it on the porch floor and sat.

"All run by women entrepreneurs I would imagine… Plain women entrepreneurs. You can find them in nearly every bakery and fruit stand—not to mention quilt shops and yarn shops. They are also house cleaners and most of our teachers. Schoolhouses aren't a business, but you get my point."

"I do. Obviously, this is a subject you've given a lot of thought."

"I have."

She raised her chin like she had in the kitchen. It almost made him laugh. She was a spunky one.

"I've offended you, and I'm sorry. It wasn't my intention."

She considered him a minute and then closed her journal. "It's possible I'm a little sensitive about the topic, being an entrepreneur myself."

"So tell me about your business."

"Not much to tell. I cater weddings."

"I thought…"

"That the family of the bride cooks the food? *Ya.* A lot of people think that. But when you consider that most of our weddings have over 400 guests…well, the mothers of the bride and groom have an increasingly difficult time cooking for a gathering of that size."

"Maybe they could invite less people."

"And put me out of business? No thank you." Her tone was serious, but she smiled at his joke. "How did you land in Goshen? We're a good ways from Lancaster, Pennsylvania."

Levi didn't respond immediately because the actual answer was complicated. He certainly didn't want to go into his family situation with this young woman he'd known less than twenty minutes. And how could he explain how he'd vowed never to return to this area when he was still just a boy? Goshen did not hold good memories for him, but here he was. He decided to go with the simplest, though less complete answer. "My family knows Simon King. He lived with us in Texas, and he's interested in possibly returning."

"Mamm mentioned you were staying with Simon. We call him Old Simon because there are two others in the congregation—Tall Simon and Young Simon. Young Simon is older than Tall Simon but younger than Old Simon." She laughed and then added, "You know how Plain communities are."

"I do, and he's not that old."

"I'm just surprised he'd be interested in moving at his age."

"I suppose that since his wife died, he's a bit lonely. We stayed in contact over the years. When I mentioned that I was raising up a group to start a new community, he was interested."

"How many families do you need?"

"A dozen is the usual number, with at least one church leader."

"And that would be Old Simon?"

"It would."

"How many families do you have so far?"

"There's myself, Simon and possibly your *dat*."

Annie covered her mouth with her hands. It took Levi a minute to realize she was laughing. It irritated him, though he couldn't have said why.

"What's so funny?"

"I'm sorry." She pulled her lips into a straight line, and stared down at her lap, smoothing out her apron with her fingertips. Obviously, she was making a huge effort to rein in her amusement.

"No, tell me."

"It's only that Dat…"

"Yes?"

"I hope he hasn't raised your hopes. Mamm says he likes to dream, that it's entertainment for him like some people might read a book. It's harmless enough. We've all learned not to take him too seriously in that regard."

Levi stood and pushed his cowboy hat more firmly on his head, but Annie was now on a roll.

"Once he was going to move us to Canada...there are Amish communities there, you know."

"I'm aware."

"Another time, it was a pig farm he was going to purchase, in Missouri, and then there was his idea to raise camels. He checked out a lot of books from the library for that one."

"I would think you'd show more respect for your *dat*. It seems that you don't take what's important to him very seriously."

"You're an expert on my *dat* now?"

"I can tell when a man has a dream."

"Like you?"

"*Ya*, like me."

Annie stood as well and moved a step closer. She gazed up into his face. She looked at him in the same way his mother often had, and it only served to increase his irritation even more. There were always some who were closed-minded, who couldn't see the possibilities of a fresh start in a new place.

"I don't mean to be rude, Levi. However, if you're counting on my family moving to Texas, you should know that's not going to happen."

Instead of contradicting her, he said, "I'm glad I'll have plenty of time to speak to your family about this."

"Speak to them?"

"Since I'll be working here two days a week."

"You're going to be working here?"

"It's nice to meet you, Annie. Perhaps we can continue this conversation tomorrow. Your *mamm* has invited me to stay for dinner."

She crossed her arms and scowled at him as he turned and made his way down the porch steps.

Levi gave her a backward wave, but he didn't look back.

He wanted to. Annie Kauffmann made a pretty picture standing on the front porch with fall leaves pooled at her feet and a cat rubbing against her legs. He didn't allow himself a last glance, though. He knew all about naysayers, people who said it couldn't or shouldn't be done. He'd been stopped by them long enough.

This time, he had a plan.

If things went well, he'd be in Texas by spring.

Chapter Two

Annie managed to avoid Levi on Wednesday when he came to help her father in the fields. They owned a mere eighty acres, but her *dat* used every bit of it. He adamantly believed in varying the crops, which increased the amount of work but also improved the harvest. The hay wouldn't be ready to cut for another two months. The sorghum would need to be harvested by the end of October, soybeans after that, and winter wheat had to be planted as well.

There was always work to be done on a farm.

It wasn't unusual for their bishop to arrange for young Amish men from out of town to find some work, and it was true that her father needed help, but she wasn't sure Levi Lapp was the kind of help he needed. Like the first day he'd spent time with Levi, her *dat* spent Wednesday evening asking enthusiastic questions about Texas over dinner.

"Big ranches there?"

"Some are. The King Ranch is bigger than the state of Rhode Island."

"You don't say."

"Many are smaller family places, though. Like we would have."

Annie and her *mamm* shared a look, but her mother merely shook her head. They'd been through this before. It was best to let the dream run its course. If this went the way of her *dat*'s other ideas, he'd move on to something else before the end of the week. So she endured dinner with Levi and tried to simply nod and appear polite. Had he swallowed an entire encyclopedia of Texas trivia? She couldn't resist commenting when he laughingly told them about the Texas state mammal.

"They have three, actually. The longhorn is the large state mammal. The Mexican free-tailed bat is the flying state mammal. And the nine-banded armadillo is the small state mammal. Those are quite a sight to see. They can run up to thirty miles an hour..."

"Why would they need to run for an hour?"

Levi seemed to consider the question seriously, and Annie was suddenly sorry she'd asked it.

"I suppose they wouldn't. My point is they're fast, and they can jump straight up too. I've seen them jump..." he held a hand level with the table. "At least that high. It's something else."

Now she was irritated. In truth, she'd been irritated since he'd sat down and started spouting facts and figures. "Aren't they just large rats with shells?"

"More like an anteater or a sloth."

"Who would choose that for their state mammal?"

"Texans would. In fact, they did in 1927." He said all of this slowly, as if she were a child and couldn't grasp the concept.

Her mother jumped in and started talking about the possibility of rain, and Annie soon lost track of the conversation. Thinking back over what she'd said as she washed the dishes, she was rather proud of herself. At least she hadn't laughed at him. She hadn't openly mocked him, but what was his deal? Why did he act as if Texas were the promised land?

She'd simply have to pray for extra strength to curb her tongue when she was around him.

Friday that wasn't so easy.

On Friday, Levi managed to tax her patience to the limit.

It didn't help that she had a wedding the next day, the florist had ordered roses instead of mums and she'd spent ten hours in the kitchen cooking and shredding chicken. When Levi and her father trotted inside, leaving muddy prints across the floor she'd just cleaned, Annie thought she might flip like pancakes on a griddle. Things went downhill from there.

She placed a dish of chicken potpie in the middle of the table. Beside it was a loaf of fresh bread, butter and a large salad. Her *mamm* came in asking about the field work, and they all sat down to eat—including Levi. The serving bowls had barely been passed when her *dat* started in on the Texas trivia points for the day.

"Levi was telling me about Texas longhorns."

Levi held his hands up to his head and then spread them as far apart as possible. "Big longhorns."

"Horns curve outward and can measure up to eight feet in length," her father said. "Sharp on the end, but apparently they're gentle animals."

"Most are." Levi reached for an extra piece of bread. "Best to check with the owner before approaching one."

Annie dropped her fork onto her helping of chicken potpie and gave Levi her most critical look. It always worked when she substituted at their local school, but

Levi simply shoveled in another forkful of chicken pie and grinned at her.

"Great dinner," he said after he'd swallowed.

She learned about the rivers that often ran dry, the terribly hot summer temperatures—her father laughed at that as if such a thing would be eons better than their pleasant summers—and even about their wildflowers.

Finally, she said, "If you'll excuse me, I need to load up my trailer."

"I can help with that," Levi said.

"*Nein*—"

"How kind of you, Levi." Her *mamm* stood and began picking up dishes. "Accept his help, Annie, and your *dat* and I can clean up this kitchen."

Annie couldn't remember the last time she'd seen her father help with the dishes. This was plainly a trick to throw her and Levi together, and she couldn't imagine what her mother was thinking. Unless…maybe she was hoping that she would set Levi straight. She could certainly do that.

"Okay then. *Danki*, Levi. If you'll pick up those boxes of cooked chicken, I'll bring the loaves of bread." The bread tray was clumsier but lighter. The chicken would have taken her at least two trips, but Levi picked up both large boxes and looked around as if he were wondering what else he could carry.

They were barely out the back door when he started in with his questions.

"You have a wedding tomorrow? I thought most Amish weddings were on Tuesday or Thursday."

He was tall and his shadow leaped out in front of them as if it was leading the way. The thought annoyed Annie, though she supposed he had no control over his shadow.

"Tomorrow's wedding is a special situation. This

family has relatives who live out of town. They couldn't arrive until late on a Friday afternoon, so we scheduled the wedding for a Saturday."

"You cater a lot of weddings?"

"*Ya*, I do…" She turned toward him when they reached her trailer, ready to confront him about this Texas issue. Then she looked over her shoulder, and the sight of her mobile kitchen eased the knot of tension in her shoulders. "You can bring those inside."

The trailer was small, but she was proud of it. Inside was a mobile kitchen—with dishes for five hundred people, propane-powered refrigerators, three stoves that provided her with a dozen burners, plus a large industrial-sized oven that was six feet tall. On the side, they'd had stenciled the words *Plain & Simple Weddings* in a black italic font.

She set the trays with loaves of fresh bread in the oven. It was taller than she was and would hold the loaves just fine. She didn't have to turn it on, because the loaves were already baked. She'd heat them before the luncheon. When he handed her the boxes of chicken, she took each platter out and set it in one of the propane refrigerators, which she'd turned on earlier in the day.

Levi's eyes widened as he looked around, and he let out a long whistle. "Wow. Some setup you have here."

"It is, and it took time and a lot of work to be able to afford it."

"You pull this with your buggy?"

"No, I don't pull it with my buggy. That would be illegal, not to mention unsafe." She nudged him back out the door of the trailer.

"Then how…"

She waved away his question. She had no intention of telling him the ins and outs of her business. He didn't need to know that she had an *Englisch* partner who owned a large pickup truck. Though she could imagine what Priscilla would say about Levi, and that eased even more of the tension in her neck. Priscilla would call him tall-fair-and-yummy.

She walked out of the trailer and said a quick prayer for patience and wisdom. She seemed to need large helpings of both around Levi Lapp. "I need to talk to you about my *dat*."

"Oh. He's a nice guy. You have a *wunderbaar* family."

"*Ya*, I do." She thought to ask him about his family, but she didn't want to get distracted. "Look, I wish you well in finding a group to start in Texas…"

"Your *dat* seems quite keen about the idea."

"That's the thing I wanted to talk to you about. Remember what I told you before? Dat gets excited about an idea, usually for about a week."

"Maybe this time is different."

"It isn't."

"How can you know that?"

"Because I know him. He's a *gut* worker, a *gut* provider and a *gut* husband and *dat*. He doesn't smoke or drink or run around."

"Which would make him a great addition to my group."

"We're not moving to Texas!" The words came out more sharply than she'd intended, and for a moment the ever-present smile slipped from Levi's face.

Finally, she was getting through to him.

Or so she thought.

"Change is hard. I understand. And you have this thriving business…"

"Which I have no intention of packing up and moving to Stephenville, Texas."

"Might not be Stephenville. It would depend on where we can find good land at a reasonable price."

"You're missing my point." Maybe she should try appealing to his sense of right and wrong. "Mamm and I like it here. My *bruders*, they live close enough that they're able to help with the harvest. My *schweschder* lives down the road. We have *freinden* and family here, and I have a thriving business. We. Are. Not. Moving."

She'd moved out in front of him, but he scooted around her and plopped down on the step which led up into the trailer. She stood there, arms crossed, waiting for the truth of what she was saying to sink in beneath his cowboy hat.

"I think what you're actually trying to say is that you'd like me to stop speaking to your *dat* about a move."

"Exactly."

"Would you also like me to quit working for him?"

"What? No. Obviously, he's satisfied with your work, and he needs the help."

"Would you rather I didn't stay for dinner?"

"Of course not. Mamm doesn't mind, and it certainly makes no difference to me."

"So I'm allowed to work here and eat here, but only if I watch what I say."

She was shaking her head before he finished talking. "I'm not the boss of you."

"That's true. You are not."

When he glanced up at her, she was discouraged to see that his normally amiable expression had changed into something more stubborn. Something probably resembling a Texas mule, if they looked any different than Indiana mules.

She cleared her throat and tried a different approach.

"I admire what you're trying to do. I'm simply asking that you consider the situation of my family. We're happy here. Don't stir Dat up with all this talk of longhorns and wildflowers."

"Okay." He stood and clamped the ridiculous cowboy hat down more firmly on his head.

"Okay?"

"*Ya.*"

"Just like that?"

"Seems a fair enough request."

"I agree. That's why I made it."

"*Gut* day to you then." With a quick smile, he turned and walked toward the lane. As if he'd just thought of something, he stopped, took off the hat, scratched his head and then turned back toward her. "Tell your parents *gut* evening, and *danki* again for the meal."

Annie stared after him, wondering what had just happened.

Why had he agreed so readily?

Why was he smiling?

What was she missing here?

Those things didn't matter. What mattered was that they could put this silly matter of Texas behind them, and she could go back to focusing on her business. Though it was only September, she'd already passed the previous year's profit. Now if she could have a strong fall, she'd feel in a good position for starting the new year.

A new year in Goshen, Indiana, not on the wild plains of Texas.

Amish families tended to eat dinner early—that way they could go out and do the evening chores before things were too dark to see well. The sun had dipped toward the west and a pleasant coolness had settled in

as Levi walked down the road, away from the Kauff-
mans' and toward Old Simon's.

He was thinking of how pretty and stubborn Annie
was, how focused she was on that catering business—as
if it were all that mattered—and the way her cheeks colored pink when she was angry. He was wondering what
it was about himself that irked her so much, when an
Amish man working on a fence line called out to him.

"You must be the fellow helping out my father-in-law."

"I'm Levi. Levi Lapp. If your father-in-law is Alton
Kauffmann, then *ya*. I'm helping him out two afternoons a week."

"Thought so."

"What gave me away?"

"You're the only Amish person I've ever seen wearing a cowboy hat. By the way, I'm Jebediah. I'm married to Alton's middle daughter, Nicole."

"Nice to meet you."

Jebediah didn't seem in any hurry to finish mending the fence. Instead he leaned against one of the fence
posts and started peppering him with questions. "Heard
you're from Texas. What was that like? Also heard you
were going back. When do you expect to do that? And do
you really think you'll convince Alton to go with you?"

Levi laughed. "It doesn't take long for word to get
around."

"You know how it is."

"I do." Levi scanned the horizon and wondered how
best to address Jebediah's questions. As usual, his enthusiasm for the subject won out over any instinct that
might have told him to approach the subject slowly.
"Texas was *wunderbaar*, and I've been trying to get
back pretty much since we left, which was twelve years

ago when I was fourteen. I hope to move down in the spring. Now that I have a church elder interested—"

"Old Simon?"

"Ya."

"He's not in the best of shape."

"He's not in the worst, either, and once we're there, I think others will come."

"Maybe."

Jebediah's comments were nothing like Annie's. He didn't sound critical of the idea so much as skeptical. A skeptic he could handle.

"You should think about going with us."

"Can't say as I'm interested myself, but if Alton goes, well that might be a different story. My wife is pretty attached to her family, which is *gut* because mine is in Ohio and we can't afford land there."

"Land in Texas is cheap."

"Is it now?" Jebediah grinned as if he'd heard that one before. "Cheap doesn't really matter if you don't have any money, which I don't. Married four years ago, and we have three *boppli* with another on the way. Every cent I makes gets plucked from my hand like a north wind snatched it away."

"That doesn't bother you?"

"Not really. We have what we need."

Levi wasn't sure how to answer that. It was a common sentiment among Amish men and women alike. He had a little trouble relating. It wasn't that he wanted more. It was only that he wanted something different than what he had.

"I don't want to keep you from mending that fence, and I best get on before Old Simon wonders what happened to me."

"See you tomorrow then."

"Tomorrow?" Levi had already turned away, but now he turned back to Jebediah. "Oh, I don't work for Alton on Saturdays. That's my day to stay and help Old Simon."

He'd even started calling the old guy that, and he'd only learned the nickname recently.

"I mean that I'll see you at the wedding."

"Wedding?"

"Beth and Avery. Old Simon will be there for sure and certain—everyone will. It'll be a *gut* time for you to meet folks."

The wedding that Annie had been preparing for. He suddenly realized that he'd like to see her in action, serving the masses from her tiny trailer. "I don't even know them."

"You're invited nonetheless. You're a part of our community now. Everyone's invited."

Those words echoed through Levi's mind as he walked the last half mile to Old Simon's house. *You're a part of our community now.* It was a simple yet common sentiment among Plain folks. You moved in; you were accepted.

So why had he never felt at home in Lancaster?

Why did he have such terrible memories of his time here in Goshen?

Maybe because he'd resented his community's decision from the day they'd abandoned the Texas community. Maybe because the move had been difficult for his parents, not to mention his siblings. The old ache twisted in his gut, but he chose to ignore it.

That was his past.

His future was to the south and moving closer every day.

He arrived home to find Simon sitting on the back

porch, an open Bible in his lap. He barely seemed to look down at the well-worn pages. In fact, Levi had surmised that the old guy's eyesight had weakened to the point that he couldn't read the words printed there, but it seemed to soothe him to hold the open Bible.

He also was a terrible driver. It was a good thing that the buggy horse practically drove itself, or they would have been killed on Levi's first day in town.

"Preparing for your sermon?"

"Ya." Simon looked up in surprise, so apparently, he hadn't heard Levi enter through the front door or the banging of the back screen door as he'd come outside. Maybe his hearing was going too, but a smile spread across his face.

He was a nice old guy, terribly lonely since his wife had died the year before. Their children were in Kentucky. Levi had written to both sons before he had accepted Old Simon's invitation to move to Goshen. He didn't want to be the source of hard feelings in the family. The eldest son had explained that they were trying to convince Simon to move, but that so far he'd resisted. Levi didn't share with Jonah his hopes that Simon would move to Texas with him. He didn't lie about it. The subject just didn't come up.

Old Simon patted the Bible. *"Gotte*'s word—it's a lamp for my feet and a light for my path."

"Is that what your sermon will be on?" Levi eased onto the floor of the porch, bracing his back against the porch column.

"Maybe," Simon said. "As the Lord leads."

"I met Jebediah this afternoon."

"He's a *gut* man and about your age, if I remember right."

"Told me about the wedding tomorrow."

Simon's expression turned to one of concern, but then he tapped his forefinger against the arm of the rocker and said, "I knew there was something I was forgetting. We have a wedding tomorrow."

"He said I was welcome to attend, even though I don't know Beth and Avery."

"Who?"

"The couple getting married."

"Oh. That's right. It is a *gut* idea for you to go. I assumed you would. Weddings are a *gut* place to meet people, and maybe a young lady will catch your eye." Simon grinned and then turned his attention out to the family garden. He hadn't put that in himself. A neighbor must have done it for him. He didn't seem to see the last of the vegetables that waited to be gathered, though. Instead he spoke of the past. "Did I ever tell you where I met my *fraa*, Tabitha?"

"You didn't."

"It was at a local wedding. I knew the minute I saw her that she was the one." He pressed his fingertips against his chest. "Something in my heart…just told me."

Levi didn't know how to answer that, so he stood and said, "I ate with the Kauffmanns. Have you had anything yet?"

Simon shook his head and turned his eyes back to the pages of his Bible. "Can't say as I'm hungry."

"I'll go and fix you an egg with some of that ham we had left over. You need to eat."

"*Ya.* Okay."

Levi walked into the kitchen and set about putting together a simple meal for the old man. Working in the kitchen reminded him of Annie's lecture about women entrepreneurs. Levi was fine with that. He didn't see any problem with women starting businesses. In his experience, they often had excellent perspectives on what customers wanted to purchase.

He actually admired her for starting an Amish catering business, but he sensed that her passion might become a roadblock for his own plans. Alton wouldn't want to leave unless his entire family was behind the idea. And Annie obviously was dead set against it. It wasn't absolutely necessary to have Alton in his group, but it would help. And it might mean that Jebediah and his family would come, as well.

All he had to do was win Annie over to the idea.

Which, he knew, would be no simple task.

As he heated the cast-iron pan, fried an egg and put it on the plate with fresh bread and a slice of ham, he thought of the words of his *daddi*.

No dream comes true unless you wake up and go to work.

He'd known it wouldn't be easy to start a community in Texas, but he was willing to work. He only had to convince ten more families and then they could send two men down to look for land. Goshen was a big community. Regardless what Annie said, he thought that Alton would follow through on this dream. Indiana Amish weren't as set in their ways like Pennsylvania Amish, or at least that was how it seemed so far.

Then again, he could be merely seeing what he wanted to see. Time would tell—though he didn't have much of that. They needed to form a group, decide on some basic rules and then send down scouts. They needed to do all of those things in the next few months. After all, planting season in Texas started early.

Chapter Three

Levi didn't have a chance to talk to many people before the wedding. Amish weddings started rather early in the day—on account of they were long and they needed to be finished in time for lunch. Then there were games for the young adults and children, and after that, most of the teens and young married folk stayed for dinner.

Beth and Avery's ceremony was taking place outside, so it was fortunate that the day dawned mild and sunny. In fact, it was a perfect fall day. He watched families assemble across the benches that had been set out in the backyard of the Stutzman farm, but his mind was on Annie Kauffmann. He'd had only one glimpse of her when he and Old Simon were walking from their buggy to the house. He was thinking of how he hoped to have time to talk to Alton again when he spied Annie darting from her trailer toward the back porch.

How did she manage to move that trailer there?

When did she find the time to cook enough food for all of these people?

Did she enjoy cooking that much?

And why wasn't she married? She was a nice-enough-looking woman and pleasant, other than her dislike of Texas. Or maybe it was him that she disliked. It was hard to tell.

He was chasing that line of thought when the hymn singing started. Old Simon led the congregation in a prayer, then there was more singing, a short sermon, and finally, the soon-to-be-married couple stood in front of everyone.

It seemed to him like they'd only been there a few minutes. He was surprised when he glanced at his watch and saw that ninety minutes had already passed.

As he watched the couple exchange their vows, his mind slipped back to Annie. Did she need help readying the wedding lunch? Probably not. No doubt she'd catered many weddings before without his help, but then again, perhaps volunteering would soften her up a little.

Before he could properly think that through, they were singing again and then the bishop—an older guy named Marcus with a beard that was more salt than pepper—reminded everyone to stay for the meal and led them in a time of silent blessing. The next thing Levi knew, Jebediah appeared at his side holding two babies in his arms and introduced him to at least a dozen people. It would take him a while to get all the names straight, but he tried to look as if he were paying attention. The names were common Amish names—Joel, Matthew, Silas, Eli, Martha, Tabitha, Naomi. He wondered how he would ever remember who was who, but then he realized he wasn't staying in Goshen. It didn't really matter if he remembered everyone's name. So he smiled politely and said hello.

Finally, a woman and a young girl moved beside Jebediah. The woman said something softly to him, as the young girl clung to her dress. Jebediah laughed and turned to Levi.

"This is my wife, Nicole."

"Oh, *ya*? *Gut* to meet you."

"Jebediah told me all about you."

He could see the family resemblance, now that he studied her closely. She had the same warm eyes as Annie, but her hair was blonder and she had her father's height. Annie was shorter with hair that reminded him of the color of autumn wheat. The word *prettier* popped into his mind, but he brushed it away. Annie Kauffmann might be pretty, but she had a lot of strong opinions that she didn't mind sharing. It might be funny except for the fact that she was standing in the way of his plans.

"I think we lost him for a minute," Nicole said.

"He drifts off every now and then." Jebediah jostled the two babies in his arms.

"I can hear you. I was thinking of how much you look like your sister Annie."

"*You* look exactly like Annie described. She's talked about you a fair amount." Nicole reached out and wiped some drool off one of the babes in Jebediah's arms. "As has Dat."

"All *gut* things I hope."

"From Dat? *Ya*. But Annie, well…you know how Annie is."

"I do? I've only known her a few days."

"She's not exactly a mystery."

"Meaning?"

"She told me she told you that she doesn't like all this Texas talk."

"I guess she did mention it."

Jebediah and Nicole both laughed at that as if he'd

told a joke. It made him squirm, not that they might be laughing at him, but that he might be up against a force to be reckoned with. Instead of delving into the details of Annie's opposition, he changed the subject.

"What are your children's names?"

"The twins are Micah and Mitchell—nine months old." Jebediah readjusted both babies in his arms. "Our oldest is Rachel."

"I'm three," Rachel proclaimed, holding up a pudgy hand and bending down her thumb and pinky.

Levi remembered what Jebediah had said about their expecting another. He glanced at Nicole's stomach, then quickly averted his eyes.

She again laughed. "I'm five months along, in case you were wondering."

"I wasn't." And now his cheeks were burning.

When everyone else surged forward to be in the first seating of folks who would eat, Levi hung back.

"You can come with us into the first group," Jebediah said.

"No need. I don't mind waiting. Gives me time to watch folks."

Annie had stepped out of the trailer to deliver two platters of food. When she stepped back inside a small tabby cat crept in after her.

"Uh-oh," Jebediah said.

His astute comment was immediately followed by an ear-piercing scream. He handed the babies off to Nicole, but Levi was already on his way toward Annie.

The scene in front of him when he stepped into the trailer was something he wouldn't forget for a very long time.

An *Englisch* woman was holding two large bowls of

side dishes up high and trying to move around Annie without dropping them. She wore a conservative dress and a handkerchief over her hair, which was red and braided into a long ponytail down her back. She most certainly was not Amish.

Annie wore a light gray Amish dress with a white apron. A fresh *kapp* covered her hair, and her cheeks were a bright red. She had a pot lid in one hand and a dish towel in the other. She was slapping at the cat with the towel and holding the pot lid like an early Christian in Rome's Colosseum fending off the hungry lions.

As for the cat, he was clearly a terrified kitten, but that didn't stop him from arching his back and hissing at Annie.

Levi wanted to see how this would unfold. He wanted to burst out laughing, but another look at Annie told him that wouldn't be a wise move.

So instead, he pulled off his Stetson, dropped it over the unsuspecting cat, scooped it up in his arms and fled the trailer.

"Who was that?" Priscilla was still holding the two dishes of corn casserole high, as if the cat might return at any moment and leap on the food.

"I'll explain later. We need to get this food out there."

The next hour passed in a blur of activity. Annie loved nearly every minute of it. She liked feeding people, liked seeing the bride and groom and families relax. This was their day of celebration. They shouldn't be worried about chicken and hot rolls and casserole dishes. The fact that she did her job well meant that they could enjoy the wedding. And she didn't mind admitting that she was very good at guiding families through these special days, when there weren't feral cats hopping into her trailer.

She sighed and stood in the doorway looking out over the tables.

"Take a break," Priscilla said. "In fact, take some food and go sit down somewhere."

"You're bossy, you know that?"

"Which is why I make a good partner."

"I guess."

"You're still staring at him."

"Who?"

"The Amish cowboy."

Annie snorted at that. It sounded so ridiculous. It was ridiculous.

"So what gives?"

"He arrived here a few days ago."

"Why?"

"Looking for families to move to Texas."

"I didn't realize there were Amish communities there."

"There's one, and it's quite small and located in South Texas. Levi wants to start another."

"Ahhhh…" Priscilla's single word said she finally understood the problem. She'd been around Annie long enough to know how excited her *dat* could be when he first dove into a new idea.

"We're not moving," Annie said.

"Have you told your *dat* that?"

"You can't tell Dat anything. You have to…wait it out."

"Like the camels."

"*Ya.* Like that."

"If it's any consolation, I have family in Texas—

Fort Worth. I've visited a few times. It's not such a bad place to live."

Annie shook her head and picked at the plate of food that Priscilla had pushed into her hand. "I need a plan."

"Uh-oh."

"What if Dat went through with it? I mean usually he doesn't, but this time could be different. I've never seen him this focused before. He even checked out some books on Texas from the library. Spent some time on their computers looking things up too."

"That does sound serious."

"I need a plan to distract Levi."

"What did you have in mind?"

"I don't know. What are men interested in…" At that moment, a swell of laughter arose from the newlyweds' table. Both Annie and Priscilla stuck their heads out of the trailer to see the bride blushing and the groom ducking his head.

"Women," they said at the same time.

"That's it." Annie reached for her glass of tea and made her way down the trailer steps.

"Do you need help?" Priscilla called after her.

Annie turned so that she was walking backward. "You already helped. You gave me the idea."

"I did?"

She made her way to an empty seat, sat down and enjoyed the plate of food. The chicken had not dried out, the vegetable casseroles were tasty and the bread practically melted in her mouth. She was a good cook, a good businesswoman, and she wasn't going to lose everything she'd built to a guy who had stumbled into town with a dream.

It was later that afternoon before she had a chance

to implement her plan. She and Priscilla had cleaned the dishes and made sure everything was ready for the evening meal. With nearly two hours before they had to do anything else, Priscilla decided to drive into town and do some shopping. Annie made her way to the pasture fence, where Beth's parents kept their small herd of goats. They were playful animals. One stuck its nose through the fence when she approached, so she reached into her pocket and pulled out a piece of carrot.

"Now they're going to stampede over here." Levi walked up and crossed his arms on the top of the fence.

"Maybe that's what I wanted."

"A goat stampede?"

She dusted off her hands and shooed the goat away. "I saw you talking to Dat earlier."

Levi raised his hands in surrender. "Not the way you think."

"So you weren't talking to him about Texas?"

"I didn't bring it up. I told you I wouldn't, and I didn't."

"But…"

"I didn't say I wouldn't answer questions. He brought it up because he had a few questions that cropped up from his reading."

"And it didn't hurt that a few other men were standing around listening."

Now Levi smiled. "Come on, Annie. It's why I'm here. You can't fault me for that."

"Except your plan could bankrupt my business."

"Ten families moving wouldn't affect you at all."

She shook her head so hard that her *kapp* strings bounced back and forth. She had promised herself she wouldn't get into an argument with him. That wasn't her plan.

But she needed for him to see what was at stake.

Suddenly she thought of the brainstorming sessions she'd had with Priscilla, before they'd started Plain & Simple Weddings. Part of their initial challenge had been convincing families that they needed their services, and that in the end, it would be less expensive for them. She was up against the same sort of thing with Levi. He simply didn't understand that he needed her services, and she wasn't talking about catering.

Levi Lapp thought he needed a fresh start, but that wasn't the case at all. When had moving away from your problems ever solved anything?

Levi didn't need to move; he needed to believe in himself.

He needed to be able to envision his future here—in Goshen, Indiana.

He needed a woman, and she knew several that were available.

Annie cleared her throat and looked back toward her trailer. "Priscilla and I started our business three years ago."

He seemed surprised at the change of subject, but he turned as she had and looked out at the trailer.

"She put up two-thirds of the initial money."

"You mean buying the trailer?"

"It's actually a mobile kitchen and cost a little more than twelve thousand dollars."

Levi glanced at her in surprise. "Seriously?"

"*Ya*. Stoves, refrigerators and enough dishes for five hundred...not to mention the trailer itself and the licensing fees."

"I had no idea."

"We broke even the first year."

"Wow."

"She's a *gut* partner too. Since she's *Englisch*, she drives a truck that can pull the trailer. She can also order a lot of what we need wholesale on the computer."

"You're saying you two make a *wunderbaar* team. I can see that. You have every right to be proud of what you've done, Annie."

"Pride goes before destruction as my *mamm* often reminds me, but I am pleased with our success. More importantly I enjoy what we do. I like making this..." She waved at the large group of people sprawled across the green yard—full, content, some of them growing sleepy. "I like making it all possible. I enjoy seeing others happily wed."

"What about you?"

"Me?" Her thoughts scrambled for an answer to his question. It wasn't the first time someone had asked her why she wasn't married, but somehow it was different coming from Levi Lapp while he smiled at her with his cowboy hat tilted at an angle.

"Doesn't being at so many weddings make you... interested in finding someone?"

"I'm only twenty-four."

"I didn't say you were an old maid."

"My *mamm* worries about that, but I'm in no hurry. I've been to my *schweschder*'s often enough to know that running a catering business is less work than three small children." She paused, and then added, "What about you?"

"Me?" His voice squeaked. He cleared his throat and

resettled his hat on his head. "I figure that will happen after I move to Texas."

"But what if you could find a *fraa* here and take her with you?"

"Now you're making fun of me."

"I'm not."

"Did you have someone in mind?" The grin he gave her reminded Annie of the cat in her trailer—mischievous and daring.

Annie had a flash of clarity then, staring up into Levi's blue eyes. There was no doubt that she could find women in their congregation interested in dating Levi Lapp, but she wouldn't be able to trick him into it. That part of her plan died before she could implement it. Levi was like competition that you had to face head-on.

So she stepped back and crossed her arms. "Do you really think you can convince my *dat* and *bruder* to move to Texas?"

"I'm not saying that I can, but it should be their decision…along with your *mamm* and your *schweschder*. If it's what they want, then you should be happy for them."

She didn't bother arguing that her *mamm* and *schweschder* were quite happy in Goshen. Levi was like a steam-engine train headed in one direction—no U-turns allowed.

"All right. I'll make you a deal."

"A deal?"

"You agree to date some of my *freinden*…"

"Date?"

"Hear me out. You're not planning on staying. They're not necessarily looking to get married, but they need…let's say they need a little experience in the dating area."

Levi groaned. "You're going to set me up with the rejects."

She felt a headache forming just at her left temple. Closing her eyes, she prayed to *Gotte* for patience, then counted to three.

"They're shy," she corrected him. "And maybe they have a lack of confidence. Dating you should help that."

"Because I'm such a *gut* catch?"

He grinned, and she realized he was handsome. Not her type, but handsome nonetheless. Yes, this plan could work.

"Let's say there's no pressure on either side. That should help. They'll know you're not staying…"

"And I'll know they're not really interested. This is a terrible plan. Why would I agree to it?"

This was the tricky part. She almost couldn't believe she was going to suggest it. But then again, what choice did she have? He was going to talk to her *dat* and Jebediah in spite of how much it bothered her. They would keep asking him questions. He'd keep painting pictures of rosy Texas sunsets.

"When were you planning to leave?"

"You get right to the point, don't you?"

"Do you even have a plan?"

"Of course I do." Levi scuffed the toe of his boot against the dirt, and she noticed he was wearing Western boots. Of course he was.

"Why does our bishop let you dress like that?"

"This?" He pointed the toe of his boot up. "These are Ariats. Very comfortable."

"And that." She pointed at his hat.

"A Stetson. All Texans wear them."

"Why are *you* wearing them? You're Amish." She said the last word slowly, in two drawn-out syllables.

"Marcus talked to me about it," Levi admitted. "He said if I decided to join the community I'd need to dress more conservatively. I assured him I was moving on, so he said it wasn't a problem."

"Back to the *when* of your plan…"

"I hope to go down before Christmas to look for land and move by early spring—my target date is February or March."

"That's not spring."

"It is in Texas."

She couldn't hold the sigh inside. She'd hoped he was planning for a move in a year, which would have been plenty of time for her *dat*'s attention to wander elsewhere. A scouting party before Christmas? That was mere months away. She'd have to work fast if she hoped to save the nice comfortable life she had. She'd already waded in too far to back out now, plus she didn't have any backup plan. It wasn't going to be easy to match Levi with someone. Who wanted an Amish cowboy? Though there was one possibility…

Levi was studying her as if expecting her to give up. He didn't know her very well. She liked a challenge. She thrived in tough situations. Tossing her *kapp* strings behind her shoulders, she plastered on what she hoped was her prettiest smile. "All right. You agree to date a couple of my friends…not at the same time, mind you."

"Of course not."

"And in return, I won't try and stop you from talking to my family about your plans."

"As if you could."

"My point is that you won't have to deal with my objections."

He studied her a minute and then said, "Seriously?"

"Ya."

"What's in it for you?"

"Me?"

"Why are you doing this? I know you're dead set against the idea of moving."

"Oh, I am not moving. I'll find a way to stay here even if you convince the whole community to move south."

Levi laughed. "That's the Annie I know."

"You don't know me."

"Uh-huh. But seriously, why are you doing this?"

"I like weddings is all. I enjoy seeing two people who are meant to be together find each other."

"I'm not getting married."

"I know, but maybe *Gotte* has different plans."

"What does *Gotte* have to do with it?"

"Maybe He brought you to Goshen for a reason…a different reason."

"So now you're a matchmaker?"

"Think of me as a concerned bystander."

Levi shook his head. "I don't know…"

"Is it a deal or not? If you'd rather, I can keep pointing out all the terrible things about your Lone Star State."

"All right. It's a deal." He held out his hand. "But you have to shake on it."

She rolled her eyes, but put her hand in his. He closed his fingers around hers, held her hand long enough that she didn't like the goose bumps running down her arm or the jumble of nerves in her stomach. She jerked her hand away.

"Great. Then it's settled. I'll give you the name of your first date when you come over on Wednesday to work."

"I look forward to it."

Of course he did. The man was conceited in addition to being stubborn. But, just possibly, she'd found a way to keep her life firmly rooted in Goshen, because she had the perfect woman in mind for Levi Lapp and this person would never consider moving away. All Annie had to do was see to it that the two of them fell in love. She was envisioning a wedding announcement before the holidays if she handled this right. No need for a long courtship at their age. It would mean she'd have to live around Levi the rest of her life, but at least she wouldn't have to do so in Texas.

Chapter Four

Annie woke the next morning determined to start right away on her new plan. Levi Lapp had invaded her dreams throughout the night—she'd found herself surrounded by wildflowers, nose to nose with a longhorn, even looking across a vast plain toward rain clouds in the distance. As if those images of Texas weren't bad enough, Levi himself had put in several appearances, always wearing his Stetson hat and that cocky grin.

It was past time to do something proactive and push Levi and his Texas trivia out of her dreams. She picked her newest Sunday dress, brushed her hair vigorously and wove it into a braid tight enough to pucker the skin along her forehead. Pulling the covers up snug on her bed, she prayed for wisdom and patience. She was bound to need both.

Her *mamm* found her downstairs making coffee before the sun was up.

"Problem sleeping, dear?" Her *mamm* stared at the coffee maker on the stove as if she could make it percolate faster.

"Go sit down. I'll bring it to you."

"All right."

Five minutes later, they were both clutching steaming mugs of coffee and sitting at the kitchen table.

"Want to talk about it?" Her *mamm* kept blinking her eyes, as if she wasn't quite awake yet.

"About what?"

"Whatever's bothering you."

"Nothing's bothering me."

Instead of arguing, her mother took another sip of the dark brew—the entire Kauffmann family enjoyed their coffee strong—and waited.

"Oh, all right. I'll admit it. This thing with Levi has worked its way under my *kapp*."

"Has it now?"

"I don't want to move to Texas, Mamm."

"Which is understandable."

"It is?"

"I want to be where your father is, and if he decides—"

Annie groaned. "Tell me you're not on their side."

"This isn't about us and them. This is about seeking out and following *Gotte's wille* for our lives. I'm not afraid of doing that even if it means living in a different place."

"I'm not afraid. It's just that if Levi had never shown up on our doorstep, Dat would never be considering a move to Texas."

"Perhaps, but *Gotte* brings people into our lives for a reason."

Annie jumped up to refill their mugs. As she turned toward the stove, she muttered, "I'm pretty sure it was a Greyhound bus that brought Levi to us."

"And yet *Gotte* put this dream in Levi's heart."

"Oops. I didn't mean for you to hear that."

"Levi's relationship with Old Simon also brought him here."

Annie refilled her *mamm*'s mug and then plopped down in the chair across from her. She needed her mother with her on this. Perhaps she should try a different tack.

"Okay. Let's assume what you're saying is true…"

Her *mamm*'s eyebrows arched, but she didn't interrupt.

"But what if Levi is confusing some unresolved business from his childhood as *Gotte*'s leading? Maybe *Gotte* brought him here for a reason—a reason other than ripping twelve of our families away to start a new community. Maybe Goshen needs Levi here, but he doesn't realize it yet." For some reason, that idea didn't sit well with her, either. In her daydreams, Levi had always ridden off toward the West, tilting his hat against the setting sun, searching for another community where he could disrupt people's lives.

"What I mean is that perhaps *Gotte* has other plans for him. We can't know."

"Indeed."

They were silent for a moment. Finally her *mamm* said, "Do you have some ideas about why Levi might be here?"

Annie picked at a fingernail. "Maybe he's supposed to meet someone here."

"Someone?"

"A woman, Mamm. Maybe he's supposed to meet a woman, fall in *lieb*, settle down and start a family." Once she said it out loud, the plan took on a new dimension. What she was suggesting was possible. It was almost as if she were doing a charitable thing for him.

"I spoke with Levi yesterday after the wedding, and he's agreed to allow me to set him up on a few dates."

"That's kind of you."

"I guess, but just think, Mamm…if he falls in *lieb*, then he might forget this ridiculous obsession with Texas."

"Mmm-hmm."

"He might decide he wants to stay here in Goshen."

"I suppose that's possible."

"And if he stays, well, we both know that Dat's enthusiasm for moving will melt away."

Instead of arguing with her, which was what Annie had suspected, her *mamm* smiled over the rim of her mug. "Who did you have in mind to set him up with?"

"Martha Weaver."

"Have you spoken to Martha about this?"

"*Nein.* I was hoping to do so after church service."

Her *mamm* drained her coffee cup, stood and pushed her chair back in under the table. Walking around behind Annie, she kissed her on top of the head, causing Annie to feel four years old again.

She thought that her mother would reprimand her, tell her to mind her own business, caution her about intervening in other people's lives. She didn't. Instead, she simply walked to the refrigerator, pulled out what she planned to cook for breakfast and began cracking eggs into a bowl—leaving Annie to wonder what she wasn't saying. If she were honest with herself, some doubts remained in her mind about this new plan. Perhaps she was foolish to think that playing matchmaker could solve her problem.

It was well after lunch before Annie had a chance to speak with Martha. She'd been friends with Martha since their school days. Though Martha was two years younger, she'd always seemed to be around Annie's age, perhaps because she'd stepped into the role of helping with her younger siblings. Annie found her watching over her disabled brother as well as a group of the younger children who were playing in a pile of leaves in the circle of three giant maple trees. The service had been held at the Bontragers' place. The old couple had raised a family of twelve in Goshen. All their children—all twelve of them—had moved to Maine, and the small For Sale sign in the front yard reminded Annie that they would be joining them soon. The Bontragers had been around as long as Annie could remember.

Why would they move?

Why did things have to change?

Plainly they were happy here.

She shook away the questions and reminded herself to focus on her mission.

Walking over to Martha, she held out her arms to accept one of the Miller babies that her friend was holding. "Joseph or Jeremiah?"

The twins were six months old, but she still couldn't tell the difference between them.

"Joseph. You can tell because he has a little strawberry mark on the back of his neck."

Annie snuggled the baby against her neck and sat down at the picnic table that had been positioned under the trees. "Where's the older *bruder*?"

"Stephen has a little cold, so Kathy took him inside to see if he'd nap. I was already watching over the others, so two more didn't seem like a problem."

There were six children of various ages running around, some falling in the leaves, some sitting on the ground and crushing the brittle red, yellow and orange leaves in their fists. Off to the side sat Martha's brother.

Annie had known Thomas all of her life. She didn't see him as disabled so much as she saw her best friend's twin brother. Sometimes, though, when they were in town shopping or splurging on ice cream, she'd notice the way strangers looked at Thomas. In those moments she'd have a tiny inkling of what it was like for Martha and why she was so fiercely protective of him.

Tommy, or Big Tom as he liked to be called, had a flat nose and small ears. He had been diagnosed with Down syndrome the day after his birth. At twenty-two, his body had grown to that of a man, but he still acted like a child in many ways.

Amish families have the highest incidence of twins of any demographic group—a teacher had mentioned that in class one day and Annie had looked around the room to spot no less than six pairs of twins. Annie understood that the bond between twins was strong, but the bond between Martha and Thomas exceeded even that. It was as if they were tethered together by some invisible line—a spiritual cord stronger than any rope made by man.

Martha seemed content to watch the children and her brother. She was mature for her age and bore an air of complete contentment. She wore glasses—blue frames she'd found on sale at the local optometrist office—had beautiful white-blond hair and blue eyes.

Those eyes were now studying her, brows slightly arched, a smile playing on her lips.

Annie jumped up, still snuggling baby Joseph and pacing back and forth in front of Martha. Another glance at her friend confirmed that she'd have a higher chance of success if she got straight to the point.

"Levi Lapp would like to step out with you."

Martha's mouth fell open, and she looked over her shoulder as if Annie might be talking to someone else.

"How do you know Levi?" Martha asked. "He just moved here…"

Annie blushed. "He was at our house last week, talking to my *dat* about Texas."

A toddler ran over to Martha and held up his arms. She shifted Jeremiah to her left arm and pulled the toddler into her lap. "Why would Levi Lapp want to step out with me?"

"Why wouldn't he? You're a pleasant person, Martha, and very eligible. Let's not forget that."

"I rarely do."

"You're pretty, and you have a good head on your shoulders."

"He couldn't possibly know what kind of head I have on my shoulders. So stop trying to butter me up and just tell me what's really going on."

Annie groaned. She should have known Martha wouldn't make this easy.

"He wants to move to Texas."

"Why do you care about that?"

"He wants to start a community there, and he's targeting our community to pull families from."

"Targeting?"

"Whatever." She waved away Martha's concern about her word choice. "He's been bending my *dat*'s ear, and now Dat is stirred up."

"Ahh. Now your concern makes sense. But what does this have to do with me?"

"I need to distract him."

"That's what you want me to do?"

"Nein. Ya. Maybe." Baby Joseph had fallen asleep in her arms, so Annie sat on the ground in front of the picnic table, crossed her legs and placed him in the crook of her knee. She quickly explained that Levi was working at their house two days a week and that he had set his sights on recruiting her father and brother.

"Jebediah and Nicole might move to Texas?"

"I don't know. Anything is possible, I guess."

"Wow."

"I know."

"Texas?"

"You should hear him talk about it. Actually, you *will* hear him talk about it if you go out on a date with him because it's his only topic of conversation."

"Hmm. You make him sound more attractive all the time."

Annie snorted. "He's good-looking enough, I'll give you that, but that's not the point. I just want you to agree to go out with him a few times."

"Again…why? You know I'm taking a six-month break from dating."

"Ya."

"After what happened with David—"

"It wasn't your fault he left the faith. He would have been willing to move to Alaska if they'd let him keep that cell phone."

They shared a smile, both remembering the way that David had carried it around, glancing at it every few minutes, tapping on it constantly with his fingers.

"That relationship was never going to work anyway,"

Martha admitted. "But the fact remains that I'm on a roll of bad relationships."

"Only three."

"Four if you count Meno."

"Years ago, and he was never right for you."

"None of them are." Instead of looking as if that thought depressed her, Martha smiled. "I'm on a break."

"Okay. All right. So don't call it a date. Call it being a friend to someone new in our community."

"It doesn't have to be romantic?"

"*Nein.* Levi thinks…"

"Uh-oh. What did you tell him?"

"I might have mentioned that you need practice dating."

"We both know that isn't the case."

"You need practice dating someone new."

"Let me get this straight. I'm supposed to go out with him and distract him…"

"Maybe mention the *gut* points about Goshen. You know this place as well as I do, and it's a fine community. He doesn't have to go to Texas to find a place to settle down."

"I'm not falling in love with Levi Lapp."

"Of course not."

"I don't want to move to Texas any more than you do."

"Exactly."

"He's bound to figure that out sooner than later."

"Later would be better. Just buy me some time for Dat to simmer down about the idea."

"Why don't you do it? Why don't you date him?"

Annie shook her head so hard that her *kapp* strings bounced back and forth. "Oh no. That would only encourage him to get closer to my family. Plus, fall and spring are the busiest seasons for my business. I have no time to waste on dating."

"Oh, but I should…"

"You know what I mean. It's fine for other people. I want other people to date."

"If they didn't, you'd be out of business."

"Exactly."

Martha placed the toddler on the ground and baby Jeremiah in his baby carrier. She stood, stretched and cast a look toward Big Tom who was still playing in the leaves, though now he was lying on his back and making a snow angel—or maybe a leaf angel. Martha smiled, and Annie was struck again by how close the two were.

Annie handed Joseph back to Martha, stood and brushed off the back of her dress.

"Will you do it?"

"*Ya, ya*, I'll do it."

"*Danki.*"

"But only because you're my best friend."

"I owe you."

"*Ya*. You do." Martha walked over to her *bruder*, who held up a hand and allowed her to pull him to his feet.

Annie glanced up in time to see Levi driving away in Old Simon's buggy. She'd missed talking to him today, but that was okay. She'd tell him the good news first thing Wednesday.

By the time Levi showed up at the Kauffmann place on Wednesday, he'd completely forgotten Annie's plan to find him a girl. He'd been focused on other things. He'd talked with several of the local families at the wedding, and three had come back to ask him questions after the church service. At this rate, he might get to Texas earlier than he'd thought. He might have enough interest to send down a scouting group before fall turned into winter.

He was mucking out the horse stalls early Wednesday morning, before they'd even had breakfast, when Annie showed up in the barn.

"*Gude mariye*, Levi."

He wiped the sweat out of his eyes and squinted at her.

As usual, she looked fresh and energetic. Normally she seemed aggravated when she saw him, as if she'd swallowed unsweetened lemonade. Today she was smiling broadly. Why the change in attitude?

Then he remembered their deal and literally slapped himself on the forehead.

"Problem?"

"Just remembering what you talked me into."

"I didn't talk you into anything. I simply made a suggestion and you agreed."

She grinned at him as she had on Saturday. He could still feel her hand in his, the way her eyes had widened as she'd glanced up into his eyes, and then how she'd snatched her hand away as if she'd been stung by a bee. What was that about?

She didn't waste any time ruining his morning. She pulled a folded sheet of paper from her apron pocket and waved it at him. "I wrote down the information you need for your date."

"My date…"

Her plan was bound to be a trap. He didn't know how, but he was sure that it must be designed to ruin his goal of moving to Texas.

"Her name is Martha Weaver. Here are directions to

her house as well as the number for the nearest phone shack."

He took the piece of paper and stared down at her tidy handwriting. "Guess I'm stuck doing this."

"You're lucky to date Martha, actually. She's level-headed, nice looking—"

"Then why isn't she courting or married? There must be something wrong with her."

"And she's my best friend."

"Oops. Sorry if what I said sounded rude."

"It did, but I'm not surprised. Men your age only want to step out with the prettiest, thinnest girls."

"That's not true."

Instead of arguing, Annie walked into the stall and around the perimeter. "Martha has a sweet tooth. You might think about taking her to the pie pantry."

"I have dated before, you know."

"Oh, you have?"

"Don't look so surprised."

"I'm not surprised."

He could tell that she was holding in her laughter, which irritated him more than it probably should have.

"I wonder if your *mamm* has breakfast ready."

"Oh, *ya*. That's what I came out to tell you."

"You could have led with that."

"And miss the chance to tease you?"

"Is that what you're doing? And why are you in such a chipper mood this morning?"

"Who wouldn't be in a good mood on such a beautiful morning?"

He had been too—until Annie showed up with her dating instructions. He hadn't fully thought this through when he'd agreed to her dating scheme. His few attempts to date back in Lancaster had been a disaster. The women he'd met were only interested in settling down and having babies. He had nothing against either, but they'd had no patience for his talk of moving to Texas, especially when they'd heard that he was saving every dime in order to make the move possible.

Dreamer.

Naive.

Immature.

He'd been called all sorts of things, always with a smile, a touch on the shoulder, and a look of pity. Well, he didn't need anyone's approval or sympathy, and he didn't need another woman who was going to try and set him straight.

"What are you frowning about?"

Instead of answering, he carried the pitchfork into the main room of the barn, then returned to pick up the muck bucket. Annie was still there, leaning against the wall, a smile on her pretty face, arms crossed, studying him.

"You don't have to look at me that way."

"I don't?"

"I promised you I'd take your friend out."

"Her name is Martha."

"I agreed to take Martha out, and I will."

He trudged toward the house, aware that Annie was practically jogging to keep up with him.

"You're looking at this all wrong. It's not like an extra chore."

"So you say…"

"She's levelheaded and—"

He turned toward her so quickly that she nearly bumped into him. "And pretty. *Ya*, I heard."

"So what's the problem?"

"No problem, Annie." Instead of backing away, he stepped closer, causing her to cross her arms and frown at him. "Just be sure you keep up your end of the bargain."

"Of course."

"No more hiding your *dat*'s library books."

She pulled back in surprise.

"He's not that absentminded, and he wouldn't have left them on top of the washing machine where he found them."

"Oh, well… I might have been looking through them and…"

"Left them there by accident? Uh-huh. Just remember that we have a deal, and you have to keep your side of it if I'm going to keep mine."

When she'd nodded once, he turned and clomped into the house. He'd brought a map of Texas, and he was eager to show it to Alton. He'd even marked the route from Stephenville to Beeville. Sure, they were three hundred miles apart, but Levi wanted him to know that they wouldn't be completely alone in their new community.

By the time he'd had two cups of coffee, breakfast potatoes, eggs and pancakes, he was in a better mood. Alton had gone to find his reading glasses so he could better study the map. Lily was humming softly as she ran dishwater into the sink. And Annie?

Annie was throwing daggers his way, which was fine with him. She'd soon accept that there was no stopping him. He'd had his dreams trodden on by plenty of women before—girlfriends, his sisters, even his mother. Annie Kauffmann didn't represent that big of an obstacle. It was a shame, though. Her sort of stubborn spirit would have been a real asset in settling a new community.

Chapter Five

The first official meeting for those interested in a Texas community was held ten days later on a Friday afternoon. The weather was pleasant—still warm though it was now October. Storm clouds were building in the west. The front would bring rain and cooler temperatures, but Old Simon said it wouldn't hit before the next morning.

They'd placed chairs in the backyard in a semicircle.

Levi had hoped half a dozen men would attend. He was pleasantly surprised when their numbers hit ten, including Jebediah and Alton.

There were three women, as well—Nicole, Jebediah's wife; Beth, who had married Avery the first Saturday Levi was in town; and Annie.

Marcus stood when it seemed everyone had arrived. "As your bishop, it's my duty to oversee any plans to split and/or begin a new community. I don't want to lose a single man, woman or child from our group. You're all vital to our church district here in Goshen, but I do want to be sensitive to *Gotte*'s leading. If it is *Gotte's wille* for you to begin a new life in Texas, then we will find a way to make it happen. These are, of course, the very early stages of inquiring and everyone here should understand that nothing has been decided. We'll move slowly, carefully and with consensus."

Marcus looked at Levi, who nodded in agreement.

They'd had this very talk the night before.

Marcus wasn't about to let any fool with a dream come in and disrupt his community, but at the same time he seemed like a fair man. And that was all that Levi could ask for. It was certainly more than he'd received from the community in Lancaster.

"How many families do you recommend we need?" Jebediah asked.

"Normally we suggest ten, at least. Since this community would be a good distance from any other—" Marcus held up his hand to stop Levi's protests. "Beeville is five hours away, by car, which you won't have and won't be able to afford to hire. Because there is a significant distance between you and another Plain community, I'm going to recommend that you have a firm commitment from a dozen to fifteen families before you purchase land."

Marcus studied the group and let the weight of what he was saying sink in. "You'll be on your own in Stephenville, and that's why it's important that you start with as much support from one another as possible. Also, I'm going to insist that you have at least three ministers so that you'll be able to hold proper church services."

Levi tried to stifle his groan, but with little success. He'd thought they would let the community begin with one minister, and he had that—Old Simon. Finding two more was not going to be easy.

"Any idea how we can find two more ministers?" Alton looked around at each person and then back at Marcus. "They're not exactly growing on trees."

The small joke went a long way to easing the tension in the group.

Avery Stutzman spoke for the first time since the meeting had begun. "We could put a notice in *The Budget* asking any interested persons, any interested ministers, to contact Levi or Marcus. I'd be happy to write that up and give it to our scribe. She could post it in the next issue."

Avery reached over and snagged his new bride's hand. "We're committed to helping make this happen. As a young newlywed couple…"

Beth and Avery smiled at each other and she blushed as the chuckles died down. "Having our own place is a real concern. My parents have land here, of course, as do Beth's parents. But we're both the youngest in our families, so there are a lot of siblings in line before us."

"We've been saving," Beth added. "But the cost of land here is a bit steeper than what we can afford at this point. At the rate things are going, it will be several years before we have our own place, and we'd rather not wait that long."

"It's a problem in nearly every Amish community." Marcus nodded in understanding. "As the group grows, as more people need and want to farm in an area, the price of land goes up. That's another thing to consider in a new community, as well. We need to do this carefully so the price per acre doesn't spike once the good folks in Texas realize we're coming."

At least that sounded more positive to Levi, though the deal about needing three ministers…it could be a problem. He didn't know if they'd be able to find two other men in leadership positions who would be willing and able to uproot their families.

It was decided that Marcus would contact bishops in neighboring communities and see if any of their ministers had a desire to help build a new group. Avery had volunteered to write a piece to give to their scribe, a girl named Naomi. Other persons attending vowed to write to relatives and friends in locations outside their county—looking for interested families as well as two additional ministers.

Levi had harbored high hopes for this meeting, but to this point, the news certainly wasn't all good. Of course it wasn't all bad, either. The folks assembled seemed eager and committed, for the most part.

It felt to Levi like they were taking two steps forward and one step back—but it was forward progress and that was all he could ask for. As the meeting progressed, his mood went from wildly optimistic to worried to cautiously hopeful. He was exhausted and ready to call it a night when Marcus asked for any last questions.

"I have a question."

He jerked toward the voice, sure it couldn't be…but it was. Pretty Annie Kauffmann had stood, squared her shoulders and faced the group. He had a bad feeling before she even tossed her question out.

"Why Texas?"

Levi had jumped up from his chair and was ready to blast a dozen reasons back her direction when Old Simon reached out, grasping his arm and pulling him back into a sitting position.

"But…"

Old Simon only shook his head and nodded toward

Marcus who was listening intently to whatever Annie was saying. She spoke demurely and with a pleasant tone, as if she hadn't cooked up what she was going to say days ago.

Levi knew better.

This was a plot to ruin his chances of moving.

This was a scheme to keep her father in Goshen. Steam must have been shooting out of his ears, but he forced himself to focus in on her last words.

"I'm just wondering, why not Missouri or Arkansas? There's plenty of good farmland between here and Texas. Plus a community in Stephenville has been tried before, and it failed. So what has changed? Why do we think it will be successful now?"

Levi again tried to jump to his feet, but Old Simon's surprisingly strong grip on his arm held him back.

"Those are *gut* questions, Annie, and thank you for bringing them to our attention. In fact, if you hadn't, I would have." Marcus stared down at the sheet of paper where he'd jotted some notes. "I had planned to ask you all to carefully consider that very thing as you go about your work in the coming days. I beseech each of you to pray about this, seek *Gotte*'s guidance, and when we meet again in three weeks I'll ask Levi to address those very questions that Annie has brought to our attention."

The meeting broke up then, everyone stretching and talk turning to upcoming harvests, plans for winter crops and the fall festival which was to take place in a few weeks.

Levi saw Annie dart around the corner of the building. Fortunately her *dat* was still speaking with the bishop. Perfect. He'd have a few minutes alone with little miss Annie. Maybe she could explain why she was trying to sabotage his plans.

"Sabotage? You've got to be kidding."

"What would you call it?"

"Asking questions. I thought that's why we were meeting." Annie had guessed he wouldn't be happy with her, but she didn't think he'd have the nerve to follow her to the buggy.

"I don't even know why you're here." He waved his arms in the direction of Simon's backyard, nearly knocking off his hat. "Why would you bother coming to this meeting when you have no intention of moving with us?"

"I'm here because I care about what happens to my community, to my family."

"You care about them? Do you care if Avery and Beth are able to purchase land?"

"*Gotte* will provide a way."

"And maybe that way is moving to Texas!" Levi snatched his hat off his head and slapped it against his leg. "You wouldn't move if the entire community was packing up and leaving."

"And why should I? This is a *gut* place to live." She stomped her foot, which at first seemed to work because Levi stopped arguing with her, but then he shook his head and after that he started laughing. Before she could figure out what was so funny he was holding his side as if he had an ache from running.

"Do not laugh at me, Levi Lapp."

"I can't help it."

She stared at him in disbelief, so he held up his hands

and repeated what he'd just said. "Honestly, I can't help it. Sorry. I'm sorry. You just look so...well, funny."

"I look *funny*?"

"I want to stay mad at you. I still am mad at you. I'm plenty steamed, but if you could see the look on your face...and then you stomped your foot like some child annoyed at not getting your way."

"Did you just call me a child?"

"I said *like* a child—not the same thing."

He moved to her buggy and rested his back against it, his hands still pressed against his stomach, his gaze on the ground. "You are one interesting gal, Annie Kauffmann."

"What's that supposed to mean?"

"You have no problem speaking your mind."

"Why should I?"

"Not exactly the meek Amish woman pictured in romance novels."

"What do you know about romance novels?"

"My *schweschdern* kept them around the house... I used to tease them about it."

It was the first time Levi had mentioned his family, and Annie felt her anger toward him soften.

"Don't you miss them?"

"Some."

"Then why—"

His look silenced her. Okay. Not a subject he wanted to talk about. That was fine with her.

"We had a deal," he reminded her.

"I haven't tried to stop you from talking to my *dat*."

"But you came to this meeting when you obviously have no intention of moving."

"It doesn't hurt to know the status of things, and I'd

rather receive my information firsthand than hear it from the grapevine."

"Okay, fair enough. Come and listen."

"I wasn't asking for your permission."

"And I didn't mean it that way."

He stared at the ground a moment before raising those gorgeous blue eyes to study her. He really was a nice-looking guy.

"But do you have to throw out obstructive questions?"

"Obstructive? Someone was paying attention in English class."

"Look me in the eye and tell me that you were not trying to throw down a roadblock."

She squirmed under his gaze and finally admitted, "Yes and no."

"I understand the yes part of that answer."

"I'll admit, you all looked like a bunch of starstruck fools—so, yes, I was trying to splash some cold water on the group."

"Finally, some honesty."

"But also no—because I didn't ask *why Texas* for the sole purpose of slowing your progress."

"Okay, then, explain it to me."

"I honestly want to know." Her hands went to her hips again, and a smile twitched on Levi's lips. It made her want to stomp her foot once more but she resisted. No need sending him into more gales of laughter. "Why Texas, Levi?"

He didn't answer her right away.

The people who had attended the meeting were walking around the corner of the house now. A few saw them and waved. Great. Now they'd think she was stepping out with Levi Lapp.

"Maybe I should have addressed that to begin with. You were correct when you pointed out that there are other places—closer places—we could move. Missouri and Arkansas are both *gut* examples, and I've been to communities in both of them."

"Let me guess. They don't measure up to your memories of Texas."

"They're *gut* places, I guess. Pretty much like Indiana. Arkansas has more mountains—a different way of life than what we have here. Missouri has plenty of farmland, and we would basically be living the life we have here in a different state. Maybe costs are less. I'm not really sure. I guess I'll be checking before our next meeting."

"Information isn't a bad thing, Levi."

"Sure. I understand."

"But…"

"But, they're not Texas, and that's something that you can't understand unless you've been there." He resettled his ridiculous hat on his head and pushed away from the buggy. When he turned back toward her the laughing friend was gone and the adversary was back—but it seemed to be a kinder, gentler adversary.

"I've been there, Annie, and it's my life dream to go back. I only hope that I have that opportunity. Did you know that Texas comes from the Native American word for friend or ally?" And without any further explanation, he turned back toward the house, shoulders slightly bowed from the weight of the task before him.

In that moment, Annie experienced a sudden and profound remorse. She'd pulled the rug out from under his feet, and although she didn't regret that, she hated to see him so dejected.

"Martha enjoyed going out for ice cream with you."

He stopped, turned and nodded once. Then he walked back toward the house without another word.

Martha had told Annie earlier that day that she'd enjoyed the trip for ice cream and the walk down the Pumpkinvine Trail. She'd gone alone with Levi on the first date, but Levi had suggested they bring Big Tom along on the second. They'd ended up eating snow cones—she'd had grape, Big Tom had cherry and Levi had settled for coconut.

"I told you I thought he was a nice guy," Annie had said.

"*Ya*, I know. The thing is…he did more than tolerate Big Tom. He actually included him."

But it was the last thing Martha had said that had stuck in Annie's mind, that she replayed over and over as she'd tried to sleep the night before. "Some people don't make *gut* couples because they're complete opposites. Levi and I would never be right for one another because we're too much alike."

Levi was like her best friend? How was that even possible?

And why did the thought of that deepen her remorse and cause her to wonder if she should be fighting Levi's plan at all? Because she still didn't want to move to Texas, and she still planned to do everything in her ability to stop her family from doing so.

The only difference was now she felt bad about it.

Annie woke the next Wednesday determined to shake her foul mood.

As she pulled out her most worn dress, she vowed not

to care that Levi had taken Martha on another date—after all, she'd asked him to, hadn't she?

Fastening a frayed *kapp* to her head she stared at herself in the mirror and scolded her image. It was time to stop dwelling on the look of hurt on Levi's face when she'd thrown cold water on his plans at the meeting. Her questions had been good ones. If settling in Stephenville, Texas, didn't work before, why would it work now? And why there? Despite what Levi thought, there were bound to be good places closer to Goshen.

Pulling on her work boots, she remembered how she'd stomped her foot at him and he'd laughed—laughed at her when she was trying to make a point. If he'd been angry, it would have been more satisfying, but to have him laugh at her? That was just insulting.

She fastened a stained but clean apron around her dress and marched down the stairs. The rain had held off, though cooler temperatures had arrived. She actually needed a sweater or shawl in the evenings. Her *dat* had informed the family that the corn harvest would begin today. Harvesting was always a family affair and two of her *bruders* would be there to help. Her oldest *schweschder* would arrive in time to help Mamm fix a big lunch. It would be a busy day filled with hard work, good food and family.

She stomped into the kitchen refusing to let the fact that Levi Lapp would be in the middle of it all ruin her mood.

It took some effort, but she held on to her complaints through breakfast and cleaning the dishes. Once she stepped outside, though—into a fall day that had dawned crisp and clear—even she couldn't help smiling.

"That's my girl," Mamm said.

So she'd noticed.

Of course she'd noticed, but her parents believed a bad mood had to be worked through on a private level. Annie didn't have them often, and they usually blew over quickly, so perhaps her parents were right.

But honestly, who could be angry when surrounded by so many of God's blessings? That would be worse than stubborn. It would be ungrateful, and Annie couldn't find it in her heart to be that.

So she smiled at her *mamm*, bounded down the steps and hurried out to the field.

Nathan and Joseph had eaten an early breakfast at home, but they were already standing by her *dat* next to the field where the corn waited to be harvested. Even the horses seemed eager to begin their work.

The sun was barely peeking over the horizon and the weather was cool. Finally, fall was here. And fall in Indiana was a special time indeed.

The stalks had been cut and stacked into tepees two weeks before. Now they were sufficiently dry to separate the corn from the husks. It would take everyone working all day to finish the job, and she'd be working side by side with Levi.

"*Gude mariye,*" he said as she walked up to join the group.

She was about to answer when her father raised his hand for quiet.

"Nathan and Joe, I want you working collecting. Levi and I will stand on the wagon and catch and stack. Annie, you'll drive. Now let's take a moment to pray that *Gotte* blesses our harvest and keeps each of us safely in the palm of his hand."

There were times when Annie wished they prayed aloud, where she could simply listen to the calming sound of her *dat*'s voice. Instead the silence forced her to speak to *Gotte*. She found herself confessing her ungratefulness, her tendency to consider her wants and needs more important than those of others, her love for her family and this day and their simple life.

After her father said, "And in His name, we pray..." and everyone answered "Amen," Levi glanced her way.

Did he just wink at her?

Annie looked at the ground, back at the house and then at Levi who was smiling broadly.

They walked together toward the wagon that was already hitched to the Percherons. Pop was the older of the two. He had a light gray coat, stood sixteen hands tall and weighed nearly two thousand pounds. Annie reached in her pocket and handed him a carrot.

"I was a toddler when Dat bought Pop. He's older, but still strong, still a *gut* workhorse."

"I've cleaned out their stalls for nearly a month now, but I haven't really spent any time with them." Levi ran his hand down the neck of the other workhorse. He was chestnut colored and nearly identical in size to Pop.

"That's Pretty Boy. We've only had him three years now."

"You'll drive careful, right?"

"I always do."

"You won't intentionally knock me off?"

"How can you even suggest such a thing?"

"It's no secret I'm like a burr under your saddle."

"We don't have saddles. We're Amish." How many times had she reminded him? This time instead of being irritated at her correction, he smiled even more broadly.

"Just remember your *dat* is riding back there with me."

He held out a hand to help boost her up onto the wagon bench seat.

She ignored it, grabbed the handle and pulled herself up.

And then they were harvesting, and she didn't spend another minute arguing with Levi Lapp in her mind. She was too busy minding Pop and Pretty Boy.

Enjoying the sounds of her brothers as they pulled the corncobs from the husks and tossed them to the wagon.

Even smiling when Levi and Dat picked up the chorus of "I Have Decided" and then followed it with "Victory in Jesus" and "Will the Circle Be Unbroken." The morning flew by, and she was surprised when the sound of her mother ringing the dinner bell echoed across the field.

Nathan jumped up onto the wagon, reminding her of the young teen he'd once been. Now he was thirty and had seven children of his own. "I'll take them to the barn."

"Are you sure?"

"Can't have my little *schweschder* watering horses."

She handed him the reins and stepped down, dismayed to see Levi waiting for her. Her father and Joseph were already walking toward the house.

"You didn't have to wait."

"I wanted to."

She started to ask why, but she didn't want to ruin her good mood by being snarky.

"You're pretty *gut* with the horses."

"Danki." She fished around for something else to say. Why did she suddenly feel tongue-tied around Levi

Lapp? It occurred to her that he was adorable in a lost puppy kind of way.

"You're smiling."

"I am?"

Instead of answering, he bumped his shoulder against hers. They walked toward the house where she could see her *mamm* and oldest sister, Mary, had set lunch out on the picnic table beneath the maple trees. The sight brought a cascade of memories to her mind—twenty-four years' worth, though she wasn't certain she could remember the early ones.

But always they'd had the fall harvest.

Always family had helped.

Always they'd had lunch under these trees.

She glanced at Levi, saw a smile spread across his face as he looked at the spread of food and gathering of her family.

"It's *gut* here," she said. "This place? This land? It's *gut.*"

He slowed and studied her for a moment, and Annie had the ridiculous notion that he was about to reach for her hand. Instead, Levi again nudged her shoulder and said, "I'll race you."

Which was completely ridiculous. After all, they were not *kinner* anymore. Laughter bubbled out of her, sounding young and hopeful and free. And then she was running to catch up, because she couldn't stand the thought of Levi Lapp beating her even at something as silly as a race to the lunch table.

Chapter Six

Levi had expected to like Annie's family from the very beginning, but he hadn't expected to feel so comfortable with them. He pushed back from the table, certain that if he ate another bite he'd be asleep in the field rather than working in it.

"I think I better walk this off," he muttered and headed toward the shady side of the lawn. He was surprised when Joseph walked out of the barn and joined him.

"Ready for the second shift?"

Levi patted his stomach. "The mind is willing, but…"

"*Ya.* The flesh is full."

"Indeed."

"*Dat* always takes a thirty-minute break after the meal is done. You'd think we were going out to swim instead of harvest." Joseph pushed his hat back on his head.

Levi thought of Annie making fun of his hat, and then it occurred to him how he and Joseph must look. Both Amish. Both relatively young men. One traditionally Amish, wearing the customary straw hat, and the other—him—not so traditional, wearing his Stetson. They were both standing at the fence, hands crossed over the top bar, watching the workhorses nod in the sun. In that moment, he felt their similarities out-weighed their differences. He felt, temporarily at least, like a part of something bigger than himself.

"Actually what I wanted to talk to you about was Annie."

"Annie?"

"We're all a bit protective of her."

"*Bruders* usually are." He'd felt that way toward his own *schweschdern* once. Then they'd grown up, mar-ried and decided it was their job to set him straight.

"It's what I wanted to talk to you about."

Levi looked at him in surprise.

"It's obvious that you like her."

"Annie? I like her fine."

"You're not understanding what I'm trying to say. It's *obvious* that you're interested in her."

"Annie?" His voice screeched like when he was a *youngie* and everything was changing. He swallowed, took a deep breath and forced himself to speak in a nor-mal voice. "*Nein*, not like that. She can barely tolerate being around me."

"That's not what it looks like from where I'm stand-ing."

Levi glanced back toward the picnic area. The women were cleaning up, and Annie was in the mid-dle of them stacking dishes into a tub.

"Maybe you need glasses then..." Levi's words trailed off as he thought of Annie working in her wed-ding trailer, Annie driving the horses, Annie running beside him across the field.

Joseph cleared his throat, and Levi forced his attention back to the conversation. "As far as Annie is concerned, you've got the wrong guy, or something."

"So you don't have romantic feelings for my little *schweschder*?"

Levi opened his mouth, closed it, opened it again. He felt like a fish out of water. He felt completely disoriented.

"Just be careful. Annie's the youngest in our family, as you know, so we all feel as if we need to look out for her."

"You have nothing to worry about with me. She doesn't…she can't even stand…you've got this all wrong."

Joseph patted him on the shoulder. "Maybe you don't realize how you feel at this point."

"And you do?"

"I'm asking you to be mindful of how you treat her. If you don't plan on staying—and from what I've heard from Dat, you don't—then it's probably best to not even go that direction with her."

"But if Alton and Lily move, then—"

"My parents moving would be difficult for her, but does that mean she will too? Not likely." Joseph crossed his arms, studying the scene before them. The fields, the picnic, the family—it could be an illustration for a book on Amish life. "Annie's always had an independent spirit. She worked hard to build up a *gut* business, and she probably won't give it up even when she marries, though she'll have to cut back some or hire other workers to help her. But moving to Texas? I don't see that happening even if Dat and Mamm go."

Joseph resettled his hat on his head. "So I'd appreciate you not leading her on." With those words, he walked away.

Suddenly Levi understood what had puzzled him since his arrival. He understood as clearly as if it had been carved on a tablet and handed to him.

He wasn't merely suggesting a move to her parents. If what he hoped would happen did happen, then Annie's entire world would be turned on its head.

Annie saw Joseph talking to Levi. She hoped it had been about the harvest, or church or even the community he'd come from. Worst-case scenario, he was asking questions about Texas, but she didn't see that happening. Joseph had a very prosperous farm as well as a woodworking business. She couldn't see him starting over again somewhere else, especially with such a large family.

But maybe she was wrong.

Maybe he was already worried about land for his sons.

Possibly Texas sounded like the promised land to him same as it did to Levi.

The thought filled her with dread. Would she lose her entire family to Levi's dream? She pushed the thought away, determined not to let her worries ruin such a beautiful fall day.

The afternoon passed even more quickly than the morning had. She spent two hours on the back of the wagon, catching and stacking corn, another hour walking along the rows and pulling the cobs from the shucks and the final two hours driving the team.

By the time her *dat* called it a day, she was so dead

on her feet that sleeping in the field seemed like a valid option.

"Tired?" Levi asked.

"How can you tell?"

"Because you're standing still staring at the house instead of walking toward it."

She glanced at him, exasperated to see that he had enough energy to tease her. Annie sighed and began plodding toward the house, and Levi matched her step for step. If she was going to have to walk with him, she might as well ask what was on her mind.

"What were you talking to Joseph about?"

"Joseph?"

"My *bruder*. The guy you stood with outside the barn after lunch."

"I know who he is."

"So what were you talking to him about? Please tell me it was not about Texas."

"Nein." His answer was soft and he avoided looking directly at her.

She didn't think he would lie to her, but something was up.

"Then what were you talking about?"

"Oh…" Levi seemed to hesitate. When had he ever minced words before? Finally, he plunged ahead. "Joseph was warning me that they're protective of you."

"Protective?" They were halfway across the field. She could see her father releasing the horses into the pasture, Nathan forking hay into the feeder and Joseph pouring water from the horse trough over his head. "Protective how?"

Levi jerked the hat off his head, and that was when

she noticed how red his ears were. Had he somehow sunburned them, or…

"They think that we're interested in one another—romantically."

Her mouth fell open. She tried to think of how to respond to that, but her thoughts were suddenly spinning in a dozen directions at the same time. She shook her head and snapped her mouth shut, though she continued to stare at him.

"I know."

"You know what?"

"That the notion is ludicrous. You can barely stand to be around me."

"That's not true."

"My hat irritates you." He waved the Stetson.

"It's not Amish."

"My boots irritate you."

"They're cowboy boots."

"And my dream of moving to Texas irritates you."

The look he gave her reminded Annie of a child who had been scolded.

"It's not your dream that bothers me, Levi."

"It's how it will affect your family. I know. I understand that now."

"You do?"

He nodded, slapped the Stetson against his leg releasing a small cloud of dust and positioned it back on his head. "And I'm sorry."

"You're sorry?" She could hear herself repeating his words like some sort of well-trained parrot, but she couldn't seem to stop. "You're sorry?"

"I am, Annie." His tone of voice, his posture, even his expression told her that he was no longer teasing.

He was serious. Levi Lapp was seriously apologizing for disrupting her life and sending her future plans into a tailspin.

She hadn't seen that coming.

How should she respond?

She had no idea. So she resumed walking toward the house.

"I was so focused on what I wanted, that it never occurred to me how it would affect you. When I came here, I only knew Old Simon. I certainly didn't anticipate meeting your family."

"And yet you were looking for families just like mine."

"I was. That's true, but maybe…maybe I should have backed off when I saw how much it upset you. Instead, I dug in deeper."

Her voice dropped, an image popping in her mind from her childhood. "There are times you remind me of our old hound dog whenever he found a bone."

They were nearly to the house. He put a hand on her arm and didn't remove it until she'd stopped and turned to face him. "I don't know how I'm going to fix this, but I promise you that I will try."

He waited a moment, maybe to see if she believed him, maybe to wait for her response which never came because she still had no idea what to say.

Then he turned and trudged toward the barn, and Annie was left trying to figure out what had just happened.

Annie thought of trying to set her family straight. But everything she came up with sounded like a *youngie* protesting that she didn't have a crush when she did. Instead, she vowed to keep quiet on the topic. She washed up, changed clothes and made it downstairs as her *mamm* was putting dinner on the table. Joseph and Nathan had headed home to eat with their own families. Mary had helped prepare the meal and then hurried home as well. As they settled around the table it was only Annie, her parents and Levi.

She expected things to be uncomfortable, and indeed, at least three different times, she caught her parents sending each other silent looks. They'd done that as long as she could remember. It was as if they had their own wordless communication system. Was that what it was like to be married? To be able to know what your spouse was thinking without uttering a word? Annie wasn't sure she was ready for that kind of intimacy. The idea that her family thought she wanted such a relationship with Levi Lapp almost caused her to laugh out loud.

"Levi, you were a big help today." Her *dat* reached for a second helping of potato casserole.

"*Danki.* I enjoy harvest, always have."

"You haven't talked much about your family other than to mention they're in Lancaster."

Annie fought the urge to roll her eyes. She'd been through this before—once when she was dating a boy from Shipshewana and another time when she'd stepped out with a boy who had recently moved to Goshen. It was as if her *dat* had a list of questions for any prospective beaus.

She barely heard Levi's reply. She was too busy trying to think of a way to derail her parents' confused ideas about her and Levi.

Her *dat* continued to pepper him with questions

about Lancaster. Bits and pieces of Levi's responses registered: sixty-five-acre farm, a few dairy cows, all the children grown and gone but an oldest brother living on the family farm.

Her *mamm* wanted to know how many siblings he had—two sisters who were older than Levi and two younger half sisters. Annie dropped her fork and stared at him at the mention of a stepfather.

"My *dat* died when I was fifteen," Levi explained. "We were living here in Goshen at the time, and then my *mamm* remarried. Not too long after that we moved."

Annie's *mamm* carefully pressed her napkin to her lips and then folded it in her lap. "I'm sorry, Levi. I don't believe I knew your parents. I guess even then Goshen was large enough to have divided into several church districts."

"*Ya*, we lived a *gut* ways from here, what I can remember of it."

"We are all sorry for your loss." Her *dat* echoed her *mamm*'s sentiment. "Couldn't have been easy for a young man to lose his father."

Levi shrugged and changed the subject, asking when they'd begin to plant the winter wheat. Soon they were deep into a discussion on crop rotation.

Annie stood to help clean the dishes, but her mother made up a bogus excuse for Annie to see Levi out.

"They've done this before," she said as she walked him toward the barn.

"Done what?"

"Decided that I'm interested in someone, and gone out of their way to be accommodating." She tried to laugh, but really it was humiliating. She didn't need her parents' help to find a beau.

"They care about you."

"*Ya*, but they also think they know what's best."

"Don't all parents? Mine certainly thought they knew what was best for me—staying in Lancaster, farming a tiny place because that's all we could afford, starting a side business to support the farm. It's what my step-dad had done and what my brothers-in-law had done. They were convinced I should stay and do the same." Levi shook his head. "They couldn't grasp the idea that the life I wanted was different from the one they had."

"I understand firsthand how frustrating that is. Mamm and Dat have been supportive of my business, but I think at first they were convinced it was a phase I'd grow out of."

"Plainly they are proud of you."

"And plainly they want me married." Her cheeks burned even saying the words. At least it was dark and Levi couldn't see.

She helped him hitch Old Simon's horse to his buggy.

"He's had this mare as long as I can remember." The mare was black with white socks. Annie stepped closer and rubbed her hand up and down the horse's neck. "Old Simon's wife named her."

"First mare I've ever known named after a flower."

"Petunia's a *gut* name. Tabitha named the milk cows too—Rosebud and Daisy and Tulip."

Levi started laughing. "You're making that up."

"I'm not."

Instead of climbing up into the buggy, Levi turned around, his back against the buggy, and stared up at the stars.

"Please don't tell me the stars are brighter in Texas."

He didn't. Instead he began to sing "Deep in the Heart of Texas." She'd heard it before. But she'd heard it as an energetic children's song that they'd sung in school when they were learning about each state.

Levi sang it like a lullaby, and for the first time Annie found herself curious about this state that had captured his heart.

She moved beside him, stared up at the sky and wondered if it could be true. Were the stars brighter in Texas? She didn't ask. She didn't want to know.

Levi nudged his shoulder against hers. "I've figured out what we should do."

"About what?" Annie was distracted by Levi's closeness. She wondered what it would be like to kiss him.

"About your family."

"Oh, *ya*. Tell me. I'm all ears. Because trying to persuade them something isn't so only convinces them that it is."

"So we should do it."

"Do it?"

"Step out together."

She squinted at him in the darkness, trying to make out his expression. Finally, she found her voice. "Did you hit your head today? Stay out in the sun too long? Maybe you're having a small stroke?"

"Why is it such a crazy idea?"

"Well…we're complete opposites."

"True."

"You're not going to be here very long if your plan works."

"I didn't ask you to marry me."

"And I didn't ask you to ask me."

Instead of becoming exasperated with her, which he had every right to be, Levi began to laugh.

"See?" He stuck his thumbs inside his suspenders. "This is what I enjoy about us."

"There is no *us*."

"You never say what I expect, and you always say what's on your mind."

"Not always."

He laughed again, as if she'd said something very witty. She was beginning to wonder if he was a little daft, but then his tone grew serious.

"Joseph warned me not to mislead you, but we're being honest with one another here. I know you're not really interested in me." He said it as if he were relating the weather forecast. "Your parents plainly want us to step out, so we'll do it, and then…"

"Then what?"

"I don't know. Show them that we're incompatible, I guess."

She wound her *kapp* string around her finger. "What about Martha?"

Levi shook his head. "I've told you. There's nothing between me and Martha. She's like a nicer, kinder version of my little *schweschder*."

Martha had said practically the same thing about Levi to Annie the day before, but she hadn't believed her. Why did she feel such a sense of relief hearing Levi confirm it? Why did she even care?

Instead of pointing out how ridiculous their plan was, she found herself saying, "It might work."

"Really?"

"I mean it might prove to my parents that we're mismatched. We can step out a few times, and then when it's obvious we don't belong together—"

"Plainly, we don't."

"Then we can say we tried, and they'll back off. This isn't the first time they've poked their collective noses in my social life. And don't say it. I know. They care about me."

"It's a deal then."

He'd climbed up in the buggy, but he leaned back down and said, "I still want to go to Texas, still plan to. I'm going to find a way."

"I'm sure you will."

"But I've mucked things up for you, and I'm going to find a way to undo that."

"You mean with Dat?"

"And your *bruder* Jebediah. Why wasn't he here today?"

"Had to get his own corn up, though his crop was much smaller and he was able to do it with the help of a neighbor. You know how it is—everyone harvests at the same time."

Levi stared out over the mare, out toward the fields they'd just harvested. "You have a nice life here. I can see that now. My future—it's to the south, but my dream doesn't have to be your *dat*'s."

"Maybe you could mention some of the bad things about Texas."

"I'll have to be a little more subtle than that, but I'll think of something." He turned to look at her then. "I promise."

He waited until she nodded, then he picked up the reins, released the brake and guided Petunia down their lane. It occurred to her that Levi Lapp was a good man, and he'd make some Amish girl a fine husband.

* * *

Levi didn't expect Old Simon to still be up when he finally made it into the house. The drive from Annie's was only ten minutes, and he often walked. Since he knew they'd be working later and he'd be staying for dinner, he'd taken the buggy. Plus, Simon rarely took it out alone anymore. Levi didn't hurry as he unhitched the buggy and cared for the horse. Those things calmed him, helped him to process all that had happened. By the time he stepped into the sitting room, it was well past the old guy's normal bedtime.

But there he sat, in his rocker, whittling on a cane.

He carved crosses into the tops of them, sanded them until they were as smooth as the softest cotton and sold them at a store in town. It was a way to earn extra money, but more than that it was something he seemed to enjoy doing.

"How was the harvest?"

Levi sank onto the couch and told him about the day in the field.

When he'd finished, Simon said, "Sounds as if our Annie has caught your fancy."

"Why do you say that?"

"Because you mentioned her quite a bit, but hardly spoke at all about her *bruders*."

"Oh, her *bruders* seem like nice people too."

Simon smiled, but he didn't comment on that. Realizing that he would hear about his and Annie's dating, Levi decided to tell him about it before someone else could.

"Actually, we're going to be stepping out together— Annie and I."

"Thought you were seeing the Weaver girl."

"*Ya*, I was, but we decided…that is, it seems like… well, what I mean is, we're *freinden,* is all."

"Love often starts as friendship."

Did it ever start as enemies? The question almost popped out of Levi's mouth, but he managed to rein it in. He and Annie hadn't been adversaries—not exactly. That was too harsh a word. It was true that they were on opposite sides of the Texas issue, but now he understood why. It didn't weaken his resolve to move there. In fact, he realized, in that moment, that he felt less anxious than he had since moving to Goshen. It no longer seemed that Annie was working against him, only that they were on separate paths.

"She's a *gut* girl, our Annie." Simon ran a hand up and down the walking stick checking for rough spots. "Seems as if only yesterday she was a young thing, running around with the *kinner.*"

"Not many Amish women run their own business."

As soon as he uttered the words, Levi remembered Annie admonishing him about how many Amish women did work to help the family budget—bakers, quilters, etc. She'd been right. He'd simply never taken the time to think about it.

But what she'd done?

The wedding trailer?

Cooking for hundreds of people at a time? *Nein.* There weren't many women that he knew who could accomplish such a thing.

"It's true," Simon said. "But Annie saw a need in our community and met it."

"Because Goshen has grown so much."

"That—and also because now Amish women are

busier than ever." Simon added a touch of oil to his rag and proceeded to rub it into the cane. "Raising a household of children, keeping the house and preparing the meals—those things are a tremendous amount of work. Plus, most families now have cottage businesses that are important to their livelihood. Unfortunately it's become harder and harder to make it on farming alone."

It occurred to Levi that Simon's thinking was remarkably clear tonight. There was none of the confusion he'd witnessed earlier. Hadn't he mixed up the Red River with the Mississippi just the day before? Perhaps his confusion only happened when he was tired or stressed.

"I agree that times are hard—even for an Amish farmer who is supposed to be self-sufficient. The cost of land is so prohibitive. It's why I want to start a community in Texas."

"*Ya.* Sure and certain it could be less expensive there, if you pick the right spot. But farming is always hard, Levi, especially dry-land farming."

"I didn't claim it wasn't." He felt the old defensiveness rise up in him—like a cat being stroked the wrong way.

"I knew you were aware. We've lived there—you and I have. You were old enough when we left to know that the farming was difficult—it wasn't all bluebonnets and rodeos."

"Are you against the idea of moving?"

"Not at all." Simon ran the rag over the cane one last time, then stood and carried it to a corner of the room where he placed it with the ones that were ready to go to town. "But I wouldn't want to misrepresent what we're doing. We're not going to the promised land, though it might appear that way from a distance."

"I'm aware."

"We work and toil in this life, live simply, try to be a good neighbor and follow *Gotte's* word. Rest assured, you'll face challenges in Texas same as here. Let's be very certain that everyone understands that."

Levi wanted to take offense at the words. It felt like the old guy was lecturing him, but a crack had opened in Levi's dreams and the smallest bit of doubt had crept in.

Was he only remembering the best parts of Texas?

Had he forgotten how difficult it was living there?

And worse yet, what if Annie was right? What if there was somewhere closer, somewhere better, that he hadn't considered? Not only would he be risking the money he'd saved, but he'd be leading a group of people right off the proverbial cliff with him.

Chapter Seven

Annie was busy on Thursday—from the moment the sun rose until it settled in the west. She barely had a moment to rest what with catching up on the household chores and setting things straight in the wedding trailer.

By Friday morning, she felt that she'd made up for the day she'd lost harvesting. As she drank coffee with her *mamm*, she made a long list of things she needed to purchase. Although Priscilla bought most of their food in bulk at the local big-box discount store, there were still items she needed to pick up at local stores.

And there was another reason she was eager to take the buggy out. On the way to town, she had to pass right by Martha's place. No harm in stopping to see if she'd like to ride along.

Her *mamm* thought it was a fine plan and added a few things she needed to the bottom of Annie's list. After they'd had breakfast and cleaned up the dishes, her *dat* brought the buggy around. She couldn't help smiling when she walked up to Bella. They'd bought the mare four years ago, but Annie still thought she was the prettiest buggy mare she'd ever seen—chestnut colored with three white socks and a sweet disposition.

She headed off to town feeling fairly optimistic about the day, though she dreaded confronting Martha. "Not a confrontation," she tried to assure herself. "More like an informational meeting."

Big Tom was off with one of his *bruders*, looking at goats.

"He's quite excited," Martha said. "We had some, years ago, and he's forgotten how much trouble they can be."

"My *dat* says if water can get through a fence, a goat can and will."

"*Ya*, I've heard that one. There's some truth to it too."

Martha was keen on spending a few hours away from the farm. They stopped by the fabric store where Annie purchased several yards of lace that she planned to use on her centerpieces the next day. Then they went to the general store for the rest of the items on her list. By the time they were finished there, Annie realized she'd skipped lunch and was starving.

"Coffee and a treat?"

"You'll never hear me turn down either of those things."

Annie ordered coffee and a cranberry-walnut scone. Martha chose coffee and a large blueberry muffin. When they sat down, both girls cut their treat in half and swapped. It was something they'd done since they were young. They didn't even think about it anymore—best friends shared, and Martha certainly was her best friend.

It was after they'd finished their food and were sipping on refills of coffee that Annie brought up the subject of Levi. She explained how he'd helped with the

harvest, how her family had misinterpreted their friendship and what they'd decided to do about it.

By the time she was done, Martha was grinning like
a child who'd caught her first fish.

"Why are you looking at me that way?"

"What way?"

"As if you expected this."

"But I did expect this."

Annie stared at Martha. She wasn't offended exactly,
more surprised. Martha had always been the more in-
sightful one, while Annie had always been the one to
jump into action. Still, she hadn't seen this coming at all.

"It's not real," she reminded her.

"Uh-huh."

"We're not truly interested in each other."

"So you mentioned—at least three times now."

"It's just that my parents are quite single-minded.
You know how they are. Once they get an idea in their
heads, it's impossible to convince them it isn't so..."
The rest of her explanation died on her lips when she
saw Martha was now outright laughing at her, though
she was attempting to hide it behind her napkin.

"What?"

"Maybe you don't realize that Levi is quite taken
with you."

"Taken with me?"

"That's what I said."

"Now you're being *narrisch*."

"I'm perfectly sane and you know it."

"Then why would you suggest such a thing?"

"Because it's true."

"Definitely is not true."

"I've spent a lot of time with him the last few weeks, thanks to the elaborate plan you concocted."

"Desperate more than elaborate."

"He talks about you all the time."

"What?" Her voice had climbed an octave and an older *Englisch* couple turned their direction, eyebrows raised. Annie forced her voice down. "What are you talking about?"

"Always it was Annie this and Annie that. He's quite smitten with you and probably doesn't even know it."

"Martha Weaver. I believe you're teasing me."

"I'm not." She leaned forward and dropped her voice to a whisper. "One day he even told me that you would make a fine *fraa*…"

"He said that? About me?"

"Uh-huh."

"What else did he say? I can tell you're holding something back."

"*Nein*, I'm not."

"Spill it."

"Well, okay. He said you'd make a fine *fraa* for someone who didn't mind an opinionated, stubborn and very strong-willed woman."

"See?" Annie sat back, satisfied that she hadn't misread the situation. "That sounds more like the Levi I know."

"If you say so. It's a little warm in here. Are you ready to go? I think I need some fresh air."

The day was drizzly, but they'd stopped by the library earlier, and she'd checked the weather on the computer. The forecast promised things would clear off during the late afternoon. Tomorrow should be sunny but crisp—perfect weather for a wedding.

She pulled in a deep breath as Martha joined her on the sidewalk, linked their arms together, and turned them toward the buggy.

Martha's voice was suddenly serious. "It's okay, you know. If you like him."

"Because you two are just *freinden*."

"Yup."

"Because you're so much alike."

"Exactly."

"I'm going to disagree with that. You're kind and giving and compassionate…"

"If you could have seen Levi with Big Tom, you'd understand that he is those things too."

"All right. I'm not saying he doesn't have *gut* qualities, but he's also more bullheaded than those Texas longhorns he's always bragging about."

"Not always a bad thing."

They'd reached the buggy. Annie fed a carrot to Bella, patting the mare and thanking her for waiting so patiently. When they were settled inside, and Annie had set the mare into a nice trot down the street, Martha said what was on her mind, what she'd probably been trying to say from the beginning.

"It's okay if you change your mind about a thing or a person. Sometimes first impressions aren't the best. Sometimes we have to see past that impression to the scars and hopes and dreams underneath, and then we understand who they really are."

"And you think that's what is happening between Levi and me?"

"Maybe."

"I don't know. Honestly when I think about Levi, my thoughts and feelings are a jumble."

"Give it time, my friend. But please, keep an open mind."

Could she do that where Levi was concerned? And did she owe it to Levi to give him a fresh start? She hadn't made the best first impression, either. She could still remember the lecture she'd given him that first night he'd had dinner at her parents' house.

So what was she supposed to do?

See past Levi's scars, as Martha had suggested?

How did a person even do that?

She puzzled over that question long after she'd dropped off Martha at her place. She was nearly back home before it occurred to her that maybe this wasn't something that she could figure out on her own. Maybe it was something she needed to pray about.

Levi kept trying to find time to speak with Annie on Sunday, but either she was extraordinarily busy or she was avoiding him. There was no church meeting that day. Instead, it was a visiting Sunday, and he and Old Simon had been invited to eat with Annie's family. The place was starting to feel very familiar to him. It was starting to feel more like home than his mother and stepfather's place ever had.

He drove Petunia right up to the barn and released her into the adjacent field as Old Simon made his way over to the luncheon tables.

Unfortunately it wasn't the quiet, intimate affair he'd hoped for. It seemed that all of Annie's family were there—two older *bruders*, two older *schweschdern*, all their spouses and plenty of nieces and nephews. He gave up trying to remember all the children's names.

For reasons he couldn't fathom, Annie was in a state

of constant motion. She was the last to sit down to eat—taking a place at the opposite end of the table from him—and the first to jump up and start clearing dishes. It was possible she was avoiding him.

The thought bothered him more than he wanted it to. He wanted not to care. It wasn't like she'd confessed her affection for him, but they had come up with a plan. He'd thought he was helping her out. Now he wasn't so sure.

Clouds had been building through the morning, so it was no surprise when the sky darkened even more and a gentle, soaking rain began to fall. The adults sought refuge on the wraparound covered porch. The children headed to the barn. After confirming that Annie wasn't on the porch, he darted across the yard, soaking his clothes in the process. It was worth getting wet because the minute he stepped into the barn he found her.

She looked as pretty as she had bustling around the table, but now her eyes were covered with a checkered dishcloth that had been folded into a rectangle and tied around her head. She held out her arms to keep from walking into anything, and a bright smile covered her face. The children called out to her as she sought to tag them.

"Can't catch me."

"You're not even close."

"This could take days."

Before he realized what had happened, she'd banged an arm against his chest and shouted "Ha! You're It." The expression on her face when she yanked off the blindfold and saw who she'd tagged was priceless.

"Where did you come from?"

"Outside. It's raining."

"*Ya.* I know. That's why we're in here." Her face was flushed and she was twirling the blindfold in her hands.

If he'd thought he would have time to talk to her, he was sadly mistaken. They were surrounded by kids. It seemed as if the number had doubled since lunch and they were all shouting, "You're It, Levi. She tagged you!"

It should have been a simple game.

One he hadn't played in many years.

Still, it was embarrassing that it took him so long to tag someone. He kept hearing Annie's laughter and lurching toward her, only to slap a bale of hay or the barn wall or one time the tabby cat that hissed and swiped at his arm. This sent the entire group into fits of laughter.

Finally, he caught the littlest nephew, a small tyke with white-blond hair and blue eyes. "I'm It? I'll never catch anyone."

"I'll help you…"

"His name is Teddy." Annie pulled the blindfold from Levi's hands and began to tie it around her nephew's eyes.

"Teddy?"

"Short for Theodore."

"I'll help you, Teddy."

"You will?" Teddy jerked his head in Levi's direction, though he couldn't see him as the blindfold was now firmly in place.

"Sure, just follow my voice and ignore everyone else."

It only took a couple of minutes.

Teddy's older *schweschder* Molly happened to trip and fall in the hay. Lucky for Teddy. He fell on her claiming, "I got ya. You're It. We did it, Levi."

They played another half hour, Teddy sticking close to Levi the entire time. When the children finally decided they were hungry again and ran from the barn, Levi collapsed on top of a bale of hay.

"Young ones wear you out."

"Oh, you're worn out, are you?"

"*Ya.* Aren't you?"

"I suppose." She glanced out the door and then back at him as if she was uncertain whether she should stay. As if she didn't know whether she should chance being alone with him.

"You can sit down, Annie. I won't bite."

"I never said you would."

"Then why does it feel like you've been avoiding me all day?"

"Avoiding you? Why would I do that?"

"I don't know. That's why I brought it up."

She rolled her eyes but sat down on an overturned crate.

"We should talk about our first date."

"We should call it something else."

"Really? Like what?"

"I don't know." She swiped at a lock of hair that had fallen free of her *kapp.* "Doesn't matter, I guess."

"I thought the point was we want your parents to think we're dating."

"Yes, yes…"

"And then it won't work, and then they'll leave you alone." He smiled triumphantly. "See? I was listening."

"Fine. So where are you taking me on this date? I was thinking a fancy restaurant…"

"What?"

"Or maybe even an *Englisch* movie. I love the popcorn and soda there."

"Do you know how much those cost?" He realized

too late that she was baiting him. Feeling ridiculous, he countered with, "This whole dating thing—where it's assumed the guy will pay for everything—is not fair."

"Oooh. Are you thinking of bucking tradition? Notice I use the word *buck*. I'm trying to make you feel comfortable with some Texas slang."

This was the Annie he liked. The one who teased him with a smile that said, *Come on, walk into this trap.*

"I rode a bucking bronco once."

"You don't say?"

"Cracked two ribs when he threw me."

"So you learned your lesson?"

"What lesson would that be?"

"To stay off bucking broncos."

"*Nein.* See, bronco riding is a sport in Texas. They really enjoy it—like we do baseball."

"People don't crack their ribs in baseball."

"Well, normally they don't, but they could. That's not the point." He started to explain rodeo competitions to her, but she held up a hand and stopped him.

"You can bore me with this on our date. Where are we going?"

Suddenly he knew where he wanted to take her. "Let's go snag some of those leftover oatmeal raisin bars."

"We just ate."

"Hours ago. I'm starving."

"Spoken like a man."

"Women don't get hungry? Come on. You barely ate anything at lunch."

Annie had stood and was brushing hay off her dress. She stopped, her hand halfway down her apron, her eyes squinting and a line forming between her brows. "You were watching me eat?"

"I was trying to find time to talk to you."

"And so you followed me out here?"

"I'm not a stalker. We needed to plan our not-date. So what about it?"

"What about what?"

"Those oatmeal bars."

"They're bound to be gone already...the kids had a fifteen-minute start on us." A mischievous smile teased at her lips—very pretty pink lips, he suddenly noticed. "I might know where some are put back in the kitchen."

"You don't say."

"I could be persuaded to show you."

Levi stepped closer, reached out and plucked a piece of hay from her *kapp*. She stood frozen, like a deer caught midstride.

"I'd like that." His voice suddenly sounded husky and low, sounded like a person he didn't recognize. He moved closer, wondering if he had the courage to kiss her. But either he was reading the mood wrong or Annie was not having any of it. She thrust the red dishcloth in his hands and said, "Stay close. If the *kinner* see what we're up to, we'll starve. We're outnumbered and don't stand a chance."

But Levi's thoughts were no longer focused on snacks or games of tag or even bull riding. He was thinking of one thing, and at the moment she was wearing a pretty dark blue dress and leading him across a rain-soaked yard.

Chapter Eight

Tuesday afternoon Annie waited on her front porch for Levi to arrive.

"Where is he taking you?" Her *mamm* was working on yet another baby blanket. They seemed to sprout from her knitting needles. This one was in pink, white and lavender.

"I don't know. He wouldn't say."

"It's so nice to see you getting out and having some fun. You work entirely too much, in my opinion."

Annie didn't answer that. She was already regretting this plan of theirs. She should be spending the afternoon sketching out ideas for the Hoschstetler wedding, though in truth she had two more weeks to get ready for that, and it was a small gathering—only a hundred and fifty guests.

"That sweater looks very nice on you."

"You made it for me."

"I remember, but you hardly ever wear it."

Annie fingered the light wool. It was a pretty burgundy and always reminded her of fall. It was true she rarely wore it, as she seldom did anything social and it was too nice for everyday clothes. Why had she even picked it for today? It wasn't like she needed to dress up for Levi Lapp.

As if thinking his name had the power to make him appear, Levi pulled into their lane.

How he'd managed to get off work early on a Tuesday, she had no idea. But he'd insisted that two in the afternoon was the best time so she'd agreed. What else could she do?

Annie tried not to blush as her *mamm* reminded them there was no need to hurry home. Before she could back out of the date, they were in the buggy traveling down the lane.

"How was your day?" Levi asked.

No doubt he was merely being polite, but she found herself telling him about the upcoming wedding and how Rachel Hoschstetler was having a small group.

"One hundred and fifty? Doesn't sound small to me."

"You've been to plenty of Amish weddings. You know what I mean."

"I guess."

"If you have ten siblings and they have ten children."

"I can do the math…"

"So you see what I mean, plus there's all the *aentis* and *onkels*. But Rachel, her family is small on her *mamm*'s side. She was an only child."

"I'm surprised they hired you if the gathering is so small."

She glared at him. Now, this was the Levi she expected, not the play-it-nice guy who wanted to know how her day had been, but the snarky one who questioned her ability to run a business.

"Why are you looking at me that way? My hat crooked?"

She didn't want to talk about his cowboy hat again. That was a ploy he often used to change the topic. She wasn't falling for it. "How could you say such a thing?"

"What did I say?"

"That you were surprised they would hire me."

"I am surprised." As if hearing what he was saying for the first time, he began to stammer, "Um...that's not what I meant."

"Oh, it isn't?"

"*Nein.* What I meant was...well, I was just wondering out loud why Amish who seldom eat out and never hire someone to help with the housework would hire someone to cook for a wedding. But now that I think about it, I guess you explained it to me that first night."

"You were actually listening?"

"Amish families hire you because a wedding is a tremendous amount of work. In fact, it's almost impossible for one family to do the work to prepare for a large wedding. But if this Rachel only has a small family, then I'm surprised they'd hire you."

He smiled in her direction, as if he'd cleared it all up.

Which he had, sort of. She was definitely too quick to jump to the wrong conclusion with Levi.

"Okay. Now I see what you mean."

"*Gut.*"

"Her *mamm* is sick. She has MS and some days are harder than others. So her *dat* offered to hire me."

"Now that makes sense."

Annie had been so caught up in their conversation that she hadn't paid any attention to where he was driving. They'd traveled through Goshen and popped out the other side. They passed the Dairy Queen and the Best Western, and then Levi pulled off the main road.

"Fidler Pond?"

"*Ya.* Have you been here before?"

"*Nein.* I've wanted to but haven't found the time."

"I thought a few hours away from the farm might be nice."

"Huh."

"And I haven't tried my hand at a paddleboat in quite some time."

"They have paddleboats?" She felt an uncharacteristic surge of excitement. She loved paddling around in the water. Had she told him that? How could he have known?

Levi was parking the buggy, careful to pick a shady spot in an area that wasn't paved over. "Don't want Petunia standing on concrete for hours."

They were going to spend hours together?

Before she could dwell on that terrifying thought, he'd tugged on her hand and pulled her toward the small rental shack. As he started to pay, she remembered his lecture about men being expected to pay for everything on a date, about how unfair it was. She hadn't thought about that much. Then again, she hadn't been on very many dates.

"I can pay half." She opened her purse to fetch some money.

"I've got this." When she started to protest, he added, "We'll do dinner Dutch and you can pay for dessert."

"You expect this date to last that long?"

"Hope springs eternal…"

His tone had turned suddenly serious, and she found she couldn't quite meet his gaze. Why was Levi always surprising her? Teasing one minute and looking at her with those blue eyes she could drown in the next.

Instead of dwelling on it, she tossed her head and said, "Fine, but I get to pick the color of the boat."

She chose the bright yellow one, and before she could stop to think about how close they were going to be forced to sit, they were out in the middle of the small pond, laughing at the fish and splashing one another with the water.

After an hour of paddling, which was more strenuous exercise than she remembered, Levi dropped her off near some shade trees and returned to the paddleboat shack for the deposit he'd paid. She shouldn't have been surprised, but she was when he came walking down the trail carrying two cold sodas, two fishing poles and a small box of worms.

"Really? You bought worms?" It sounded critical even to her ears, so she bumped her shoulder against his and said, "Big Tom would have been happy to dig some up for us."

"*Gut* point." He popped the soda and handed it to her, then opened his own and drank down half of it. "But Big Tom isn't here, and I want to know if you can fish."

"Of course I can fish."

"Bet you don't know how to put a worm on a hook."

"Seriously?"

"Show me."

When she'd done so, he wiggled his eyebrows and said, "Little Annie is full of surprises. Now do mine. I can't stand to touch the things."

She couldn't help laughing at his expression of disgust as she threaded another worm on his hook. A guy who didn't like baiting a hook? Maybe in Texas they did it differently. Maybe there the fish jumped out of the water and into the boat with a little coaxing.

They caught a dozen perch in the next hour, then returned their poles and gave the remainder of their worms to a pair of *Englisch* boys. They looked to be under ten years old and had cane poles but only a couple of worms in a tin can.

"Thanks," the boys exclaimed, dashing off toward the water.

As they were walking back toward the buggy, Levi bumped her shoulder and asked, "Ready for some dinner?"

"You don't have to do that, Levi."

"I don't have to take you to dinner? So you think I'd take you home hungry?"

"I think I know your opinion on the terrible cost of dating."

"*Ya*, for sure and certain it's expensive. I paid two bucks for those worms." Waiting to be sure that she knew he was kidding, he added, "Your parents would never believe this was a real date if I took you home without feeding you."

They ate at the Dairy Queen, which had the added benefit of buggy parking. Sitting in the booth, watching Petunia munch on fall grass, Annie marveled at the odd twists and turns her life seemed to take. A month ago, she hadn't even known Levi Lapp. Now she was on a pretend date with him. Would wonders never cease?

"That's one thing they don't have in Texas." Levi wadded his wrapper into a ball and tossed it on top of the tray.

"Say that again."

"That's one thing they don't have in Texas—designated buggy parking."

Annie pulled on first one ear and then the other. "You must have splashed water in my ears when we were on that paddleboat. I thought you just said there's something Texas doesn't have."

"Go ahead. Make fun of me, but it's true. They don't have everything."

"They don't have Dairy Queens?"

"Of course they do. Actually, Texas has more DQs than any other state."

"You're making that up."

"*Nein*, I'm not."

His mind was like a buggy wheel stuck in a rut. Everything he saw, thought or heard he twisted into something about Texas. He was incorrigible.

"Tell me three things you don't like about Texas."

"Let's get dessert first."

They'd both had a burger and shared fries at a table inside. Levi bussed the table while Annie stood staring at the ice cream options. When he pulled out his wallet to pay, she stopped him.

"No way. You paid for dinner. I'm buying dessert. I intend to pay my way in this relationship."

Levi shrugged and ordered a large sundae. She settled for a dipped cone.

They took the ice cream outside and sat at one of the picnic tables, watching the *Englischers* and Amish come and go.

"That's one thing I enjoy about Goshen that I'd sort of forgotten." He pointed at a buggy, waiting in the drive-in behind a pickup truck.

"I'm not following."

"The two parts of the community have become used to one another here. Sure we have the occasional tourist trying to snap pictures…"

"Happens every time I come to town."

"And some *Englischers* still complain that Amish are willing to work for too low a wage."

"There was an article in the paper on that this week."

"But overall, it seems the Amish here have figured out how to remain separate while they also work seamlessly with the *Englisch*."

"I don't know if it's seamless." Annie paused to lick at a bit of ice cream that was running down her cone. "It's true though that we do work well together. Employers understand that we don't work on Sundays. And Amish understand that *Englischers* are simply trying to run a profitable business, which is important if we want the jobs."

"It's a *gut* situation for both groups. It's what I hope and pray we can have in our new community."

"Uh-uh. You don't get to jump into daydreaming. Now tell me three things that you don't like about this great state of yours."

Annie thought he'd brush her off, that he'd claim he needed to get back to Old Simon. She honestly wasn't sure he could do it. Look at his dream realistically? Was that even possible? Or did it stop being a dream at that point? But instead of changing the subject or claiming he needed to leave, Levi seemed to be thoughtfully considering her question.

Levi was surprised to find he was enjoying the pretend date with Annie. He'd grown used to her skepticism about Texas, so it no longer irritated him as it once had. Unlike when he'd first met her, he no longer took it personally. It helped that he understood her reasons for wanting to stay in Indiana.

"What you're asking, it's hard to do," he admitted.

"Hard? Why is it hard? Every person, every place has negative qualities."

"It's kind of like your grandparents."

"My grandparents?"

"Do you remember them?"

"Of course."

"So tell me about them."

"Dat's parents were quite a bit older, so they passed when I was young. Mamm's parents, they lived down the road. It hasn't been that long since Mammi and Daddi passed. I grew up as much at their house as I did at my own. I used to go there after school sometimes instead of going home. I'd help Mammi with her garden or work on a quilt with her."

"Tell me three things you didn't like about your *mammi*."

"I loved my *mammi*."

"Of course you did, but every person, every place has negative qualities."

She ducked her head and gave him a look when he quoted her words back to her. But he knew Annie well enough to know she wouldn't back away from a challenge.

"Okay. I see what you're doing. It is hard to remember the negative, or maybe we just choose not to remember." She stood up, walked to a trash barrel and tossed her napkin into it. When she came back to the picnic table, she was smiling. "Mammi was a sweetheart. I loved her dearly, but she wasn't perfect. She always wore this smelly lotion that she was certain helped with her arthritis. I remember being embarrassed at church thinking everyone else must be able to smell it, that surely she could go one day without putting it on."

"Probably other people wore it too."

"Oh, they did. In fact, they still do. When I catch a whiff of the stuff now, it always brings back *gut* memories of sitting by her side."

"But don't you see? Time changes the way we think of something. We tend to remember all the positive aspects or all the negative aspects. We don't have a very balanced view of things in our past."

"We see the past with rose-colored glasses."

Was that what he'd done for the last twelve years? If so, he needed to stop right now. He was convincing other families to risk a lot in order to move with him. How could he do that if he wasn't willing to look at what they were doing objectively?

"I was only fourteen when we left Texas. By that time, my *dat* was sick. He had prostate cancer, though he wasn't diagnosed until we'd been back in Goshen for six months."

"I'm so sorry, Levi. I didn't know."

"I was a rambunctious teenager who was happy where he was. I had friends in Texas, and I had Tate Calloway—"

"Who was that?"

Levi sighed. He hadn't allowed himself to think about Tate in a long time. When he did, the pain still felt fresh. The man had been like family to him, and he hadn't even been able to attend his funeral. "He was our neighbor. He was a *gut* man."

"Sounds as if he was more than a neighbor."

"*Ya*. My *dat*…he had a hard time farming in Texas. It was nearly impossible to do so successfully, especially then. The bishop allowed us to try…not modern technology exactly but some irrigation techniques that helped. But Dat was stubborn and insisted on doing things the old way, and the old ways didn't work in the Texas dirt, especially during a drought."

The sky was growing dark, and Levi realized that the dinner crowd was thinning out at the Dairy Queen, but he wasn't ready to leave. The October evening was a perfect temperature, and Annie seemed like a different person tonight. She almost seemed to be enjoying her time with him. As goofy as it sounded—even in his own head—he didn't want the night to end. So instead of suggesting they drive home, he leaned back against the picnic table and found a comfortable position.

"Tate was your stereotypical Texan. He had calloused hands, a farmer's tan, and a slow way of talking. He worked hard and was faithful to his friends and family. I guess he became like a father to me. We didn't have any other family there, and the farms were spread out a bit which made it difficult to see one another during the week."

"There's one negative thing."

"*Ya*, I guess it was. It was probably natural to become close to any neighbor within shouting distance—even if he was a crusty old *Englisch* cowboy."

"He became like an *onkel* to you?"

"I guess he did." He glanced at Annie, surprised that she had understood the situation so quickly. He barely understood it himself. "Tate taught me how to ride a horse proper-like. He gave me my first Stetson. He even paid my entrance fee in the rodeo."

"And your parents were okay with that?"

Levi shrugged. He couldn't really remember his parents' response. "They didn't seem to notice what I was doing then. I guess they were too busy trying to pull a living out of the Texas dirt."

"A second negative thing."

He would have taken offense, but Annie didn't sound gleeful about pointing out the undesirable aspects of Texas. She looked completely caught up in his story.

"I guess. Anyway, my point is that those years were the best time in my life, so I remember the positive, like you do with your *mammi*."

"What happened then? Why did the community dissolve?"

"Drought, I think, and *ya*, that would be a third thing that's not so great about Texas. Here in Indiana, if it doesn't rain for a week we think we're having a drought. In Texas, it can go months with no rain, and then it comes all at once, flooding everything in sight."

"You really know how to sell a place." Her words didn't surprise him, but when she reached out and squeezed his hand, he almost jumped out of his suspenders.

"Don't worry, Levi. I'm not flirting with you." She smiled at him as if he'd just offered her a new pony. "But I understand now that those years in Texas were special to you. How long did you stay here in Goshen? Because I don't remember…"

"You were still a *youngie* then, and we would have been at different schoolhouses."

"I should be able to remember something of your being here if it was only twelve years ago."

"Twelve years is a long time." The calendar in his

head never forgot that date. He'd been trying to get back to Texas since the day they'd left. "You were probably still in school."

"*Ya.* I was."

"We came back here, and before we could really settle in, Dat was diagnosed. Prostate cancer usually moves slowly, but the kind Dat had moved fast. I can see now that was probably a blessing. At least he wasn't in pain for a long time."

He stood and nodded toward the buggy. They walked close together across the parking area. It felt strangely intimate, as if they were on a real date, as if he should reach out and take her hand. "He died three months after his diagnosis. Those were…they were tough months."

"I can't even imagine."

"My *mamm* was grieving, and my family was renting a place that was in pretty bad shape. Then my *mamm* met my stepfather—he was visiting his family here in Goshen one Sunday. Next thing I knew, we were packing up and moving to Pennsylvania."

He checked the horse, then helped Annie up into the buggy. Once they were on the road, he glanced at her, a little embarrassed that he had shared so much.

If it bothered her, he couldn't tell.

Their ride home was a quiet one, but it was a comfortable silence. He didn't feel the need to jump in and talk about horses or boots or crops.

When he pulled down her lane, she said, "My life, I guess it's been pretty easy compared to yours."

"Every life has its burdens."

"Maybe, but you've been through a lot for someone so young. It's no wonder that you want to go back to a time, to a place, where you were happy."

"So you'll help me?"

"Nein."

He could feel more than see her smile as he pulled the horse to a stop in front of her house.

"But maybe I'll stop fighting you so hard."

She hopped out of the buggy. He leaned over before she could close the door. "Don't you think you should stay here a few minutes? Maybe we should kiss a little so your parents will believe this is a real date."

Her laughter was soft and sweet, and instead of it hurting his feelings, he found himself whistling as he turned the mare toward Simon's. He probably wasn't any closer to his dream, but something had happened tonight. He'd found a friend, and that didn't happen every day. Friendship, he'd learned over the years, was a precious thing. He could pause in his quest long enough to appreciate that *Gotte* had put Annie Kauffmann directly in his path.

The only question was, what was he supposed to do now?

Chapter Nine

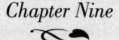

Annie's plan was working, perhaps a little too well.

"You two were out late last night."

"I was home by dark, Mamm."

"Nearly."

"Okay, it was a few minutes after dark."

"I guess you had a *gut* time."

Annie stared over the rim of her coffee cup at her mother. Perhaps if she drank down the entire thing before answering, she'd find the patience to keep up this little charade of being romantically interested in Levi.

Then she remembered about his *dat*, dying when Levi was only a *youngie*.

She remembered telling him about her *mammi*, and how much she missed the dear woman.

She sipped her coffee, offered up a prayer of gratitude that she still had her parents around to meddle in her affairs and smiled at her *mamm*.

"We went to Fidler Pond, walked a little, fished a little…"

"You fished?"

"I even baited Levi's hook for him. Turns out, he's a bit squeamish."

Which started them both laughing and suddenly her irritation melted away. Later, as she was setting the table for breakfast, Annie realized that part of her bad mood was her own fault. She didn't like deceiving her parents. She should just tell them that she wasn't interested in Levi as anything but a *freind*.

But then they'd point out what a fine young man he was.

They'd bring up that she wasn't getting any younger.

They would insist that there was no hurry, but really how many chances did she expect to have?

Nein. She wasn't going through that conversation again. Better to pretend to like Levi in a romantic way, then after a few dates she could explain that they simply weren't compatible.

It was a deception, and she felt guilty about that.

But it was the easiest path for everyone.

Levi didn't eat breakfast with them, claiming he'd eaten at Old Simon's. She couldn't imagine what type of food that might have been, but she shrugged as if it didn't bother her and handed him a mug of coffee.

"Mind if I carry this to the barn?"

"Suit yourself."

He'd been avoiding eye contact, but now he looked at her, smiled and touched the brim of his cowboy hat.

That hat.

She'd closed her eyes and was thinking of how to get it away from him, how to casually replace it with a proper Amish hat, when he turned and walked away. After breakfast, she saw Levi and her *dat* head out to the south pasture. Probably planting the winter crop. If her *dat* had talked about his plans for that day during breakfast, she hadn't been paying attention.

Not that it mattered to her what Levi Lapp did all day.

She went out to the garden to harvest the last of their vegetables. A half hour later, she was digging up the last of the potatoes when her sister Nicole called out to her.

"I didn't hear your buggy pull up."

"We walked."

"You're a brave woman venturing out alone across the pasture with that group."

She looked up into the kitchen window and saw Nicole's three children sitting at the table. No doubt they were being treated to cold milk and a good-sized peanut butter cookie by Annie's *mamm*.

"They were full of energy this morning," Nicole explained. "I decided a walk would tire them out…"

"I hope you used the stroller."

"I did. Anyway, I was hoping the time away would help everyone take a nap this afternoon."

"How are you feeling?"

"Gut." Nicole placed a hand on top of her stomach as she sat down in the dirt next to Annie. "This is the *gut* part, before my ankles start to swell and I have constant indigestion from the baby taking up the space where my stomach is supposed to be."

"You make it sound lovely."

Nicole picked up a handful of dirt and sifted it through her fingers. "It's better than that—I think it may be the most amazing thing a woman can experience."

Annie didn't bother answering. She'd seen her *schweschder* in this phase before—two times before.

She'd also seen her when she could barely waddle down the steps, and when she'd been carrying the twins she'd looked positively huge. Pregnancy wasn't a picnic in the park, but for now Nicole was enjoying her condition so why argue with her?

"Heard you went out with Levi last night."

"Oh, good grief."

"What? It's not like anyone was gossiping."

"Right. So a little bird must have told you, *ya*?"

"Beth saw Levi turn into the park when she was coming home from work. Martha saw you at the Dairy Queen as she was leaving. Guess you didn't notice either one of them."

"Guess I didn't."

"She said you only had eyes for Levi."

"Oh, come on. Does that even sound like me?"

"It doesn't, which is why I'm sitting here asking you questions."

Annie pushed her shovel under a particularly stubborn potato and pulled from the top. She was rewarded with a spray of dirt. Seeing her covered in dirt, Nicole began to giggle. Annie wanted to be offended, but she couldn't pull it off. Before she knew it, she was laughing along with her. It felt *gut* to relax with her *schweschder*, and she knew deep in her heart that it would feel even better if she were to confess the truth to her.

"I'm going to tell you something, but promise to keep it to yourself."

Nicole nodded. "I promise."

So she told her about the harvest, how her parents had begun giving her *the look* and whispering when they thought she couldn't hear, how she'd come up with a plan to pretend to date Levi.

"And they fell for it?"

"Well, *ya*, because they already think we're falling for each other. People see what they want to see."

"How long do you expect to keep this up?"

"I don't know—three or four dates, I guess. That's about the longest any relationship I've ever had has lasted."

"And you can't just tell them that you're not interested?"

"You know I've tried that before. They don't listen."

"It's because they worry about you. We all do."

"Why? Because I have a successful business and I'm a happy, single Amish woman?"

"Don't twist your bonnet strings into a knot. I'm just saying that we care about you, and we want to see you happily settled."

"I'm only twenty-four. It's not like I'm ancient."

"And no one is suggesting that you are."

Annie stood, brushed the dirt from the back of her dress, then reached down and helped Nicole to her feet. She thrust the basket of vegetables into her *schweschder*'s hands and picked up her gardening tools. They walked toward the back porch in silence, but before they climbed the steps, Nicole stayed her with the touch of her hand.

"Just be careful."

"How do you mean?"

"With your heart. Beth and Martha both said that you looked happy, and when you talk about Levi, your eyes light up."

"You've been reading too many romance books again. Eyes don't actually light up."

"It's just… I don't want to see Levi break your heart."

"You think I'll have a broken heart? I thought you liked Levi."

"Sure, I do, but everyone knows how you feel about moving to Texas."

"I can't believe you're even considering it."

Nicole didn't address that. She was apparently bound and determined to issue her warning. "It doesn't seem likely that Levi will change his mind and stay here in Goshen."

"And I wouldn't want him to. It's obvious Texas is where he belongs." Which sounded so strange coming out of her mouth that she almost pinched herself to see if she was awake or in some bizarre dream.

As she followed Nicole into the house, she realized that it was true. Levi did belong in Texas. That much was obvious from their long talk the evening before. Which left her in quite an awkward position—finding a way to stymie his plans or at least remove her family from the details at the same time that she was hoping and praying he would be able to move forward.

Levi didn't see much of Annie on Wednesday, and was surprised when she wasn't at the breakfast table on Friday morning. If he were honest with himself, he would admit that he had been avoiding her on Wednesday. He'd even skipped breakfast so he wouldn't have to sit and make idle chatter. For some reason he wasn't sure he could do that, not after they'd shared so much with each other on their first date.

He'd agreed to work for her *dat*, and he'd agreed to this pretend dating plan, but he'd expected to be able to keep himself aloof from it all. It wasn't working. He could feel his wall of disinterest caving. He could feel himself becoming distracted.

The less time he spent around her, the better. Then again, they were supposed to be stepping out together.

So as he accepted the mug of strong coffee and sat down at the table, he caved in to his curiosity and asked her parents where she'd gone so early in the day.

"She's helping Priscilla prepare for a wedding they are catering tomorrow."

"Another Saturday wedding?"

"*Ya.* I remember when most weddings were on Tuesdays and Thursdays, but we've grown so much that Saturday weddings are becoming a common occurrence."

"Oh."

"Would you like me to give Annie a message?"

"I didn't realize she would be working, though everyone knows that October is the marrying season around here. I should have thought of that."

"What were you going to ask her?" Alton reached for the platter of bacon and put four pieces on his plate.

"I thought she might want to go to town with me tomorrow night. You know, since we're stepping out and all."

Annie's parents shared a look, and Levi wanted to hide under the kitchen table. Why had he even brought it up? Now they were looking at him as if he'd invented the hay baler.

He thought they might give him the standard talk of always being respectful to their daughter.

Or maybe they'd bring up what a fine *fraa* she would make, as if he couldn't see that with his own two eyes.

Instead, Lily scooped another helping of eggs onto

his plate, and Alton started talking about the fence work they needed to do that day.

When he was leaving to follow Alton to the barn, Lily pulled him aside. "Annie's wedding tomorrow is an early one, and they're only having the noonday meal, not the evening."

"Ya?"

"I suspect she'd enjoy some time out after that. You could leave her a note, and I'll give it to her."

"Danki, I'll do that."

He borrowed paper and a pen and worked on the message at lunch, eating his sandwich out at the picnic table. He ruined three good sheets of paper before he settled on what to say. Reading back over it, he wondered how he'd ever had a date in his life. He certainly wasn't very good at this.

Annie,
I know you're working tomorrow morning. Would you like to go out for pizza tomorrow night? The fall festival is happening in town and we could walk through the booths, listen to the bands, stuff like that. If you want. If you don't, I understand. In fact, you probably don't, so you can just ignore this letter. But on the off chance you do want to, leave me a message at the phone shack. I'll check it around noon.
Yours,
Levi

Yours?
What did that even mean?
Why did people sign letters that way?

And under that was a deeper worry. Was her mother going to read it before giving it to her? Should he have added a heart or said something about kissing her so they'd believe that something romantic was going on?

"We're not *youngies*," he muttered to himself, folding the letter and sticking it into his pocket. He'd hand it to Lily before leaving. Annie had said they needed to go on three dates, and if it helped her out, then he'd do it. Though this letter-writing thing was nothing short of humiliating.

The afternoon passed more slowly than seemed possible. He kept checking his watch to see if it was time to go. Finally, he finished the last of the chores Alton had asked him to do and bounded up the steps and into the kitchen. On Fridays, Lily always had his pay for the week ready for him, and he'd need that if he was going to take Annie to the festival. The wages he'd earned the previous weeks were already in the bank, in what he thought of as his Moving-to-Texas account, and he didn't want to use any money from it. Folks thought that Amish didn't use banks, but it wasn't like he could keep money under his mattress. Well, he could, but it would be a silly thing to do.

So he needed his week's pay if he was going to take Annie out the next day. Not that he expected her to say yes, but better to be prepared than not.

Lily had wrapped up some of the dinner she was cooking. She handed it to Levi. Apparently, everyone thought that he and Old Simon were starving. It was true that both of them were growing tired of egg sandwiches, but they certainly weren't going hungry.

Levi stared down at the basket full of freshly fried chicken, baked potatoes and some sort of dessert. He should feel hungry, but instead his stomach felt as if he were coming down with a bug.

"I'll give her the note," Lily assured him.

"Danki." He turned to go, but turned back around when Lily called his name.

"We appreciate your help around here. You've been a real blessing to us."

He nodded, his throat suddenly feeling as if he were choking on something. Had his own family ever said those words to him? He didn't think so. He thought they were probably glad he'd left. So why did it seem that Annie's family was always so glad to have him around? And why was he letting himself get closer to them when for sure and certain he'd be gone in six months?

Levi was completely surprised when he checked the phone booth on Saturday afternoon and he had a short message from Annie. She must be more eager to get their three dates over with than he thought.

When he arrived at her house, she was dressed in a freshly laundered dark orange dress with a white apron. She looked as pretty as the fall leaves dancing across the porch.

"You're sure you feel like doing this?"

"After today's wedding? *Ya.* I'm sure."

She proceeded to tell him of the squirrels stealing the nuts on the tables, a bridesmaid who broke out in hives and a young nephew who decided that putting his finger in each of the wedding cupcakes was a fun idea.

He was laughing so hard by the time they reached downtown Goshen that he'd forgotten all about being nervous. Had he been nervous? Maybe he'd built this up to be more than it was. They were becoming *freinden*, and that was *gut*. The fact that they were pretending to be something else, that wasn't great but he thought he could live with it.

He actually relaxed and started having a good time.

That is, until they ran into the newlyweds Avery and Beth.

"We'd heard you two were stepping out."

Beth clasped Avery's hand as if she were afraid to walk through the fall festival alone. Or maybe that was what love looked like. Levi wasn't sure.

"*Ya.* We're dating for sure and certain." Levi ran a thumb under his right suspender. "I'm looking for a missus to take to Texas, so it seemed a smart thing to do."

Annie's elbow in his ribs caught him by surprise.

"Not that I'm thinking of moving to Texas," she corrected. "But anyway, let's not talk about us. How are you two?"

The next twenty minutes they spent walking through the fall booths, listening to Avery describe his new mare, new buggy and new home. Had these two waited a long time to marry or were they simply fortunate enough to be given everything a young couple could possibly want? Levi was so irritated he could barely concentrate on what everyone was saying.

Plus, his mind was distracted by Annie.

She was standing shoulder to shoulder with him. He wasn't used to being in such close proximity to a beautiful woman.

And she'd been holding his hand since they'd run into Beth and Avery. He wasn't great at holding hands—not that he had a lot of experience with it. He never knew if you should lace your fingers together or simply clasp each other's hand. And what happened when your hands started sweating like his were now? Should he pull his hand away and wipe it on his pants? Or pretend he didn't notice?

On top of those questions, he kept worrying he was squeezing her hand too hard.

Why did everything feel so awkward?

He even tripped twice over absolutely nothing.

Finally, Beth and Avery hurried off to ride the merry-go-round together, which sounded ridiculous to Levi. Weren't the rides for *kinner*? Why would an adult ride one? Slapping his hat against his leg, he voiced his irritation with the two.

"They're all right. They're just in *lieb*." Annie looked down at her hand clasping his, dropped it like a hot potato and muttered, "Sorry about that. Just trying to look authentic."

"They even have a new halter for the horse. If I heard of one more new thing, I think I might have had to do something desperate."

"Like?"

"I don't know…challenge him to an apple-bobbing contest, then reach over and push his head under? A good dunking in cold water might help him come to his senses."

Annie was smiling at him and shaking her head, so he kept going.

"Or I could suggest he get in the pie-throwing contest and then buy three pies to throw at him? Maybe I could have sent him into the corn maze and hoped he got lost for a few minutes. I was ready to pay for the merry-go-round just so they'd go."

"While you two were checking out the woodcraft

booth, I had to listen to Beth talk about her new dishes, new bedding and new furniture."

"Were they both born with a silver spoon in their mouths?"

"They're Amish, remember. Just on the upper end of the simple scale, and they are usually very nice about it. I guess they're rather caught up in being newlyweds."

"I guess. We'd never act like that, though. You and I wouldn't lose our common sense or our manners just because we decided to get hitched."

Annie stepped back and nearly tripped over a hay bale that was painted like a pumpkin. Levi reached out for her arm, steadied her and then dropped his hand when she assured him she was fine.

"This date is not turning out like I planned," he said.

"It's a pretend date. How did you expect it to turn out?"

But before he could answer that, they bumped into the bishop and his wife. Annie once again stepped close to his side, slipped her arm through his so that they were like links in a paper chain. He could smell the soap she'd used to shampoo her hair, some sort of flowery-smelling lotion and, if he wasn't mistaken, perhaps a touch of cocoa. When he asked her about it, she started laughing. That was one thing he really liked about Annie. She laughed easily.

"That would be from the chocolate cake I made for the wedding."

"Chocolate cake?"

"It was a spur-of-the-moment decision. I had to replace the ruined cupcakes and we had plenty of flour, sugar and cocoa on hand."

They'd stepped away from the bishop and were headed toward the food booths.

"What did you mean before?" she asked. "You said this date wasn't turning out like you expected."

"I didn't count on running into so many people we know."

"*Ya*, Goshen is still a small town."

"I know what will cheer me up." He snagged her hand and pulled her toward the food booth with the longest line. After they'd purchased a turkey leg, corn dog, large fries, funnel cake, hot chocolate and sweet iced tea, they found a seat at one of the picnic tables toward the back. She started to sit across from him, but he shook his head and pulled her over to his side—so they were both facing the band, not because he wanted to sit next to her.

"This is perfect." Levi finally felt like he could talk at a normal volume. "We can hear the band but not be overpowered by it. Have you ever noticed how loud *Englischers* play their music?"

But Annie wasn't paying attention to the band on the stage. She was staring at the tray of food he'd plopped on the table. "Are you really going to eat all of that?"

"Of course not. I bought half of it for you."

"Which half?"

"You said you like turkey legs…"

"I do."

"So do I. You can have the first half and I'll take what's left."

"We're splitting a turkey leg?"

"I had to try a corn dog. Fall festivals require corn dogs."

"So you get half the turkey leg and all the corn dog."

"I'll save you the second half."

"I've never shared a meal this way."

"Have you ever shared a meal at all?"

"Well, I had *bruders* growing up. They'd sometimes steal food from my plate when we were out in public."

"They did not."

"*Ya*, they did. Nathan was the worst about that. He'd always claim I wasn't going to finish it anyway."

"I like hearing about your family."

"You do?" She carefully chose a fry and put it into her mouth.

"Sure. They sound so…happy."

"Was your family not happy?"

"I don't know. I always thought the tension was normal, but maybe it wasn't. Maybe it was just that times were tough while we were in Texas, and then Dat getting sick and all as soon as we moved back here." He bit into the corn dog and groaned. "You have to try this."

Annie squirreled up her nose.

"What? Afraid of my germs?"

"Of course not."

He leaned toward her and lowered his voice. "If we were kissing…"

She scooted away as if he had chicken pox and she was afraid of catching it. "I think you must be really hungry because you're acting a little crazy."

"I am?" Levi could feel the smile growing on his face. He liked teasing Annie. He especially liked it when she blushed and seemed flustered. He slipped across the bench, pulling the tray of food with him. "We should sit closer. So we look authentic."

Instead of answering, she accepted the corn dog he

was still offering her and took a big bite. "That is *gut*," she said with her mouth still full.

And then they were both laughing, and Levi thought the night was turning out all right, maybe even better than he had imagined.

They finished their meal, took a stroll through the corn maze and watched children having their faces painted. They ran into a few more people they knew, and each time Annie stepped closer and reached for his hand. The last time, she didn't let go, so maybe she was trying to be prepared.

Or maybe…

Before he could finish that thought, he noticed Bishop Marcus hurrying toward them across the parking area.

"Levi, I've been looking all over for you."

"Why?"

"It's Old Simon. He's in the hospital."

Chapter Ten

Annie sat in the waiting room of the Goshen Medical Center. It wasn't her first time there. Over the years, they'd visited the facility whenever someone in their congregation was ill. Now Amish folks from their church filled the waiting room, a testament to how many lives Old Simon had touched.

"Still no word from Levi?" Nicole asked.

"*Nein*, and I can't believe you're here. Shouldn't you be home resting?"

"I'm pregnant, not sick."

"But the kids…"

"Mamm was happy to stay with them. She wanted me to come and sit with you."

Annie resisted the urge to roll her eyes.

"Someone needed to bring you home if Levi decides to stay."

"This room is full of people from our church. I think I could have found a ride home." The words came out snippier than she'd intended, so she bumped her *schweschder*'s shoulder and added, "But thanks for coming. I appreciate it."

She felt as if her emotions had been through a clothes wringer. She wasn't sure what she was feeling, and her mind kept returning to Levi.

To the look on his face when the bishop had first told them Old Simon was ill.

His profile as he drove the buggy toward the hospital.

The way he'd reached out for her hand as they'd hurried toward the emergency room entrance.

She'd sat with him for two hours as the waiting room had slowly filled with people from their congregation, everyone eager to hear an update on Old Simon's condition. The only thing anyone knew was that a neighbor had found him collapsed in the kitchen when they stopped by to deliver fresh eggs.

"He was fine when I left him," Levi had insisted when they'd first sat down onto two plastic chairs. He picked up a magazine from the table which he continually rolled and unrolled in a tube.

Annie was certain it would never be flat again, but she didn't have the heart to correct him. Perhaps it was one reason they put the magazines there, so people would have something to do with their nervous energy.

An hour later, one of the doctors called him back to Old Simon's room.

"I'm surprised they let him go in to visit." Nicole had brought her knitting bag and proceeded to work on a baby blanket—yellow with blue-and-pink flowers. "You know how strict they are about only allowing family to see a patient."

"Levi has been in contact with Old Simon's eldest son, even before he moved here. He wanted to make sure it was all right for him to do so. He didn't want anyone thinking he was taking advantage of Simon."

"I didn't realize that. It was thoughtful of him to reach out that way."

"As soon as we arrived here at the hospital, he called Jonah, who gave the doctors permission to speak with Levi."

They waited another thirty minutes, the clock creeping past midnight. Somewhere around one in the morning, Levi came out, spoke quietly to Bishop Marcus and then sat down next to Annie.

Marcus raised a hand to quiet everyone. "Levi has met with the doctors, spoken on the phone with Jonah, and he's visited with Old Simon. It would seem that Simon has suffered from a stroke."

Murmurs of "mercy" and "*Gotte* be with him" and "we'll keep praying" wafted through the group. When they'd quieted down, the bishop continued.

"The stroke mainly affected his left side, so Simon is considered a fall risk at this point. The doctors will monitor him another forty-eight hours, then he'll be sent to the rehab facility here in Goshen where they can work on restoring his strength to his left side. He is able to speak, and he's thanked all of you for being here and asked you to go home."

Soft laughter echoed around the room. Slowly in ones and twos, people began standing and gathering their things. Several offered to give Annie a ride home, but she told them she'd wait and go with Levi.

Nicole pulled her into a tight hug and said, "Remember what we talked about—guard your heart."

Soon the only three who remained were Levi, Annie and Bishop Marcus.

No one spoke for a few minutes. Levi broke the silence, leaning forward with his elbows propped on his knees and his fingers interlaced. "I should have noticed. He's been more forgetful than usual. Said we should drive over to Stephenville one day. Another time he confused the Red River with the Mississippi River."

"No reason for you to suspect that it was anything more than a slight forgetfulness," Annie tried to reassure him.

"*Ya,* but I could have insisted he see a doctor."

"I've never known Old Simon to respond well to such suggestions." Bishop Marcus was sitting in the chairs across from them, but the room was small and it felt as if they were in someone's living room.

"I'm so relieved that he's going to be okay." Annie wanted to reach out and clasp Levi's hand, but she stopped herself when she realized that might not be appropriate. They weren't promised to one another. They weren't even really dating.

The bishop cleared his throat. "It sounds as if he is...for now."

Levi's head jerked up suddenly. "What do you mean for now?"

"I've seen this before, is all I'm saying. Strokes are caused by cardiovascular disease. The condition is actually a cluster of diseases. Events such as a stroke are often followed by heart problems that require surgery for stents or bypasses. That's on top of the danger that another stroke might occur or even that he could develop a blood clot."

"But the doctor said—"

"That they'll rehab him. Yes, of course, but what I want you to realize is that this isn't something that will go away. It's something Old Simon is going to have to deal with from now on. Ultimately it means that Jonah is going to have to make a decision about where his father should live."

"What you're saying is that he's not going to Texas."

"Do you think that would be a wise decision? If he were your *dat*, would you want him moving to a smaller community and tackling the difficult work of starting a new district?" Marcus studied Levi, but he didn't rush him. Instead, he sat back and waited, patiently.

Levi dropped his head between his hands, and it seemed to Annie that a giant burden had been placed on his shoulders. Instead of letting it defeat him, though, Levi sat up straighter, squared his shoulders and looked Marcus straight in the eye.

Annie realized in that moment that she could love Levi Lapp—if things were different, if she'd met him five years earlier or five years later, if he were looking to marry and settle in Goshen.

"Nein," Levi said. "I don't believe it would be wise for him to go to Texas. He needs to be here, near his *freinden*. Or with his son. But he doesn't need to try something so physically taxing as moving and starting a new community."

Marcus nodded in agreement.

"He was the reason I came here. I thought… I thought it would be possible to finally realize my dream if I had the help of someone like Simon backing me."

"What you're trying to do, it might still be possible, Levi. But the Bible never said that our path would be easy, and your path just became a little harder. Pray about what has happened as well as what lies ahead, read the scripture, look to the wisdom of family and *freinden*. You will know what it is that you should do next."

The bishop stood, stepped closer and reached out a hand which he placed gently on each of their shoulders. "*Gotte* guide you through this difficult time," he said softly, and then he was gone.

Twenty minutes later a nurse came out and told them that Simon had been given something to help him sleep. She suggested they go home and get some rest, then come back in the morning. When they stepped out into the night, Annie looked up at the stars and marveled that only a few hours had passed. It seemed as if they'd been in the hospital for days.

They rode in silence. The sway and rhythm of the buggy and the clip-clop of the horse calmed the emotions churning through Annie's heart. She found her thoughts drifting to how Levi seemed to have matured since she'd met him. He no longer rushed at top speed into something. He'd been able to admit that it wasn't the best thing for Old Simon to move, even though it would be a setback to his own plans. He'd held up admirably to the pressure of the evening.

She thought she detected a softening in his attitude.

Perhaps he was beginning to see that his happiness and future weren't dependent on an ill-advised move to Texas.

At the very moment that thought passed through her mind, Levi sat up straighter and pushed his hat down on his head.

"Something wrong?"

"Only that I realize what a fool I've been."

"Fool...what do you mean?"

"The last few hours I've been thinking this was the end of everything that I've worked for."

"You're not going to move?"

"But now I realize it's *Gotte* testing me, same as he tested Job, same as he tested Abraham."

"I'm not following the comparison."

"This." His hand waved to include the horse, the road, the cold October night. "Certainly it was unexpected that Old Simon would take ill—though perhaps I should have been prepared for it. You all call him Old Simon for a reason."

"Many people are old but don't have strokes."

If Levi heard her he gave no indication. It was almost as if he were speaking to himself, as if he were working out some puzzle and he needed to verbalize the solution.

"Simon's illness doesn't mean I'm supposed to give up. It means I'm supposed to stay the course."

"That's what you took away from what Bishop Marcus said?"

"He reminded me that the Bible never said that our path would be easy."

"*Ya*, but—"

"We're to run the race set before us."

"Once we're certain what that race is."

"Fight the good fight."

"I'm not sure that verse refers to chasing a childhood dream."

"*Gotte* has plans for me. Plans for a future."

"*Ya*, but Levi, are you absolutely certain that future is in Texas?"

He glanced at her, studied her a moment, then looked away.

"You don't believe in my dream, Annie?"

"I didn't say that."

"I thought we were becoming friends."

"Of course we are."

"Then as my path becomes more difficult, I would think you would encourage me, not question me."

She didn't answer immediately. In truth, her temper had claimed her tongue. How could he be so stubborn and bullheaded? But she didn't think now was the time to share that question.

"The old ones, their proverbs come back to us at times like this. I used to laugh at my *daddi* when he quoted them, but now I can see that he was wise and trying to raise me up to be a *gut* man."

"Your *daddi* told you to move to Texas?"

"One of his favorite sayings was *No dream comes true until you wake up and go to work.*" He shook his head as if he couldn't believe what he was hearing or thinking or seeing. "I've been walking around like a *youngie*, head up in the clouds, wishing things would go my way. Now I see that it's time that I wake up and go to work."

Annie couldn't believe what she was hearing. Just when she thought Levi was finally coming to his senses, finally growing up and abandoning this ridiculous plan, he was in fact doing the exact opposite.

"Are you forgetting that you need three ministers?"

"And now I have none." Instead of hanging his head in despair, Levi stretched the muscles in his neck. "It's going to be a challenge. I need to get busy writing letters, visiting communities that are adjacent to ours. I can see now that I've been…distracted."

He flicked a glance her way, and Annie felt her temper ignite like a firecracker on the Fourth of July.

"Oh really? I'm so sorry if I've *distracted* you."

"Not your fault. I let it happen."

"You're telling me that's what this has been—what I have been—is a mere distraction."

"You said yourself that you're not interested in marrying." He pulled on the reins, directing the mare to turn down the lane that led to her house.

"Oh, trust me. I'm not, and if I were, it wouldn't be with someone who still thinks like a *youngie* on his *rumspringa*."

"And the fact that you continue to see it that way is proof that we're not intended for each other."

"I'll agree with that."

"As far as your parents thinking I'm *gut* dating material—"

"I will have no trouble setting them straight in that regard." The buggy had barely come to a stop, but Annie needed out of it immediately. She opened the door and practically jumped out.

If Levi was surprised by her abrupt departure, he didn't say anything. He certainly didn't call out after her.

How could he be so stubborn? So willful? So illogical?

She couldn't resist one last jab. Leaning back into the buggy she said, "Don't forget you'll need twelve to fifteen families."

"I haven't forgotten."

"And all those answers to my questions. Bishop Marcus said to be ready when we meet this Friday."

"Oh, I'll be ready." Now there was a gleam in his eyes that she could see even in the dim light of the moon hanging above them.

"And so will I."

"I didn't think you'd give up trying to stop me,

Annie." His voice softened, and for just a moment she was reminded of the Levi who had held her hand at the fall festival. "Do your best, but don't blame me for holding tightly to my dream."

"You can hold as tight as you want. It doesn't mean it's going to happen. It doesn't make it the right thing for our community." She was so angry that her heart was racing and she could barely spit out the words. She heard her *mamm*'s voice in her head, reminding her that a handful of patience was worth more than a bushel of brains. The problem was that she was out of patience, and Levi was determined to ignore his brain.

"I guess that's for Marcus to decide," he reminded her.

"*Ya*. I guess it is."

"Then I'll see you at the meeting Friday."

"I'll be there." She slammed the buggy door hard enough to startle poor Petunia, and she was tempted to stop and apologize to the horse. Her pride pushed her up the porch steps and into the house. As she heard Levi drive away, she felt a nearly overwhelming flood of various emotions—relief that the farce of their dating was over, disappointment that he couldn't see what was so painfully obvious to her, and a tiny bit of regret that she'd allowed an Amish cowboy to work his way into her heart.

Annie gave up on trying to sleep a few minutes before five the next morning. All she'd managed to do was toss, turn and twist her covers into a knot. By the time she dressed, made her bed, and took care of her morning toiletry, she'd moved from a random sort of resentment to a very pointed, particular anger.

Not that she would let it affect her day.

She wasn't going to waste another minute stewing over Levi Lapp. She made the coffee, squeezed fresh orange juice, put up the dishes that were in the drainer, fried bacon and potatoes and was cracking eggs into the skillet when her mother walked into the room, yawning and widening her eyes as if to try to make sense of what she was seeing.

"Something wrong, dear?"

"Nein."

"You're up rather early."

Annie looked around in surprise. The table was set. She'd made fresh cinnamon rolls. Juice was in a pitcher and glasses at each place. Steam was coming from the pots and pans on the stove. She didn't remember doing any of it.

Annie shrugged and said, "Thought I'd get an early start on the day is all."

"You do remember it's Sunday, right?"

"Sure, *ya.* But…we still need to eat."

"Indeed." Her *mamm* added cream to her coffee and shuffled over to the table, still trying to fully open her eyes.

"Did I wake you?"

"I woke when your *dat* went out to the barn, but usually I take my time to get in here. Usually no one else is awake."

"Sorry."

"If I didn't know better, I'd think our kitchen cabinets had done something to offend you."

"The cabinets?"

"You were…" Her *mamm* gulped down more coffee and waved at the cabinets. "You were slamming them."

"Oh. Sorry."

"You already said that."

"*Ya*. I know."

"What's wrong? Is it Old Simon?"

"*Nein*. His condition is stable."

"And the outlook?"

"Rehab, probably followed by reduced activity." She grabbed a spatula and attacked the potatoes with it. They were browning nicely, but she needed to do something with her hands.

"Why don't you come and sit down?"

"I can't. Breakfast will burn."

By the time her father returned to the house, she had so many breakfast dishes on the table that it resembled Thanksgiving dinner.

"Well, what's the special occasion?" he asked.

"Annie is a bit agitated this morning," her *mamm* murmured.

"I heard that," Annie said.

"I should hope so, dear."

She rolled her eyes, petitioned God for patience and then sat down at the table. She had to admit, it was a lot of food for just three people.

"Let's pray." Her *dat* bowed his head.

One thing that Annie both loved and hated about their Amish tradition was that they often prayed silently. If someone else was praying aloud, she could sometimes distance herself from the things troubling her soul. At the moment, her options were to shut her eyes and only pretend to pray or bare her heart before God. So she did just that—admitting her anger and her humiliation and her fear. She didn't like those things about herself. She didn't want fear and embarrassment to rule her emotions or actions, but she also didn't see a way around the emotions that threatened to consume her. She asked *Gotte* for guidance, for patience, for wisdom and for strength.

She might have stayed with her head bowed for a much longer time, but her *dat* cleared his voice and said, "*Danki* for this day you've given us to rest, to draw closer to you and to spend time with those you've given us to love and care for. Amen."

Her amen coincided with her *mamm*'s. Tears pricked Annie's eyes, and she stared down at her lap.

She heard her *mamm* and *dat* speaking to one another, the words passing over her like clouds scuttling by on a summer day.

"Haven't had potatoes for breakfast in ages."

"Plus she cooked ham and bacon."

"Might be too full for lunch."

"We'll have to pretend to be hungry so as not to hurt Nicole's feelings."

"'Course that is hours away, and I used a lot of energy taking care of the chores."

"You always do, dear."

Annie pushed back her chair and stood. "I'm... I'm not hungry. I think I'll go to my room for a few minutes."

As she fled the kitchen, she heard them lower their voices. She had no doubt they were talking about her, were worried, but she couldn't think about that right now. Instead of going to her room, she rushed outside, down the porch steps and out to the pasture.

Perhaps a few moments alone, appreciating an absolutely perfect October Sunday, would calm her turbulent emotions.

* * *

"So you're mad at him because he still wants to move to Texas?" Nicole kept her attention focused on her three children. They were all sitting under a maple tree that was resplendent with red, gold and brown leaves. At the moment, Nicole's oldest child, Rachel, was covering Micah and Mitchell with leaves. The twins were sitting up and staring at their big *schweschder* as if she were the most entertaining thing they'd ever seen. When she'd dump more leaves on them, they would giggle, slap the leaves with their open hands and call out, "More," one of the few words they knew.

"I'm mad because obviously everything I thought was happening, wasn't. He was stringing me along…"

"But it was your idea to pretend date."

"I know it was."

"And you've known from the first day you met him that his goal is to move to Texas."

"Yes, but…"

"But what?"

Annie avoided her sister's gaze. For as long as she could remember, Nicole had been able to read her every thought, every feeling, simply by looking at her. Maybe that was Nicole's gift—an ability to see into the hearts of people. The problem was that Annie wasn't sure she wanted her heart to be seen. She wasn't sure she had the courage to admit her dreams and heartbreak to herself. But she did know that she hated these feelings—this pent up anger and frustration and disappointment.

Finally, she raised her eyes to her sister. "My heart hurts." The words brought a fresh cascade of tears.

"Oh, honey."

Nicole scooted closer and pulled her into a hug, rubbing her back and giving her a few moments to compose herself.

Annie finally pulled away, swiped at the tears running down her face, and attempted a laugh. "You warned me."

"I did."

"This is why I cater weddings instead of trying to have one myself. It's too painful."

"Not always."

"I guess."

Rachel ran toward them, her arms filled with leaves. "Want some?" she asked.

She skidded to a stop when she noticed the expression on Annie's face. "You're sad," she whispered, and then more loudly, "I'll get more leaves!"

Annie and Nicole both laughed.

"If only leaves could fix things." Annie sighed and closed her eyes. This day seemed as if it would never end. She was exhausted, and she wanted to go home and crawl under the scrap quilt on her bed that her *mamm* had made for her when she turned twelve.

"Does Levi know how you feel?"

"I don't even know how I feel."

"But you care for him."

Annie nodded, the misery of her situation falling on her anew.

"It'll work out."

"Don't say that."

"But it will."

"*Nein.* It won't. How can it? Levi is bound and determined to move to Texas, and more than likely he'll take you all with him."

Nicole shrugged. Earlier she had shared that they still hadn't decided whether to commit to the move. They were waiting to see what happened at Friday night's meeting.

"I can't move," Annie continued. "I won't, even if it was a possibility which it's not. After all, Levi hasn't exactly declared his love. In fact, I think he sees me as an adversary now more than ever."

"Are you?"

"Am I what?"

"His adversary."

"I don't know. I don't know what I am to him, but before the night fell apart, before Bishop Marcus came running to tell us about Old Simon…it all seemed like a dream." She rested her fingertips against her eyelids which felt swollen and warm. "I've never felt so comfortable with someone before. I've never enjoyed myself like that when I was on a date with a man—and it wasn't even a real date."

She thought of sharing the turkey leg and corn dog with Levi, and she wanted to cry all over again. If only she'd stayed home last night, maybe she wouldn't have fallen in love with him. But even as that thought entered her mind, she knew it wasn't true. Her feelings for Levi had probably begun the first day she'd seen him sitting in her parents' kitchen wearing that ridiculous Stetson.

The date the night before had simply allowed her feelings to blossom, but that would have happened regardless. It might have taken longer, but it would have happened. She didn't know when she'd become such an expert in love, but suddenly she felt as if she could write a romance story—albeit a heartbreaking one.

"Honey, listen." Micah had begun to cry, so Nicole stood, scooped him up in her arms and walked back to where Annie was sitting. "You're right. I don't know the particulars of how it can possibly work out. You and Levi always seem to be at odds with one another—your dreams for the future seem completely opposite."

"They are completely opposite."

"I think you had a dream to build a business."

"And I believe *Gotte* put that dream in my heart."

"But now I think you have a different dream—a dream of love and marriage and maybe even a family. I'm not sure that you have to give up one for the other."

"I won't do it."

"That's my point. Maybe you won't have to."

Mitchell suddenly began to cry as well. Nicole handed Micah to Annie and turned to scoop up her other son.

Annie realized in that moment just how important her niece and nephews were to her. Rachel continued to flop into the leaves—giggling, burrowing under and then popping out and shouting, "Surprise!" Micah had stopped fussing and was putting Annie's *kapp* strings in his mouth. Mitchell was sucking his thumb and snuggling close to Nicole. They were such a precious sight, so innocent and sweet and yes—beautiful—that Annie felt tears sting her eyes again.

Was this what being in love was like?

Emotions seesawing between tenderness and despair?

No wonder she'd avoided it for so long.

"I'm not saying you will or won't have to give up one dream for the other. I don't know, but I do know this. *Gotte* has a plan for you, Annie." Nicole reached over and squeezed her hand.

It wasn't lost on Annie that Levi had referred to the same verse the night before.

"And who can thwart *Gotte*'s plan? Who is big enough to do that? No one. No one can. So it will work out. Your job is to believe that, and continue to go about your day doing that day's work."

"When did you become so wise?"

"Sometime between Rachel and the twins I suppose."

Annie didn't know if she believed that things would work out. Did the Bible promise that? It seemed to her that there was a lot of heartbreak and tragedy and pain in the Bible—even for *Gotte*'s people. Perhaps when they returned home, she'd spend some time reading through her favorite passages in the New Testament or the Psalms. The Psalms always calmed her heart. Maybe it was time to accept her situation and trust that *Gotte* could and would do whatever was best for her.

Chapter Eleven

For Levi, the next week was a blur of activity.

Sunday had been a visiting day, so he'd spent it at the hospital. Old Simon was improving faster than he could have imagined, and the doctors moved him into the rehab facility on Monday. Levi went about his scheduled work each day at the Kauffmanns, always arriving one to two hours early so he could tackle the day's work before the sun had even peeked over the horizon. Each day he finished by noon, and then he took the bus to Nappanee, Middlebury and Shipshewana. He met with the bishops there, shared his vision and asked them to mention the opportunity to any family who was looking to make a move. Before leaving he requested they pray for his success.

He tried to stop by the rehab facility in the late afternoon to visit Old Simon, and in the evening he would go back to Simon's house, make an egg sandwich and write letters. He wrote to anyone he had an address for. He tried to make the upcoming move sound exciting and a wonderful new opportunity and a near-certain success—and it was all those things.

But beneath all of his optimism was a kernel of doubt.

Bishop Marcus had told him to pray, and he tried. But it often felt as if his prayers stopped at the ceiling, if they even made it that far.

The bishop had also told him to look to the wisdom of family and *freinden*, but his family had already turned their backs to him. And his *freinden*? Well, that had been Annie, and he'd successfully managed to push her away.

Lastly Marcus had advised that he dedicate himself to reading scripture, and Levi tried. But each time he'd find himself staring off into space, thinking about holding Annie's hand, sharing a corn dog, hearing her laughter.

On Thursday evening, Jebediah showed up with a casserole dish that Nicole had made.

"She figured you were getting by on sandwiches."

"Pretty much."

Levi didn't bother heating the chicken casserole up. He could feel it was still lukewarm through the cloth Nicole had wrapped it in. He walked to the kitchen, fetched a fork out of the drawer, sat down at the table and dug in.

"No plate? Wow."

"You've forgotten what it's like to be a bachelor." Levi scooped up another forkful. The casserole was filled with noodles and chicken and cheese. He wasn't sure he'd ever tasted anything better in his life.

"If being a bachelor means that you eat out of the casserole dish and never clean the kitchen, I'm glad that part of my life is over." Jebediah pulled off his hat and dropped it on the table. "Nicole would be happy to get a ladies' group over here to help you clean."

"*Nein.* Old Simon won't be back for another week at the earliest. I'll have everything straightened up before then."

Jebediah clearly had his doubts. He glanced again at the sink that was overflowing with dishes, the dirty clothes that were spilling out of the mudroom and the floor that was tracked with dirt.

"Okay. If you say so."

"I do."

"You seem kind of put out. How are things going?"

"Things are going fine." Levi filled him in on all he'd done since Sunday. "I'm ready for tomorrow night's meeting. I've actually had some good results this week, better than I expected."

"So that's the reason for your good mood." Jebediah sat down across from Levi and waited.

Clearly he wasn't going to leave until he found out what was going on. Probably Nicole had sent him over to extract information, or maybe Annie had. That thought caused his mind to trip back to the night of the festival, the way her hand had felt in his, the way she'd looked at him as they'd swapped half a turkey leg for half a corndog.

Levi took a few more bites, then reached for a glass of water that had been sitting on the table and drained it. "Hopefully I'm even ready for all the negative research Annie's been doing."

"What happened to you two?"

Levi shrugged as if he had no idea what Jebediah was talking about.

"Come on. I can keep my mouth shut."

"There's nothing to tell."

"You were dating and now you're not."

"It just didn't…you know. It didn't work out."

"That's all you've got?"

"Nothing more to say." He heard the edge in his own voice and tried to lighten up a bit. "Told you I was no good with women. Maybe I'll have better luck in Texas."

"If you say so, but from my point of view you're acting like a man on a mission."

"I am."

"I didn't mean that in a *gut* way. Maybe I should have said like a crazy man on a desperate mission."

Levi looked down and realized he'd eaten half the casserole. Suddenly it felt like a brick in his stomach. He put the lid back on the dish and pushed it away.

"I'm not crazy and my mission isn't desperate."

"Have you found any ministers yet?"

"I had one call me yesterday and another send a letter. They both seem very close to committing."

"Only one to go then…"

"And three more families have signed up. If you and your *dat* would make up your minds, that would bring our total to ten."

"I'm leaning toward it, but both Nicole and I want to be very sure." He crossed his arms on the table and studied Levi. "We have *kinder*, you know."

"I'm aware."

"We can't make hasty decisions now. We need to consider a thing from all sides."

"Just come to tomorrow night's meeting. I have some *gut* news to share, and I think it might help you see things more clearly."

"Huh."

Levi stood and stretched. "I need to go muck out the barn, but thanks for bringing the food by."

"Sure." But apparently Jebediah just couldn't leave it alone. "Any message you'd like to send to Annie?"

"*Ya.* Tell her to be ready for tomorrow night, because I plan to be."

Levi was as nervous as a cat in a room full of dogs. Friday night there were even more people in attendance than at their first meeting. He kept looking out the front door, out the window, across the room. Just when he'd convinced himself that Annie wasn't going to show, she rushed through the door of Old Simon's house, breathless, clothes spattered with rain, and looking more beautiful than ever.

It took a sheer act of will to tear his eyes from her.

He needed to focus.

Tonight was important. It was crucial, and he wasn't going to let an ill-advised crush ruin his chances to finally achieve his dreams.

Annie sat in the back, between her *dat* and her *schweschder.* On the other side of Nicole was Jebediah who leaned across and said something that Annie obviously didn't like. She looked as if she was going to argue with him when Bishop Marcus stood and called the meeting to order.

"Welcome. It's *gut* to see everyone on this cold and rainy evening. It would seem that fall has finally arrived…"

"Or winter," someone called out from the back.

"Wonder if they have this kind of weather in Texas," someone else joked.

"*Nein.* In Texas, it's always sunny." Levi couldn't resist, though the look on Annie's face made him wish he'd held his tongue.

The bishop opened the meeting with a word of

prayer, asking for guidance and wisdom, and then he nodded at Levi.

"Before we begin, I'd like to update you all on Old Simon. He's been moved to the rehab center, as most of you know. Today we learned that he may be able to come home as early as the end of next week."

The news was met with nods of approval and even a few hands lifted heavenward followed by a hearty "Hallelujah."

"We would like to have a workday here on Monday," Marcus said. "We need to install some handrails and ramps. Anyone who can help, it will be much appreciated."

"What does his son Jonah say?" a man in the back asked.

"He wanted to come and see his *dat* this week, but he had to get his crop in." Levi knew that everyone in the room understood that crops couldn't wait. You helped when you could, but if at all possible crops had to come first. "He hopes to be here within the next ten days. At that point, he'll meet with Old Simon's doctors and together they will decide how best to proceed. What is certain, and I know this because I've spoken with Jonah, is that Old Simon will not be moving to Texas."

It seemed a somber note to start the meeting on, but it wasn't as if he hadn't anticipated the reaction those words would have on the group. He'd known since talking to Bishop Marcus the night in the hospital that Simon wouldn't be moving. He'd probably known it earlier when he'd spoken with the doctors, only he hadn't wanted to see it. He'd resented Marcus's brutal honesty at the time, but now he was grateful for it. The bishop had caused him to accept the way things were, deal with it and move past it.

Unfortunately, not everyone had.

Marcus was about to sit down, but he looked across the room and called on Annie. "You had a question?"

She jumped to her feet. "If we know that Old Simon can't move, and we have no other ministers who have shown an interest, what's the point in this meeting? We might as well go home."

"I was going to let Levi share this, but since you brought it up, we've actually had two ministers express a strong interest in moving to Texas."

Levi almost laughed at the look of dismay on Annie's face. Not that he wanted her to be dismayed, but it was somewhat precious. This was turning into some sort of twisted game. She'd obviously been angry with him Saturday night, though he had no idea why. Then she had pointedly ignored him during the week, and now she seemed determined to derail his plans.

Well, he couldn't be so easily dissuaded.

He was made of tougher stuff than that.

But even as those thoughts flew through his mind, Levi met Annie's gaze and his breath caught in his chest. He saw a vulnerability in her expression that melted some of the ice around his heart. He tore his eyes away and looked down at his notes. He needed to stay focused.

"*Ya*, it's true. One minister from Shipshe and another from Ohio have expressed an interest. So we still need one more, but I feel confident we will have that commitment within a few weeks."

Annie leveled him with a pointed stare, and she only sat down when Nicole reached up and tugged on her arm.

He went on to tell the group about the letters he'd received from families who had responded to his notice in *The Budget*.

"So what you're saying is that we might have more than the dozen families?" This from Jebediah, who was holding one of the twins in his arms.

"*Ya*, if even half of the people here tonight are serious about moving, then I'd say we have our dozen families."

Annie was on her feet again. "But what about the cost of land there? You were going to report back on that."

"Thank you, Annie, for bringing that up. I actually do have some numbers to share." The price of land was more than he had remembered, more than he had guessed, but it was still significantly less than the cost for a farm in Indiana. He spent the next ten minutes laying out the cost per acre and the amount of acreage he'd found available from a cursory search on the library's computer.

The room filled with an animated discussion of what crops would yield the most given the Texas heat.

Annie's *dat* stood and waited for everyone to quiet down. "It sounds to me that we can do this in the next few months, and though we might be late getting started on spring crops, the growing season is longer in Texas."

"It's true, but remember there is the matter of less rain so we may have to adjust our stance regarding irrigation."

"I won't abide electricity on my farm." One of the men positioned near the front of the group stood and turned to survey everyone in the room. "I personally won't have it, even if the bishop makes an allowance for such."

Levi jumped in before the discussion could be derailed with an unending wave of *what-if* scenarios. "And I respect that—however, it doesn't have to be an either/or proposition."

"What's that supposed to mean?" Annie asked.

"Simply that. There are other ways to irrigate. Advances have been made in both solar and wind energy. Water can be gathered in a cistern or from a well, and the pump can be solar or wind powered."

A discussion ensued as to the advisability of using solar power. Levi was relieved when Avery Stutzman brought up the fact that the Amish community in Colorado had allowed solar energy. He had that in his notes, but it seemed better when someone else pointed out the positive things.

He let the discussion continue for a few more minutes before he raised his hand to silence everyone.

"There is one more thing I want to bring up—something that was asked last time we met." He looked directly at Annie, who glowered back at him. Even with her eyes squinting and a frown on her lips, he thought she might be the prettiest thing he'd ever seen—prettier even than a Texas sunset.

"Actually there are two things I'd like to address. The first is whether there is a place between here and Texas where we could start a new community—a closer place. The answer to that—I realized even when Annie first asked—is of course there is. There's plenty of land between here and Texas, and no doubt some of it would be *gut* farmland. Some of it would be a fine place to build a new community. But that isn't my dream. That isn't what *Gotte* has put into my heart."

Everyone was looking at him now, but Levi didn't shy away from what he wanted to say, what he'd stayed awake the night before thinking about. "I can't say if this move is right for any of you. That's something that you have to pray about, discuss with your own families and ultimately decide for yourselves. I can only say that it is something that's been in my heart since I was a young boy."

He looked down at his notes, then folded the sheet in half. He didn't have to look at lines he'd scribbled on a sheet of paper to say what was on his mind, what filled his heart. "It could be that I made Texas into something larger than life, because I was happy there as a boy, because those years were some of the best years of my life."

The room fell silent as each person focused on Levi.

"Or it could be that it is a special place, a place where we can have room to spread out and raise our sons and daughters. So when Annie asked her second question— when she asked *why now* when it didn't work before—I had to spend a lot of time thinking about that. The only answer I've found is that now is best because it seems the time is right. To me it does, and I hope it does for you too."

He sat down then. He didn't know what else to say, how to share the feelings and thoughts and hopes and dreams that he'd carried for so long. How did a person put such things into words in a way that another person could understand? A dream shared didn't need to be explained, and a dream that wasn't shared couldn't be explained.

He couldn't look at Annie. He couldn't bear to see the disappointment in her eyes again. He understood in that moment that he had dared to hope that she would be the woman to share his dream, that she would care enough about him to come around to his point of view.

But she'd made it quite plain that such a thing wasn't going to happen.

All he had to do now was learn to live with that.

* * *

Annie's business naturally slowed down in November. Amish weddings typically took place in the spring and fall, some occurred in the summer, but very few happened between November and February. Most families began focusing on the holidays. Both Thanksgiving and Christmas were a time for family, a time to gather together, a time to pause and appreciate all that *Gotte* had done in their lives.

Also, holding an Amish wedding in the winter was complicated by the fact that it was difficult to find a place large enough to hold such a gathering once the temperatures fell to below freezing. Her business practically came to a stop when snow was on the ground. She'd never been bothered by that before. November was a good time to help her mother with canning. She also met with her business partner Priscilla once a week to go over their accounting as well as their business plans.

"I still think we should spend some of our profits on advertising," Priscilla said. "It would be nice to have more weddings scheduled, and to have families committed to using us further in advance of the actual wedding date."

"What are you going to do? Run a television ad? Amish don't watch television." Annie meant it as a joke, but her words came out with a sharp edge. They were sitting in the coffee shop in downtown Goshen, a steady rain falling outside the window. The shop was decorated with Thanksgiving decor—pumpkins and a scarecrow and even a cornucopia filled with plastic fruit. It reminded her that this was the time of year when they were supposed to be filled with gratitude.

"I was thinking more like an ad in *The Budget*, or placing flyers at local quilt shops, dry goods stores, that sort of thing."

"Uh-huh."

Priscilla tapped the table between them. "Hello! Earth to Annie."

"I'm right here." Annie turned her gaze from the harvest display to her best friend. Funny that she never would have imagined having an *Englischer* as a business partner and a friend, let alone her closest friend. *Gotte*'s ways were sometimes mysterious.

"But your mind seems to be far away. I'm going to guess your thoughts are approximately twelve hundred miles away."

Annie proceeded to crumble her scone into tiny pieces. "I'm not thinking about Levi if that's what you're saying."

"You're not?"

"Nuh-uh."

"Because I know you believe it's a sin to lie, and you wouldn't intentionally lie to me anyway since we're friends. But you might lie to yourself. That's what worries me."

Annie sank back against her chair. "They left two days ago for Texas."

"Levi and who else?"

"The minister from Shipshe...and my *bruder*."

"Ouch."

"*Ya*. My *dat* can't stop talking about it. With this rain, he has more time to read the books he continually checks out from the library, which means I'm subjected to a near-endless stream of Texas trivia. Did you know that the largest rose garden in the world is in Tyler, Texas?"

"I didn't."

"It's a big place—the Lone Star State. It holds more than seven percent of the nation's area. Hard to imagine a place that vast." She clasped her hands around her mug and finally looked up at Priscilla. "They've pretty much committed to a move in the spring."

"I'm sorry, Annie. I didn't realize things were moving so quickly."

"Indeed. Levi's a real go-getter. He could start a business moving people to Texas. Maybe the Stephenville tourism bureau would hire him."

Instead of responding to that, Priscilla sipped her coffee and allowed a moment of silence to pass between them. Annie appreciated that about her friend. Sometimes she desperately needed those moments of quiet.

They finished their drinks, bussed their table and headed outside, but they didn't immediately turn toward Priscilla's truck. Instead they stood there, pulling their coats tighter and watching the rain. Annie noticed that some of the shop windows already held Christmas displays—snowmen, angels, Christmas trees, and brightly wrapped presents. She'd always loved Christmas, loved everything about it. She often went about humming Christmas hymns and squirreling away presents for her family.

But this year was different.

This year she wasn't feeling the joy of the season. Instead, looking at the *Englisch* displays made her heart hurt. Why did so many things cause an ache deep inside her chest?

"Have you told him how you feel?"

Annie might not have answered back in the coffee shop when she had to look Priscilla in the eye. But standing out in the rain on a cold November day, she couldn't find any good reason to avoid the subject. "I haven't. What's the point?"

"What's the point? He might feel the same, that's the point."

"If he felt the same, he wouldn't be in Texas right now, and he wouldn't be taking my family with him."

Priscilla looped her arm through Annie's and they began walking down the row of shops, under the blue canopies, toward the parking area at the end of the block. "I'm not sure that's true. It's possible to want two things at once—two things that seem completely opposed to each other."

"I guess."

"There's a reason you fell in love with him. Levi's a good person."

"I know that, and I'm not angry with him anymore."

They hurried through the rain toward the truck. Once they had fastened their seat belts and were driving through Goshen, Annie started talking, really talking, about Levi for the first time since the night they'd gone to the fall festival. She described their date, the food they'd shared, how she'd felt each time they'd held hands.

She paused to gawk at a particularly large inflatable display in an *Englisch* front yard—penguins dressed in bathing suits and holding surfboards. She wasn't sure how that related to Christmas, but it was definitely bright. Oh, and there were Christmas scarves around the penguins' necks. She pulled her attention back to Priscilla, who was still waiting for her to finish. "Did I tell you he's helping to prepare Old Simon's house for sale?"

"He is?"

"*Ya.* Old Simon had initially done well in rehab, and they thought he'd come home—even readied the house for him."

"What happened?"

"He came down with pneumonia, which he's over now, but he's weaker than before. The doctors say that he shouldn't live alone. Since Levi doesn't plan to stay here, he thought the least he could do would be to help Simon's son Jonah prepare to sell the place."

"Levi told you that?"

"*Nein.* We don't talk, not really. I heard our bishop telling my *dat.*"

"What will Levi do if the farm sells before he's ready to move?"

"He says he'll move ahead of everyone else. Stay with the family who used to be their next-door neighbors, help negotiate the purchase of farms."

"The way you describe him, he sounds more like a man now, less like a boy with some crazy plan."

"*Ya*, you're right. He's changed for sure and certain."

"And you're absolutely certain that your parents are moving? They've told you that? Because sometimes your dad can be excited about a thing but not, you know, follow through."

"I haven't outright asked them."

Priscilla took her eyes off the road for a moment to give her a shocked look.

"What?" Annie shifted in her seat.

"You need to know. You need a plan."

"Uh-huh."

"Remember when you insisted we have a business plan that first year? And I just wanted to make cakes and cook and buy cool stuff."

"You had a lot of enthusiasm."

"And you had a lot of common sense. So what's happened to it?"

Instead of being offended, Annie started laughing. She could always count on Priscilla to be honest with her. "I guess I'm scared to hear what my parents will have to say. Once I know for certain, I can't un-know it."

"You also can't stick your head in the sand. Well, you can, but I don't recommend it."

They were near the farm now. When Priscilla had turned down the lane and pulled up close to the porch, she put the truck in Park and turned to study her.

"You know you could live with me, if your family moves."

"*Ya*, I know, but…"

"I'm not Amish. I'm aware." Priscilla reached over and tugged on one of her *kapp* strings. "I just want you to know you have options, until you figure out what you're going to do."

"You're a *gut* friend."

"Hey. I don't want to lose my business partner."

Annie smiled, and she actually felt a bit better for the first time in a long time. Life wasn't all gloom and doom, she realized as she dashed from the truck to her front porch. There were good people all around, and she was fortunate to have friends who cared.

Her heart might always feel bruised, but life contained other joys than romantic love. Funny thought for a wedding caterer to have, but she believed it nonetheless.

She'd nursed her hurts long enough.

As Priscilla had so aptly pointed out, it was time to take her head out of the sand. For the first time she felt like going to her bedroom and cataloging what Christmas gifts she'd purchased or made so far. They celebrated simply, swapping names among the adults and giving one gift to each grandchild, but with their growing family that still added up to quite a few gifts. She needed to make sure there was enough time left to finish up everything before the family met for the holidays. She seemed to remember a pink and purple blanket she'd started for her niece, Rachel.

Had she finished it?

Where had she put it?

Her heart still felt heavy whenever she thought of Levi, but perhaps it was time to move on. It wouldn't be a perfect Christmas, but it could still be special.

It had taken a full day's bus ride to make it from Goshen, Indiana to Stephenville, Texas. The ride was longer than it should have been because they weren't able to take a direct route. Time and again they detoured through downtown areas to drop off and pick up passengers. Still, the hours passed pleasantly enough, and Levi was able to read the book on dry-land farming in Texas that he'd borrowed from the Goshen library. They finally checked into a hotel in downtown Stephenville and slept for ten hours. The next day they spent with a Realtor, traveling from one acreage to another.

Now they were having a bite to eat at the diner attached to the hotel.

"Everything we saw today was too expensive," Adam said. He was a minister in the Shipshe district, with five young sons. He was concerned about where and how they would be able to farm, to continue their simple traditions, and he'd said more than once that he didn't want them working in the RV factory. "It's *gut* pay, but a man should be near his family, near the land, not inside a building working with machines all day."

It was a refrain that Levi had heard before, and though he had no children of his own, he understood the concern. Adam knew at least three other families who were in similar situations and had said they'd consider a move. Their numbers for the Texas settlement were growing.

"The problem is that this is horse country." Jebediah stirred a teaspoon of sugar into his coffee cup. "Instead of paying the agricultural value, owners are asking for the grazing value in an area that is apparently well-known for its horse stock."

"We wouldn't have any trouble purchasing buggy horses."

"The workhorses—now that will be a problem."

Levi heard them, but his mind was elsewhere. If he were honest with himself, which he'd been avoiding, he was thinking about Annie. Everywhere he looked there was something he wanted to show her—the quaint shops in the downtown area, the vista that stretched as far as the eye could see, the rolling hills and deep blue sky. The area was actually more picturesque than he had remembered. He had to fight the urge to call her and tell her that it was too warm to wear his jacket and that he'd seen children playing in shorts—the week before Thanksgiving.

But then maybe she would miss the snow and cold days and rain.

Why was he torturing himself this way? Annie had

made it abundantly clear that she wasn't interested in moving and she wasn't interested in him.

"I need to stretch my legs," he muttered, grabbing his Stetson off the seat next to him and heading outside. He stood in the parking area for five minutes, getting his emotions under control before he turned to go back inside. As he waited for a couple in front of him to enter the café, the woman, who appeared to be in her fifties, stopped and pulled a magazine from a rack positioned outside the door. Turning to her husband, she said, "Maybe we'll find our dream place listed here."

"Anywhere you are is my dream place, darling."

Levi winced at the tender words. They would have sounded glib in any other situation, but the look on the man's face as he touched his wife's arm and held the door for her convinced Levi that the man meant every word.

Had he looked at Annie like that?

His mind flashed back to the night at the hospital, but he pushed that memory away.

Best to focus on what was possible.

He grabbed three of the magazines from the rack and carried them to the table where Jebediah and Adam were finishing up their meal.

"Have any revelations while you were out there?" Adam asked.

"Not personally, but I heard someone say they were looking for a place as they picked up these." He dropped the magazines on the table.

"Central Texas Real Estate?" Jebediah shrugged and pulled a copy closer.

Adam did the same. The conversations around them faded into the background as they each studied the listings.

"I keep seeing listings in Hamilton, and the prices

are much less expensive." Jebediah glanced up. "Any idea where that is?"

Levi turned to the map page while Adam peered over at the list that Jebediah had been studying.

"Here," Levi said. "It's less than an hour south of here."

"Do you think the Realtor will take us there?"

"It sounded like his area is primarily limited to Stephenville, and he had other appointments today." Levi waved at the waitress as she walked by with a hot pot of coffee.

"You folks need a refill?"

"*Nein.* That is, we're *gut* as far as coffee. I was wondering if you could tell us how to get to Hamilton."

"Oh, that's easy. You get on Highway 281, which veers right when you reach Hico. Keep heading south and you'll be there in no time."

"We're visiting from out of town. We don't have a vehicle…"

Jebediah laughed at that. "And we're Amish, so we wouldn't own one even if we lived here."

"I thought you might be," she said with a smile.

"The suspenders and beards must have been a dead giveaway," Jebediah joked.

"Pretty much. My aunt lives in Pennsylvania, and I stayed with her a few summers." She pulled a cell phone out of her apron pocket. "I know you don't own phones, so you can use mine if you want."

"And call whom?"

"Uber, of course."

Fifteen minutes later, they were headed south.

Chapter Twelve

Annie planned all afternoon what she wanted to say to her parents, but she waited until they'd all sat down for supper. Her *dat* looked tired from his long day working in the barn, and her *mamm* had spent the afternoon helping a neighbor who had fallen and broken her leg. She let them talk about their day, remembered to ask the occasional question and tried to actually eat the ham, potatoes, corn and fresh bread on her plate.

She succeeded marginally.

If they noticed, no one said anything.

Finally, her *dat* pushed his plate away and reached for his coffee cup.

"Let me refill that." Annie jumped up and filled both his cup and her *mamm*'s.

They shared a look which said they knew something was up, but waited for her to take her seat again and clasp her hands in front of her.

When she couldn't seem to find the words to start, her *mamm* reached toward her and brushed her *kapp* string back, as she'd done when Annie was a small child, as she'd done a million times. "Did you want to talk to us about something, dear?"

"*Ya*. Actually, I did. I wanted to ask, that is, I'd like to know your intentions regarding moving."

Her *mamm* looked to her *dat* as if she were passing the ball to him. That was when Annie knew her fate was sealed. They'd already decided. They'd spoken about it, perhaps when she was sitting in this very room but too absorbed by her own problems to pay any attention to them.

Her *dat* sipped his coffee, took his time framing his answer. "Your *schweschder*…"

"Nicole?"

"*Ya*. Both she and Jebediah are worried about the cost of land here—he's worried his boys won't be able to afford it and that his girls will have to move away in order to marry and start a family."

"Plenty of young people marry and stay in the area."

"True, but how many of those couples are living on their parents' land? Not that Jebediah would mind that, and he certainly has many years before the boys are ready to marry…"

"The twins haven't turned one yet," she whispered.

"Next month," her *mamm* said. "I understand his concerns must seem premature to you, but trust me, the years will fly by. Plus, a move will be easier while the children are young."

"It doesn't mean *you* have to go."

"*Nein*. We don't have to, but we feel the Lord calling us to do so." Her *mamm*'s voice was gentle but firm.

"So it's decided? You are going?"

Her *dat* nodded and though he was probably trying to contain his enthusiasm for her sake, he didn't quite succeed. A smile spread across his face, and he began drumming his fingertips against the tabletop. "We'll wait and hear the report, but if there's affordable land to purchase, then *ya*. We will be moving when your *schweschder* does."

The words sliced through her heart, but she had a moment of clarity at the same time. She could fight this and be miserable for the time they had left or she could accept the situation for what it was. In some strange way she also felt lighter from hearing their plans. The worst had come about. She could stop worrying and start dealing with it.

"I plan to stay."

Her *mamm* reached for her hand and covered it with her own. "Your older *bruders* and *schweschder* will still be in the area, for now, and they've all said they'd be happy to have you live with them."

It had gone that far?

They'd decided where she was going to live?

Annie felt her old stubbornness rise, and it was like a coat that she'd pushed to the back of the closet and just recently rediscovered. She was tired of crying, tired of worrying, and suddenly she knew that she would find a way to deal with this and she'd do so on her own terms.

"Priscilla said that I could live with her."

Her *dat* stared into his coffee cup. When he glanced up, she saw nothing but concern in his eyes, and she felt bad for causing them so much worry.

"She's a *gut* person. You both know that. You both like her."

"You're not thinking of leaving the faith, are you?" Her mother watched her carefully.

"*Nein*. I like being Amish. I am Amish, but I need

somewhere to live, and our catering business is really taking off. I don't want to move to Shipshe or Middlebury. I like it here." She realized the absurdity of that. Her parents were going to move twelve hundred miles away, and she was insisting that a ten-mile change would be too much. "I know I don't need your permission, but I'd like your blessing."

"That you will always have, Anna Marie." Her *dat* so rarely used her full name that it always brought a lump to her throat. The words were like a caress and a blessing all in one.

Her *mamm* stood, began picking up dishes and then paused to kiss Annie on the top of the head. "You must promise to come and visit us—at least twice a year."

"*Ya*, of course."

"And who knows, maybe when you do, you'll like it enough to stay."

Annie didn't think that was likely.

She could only imagine how terrible it would be to visit her family in their new home, meet neighbors that she didn't know and hadn't grown up with, continue to see Levi after he settled down and married. *Nein*, she did not picture herself visiting Texas twice a year. But she didn't voice her concerns. Now wasn't the time. She had moved from grieving into planning in the space of a heartbeat.

"Have you talked about a date…for the move?"

She hadn't attended the last two meetings regarding the Texas settlement, and she'd avoided being alone with Nicole. She hadn't been able to bear her *schweschder*'s talk of a new life. Now she regretted the distance she'd put between them, and she vowed to spend as much time as possible with her niece and nephews in the next few months.

"We'll go in the spring, if Levi and Jebediah have been able to locate farms we can afford to purchase. It could be as late as summer if it takes a long time to sell this place."

They all knew that wasn't likely.

The reason they were moving was because there were more people who wanted to buy land in the area than there was land for sale. The farm was tidy and profitable. It would probably sell as soon as they stuck a sign in the ground. This time next year her family would be celebrating Christmas in Texas, and she would be here.

Alone.

Levi, Jebediah and Adam stood at the crest of a hill, an elderly *Englisch* farmer at their side. Buddy Johnston had just celebrated his eighty-eighth birthday. He was nearly as round as he was tall, but he had the hands and the bearing of a farmer.

"It's *gut* land," Jebediah said.

"Yes, it is, and it pains me to sell it." Buddy hooked his thumbs under his belt and shrugged. "My boys, they all work in the city now. They're not farmers, and neither of them has any use for this place. Also they could use the money from the sale—though they're in no hurry for it. Still, when me and Betty pass on, the money will be a nice amount to give to them."

"Hopefully that won't be anytime soon," Levi said.

"Eh. It's in the Lord's hands, and I'm good with that."

Which seemed to confirm that this was a place they were meant to be, on land that had been farmed by a God-fearing man, passed on to God-fearing men. It didn't always happen that way, but when it did Levi sensed a special blessing.

"Would you mind if we took a moment to speak among ourselves?" Adam asked.

"Take your time, and join me for some of Betty's coffee and pecan pie when you're done. Trust me. Betty's pie is not something you want to miss."

They watched him toddle down the lane which led to the house. An old hound dog had been lying in the sun, but it jumped up and trotted over to walk beside him, something they'd probably done together a thousand times.

"Should one of us go with him, make sure he doesn't fall?" Jebediah was like that—a caretaker in more ways than one.

"He's been walking this farm longer than the three of us have been alive," Adam said. "I think he'll be fine."

They turned and stared out at the land, which stretched to the horizon. There was a high plateau to the east. They could just make out a cut between the hills, which was the road they'd travelled on from Stephenville. What might have been the remnant of an ancient volcano shimmered to the south, and farmland as far as you could see spread to the west.

"This is a big place." Adam turned in a circle, trying to take it all in.

"A thousand acres—" Levi pulled off his hat and held it in both hands. "It could be divided into ten, maybe eleven farms."

"We have fourteen families," Jebediah pointed out.

"And we passed three other farms for sale on our way here."

"Speaking of which…" Adam glanced back toward the farmhouse. "How are we going to get the Uber driver back?"

"I paid him twenty dollars to go to town and get dinner. He had a few errands to run and said he'd be back here by dark."

The three fell silent, each contemplating the enormity of the decision they were about to make.

"We've been given the duty of finding land for our community. It's a solemn and weighty thing to make such a decision, and it's important that we be in complete agreement." Adam fell into the role of leader easily.

Levi thought he'd make a good bishop, a fair one who would make the physical and spiritual health of their community his priority.

"Any hesitation, any doubt at all—now is the time to voice it."

"I can't think of any reason not to make this deal." Jebediah pulled his gaze from the horizon and nodded at Levi. "Can you?"

"*Nein.* It's all I've dreamt of, all I've hoped and prayed for."

"Then we're in agreement," Adam said.

"*Ya*, I'm in agreement." Jebediah shoved his hands into his pockets, a smile spreading across his face. "I can see my boys growing up here. The land is less expensive than Stephenville, the barns not as well cared for, but we can easily rebuild a barn."

Levi had waited for this moment for so long that he felt a lump rise in his throat. "*Ya*, I agree," he said, which seemed to be all there was to say. He was aware that with those words, he not only changed the direction of his own life, but he also was changing the lives of all of the families who would be moving. And of course it would affect one pretty young lady who would not be coming to Texas.

Why was life so full of difficult decisions?

Why were his feelings for Annie so strong at a time

when he should be focused on this land and the families he had committed to bringing here?

He knew in his heart that this move was good and right and something they should do. For Levi, it was like coming home again, the fulfillment of years' worth of planning and working.

So why, when they turned toward the house, to tell Buddy Johnston and his wife that they'd gladly purchase their land at the suggested price, did his heart ache with another dream that died even as this one was born?

Thirty minutes later, Buddy's neighbor had arrived. The man also happened to be his lawyer.

"We called him while you were surveying the place," Buddy explained. "Seemed to me that you liked it."

"This is a preliminary notice of intention to purchase that I downloaded from the internet." Raymond Cole was probably in his fifties, had the soft, cultured voice of a man with an advanced education and the calluses of a farmer. His skin was ebony black, his hair graying at the temples, and his manner serious.

"We would have been happy with a handwritten receipt and a handshake," Adam said.

"And it says something about you folks that you would have been." Raymond accepted the three copies that they all had signed and added his own signature under the word *Witness*. "I'm not sure I'd recommend carrying twenty thousand dollars in earnest money around in your pocket, but it certainly speeds things up that we don't have to wait three days for a transfer of funds."

"We wanted to be able to show that we were serious about our ability to purchase such a large parcel."

"I say it's time to celebrate." Betty set the pecan pie in the middle of the table. Like Buddy, she was in her eighties. Her hair was whiter than the cotton they'd seen in the fields on the drive down, and her skin thin as parchment. Whereas Buddy was short and round, Betty's build was slight and her posture ramrod straight. They both seemed at peace with the decision to move off the farm.

Levi glanced around the kitchen, saw a rocking chair in the corner and beside it a small table with an open Bible resting on it. So they were truly people of faith. That might explain their calm and confident nature. He remembered Buddy's comment, *It's in the Lord's hands, and I'm good with that.* What more could a person ask for than to be at peace with the Lord's guidance in their life?

The pie had already been sliced into pieces. Betty placed a tray with six mugs, sugar, cream and a pot of coffee in the middle. "You folks help yourself."

"Where will you go?" Levi asked.

"Our sons have already picked out a place in Sun City—it's a development for old folks, but they have a fine golf course there."

"And is it closer to your sons?" Jebediah asked.

"Yes, it is. Our oldest has three pretty grandbabies, and they live in Georgetown. We'll be able to see them as often as we want. At our age, that's more important than having a field to plant winter oats in."

Levi had enjoyed Mrs. Calloway's pecan pie growing up, and Betty's was every bit as good as hers. He couldn't help laughing when Jebediah took his first bite.

"Your eyes nearly rolled up in your head."

"This is as good as shoofly pie. I didn't think anything was as good as that."

"Your wife and I will have to swap recipes, in that case. Buddy's never had shoofly pie."

"Doctor says I'm supposed to cut back, but then he's never tried Betty's cooking or he wouldn't ask me to do such a thing."

There was talk of farming and families and the upcoming Thanksgiving holiday. When they'd all finished their pie, Raymond sat forward, crossing his arms on the table and looking at each of them in turn. Levi had the sense that this was the real test—not how much money they had or their knowledge of farming.

Raymond was assessing them.

If they were found wanting, in his estimation, then their time in Texas would be difficult because word would spread. Call it gossip or call it being neighborly, one man talks to another who then talks to another. It was the way of things, and Levi didn't hold it against the man, though he did hope that they'd pass with flying colors.

"I've read a little about you people."

"Have you now?" Adam nodded as if it had been wise for Raymond to check them out before accepting their money. "And do you have any questions?"

"I do."

"Fire away."

"Is it true that you have extremely large families?"

"It is."

"Eight to ten children?"

"Not unusual."

Levi nodded, but it was Jebediah who jumped into the conversation.

"My wife and I have a three-year-old girl and twin boys who will turn one next month..."

Raymond let out a long whistle.

"And they're expecting another," Levi added.

Raymond's eyebrows shot up. "Four children under four? Is that normal?"

"It's not unusual."

Adam nodded toward the Bible that sat near the rocker. Levi wondered if Betty had been doing some reading before they all traipsed in. He marveled again that they would be buying the land from fellow believers of God's word. "Our understanding of the Scripture teaches us that the Lord grows each household as He sees fit."

"I was one of ten," Buddy commented.

Betty added, "It was normal in our generation, but our children all think that two or three are a handful, and perhaps in this day and age, in our modernized way of life, perhaps they're right."

Raymond nodded as if that all made sense and moved on to his next question. "You're not allowed to use technology—cars or electricity or computers?"

"It's true that we prefer the old ways," Adam said. "Though it's not a matter of being allowed so much as it is that we prefer to not have the distractions of a television set or the expense of an automobile. Each community has its own guidelines. For instance, we may decide that solar energy would be beneficial, even necessary, in order to irrigate our crops."

It seemed to be a good enough answer for Raymond who nodded and then distributed the copies of the papers they'd signed and slipped his into a battered old leather bag.

Levi wasn't sure if they'd passed the test until they were all walking out to the front porch and Raymond said, "How much more land do you think you'll need?"

"At this point—two or three hundred additional acres."

"I think I know two other families who would be interested in selling. Their land is close to here. One is a hundred and twenty acres. The other is a hundred and thirty. If you'd like, I could contact them."

"*Ya*, we'd like that," Adam said.

Levi released a breath he didn't realize he'd been holding. Finally he dared to believe it was actually going to happen—after twelve long years he was moving back to Texas.

Annie was sitting at the kitchen table planning their Thanksgiving dinner when Nicole arrived with the news. Jebediah had left a message at the phone shack. They'd found land. Soon Annie's *dat* and *mamm* were gathered around the table, and they were all studying a map of Texas. They wouldn't be living in Levi's beloved Stephenville, but they'd be close. She could only imagine how happy he was.

The next week both farms went up for sale, and Annie helped her sister make lists of what she needed to pack in what order, what could be sold and what would need to be purchased in Texas versus what should be moved. The horses would stay. There simply wasn't an economical way to move them, but they'd have good homes. That was one thing for certain—as long as there was an Amish community nearby, any horse would have a home.

Annie wondered if they would move before Nicole gave birth. She'd been present when Rachel, Micah and Mitchell were born. She'd presumed she would be there for all of her *schweschder*'s births, but in the future she would have to be satisfied with reading about them in letters and the occasional visit.

Her *dat* was over the moon with enthusiasm. She'd never seen him so focused. Her *mamm* had been right, and even Annie could see it. The move was going to be good for him. Sometimes change was exactly what the doctor ordered. Sometimes change was what you needed when you didn't even realize you needed anything.

Moving plans halted long enough for them to prepare for Thanksgiving. All of her siblings and their families would be coming as well as Levi. Annie had done her best to avoid him, and she hoped the size of the crowd at her house would negate any awkward feelings.

But as soon as he walked inside, sporting his Stetson and those old cowboy boots which she noticed he had at least bothered to shine, she walked straight up to him. What was the point in remaining angry? Soon he'd be gone, and she would wish that she had settled things between them.

"Congratulations. You're going home to Texas."

The room was crowded with family, children running in circles and a large number of coats and scarves and gloves and mittens piled on the pegs near the front door. He pulled her out onto the porch. A light snow was falling, and she realized with a start that Christmas was just around the corner. It made her feel both amused and sad that she'd thought she could be a matchmaker for Levi. She'd thought she could have him promised off to another woman by Christmas.

"Are you sure you won't go with us?" Levi asked, staring at her, watching for any sign of hesitation.

"*Nein*, but I'm happy for you."

He didn't smile, didn't respond to that remark at all.

Instead he turned and placed his hands on the porch railing and stared out at the fields that were slowly turning white.

"What's wrong?"

He shook his head, reminding her of their workhorse Pretty Boy, tossing his mane as he headed across the field.

"Isn't this what you wanted?"

"Yes and no."

"I don't understand."

"Neither do I."

And then he turned to look at her, his eyes searching her face as he stepped closer.

She stepped back. Heat crept up her neck. She wiped her sweating palms on her apron, and wondered if she might be coming down with something.

And why was Levi watching her so intently?

What was he trying so hard not to say?

Levi cleared his throat. "I guess I didn't account for all that would happen to me when I moved here to Goshen."

"Is that so?"

"It is."

"I hope they were *gut* things."

"The verdict's still out."

"Anything I can help you with?"

Her heart had started thumping like the drummers in the Goshen High School band in the Christmas parade. She clutched her hands in front of her, not because she was afraid but because she had the sudden urge to reach out and touch him before he disappeared like a mirage that she couldn't prove had ever been there.

Levi stepped closer, ducked his head, and she had

the startling realization that he was going to kiss her when the front door burst open and three of her nephews tumbled out—laughing and running and determined to make snowballs out of the slight amounts of snow.

"I better go and help Mamm," she murmured, her cheeks burning and her voice sounding like someone else completely.

He stepped back, smirked, and tipped his hat.

That hat!

It brought her to her senses faster than anything else could have.

Levi Lapp was determined to be a cowboy, and to think that he had any other plans at all—that was the way of folly.

Dinner was a boisterous affair that they held in the barn on tables made from sawhorses.

It had been this way for years—as their family had grown, as the children had multiplied until it seemed they could fill a one-room schoolhouse with the Kauffmann family alone.

She'd hoped they could enjoy the food with no mention of the move, but it was on everyone's mind, and her *dat* addressed it before the first bite was taken.

After their silent prayer, he stood, his head still bowed, and she realized how much she loved this man who had raised her, how much she respected him and how much she would miss him.

"*Gotte*, we thank You for all the *gut* things You have provided us—for the food on this table, for the daughters and sons, grandchildren and *freinden* around it. We thank You for the ultimate gift of our Lord and Savior Jesus Christ, and Father we thank You for the dreams

You have put in our hearts. We ask that as we begin to make our way on this grand adventure, that You will guide our every step, that You will provide our safety and that You will hold our hearts together as one."

Amens rippled around the table, but Annie had to stare at her lap, tears pricking her eyes, and her *dat*'s words, *hold our hearts together as one*, echoing through her heart.

The rest of the meal passed in a flurry of laughter and good-natured teasing. The adults spoke of the move. The children talked of Christmas and the upcoming holiday from school. If she closed her eyes, Annie could almost pretend it was a normal Thanksgiving meal. It was followed by dessert and games and more food to set out for dinner.

If she'd thought that she had successfully managed to avoid Levi Lapp, she was sorely mistaken. It was nearly evening when she stepped out the back door to look up at the stars. The snow had stopped. The clouds had moved off to the east and left behind a scene that looked like something from a child's storybook.

"Beautiful, isn't it?"

Annie jumped, a squeal escaping her lips.

"Didn't mean to scare you."

"I thought I was alone." She raised her chin, feeling ridiculous but needing to at least appear to have control of her emotions. Pulling her coat more tightly about her, she marched out to the swing, hoping Levi would take the hint and allow her some time alone.

He didn't.

Instead he sat next to her and set the swing in motion.

"Do you need a little time alone?"

"It was a goal."

"You have a lot of nephews and nieces."

"And I love every one of them."

"But…"

She couldn't help laughing. "They're a rowdy bunch. I'm not quite used to that much motion and commotion."

"Timothy put a snowball down the back of my shirt."

"Did he now?" She'd have to be sure and give Timothy an extra cinnamon roll in the morning.

"Deborah insisted I sit in a barn stall and hold the newborn kittens."

"She's a precious one."

"Did you know she's named all nine of them?"

"I'm not surprised."

"I like your family, Annie."

Well, you can't have them.

The thought popped into her mind, and she instantly regretted it. Levi cared for her family, and they cared for him. Her father had accepted him as a son; that much was obvious.

"Do you miss your family?" she asked.

"I suppose, but being here…it helps me to realize how unhealthy, how unnatural that situation has been and continues to be. I can only hope and pray that they find a way to love one another, a way to forget the hurts of the past."

"You could pray for them."

"I do, and I write to them. Not enough, but I plan to do better."

They sat in silence for a while, and Annie felt the tension inside of her unwind like a child's rope swing. The night was cold but not bitterly so. The stars sparkled as if the light winter storm had brushed the dust away and left them with freshly cleaned constellations.

A slight moon shone across the snow-covered fields. She could just make out tracks leading from the back door to the barn, no doubt momma cat in search of her evening meal.

She sighed, her heart both happy and hurting at the same time.

"I'm going to miss it here when I move to town."

"I know you will—and I'm sorry, I really am—for any grief that my actions, my dreams have brought to your life."

When he placed his hand over hers, she nearly catapulted off the swing. But his apology seemed sincere.

"Danki," she whispered.

"You won't consider going with us?"

"Nein. I need to be here."

"What if…what if you met someone, fell in *lieb…*"

"If I did…" She looked at him then, thinking that she'd never seen eyes so kind and so troubled at the same time. "If I did, he would understand."

"Understand what?"

"That I need to be here, at least for now."

The last wedding of the year was the second weekend in December. Widow Schwartz was marrying Clyde Gold. Annie kept referring to her as Widow Gold, which made Levi laugh every time.

"Neither has exactly stored up a pile of money," he'd explained when Annie had finally asked him why he was laughing. "I just find the name Gold funny and a little ironic for Amish folk."

Annie shook her head. "Keep acting silly and you won't receive a single Christmas present."

"Does that mean I *am* receiving a present?"

Instead of answering, she'd given him a pointed look and sauntered off. He thought of the snow globe he'd purchased for her in Texas. Inside the globe was a field of Texas bluebonnets, and when you shook it, they became covered with snow.

Since that night on the swing, there had been a change in Annie's attitude. She'd settled somewhere between the sweet girl he'd taken to the fall festival and the frightened woman who had tried to stop the move. He spent every free moment he could find around her, trying to soak in her Annie-ness. Trying to store up enough memories to get him through the year ahead until she came to visit her parents.

Things were changing quickly in their community.

Old Simon's place had sold, and Levi was now living with Bishop Marcus.

He'd rather have stayed with Annie's family.

He wanted time to be with her, to persuade her that they could have a future together.

She'd seemed to at least consider the idea on Thanksgiving night as they'd sat on the swing. Each evening as he went to sleep, that was the thing he thought of—not Texas, which had once been so important to him, and it still was. It was hard to admit that the idea of moving didn't bring the excitement and joy it once had.

Was that how life was?

You worked for and sought after a thing and then when you achieved it, the thing didn't matter as much?

Or was something else happening here?

Had he fallen in love with Annie Kauffmann?

And if he had, what was he going to do about it?

He realized with a start that she was talking about the upcoming wedding and he hadn't heard a word.

"I'm surprised they're even having a wedding celebration," he blurted out.

Annie was helping him brush down the horses. She'd taken to doing it every evening since the Thanksgiving dinner, and it certainly wasn't necessary. He'd told her so every night that he worked at their farm, and every night she'd insisted that she needed time out of the house. All day he looked forward to these moments they shared together, even if there was a nine-hundred-pound horse between them.

"Why would you be surprised?"

"They're so old."

"Younger than my parents."

"Still."

"What would you have them do? Amish don't elope."

He rubbed his jawline as if he needed to seriously consider the idea. "They could. They could ask the bishop to say a few words of blessing, then slip off to Niagara Falls for a little vacation. No need for all the fuss and planning."

"Hey. That's my job you're doing away with."

She smiled at him, and Levi lost another piece of his heart.

He'd thought of skipping the wedding. There was still much to do to get ready for the move. At the moment, he was trying to negotiate the shipment of a dozen buggies, which was difficult enough. Explaining that they needed to be left at Buddy and Betty's farm, where no one was currently living, was even harder.

But a clock had begun to tick in his mind, a countdown clock of how many days he had left with Annie.

For sure and certain he would go to the wedding.

Chapter Thirteen

It was a cold, blustery day so the festivities were held in the barn on the Saturday before Christmas. It was Annie's last wedding until March. She'd told Levi that she would focus on helping her *mamm* to pack and moving her own things to town.

The weather certainly wasn't unusual for December in Indiana, but the wedding venue? He'd never seen anything like it. He'd come to accept that Annie rarely did things in a usual way—the rustic setting hadn't stopped her from decorating as if they were spread across a majestic lawn. There was more greenery inside the barn than out, plus the addition of pinecones filled the air with a nice woodsy scent. Add to that miles and miles of some kind of sheer fluffy white fabric wrapped around anything that wasn't moving and you had a pretty swanky setting.

The ceremony was simple with only a few songs and a short sermon by Bishop Marcus. Levi had mocked the thought of the older couple having a wedding, but seeing them stand at the front of the crowd tugged at his heart and twisted something in his gut. The way they looked at each other, the years fell away and they were simply a man and a woman in love.

They were pronounced husband and wife to much cheering and clapping, and then everyone began moving the benches to where tables had been made out of planks and sawhorses. They were adorned with white tablecloths and small jars of fragrant cedar mixed with white carnations. Fragrant holly berries had been woven like a ribbon along the length of the tables. It reminded him of Christmas, the last holiday he would spend in Goshen. He was moving to Texas after the first of the year.

Tiny lights sparkled along the rafters of the barn.

"How'd she do that?" he asked Nicole.

"The lights? Annie purchased a generator that they carry in the back of the wedding trailer."

The wedding trailer—something he'd laughed at the first day he'd arrived at her parents' farm. Now it was pulled up next to Clyde Gold's barn. When Levi went outside and looked, an extension cord ran from the trailer toward the barn.

"Next thing we know you're going to hire a string quartet," he teased as Annie popped out of the trailer juggling two trays of food. "Let me take those."

He spent the next half hour helping to carry food into the barn.

"We might need to hire him," Priscilla quipped.

But it wasn't until the meal was over and the happy couple was preparing to leave on their short honeymoon—to Sarasota, Florida, not Niagara Falls—that Levi managed to catch a few minutes alone with Annie.

She was standing at the far end of the barn, arms crossed, surveying the crowd.

"*Gut* wedding."

"*Ya.*" She continued watching the group, but finally she sighed and turned toward him. "It's been a *gut* year. Lots of happy couples now sharing cozy little homes, starting new lives together, and some of them are already having babies."

"We could do that."

For a moment he feared that she would laugh at him, but then her expression turned tender and she reached out and tapped the top of his Stetson.

"Long-distance romances rarely work. Long-distance marriages surely wouldn't."

"Come to Texas with me."

"I can't, Levi. I can't do that."

He'd expected that answer, but he'd also feared she would deny having any feelings whatsoever for him.

So instead of focusing on the negative, he stepped closer, waited for her to look up at him, and then he did what he'd wanted to do since that first night when he'd sat on the steps of her trailer. He kissed her, and she tasted like summertime and lemonade and pecan pie.

She didn't move away, so he touched her face with his fingertips and kissed her again.

Finally she began to laugh, and stepped away.

"You are one bold cowboy."

"Or a desperate one."

"I have to go. Night falls early, and Priscilla and I still have to pack up everything."

"I'll help."

But for a moment they simply stood there, as he drank in the sight of her, fearing she might disappear if he dared to look away. He was a man dying of thirst, and the only things that could slack it, the only things that could ease the ache in his throat, were Annie's smile, Annie's touch, Annie standing next to him. She caught him staring, and he held out his hand, held it out between them, palm up.

She placed her hand in his, and they turned and walked back toward the group. Levi had the strangest sensation that she'd done so much more than put her hand in his, that she'd finally put her trust in him. Her words had said one thing but her actions and her expression—well they had said something completely different.

As clearly as if she'd spoken the words, he heard, *Levi, I trust you to find a way to make this work.*

And the fear and the loss and the ache that he'd been dealing with since that night in October when he'd sat in the hospital not knowing Old Simon's condition, those things melted away as if they'd never existed.

Once they'd packed everything up, Levi followed behind Annie's wedding trailer. He was driving Old Simon's buggy again, because it still didn't make sense to purchase his own, especially given the impending move. There were days though, when he was tempted. Old Petunia wasn't exactly spry. Sometimes he feared the mare would fall asleep in the middle of the road. So it was that he was lagging a bit behind.

He caught the light that Priscilla sailed through and more cars turning from the cross street filled the space between them.

It wasn't like he didn't know where they were going—Priscilla was driving the trailer back to Annie's farm. They would store it there until spring when they would move it to a storage facility they'd checked into renting. They definitely couldn't park it at the duplex where Priscilla lived—where Annie planned to live.

Levi had offered to follow them because he wanted more time with Annie. He wanted to explain what he'd meant when he'd said he was desperate.

He hadn't planned on saying that. The words had slipped out of his mouth before he'd considered how they'd affect her. Or maybe he hadn't thought they would.

Did she care about him?

Did she want him to stay?

Did she expect him to give up his dream of Texas?

And beneath those questions, a more important one…would she ever consider moving with him?

He pulled in a deep breath, certain he was building castles in the sand. There was no way that Annie Kauffmann was falling for him. He'd be better off forgetting the kiss they'd shared, the way she'd looked up at him in the moonlight, the ache in his chest when he thought about leaving.

He'd be better off sticking to his original plan.

Or would he?

Glancing out the buggy's window, he saw a man dressed in a Santa Claus costume walking into a bookstore where a group of children were waiting.

Children's wishes were so simple—a new doll, a baseball bat, maybe a set of clothing.

What Levi wished for, what he desperately wanted for Christmas, was Annie by his side for the rest of his life. But how could he ask her that? How could he ask her to give up everything she'd worked so hard to build?

The traffic had begun to move, and Levi was thinking about all of the questions circling his brain and the confusing turns his life seemed to take, when he heard a thunderous crash. He glanced around, uncertain what had happened. Then the car in front of him slammed on its brakes. Levi jerked hard on Petunia's reins, and she stopped so abruptly that he was thrown forward in the seat.

"Whoa. Easy, girl. It's all right."

But it wasn't all right. He realized that several people were screaming, and they were all running forward, running toward the intersection that was up ahead. Some people slammed their car doors shut, while others simply abandoned their vehicles. Everyone was streaming forward in the direction of the next block.

He attempted to guide Petunia forward, but the traffic was at a halt. He jumped out of the buggy and climbed up on the hitch, attempting to see.

"What is it?" he asked an *Englischer* who was hurrying back in his direction.

"Eighteen wheeler sideswiped another vehicle. Ambulance and fire truck are on the way."

"Vehicle...what type of vehicle?"

"Some kind of truck," the man said. "White, I think. It was pulling a large trailer. There's debris all over the intersection. A doctor who saw it happen is working on the woman..."

Levi didn't stay to hear another word.

He scrambled up into the buggy, threw on the brake, called out to the mare and vaulted out of the buggy, leaving the door wide open.

An accident.

White truck and trailer.

Debris everywhere.

And a doctor working on a woman.

"Please, *Gotte*, please..." The cry of his heart rose up into his throat. As he pushed his way through the bystanders, he heard someone say, "I need you people to step back and give the doctor some room."

He saw the words *Plain & Simple Weddings* on the side of the trailer.

His hands began to shake and a buzzing noise filled his head.

The trailer—Annie's trailer—was barely distinguishable as such. The impact of the semi into the truck had caused the trailer to jackknife. It lay on its left side, the doors thrown open, the sidewall crushed. Plates and dishes and food littered the road as if someone had tossed everything out of the trailer.

But he didn't care about any of that.

Legs trembling, he pushed forward.

Now he could see what had happened. Priscilla had pulled into the intersection and her truck had been hit by the eighteen wheeler. The truck had broken away from the trailer, spun around and was now facing back toward the way it had come. He could see the shattered windshield. Someone was helping Priscilla out of the driver's seat. She was in obvious pain, holding her arm at an awkward angle, but she was able to walk with assistance.

Levi pushed through the crowd to the other side of the truck—the side that had taken the brunt of the collision.

Annie had been pulled from the wreckage and laid out on the street. A man knelt beside her, one hand on her wrist.

"Has anyone called 911?" The doctor's voice was calm, but the expression on his face said everything—lines drawn between his eyes, attention focused on Annie.

"They're two minutes away," someone said.

"I saw it happen. The semi sailed through the red light, didn't even slow down."

"It's a miracle she's alive."

Levi heard all of these things, but his mind couldn't grasp and hold on to them. He only knew that it was Annie who was in danger. It was Annie that he had to get to.

Forcing his way through the crowd, he crouched next to the doctor.

"Annie. Annie, can you hear me?" He reached out, touched her hair where the *kapp* had slipped away, prayed that she would open her eyes.

"Do you know her?"

"*Ya.* Her name's Annie, Annie Kauffmann. Is she…"

He couldn't say the word, could barely see through the tears that he swiped away.

"Look at me. Sir, look at me." The doctor's eyes were compassionate, understanding. "She's hurt, but help is on the way. She's unconscious at the moment. Do you know if she has any underlying health conditions?"

"Underlying?"

"Epilepsy, heart condition, pregnancy…anything the paramedics should know about."

"*Nein.* Nothing like that."

Annie's eyes remained closed. She almost looked as if she was sleeping, except for the cut on her forehead, the blood trickling down her face and the way her legs were splayed at an unnatural angle. He glanced over at Priscilla's truck, trying to comprehend that she'd been sitting beneath what was now wreckage.

How had she survived?

Sirens split the afternoon, and then they were surrounded by paramedics insisting that he step back. A fire truck arrived. Before he could comprehend what had happened, they'd placed her on a gurney, covered her with a blanket and the ambulance had sped away.

He reached out for the arm of the man who had been checking her vitals. "Where will they take her?"

"To the hospital here in Goshen. Do you need a ride?"

"*Nein.* I have a buggy." Which was when he realized he'd left Petunia in the middle of the road. He jogged back toward the buggy to find that it was gone. An Amish woman—he couldn't remember if he had met her before or if she was even a member of their congregation—waved at him.

"My husband saw what happened. He moved your buggy around the corner. That way."

"*Danki.*" He took off at a jog and had no problem spotting the rig a block down the road and on the right.

"We saw the accident," the man said as he approached. "Annie was in the truck?"

So they were a part of their congregation, or maybe they knew her from a wedding they'd attended.

"*Ya,* she's hurt and so was the driver, Priscilla. Annie was unconscious. They're taking her to the hospital. I'm going to follow."

"We'll call the bishop and her parents."

"*Danki.*" The words were perfunctory, but he realized he meant them. He was grateful that he didn't have to stop to make a call, didn't have to slow down for even that important errand, because the only thing that mattered was getting to the hospital. The only thing he cared about was Annie and being with her.

Annie woke to the noise of machinery she couldn't identify. There was a swoosh-swoosh sound and a feeling that someone was gripping her arm. She wanted to ask if Levi was there, but she couldn't form the words to do so. Another machine beeped. Soft footsteps echoed close by. She tried to open her eyes, but her eyelids were so incredibly heavy.

Perhaps if she slept a little longer…

Annie stared at a yard full of wedding decorations—the tables covered with cloth and sporting spring flowers and cats. There seemed to be cats everywhere. They wound their way down the tables, stopped to sniff at the celery in the mason jars, batted at the flowers. One large tabby collapsed on the bride's table as if the place had been decorated particularly for his benefit.

Levi laughed and said, "We grow them bigger in Texas. Most cats there are the size of mountain lions."

Were there mountain lions in Texas?

Were there mountain lions at this wedding?

She couldn't think about that. She needed to get rid of the cats. She'd shoo away one, and it would be replaced by three more. Where had they all come from? And why couldn't she reach out and pick one up? Then the rain started, and the cats began to meow and brush up against her legs. Finally they settled, a nice warm pressure, comforting in a purring kind of way.

She knew that she needed to get to work, to pull off the linen cloths before they were soaked, but instead she sank to the ground and the smallest of the kittens climbed into her lap, turned in a circle, plopped down and began to methodically clean its face. The kitten's weight was comforting, and she allowed herself to close her eyes for just a moment.

A pulsing ache in her leg brought her out of the dream. Someone stood over her, shining a bright light in her eyes. She tried to resist, to move her head to the right or left. Her heart rate accelerated and her mind searched for an explanation of what was happening. Still the person with the light persisted. Perhaps if she opened her eyes, just for a minute, the person would go away.

"There she is. That's good, Annie. I know it hurts."

Great. She'd done it! She squeezed her eyes shut, hoping the woman would go away.

"One more time for me. That's excellent."

"Could you…turn out the lights?"

Her voice was scratchy and her throat sore, but all that was nothing compared to the piercing pain in her head.

Why was she in a room with such bright lights?

Why wasn't she at home?

"Can we…" Her *mamm*'s voice calmed her rising panic, but her confusion only increased. Where was she? Why did her *mamm* sound as if she was at the end of a long tunnel?

"Could we please cut the lights?"

"Of course."

Someone jumped up, turned them off and Annie breathed a sigh of relief.

Her *mamm*'s face popped in front of her field of vision. She looked pale and tired and about to cry. "Oh, Annie."

And then her *dat* was there, patting her *mamm*'s shoulder and assuring them both that everything would be okay. She sensed more than saw that someone else was in the room, and then she looked past her *mamm*, past her *dat*, and saw Levi. He offered a little wave. He looked as if he'd been crying too, and as if he hadn't slept in quite some time.

She wondered what had happened, why they all looked so bereft and relieved at the same time.

Where was she?

She glanced to the left of her bed, where a doctor was smiling and tapping something into a tablet computer. Looking back at her family, she asked, "What happened?"

Her *mamm* and *dat* and Levi all looked at one another, and seemed to silently come to the agreement that her *mamm* would be the one to tell her. "You don't remember?"

"*Nein.* Nothing."

"You were in a wreck. A truck hit you."

"Bella?" She tried to sit up, but it felt as if an invisible hand pushed her back. "Is Bella…"

"The horse is fine. You were in Priscilla's truck, pulling the wedding trailer."

And suddenly she did remember—the wedding, the conversation with Levi, leaving in the truck. Explaining to Priscilla how confused she was about her feelings.

"Priscilla?"

"She's *gut.*" Her *mamm* smoothed the white hospital blanket. "She suffered a broken arm as well as some cuts and bruises. Her arm has already been set in a cast, and they released her the same day. She comes by every afternoon to check on you. We've all been…worried."

"How long have I been here?"

"The accident was three days ago. Christmas is tomorrow."

She looked past her *mamm* to Levi, who nodded, held her gaze.

"I'd like to check a few things, and then I'll answer any additional questions you have." The doctor placed the tablet on a small table. "If Dad and Boyfriend could give us a few minutes…"

Boyfriend? She still couldn't remember the accident at all, but there was one thing she knew for certain—Levi wasn't her boyfriend. Before she could protest, though, Levi glanced down at her leg which looked huge.

Was her leg in a cast?

Had she broken it?

And why couldn't she remember what had happened over the last three days?

"We'll be right outside," Levi assured her.

None of it made any sense.

She had so many questions. Before she could decide which one to ask first, the doctor—whose white coat was embroidered with the name Dr. Tallman—helped her sit up and told her to lean forward. She placed the cold stethoscope on her back and said, "Take a real deep breath for me."

Levi probably should have left when Annie's parents did, but he couldn't. He needed to be certain that she was okay. He needed to talk to her.

At first there had been too many people in the room. Confessing feelings for a girl wasn't something you could comfortably do in front of her parents. He wanted to talk to her, and he wanted to do it before going back to his room at Bishop Marcus's.

But was now even the right time?

Maybe he should wait. He hadn't told her at the wedding and then there had been the accident. *Nein.* He wouldn't put it off again. He wouldn't take that chance.

He didn't understand his feelings himself. How was

he going to explain them to her? She might reject him. She probably would, but at this point he had to try.

Her parents had left when they'd brought in her dinner tray. She'd eaten four bites—he'd actually counted—and then fallen asleep. She'd been sleeping for three days straight. It seemed to him that she'd be all rested up. But as the doctor reminded them all, Annie had been through quite a shock and her injuries would take time to heal.

"Sleep is the best thing for her," Dr. Tallman had said more than once.

He'd wait all night if he had to. If they didn't kick him out. Priscilla stopped by after the abbreviated dinner, toting a ridiculously large teddy bear wearing a Christmas sweater. Levi stood out in the hall with her, watching nurses walk back and forth, families coming in for visitation, even a woman with a dog that wore a vest proclaiming the Labrador was a *Comfort Dog*.

"She seemed okay?" Priscilla adjusted the sling which cradled her broken arm. "You're sure?"

"*Ya*. When we told her about the accident, she asked about the horse and you…"

"She didn't remember being in my truck?"

"*Nein*. She didn't remember anything about the accident. I thought she'd be upset about the trailer, but she waved it off after reminding us it was insured."

Priscilla smiled—the first time he'd seen her do that since the accident. "Annie insisted that we have a business plan and do all this research. If you could have seen the books she brought home from the library…"

"Sounds like Annie."

"Of course I had auto insurance, and the loan we took out for the trailer required that we have insurance for it as well." She shook her head, resting her back against the wall and closing her eyes. "Annie insisted on business insurance—it covers the trailer, its contents and any gigs that we miss because of an accident."

"Wow."

"Yeah." She stood up straighter, opened her eyes and smiled.

"Doesn't sound very Amish. We usually go with *if it's Gotte's wille…*"

"Uh-huh. She told me that, but she also said most Amish folk didn't invest as much as we had in something that could be demolished by one teen texting while driving."

"Only it was a middle-aged male truck driver, not a teen."

"And it was a mechanical failure, not inattention."

They both thought about that for a moment. Levi was reminded again how the truck had hit Annie's side of the vehicle. She could have been killed. That thought ran through his mind constantly. She could have been, but she wasn't.

The fact that Priscilla had walked away relatively unhurt and Annie was mending rapidly truly was a miracle.

After watching Priscilla show up at the hospital every night, even staying the night of the accident though she was in obvious pain herself, he understood that they were more than business partners. They were friends and close ones at that.

"How did you two meet?"

"We took a cake-making class at the same time."

"Cake making?"

"Fancy cakes for big parties and important birthdays and anniversaries and weddings."

"You both took a class together?"

"At the library, yeah. I had this vague idea that I'd like to host parties for a living, and Annie—well, Annie already had a wedding business detailed in her little notebook."

He'd seen that notebook, the first day he'd been at her house.

"I've never been a great baker and taking that class confirmed as much. My cake fell so that there was this giant crater in the middle. My sugar roses looked like lumps of frosting. Annie started laughing and couldn't stop." She wiped at her eyes. "It didn't matter that she was Amish and I wasn't. We've been best friends from that first night."

"I understand."

"Do you?"

"Sure. Sometimes friendship surprises you. Sometimes it grows out of a relationship that you'd never have thought could become so close."

Priscilla studied him a minute. "Have you and Annie talked?"

"About what?"

"About how you feel?"

"How I feel?"

Now she laughed outright. He would have been offended if he hadn't been so surprised.

"Don't ask me how I know. It's as plain as the suspenders you're wearing."

"It is?"

"To me, anyway. To someone who knows Annie as well as I do. She talks about you all the time."

"She does?"

"Talk to her, Levi."

"We have—sort of."

"You've discussed your feelings?"

"Not really. I mean a little, but nothing personal. Her parents were in the room, and then the doctors and nurses are coming in and out constantly. So we've talked but not about my feelings—not really, no, we haven't."

She stood straighter and squeezed Levi's arm. "So why are you standing here? Go in there and wait for her to wake up and then say what you need to say."

"*Ya*, I plan to."

"Just do it." She pushed the teddy bear into his arms and adjusted the strap of her purse over her shoulder. "Oh, and when she does wake up, give her the bear. And tell her I'll be back tomorrow night. Tell her I'll bring the Scrabble board."

He watched her walk away, and then he went back into Annie's room.

Chapter Fourteen

The lights were low and the television was off. Come to think of it, the television hadn't been turned on as far as he knew. He settled into the chair that could be adjusted to form a small bed, though he didn't bother with that. Instead he covered himself with the blanket the nurses had kindly left, stared at the wall and tried to decide what he'd say when Annie finally woke.

An hour later, she tried to turn over in her sleep and let out a yelp.

He catapulted from the chair.

"You can't do that."

"Why?"

"Your leg…it's broken and in a splint."

"Oh."

"They're planning to put a cast on it tomorrow. The doctor said she was waiting for your swelling to go down, and then they didn't really want to move you around a lot until you were awake—if they didn't have to."

She stared at him a moment, then nodded and closed her eyes. He turned to go back to his chair, but she reached out and claimed his hand.

"Can I get you something?"

"A cup of water?"

"Sure, there's some right here." His hand shook as he poured water from the small pitcher into the cup. He showed her how to raise the head of the bed, and he made sure the straw was where she could reach it. Seeing her hand, still bandaged and sporting the IV, caused a lump to rise in his throat.

She handed the cup back to him. "Maybe pull a chair up closer."

"*Ya*, of course."

"Why are you holding a teddy bear?"

"This?" He hadn't realized he'd been holding it since she'd first yelped. "It's from Priscilla. She came by to see you."

He settled it in the bed beside her, even covered it up with the blanket, and was relieved to see a smile tug at the corners of her mouth.

"My parents didn't tell me everything. What were they holding back?"

He thought about that a minute. They'd answered all of her questions, but they had downplayed how much danger she'd been in. "I guess they didn't really describe how scared they were—how scared we all were. The bishop was here. Actually, the waiting room was filled with people from our district."

"I don't remember seeing any of them."

"The doctors weren't sure why you weren't waking up. None of their tests indicated a concussion. One doctor was worried that you'd slip into a coma, but then the other one—Dr. Tallman—said she'd seen this before and that your body just needed rest. She said that as long as your blood pressure and pulse were strong, to let you sleep."

"Three days?" She stared out the darkened window. "It's strange how you can lose a chunk of your life and never even realize it."

Levi didn't know how to answer that, so he didn't.

"You're sure Priscilla is okay?"

"*Ya.* She was here earlier. Brought the bear..." He cleared his throat—thinking of all she'd said. Thinking of her admonition for him to talk to Annie now, while there was time. Basically reminding him not to take anything for granted. As if he needed that reminder. "She said she'd be back tomorrow and that she'd bring the Scrabble board."

Annie nodded as if she expected as much. "How is the truck driver?"

"He didn't even have to go to the hospital."

"I wish I could remember."

You're better off not knowing, he thought.

But then he realized that he would want to know if it had happened to him—so he told her everything. He described hearing the crash, not understanding that it was Annie and Priscilla, leaving Petunia and the buggy in the middle of the road and running toward the tangle of cars in the intersection. When he reached the part about pushing his way through the crowd to her side, about the doctor who happened to be two cars back, his hands began to shake.

"It scared you," she said.

"Of course it did."

"Maybe it's one of those things that's worse to watch than it is to experience."

"Maybe."

"I'm not looking forward to dragging a cast around for the foreseeable future."

The splint on her leg was large and awkward. Levi realized it must be very difficult for her to get comfortable at all. "Do you need it moved or something?"

"*Ya.* Maybe a little."

So he moved it left, then right and then left again. He moved her leg as gently as if it had been a newborn baby. He was so afraid of hurting her, of making things worse. Was that why he hadn't talked to her of his feelings? Was he worried that doing so could make their relationship worse? But keeping it inside, well that wasn't going to work, either.

Finally Annie sighed and waved him back to the chair.

"I've never had a cast," Annie admitted. "It always looked like fun, when someone in school would have one and everyone would sign it."

"We're not in school, but I'll sign your cast."

Her eyebrows shot up, but she seemed to detect the underlying fear beneath his banter.

"Tell me the rest."

"I wish… I wish you could have seen Priscilla's truck. Maybe someone took pictures. I don't know. But if you'd seen it, how completely demolished it was, I think you'd be grateful for just a splinted leg or a cast. You both could have been killed."

She nodded as if she understood and maybe she did. She rubbed her temples, and he wondered if even sitting up was painful for her.

"Do you want me to call the nurse?"

"*Nein.*"

"It's understandable if you'd like some pain medication—"

She shook her head as if to dispel his concern. Finally she turned her brown eyes toward him and pinned him to the spot with a look. "I'm tired of sleeping, but I'm still tired. Does that make sense?"

"Ya." He knew about that sort of weariness, only his had come from the problems with his family, from always looking for the next spot where he was sure he'd find peace and contentment, from trying to scratch the itch that was his broken dream.

"Why are you still here?"

"Excuse me?"

"Mamm and Dat went home. Priscilla came and left. Why are you still here?"

"I didn't want you to spend Christmas Eve alone." He glanced around the room. A volunteer had come by with a tiny Christmas tree, and another had brought some artificial holly that had been draped across a shelf. There were no gifts, none of the normal things they would equate with Christmas, but he knew that the next morning her family would bring gifts and handmade cards from the children.

"Have you been doing this every night?"

"Ya, but..."

"What's going on, Levi? What aren't you telling me?"

He realized he couldn't put it off any longer. He was terrified, nearly as afraid as he'd been as he ran toward the truck. But in that moment he understood that the only thing worse than being rejected by her would be never taking the chance, and so he stood, poured himself a cup of water and drained it. Finally he sat back down on the chair next to her bed.

He wasn't sure exactly how he was going to say it, but he knew that it was now or never.

* * *

Annie felt her pulse begin to beat more rapidly. Had the accident somehow damaged her heart? Was she about to pass out? But she somehow knew that what she was feeling had nothing to do with her physical condition. It was the way that Levi was looking at her that made her pulse race. It was something tickling her memory that was causing her hands to sweat. Something she couldn't quite pull to the front of her mind.

Levi finally put down the cup he was fiddling with and perched on the chair next to her bed.

"I've been struggling with this a while now. I can see that, and I'm tired of it. Tired of going to sleep wondering if it's just a crush, if tomorrow I'll wake up and feel differently."

"A crush?"

"Only it's not. Somehow I know it's not going to pass like a bad cold."

Did he just compare his feelings for her to a bad cold? She wanted to laugh. She wanted to grab his big shoulders and shake him. But what she wanted most was for him to look at her and say what he meant.

"How I feel about you—it isn't going away. I guess I've known that for a while now."

His eyes met hers, and suddenly she remembered the kiss they'd shared, the way her heart had soared and her stomach had dropped, the certainty of her emotions when she'd confessed her feelings to Priscilla.

"I definitely never thought we'd be friends." She plucked at the blanket. "You and that ridiculous cowboy hat and boots and stories of Texas."

"We are *freinden* now." He smiled at her. "I guess neither of us saw that coming."

"I wasn't very kind when you first came to Goshen. I was so afraid of your dream, of your certainty that life would be better somewhere else. For some reason I'm not afraid of that anymore."

"I'm persuasive in that way." He gulped so hard that she saw his Adam's apple bob. "Or maybe *Gotte* has been the one doing the persuading, working on both of our hearts."

He reached for her hand and traced a finger down the inside of her palm causing goose bumps to pepper her skin.

"But what I'm feeling…" He cleared his throat and tried again. "It's more than friendship and it's more than a crush."

"It is?"

"How I feel about you, Annie, it's different than I've ever felt about anyone else."

"It is?"

"And what I want, what I dream of, is our being more to each other. I'm not satisfied with being your friend. I don't want to play it safe anymore. I'm ready to take a chance."

She shook her head, reached for her *kapp* strings and then realized she wasn't wearing one. Brushing back her hair, she met his gaze. "You're ready to take a chance on what? Levi, maybe it's my head injury, but I need you to speak more plainly."

"I want to close the distance between us. I want to be the other half of you—like two pieces of a puzzle that fit perfectly together."

"Are you saying you love me?"

"Yes. Annie Kauffmann, I love you." His gaze held steady, and she found that she had to look away. It was what she'd wanted to hear, what she'd told Priscilla that he was afraid of. Only now he wasn't. Now he was sitting here confessing his love after sitting by her side for three days.

"You're sure? Because after our kiss you said…"

"I said I was desperate. I was scared. I'll admit that." He stared at the floor a minute, then sat back and allowed a silence to settle over them. Finally he cleared his throat and chuckled.

"I was talking to Jebediah when he came up to check on you. I guess he helped me to see what should have been obvious."

"My *bruder*?"

"*Ya.* He asked me how I felt when we're apart. He asked me, did I miss hanging out or did I miss your face, your touch, your laugh."

"I never knew my *bruder* was such a romantic."

"He said there's a difference between wondering what's going on in your life and needing to know how your day was. There's a difference between caring about you and wanting—*nein*, needing to spend the rest of our lives together."

Annie nodded, a lump forming in her throat, wishing he would stop because she was about to cry, and praying that he wouldn't stop because she wanted to hear… to finally hear what was in his heart.

"And then I realized there's a difference between loving someone like a *schweschder* in Christ, like a family member or a friend, and loving someone so much that you feel a little sick in your stomach."

"Like you have a bad cold."

"Exactly." He grinned and she was reminded of that first night, of him following her out to the wedding trailer and rambling on about Texas. "There's a difference in loving someone in a general sense, and needing to say the words *I love you*. I do love you, Annie, and if you feel the same…"

"I do." The words slipped from her lips as simply as rain falling to the ground, and suddenly the weight on her heart was gone. Just like that. The burden of her love for him, it was lighter because she'd shared it. Why had she waited so long to tell him?

"You do?"

"*Ya.* I think I have for some time now."

"Why didn't you say something?"

She shrugged and remembered suddenly all that stood between them. She remembered afresh the grief at realizing she could have her dream of a successful wedding business or she could have Levi—but it didn't seem that she could have both.

Tears slipped down her cheeks and she brushed them away. "It's just that I didn't see how…how we could make it work."

"Why, Annie? Tell me why." When she didn't answer, he pushed a little harder. "Is it because of Texas?"

"Yes and no."

"Maybe I'm the one with the head injury now, but I need you to explain it to me."

"I don't want to move. I don't think I want to move. I'm willing to admit that I'm terrified of that possibility. I love you, Levi, but I also love what I have here, my business with Priscilla. It's more than just a job."

"I know it is."

"We make a real difference in people's families. We help them to celebrate one of the most important days of their lives. It's a real blessing to do that."

"I understand."

"Do you?"

"Yes, and I'm willing to stay in Goshen."

"You are?"

"If that's what it takes? Then I'll stay. We'll live here, and we'll make it work."

"But I can't do that." Now she rubbed a fist against her chest. It was all coming back. Confessing her feelings to Priscilla, looking up and seeing the truck sail through the light, the split second when she knew they were about to be hit, wondering if that was it—if her life was going to end before she'd known the love of a husband, or the joy of children or the satisfaction of caring for a family.

"I can't do that to you. I don't understand why *Gotte* put Texas in your heart, but I understand that he did. You wouldn't be…wouldn't be the man I know, the man I love, without that ridiculous hat or those silly boots."

"You like my boots?" His voice was soft and teasing. The expression in his eyes was anything but.

Had anyone ever loved her as much as he did?

Had anyone ever looked at her that way before? She didn't think so, and the realization of it took her breath away.

"I want to put my arms around you," he whispered.

"But you can't." The tears were falling like a cleansing rain now. "I'm all hooked up." She raised her arm with the IV drip as proof.

He settled for reclaiming her hand between both of his.

"Annie, I don't know the solution to where we'll live or how or when. I'm not going to lie to you and tell you that I have any of those answers."

"That's not what I want. I don't want you to lie to me just so I'll feel better."

"The thing is that you're more important to me than Texas. You're more important to me than any dream I had before I met you. *Gotte* replaced that desire of my heart with a better one—something true and lasting."

"But you'll always resent me if we stay here."

"I won't. That's the miraculous thing, because Texas without you…well, it wouldn't be worth having." He scooted forward and thumbed the tears from her face. "Do you believe me?"

"*Ya.* I do."

"So will you?"

"Will I what?"

"Will you marry me, Annie Kauffmann? I can't imagine a better Christmas gift than your saying yes."

"I made you a wool scarf."

"Did you now?"

"It's blue, like the wildflowers in Texas."

"Which reminds me of something." He jumped up, retrieved his coat, and handed her a snow globe.

She shook it, gazed at the bluebonnets and the snow, thought of Christmas and what did and didn't make it perfect. It was the people in your life that mattered. It was having those that loved you near, and it didn't really matter what state you lived in, only that you were there for one another.

She shook it again and then raised her eyes to meet his. "It's beautiful."

"You're beautiful."

"Have you been carrying this around in your pocket?"

"Jebediah fetched it from my place. I wanted to have

it here, for when you woke up. I wanted to make you smile at Christmas."

The tears began to slip down her cheeks.

"Will you be my bride and have my children and share my dreams and trials and all of my tomorrows?"

"I will."

"Then the rest we'll figure out." He stood, leaned over her bed and kissed her softly on the lips.

The ache in her chest disappeared.

The tears stopped.

The fear she'd been harboring evaporated.

And all that was left was the certainty that whatever they faced in the future, wherever they faced it, they'd do so together.

Epilogue

Three years later

Annie picked Eli up out of his crib and carried him to the front porch. An east wind was blowing, cooling the Texas afternoon. She sat in the rocker and watched Levi walk across the field toward home.

He bounded up the front porch steps, kissed her on the lips and then kissed the top of Eli's head.

"Did he just wake up?"

"He did."

"So he probably won't go down until late."

"He probably won't."

"Which means we won't be going to bed until late."

"Exactly."

Levi pulled off his hat, an Amish hat made of straw with a wide brim. He dropped it on the porch floor and ran his hands through his hair. She'd need to cut it again soon. It was already tickling his collar.

"I suppose that'll give me another chance to beat you at Scrabble."

"You wish."

He went into their house and fetched two glasses of lemonade. She should have thought of that, but the truth was, she'd slept while Eli had slept, and she wasn't fully awake yet. The doctor had said her tiredness was completely normal given the twins she was carrying.

"I spoke with Jebediah today."

"Ya?"

"He said he's going into Hamilton tomorrow for the animal auction. Believe it or not he wants to buy a colt for his son."

"Joshua is hardly old enough for that."

"So I told him." Levi grinned at her. "He asked if I wanted to go along."

"And do you?"

"Of course. Your older *bruder* is going to need a buggy horse."

Slowly her entire family was moving to Texas. They'd settled on the same land that Levi had first scouted—the land that had belonged to Betty and Buddy Johnston. Dry-land farming was difficult, even more difficult than in Indiana, but they were making it. Her parents had been with the first group that moved. She and Levi had moved with the second group, though he'd put his deposit down on a portion of Buddy's land. Profits from her wedding business had helped to pay off the loan.

They hadn't moved as soon as they'd married, partly because Annie had been pregnant with Eli by that time. Instead they'd waited, corresponded regularly with the dozen families who had set up the community, and prayed about what to do next.

Eighteen months ago they'd made the move. The new community wasn't so small anymore. It had grown to nearly twenty families—families that were adding little ones regularly. By the time Eli was a grown man, *Gotte* willing, they'd be ready to split into two districts.

For now, they were still small enough that they didn't need a wedding trailer, not yet. But she wrote to Priscilla every week. Her friend would be moving to Texas in a few months, and they had plans to start a smaller catering business that included an Amish bakery the following spring.

The sun dropped farther down the wide expanse of Texas sky, sending out bands of pink and purple and lavender.

"It's beautiful," Levi said.

"*Ya*, it's as *gut* as you described back when you were trying to convince us to come to Texas."

Levi laughed, drained his glass and placed it on the wooden crate between them. He stood and walked over to her rocker—stopped behind it and placed his hands on her shoulders, leaned down to whisper in her ear.

"I wasn't talking about the view."

"You weren't?"

"Or the sunset."

"It is beautiful, though."

"I was talking about you." He kissed her cheek, then said softly, "Stay where you are. Supper can wait. I'll take this little one and go clean us both up."

As he walked into the house, she did what he said.

Dinner could wait.

She could hear Eli talking in his baby language to Levi.

She placed her hands on the mound that used to be her stomach. "Promise me you won't ride in the rodeo," she said to the babies. She'd been to see several, and she couldn't imagine letting any boy of hers ride a bull, or any girl of hers chase lambs. She wanted to keep them safe. She wanted to protect them against anything and everything.

Of course that wasn't her job to do. *Gotte* would do that, the same way He'd kept her safe during the accident, the same way He'd brought her and Levi together.

She sat in the rocker, watching the first of the stars make their appearance, and realized—again—just how happy she was. She didn't have to worry about whether her oldest *bruder* would like Texas as much as they did, or if it would rain the next week. She could do her best each day and that was enough—which at the moment meant sitting on the front porch rocking and soaking in the blessings of her life.

* * * * *

AMISH CHRISTMAS SECRETS

Debby Giusti

This book is dedicated to my wonderful readers.
Thank you for your support and encouragement.
You are the reason I write!

Who hath delivered us from the power of darkness, and hath translated us into the kingdom of his dear Son: In whom we have redemption through his blood, even the forgiveness of sins.
—*Colossians* 1:13–14

Chapter One

"Ach," Rosie Glick moaned as the December wind whipped the *kapp* from her head and sent it tumbling through the air. She stopped pedaling her bike, then propped it on the kickstand and ran to where the starched headgear had landed, only inches away from the steep drop-off that edged the North Georgia mountain road. She retrieved the *kapp* and brushed the dust from the stiff fabric, then glanced at the churning water, raging at the bottom of the ravine some twenty feet below. Her stomach roiled at the sharp downward slope and the bevy of boulders positioned along the sides of the incline.

Another gust of wind sent her scrambling back to her bike, all too aware of the growing darkness and encroaching storm. Rosie repositioned the *kapp* on her head and secured it with hairpins before she climbed on her bike, determined to get home before the sky opened and the rain commenced.

The nervous unease within her that had started in town continued to grow. She thought again of the man in the white sedan, talking on his cell phone. Pedaling past his parked car, she had noticed how much he resembled a person she had seen once and never wanted to see again.

Surely her eyes were playing tricks on her.

Thoughts of that horrific night rolled through her mind. The door to Will MacIntosh's trailer had pushed open, and the man with the gun had forced Will outside. Rosie had escaped, but she had not run fast enough.

Chilled by the memory, she glanced over her shoulder, relieved to find the road empty of vehicles. The last thing she wanted was to be followed. She felt sure the man in town had not seen her, yet she needed to be careful.

Datt would probably question her late arrival. He had never been a man of compassion, and since she had returned home seven months ago, he seemed increasingly short-tempered.

Even her sweet *Mamm* struggled with his behavior.

Regrettably, her father would never forgive Rosie for the mistake she had made. Baby Joseph was not the problem. Her own stubborn independence had gotten her in trouble, along with her desire to experience life to the fullest, even if it meant running away with an *Englischer*.

But Will MacIntosh had been murdered, and she had been trafficked and held captive for eight months. She had spent the last month of her confinement in a dank and dark root cellar where she had given birth to Joseph. The memory of their rescue and reunion with her parents had been bittersweet. If only her father had rejoiced at their homecoming.

Hearing the sound of a car engine, barely audible

over the gusting wind, Rosie glanced over her shoulder. A white sedan raced down the hill.

She gasped and pedaled faster.

White automobiles were common among the *Englisch*, she told herself, hoping to calm her rapid pulse and thumping heart. Her legs burned from the exertion. The roar of the engine filled her ears.

The car's headlights illuminated the roadway, catching her in their glare. She inched as close to the edge of the road as possible and glanced back. Her heart stopped. The car was headed straight for her. She raised her hand to wave off the driver, but he continued on course.

The front wheel of her bike slipped off the pavement and onto the rocky berm. She lost balance and crashed to the ground. Pain ricocheted through her shoulders as she skidded across the hard-packed earth.

The car stopped. A door slammed. Before she could catch her breath and climb to her feet, the man she had seen in town was leaning over her. Dark brown hair with a long brushstroke of white near his left temple. Narrow eyes and a thin mouth. The same man who had come to Will's door sixteen months ago.

He grabbed her arm.

"Where is it?" he demanded. "Where's the information Will stole from me?"

She tried to pull free from his hold.

He slapped her face and twisted her arm. "Tell me."

She grimaced with pain.

"You were Will's girlfriend and his accomplice."

"What?"

"Don't act dumb. All this time, we didn't realize what he had taken until the last few days. When I saw you in town, it all became clear. He gave it to you for safekeeping, only we need it back."

Rosie tried to pull free. "I do not have anything you want."

"Don't act like a stupid Amish girl," he snarled. "You fooled us once, but you can't fool us again."

Tears burned her eyes.

"Will needed to be taught a lesson. Maybe you do, too." He reached for her throat.

"No!"

She clawed at his hands, which he had wrapped around her neck. Her lungs burned like fire. She tried to breathe.

Suddenly, as if hearing someone approach, he eased his hold and cocked his head. His eyes widened as he stood upright and stared for a long moment at the crest of the hill.

Gasping for air, she scooted to the edge of the incline. If only she could escape. But how?

Turning his gaze back to her, he grabbed her arm and pulled her to her feet. "You're coming with me."

The thought of being held captive again was too much to bear. She kicked his leg and gouged her fingers in his eyes.

"Aagh!" He dropped his head into his hands.

She turned to flee. He grabbed her shoulder. She jerked free, then tripped and fell to the ground.

"I need that information." He kicked her once, twice. Air whooshed from her lungs.

She rolled over and saw him raise his work boot again. Cringing, she anticipated the blow, until with one last thrust of his mud-covered boot, he pushed her over the edge of the cliff.

Her head hit a boulder. Prickly thistles and scrub brush scraped her hands and legs. Rocks battered her as she slipped and slid to the bottom on the steep ravine. "*Gott*, help me," she moaned until she no longer saw or heard anything.

Ezra Stoltz jiggled the reins and encouraged his mare over the crest of the hill. A car sat parked on the downward slope of the road. A tall man with a thick build stood in the glare of the car's headlights. He glanced Ezra's way, then quickly picked up a bike and hurled it over the edge of the roadway. Hurrying back to his car, he climbed behind the wheel, gunned the engine and headed north along the narrow country road.

With a flick of the reins, Ezra urged Bessie forward, the clip-clop of her hooves on the pavement in sync with his rapidly beating heart. Ezra had seen Rosie Glick pass the hardware store on her bike. With the fast-approaching storm, he had wanted to ensure she got home safely and had followed in his buggy. Seeing the man made him all the more concerned for her safety.

Nearing the spot where the car had parked, he pulled Bessie to a stop and jumped to the ground. Peering over the edge of the drop-off, he spied the bike, about ten yards below, and quickly descended to where it was lying.

He glanced at the steep downward slope and the boulders that pocked the hillside. Something near the rushing water caught his eye. He moved closer.

Blue fabric and a white *kapp*.

Rosie!

He scurried down the hill and knelt beside her. His heart wrenched as he saw the blood that seeped from her forehead. Her arms were scraped, the hem of her dress torn. He touched her cheek.

"Can you hear me? It's Ezra Stoltz. Open your eyes, Rosie."

Ezra's heart stopped when she failed to respond. *Please, Gott, do not let another person die.*

Rose blinked her eyes open and gasped, seeing with blurred vision a man's face close to her own. "No," she cried.

His hand touched her shoulder. "You took a bad fall."

She shook her head, trying to identify the voice.

"I will take you home in my buggy."

Buggy? She blinked, noting his blond hair and blue eyes, which stared questioningly down at her.

"We went to school together. Remember me? Ezra Stoltz?"

Ezra? Not the man in the white car. She breathed out a sigh of relief and raised up on one arm.

The Ezra Stoltz she remembered had been tall and thin and nothing like the broad-shouldered man hovering over her.

He helped her sit up. "Are you dizzy? Does anything hurt?"

Her whole body ached. She touched the tender spot on her forehead.

He leaned closer. "It is a bad cut. You hit one of the rocks as you fell."

"Did you see what happened?" she asked.

"I saw a man on the side of the road. He tossed your bike down the ravine before he drove away."

She glanced up the hill. "Where is my bike?"

"I will put it in the buggy, but first, we must tend to your needs."

Grateful for his help, she tried to find something positive on which to focus. "I am scraped and bruised but not broken."

"This is something for which we can be thankful." He smiled, easing a bit of the fear that had tangled along her spine.

Helping her to her feet, he asked, "Are you able to climb the hill?"

"I—I think so."

"Lean on me," he suggested.

She had no choice but to accept his help. The incline was steep, and her legs felt like the congealed gelatin she made for her molded salads.

"Oh." Her knee nearly buckled under her.

"I will carry you."

Before she could decline his offer, Ezra lifted her effortlessly into his strong arms.

"I am too heavy," she said, embarrassed by his closeness.

He chuckled. "You are too light. Your *mamm* must not feed you enough. Hold on, and we will climb this hill together."

She wrapped her arm around his thick neck and dropped her cheek against his shoulder. Inhaling the masculine scent of him, she questioned her own good sense for allowing a man she barely knew to carry her in his arms.

As Ezra had mentioned, they had been in school together, but he was three years her senior, and she had seen him only a few times after he had completed the eighth level.

Once they reached the roadway, Ezra lifted her into the buggy. "Wait here a moment. Then Bessie and I will take you home."

Working quickly, he retrieved the bicycle and placed it in the rear of his buggy. "I can fix your bike," he assured her as he climbed into the seat next to her.

Grateful for his help, she relaxed ever so slightly. He lifted the reins into his hands and encouraged Bessie forward.

Ezra studied the road and then flicked his gaze to her as if to ensure she was all right. "Your mother will be happy when you are home, *yah*?"

Rosie rubbed her arms and lowered her gaze, thinking of her father's verbal attack and pointed questions.

"Thank you for your help, Ezra."

He nodded, perhaps as embarrassed as she was after carrying her in his arms. She brushed the dirt from her skirt and thought of the root cellar where she had been held captive.

She would not go back there. No matter what happened.

The clip-clop of Bessie's hooves soothed her frayed nerves, and she settled back in the seat, trying to think of what she could tell her parents when they saw the gash on her forehead and her scraped arms and soiled skirt.

Her own clumsiness and being too close to the road's edge would be truthful. She would not mention the man in the white car. Her mother worried about her wellbeing. The thought of being run off the road would be too much for *Mamm* to bear.

Lightning cut across the sky, startling Rosie. Rain

pinged against the top of the buggy. The temperature dropped even more, and she shivered in the cold.

Through the steady downpour, she saw the headlights of an approaching vehicle in the distance.

Her heart thumped a warning.

"Do you see the lights?" she asked.

"*Yah*. You think it could be the man who threw your bike into the ravine?"

"Am I foolish to think he would return?"

"Not if you know the reason he wishes to do you harm."

Unwilling to share her past with Ezra, she sighed. "I—I am not certain."

He stared at her for a long moment.

"I was involved with the wrong person," she finally admitted. "It is too much to tell now, but that might be the reason."

Ezra flicked the reins and encouraged Bessie to increase her pace, which only troubled Rosie more. Instead of turning around in hopes of eluding the vehicle, Ezra was driving the buggy straight toward the approaching danger.

Fear gripped her anew. "Ezra, stop the buggy so I can run into the woods and hide."

He ignored her request and hurried the mare even more.

Lightning illuminated the sky and a crash of thunder sounded nearby. Bessie's ears raised. She snorted, no doubt skittish because of the storm.

"Please, Ezra." Rosie nudged his arm. "Stop the buggy."

The car was fast approaching. She could hear the roar of the engine just around the bend and could envision being caught in the oncoming glare of headlights.

She swallowed down the fear that clogged her throat and grabbed Ezra's hand, trying to make him realize the seriousness of her plight.

He pushed aside her hand.

Her heart crashed. Accepting a ride from Ezra had been a bad decision. The boy she remembered from school was cocky, but always considerate of others.

She raised her voice. "Stop the buggy now, and let me out."

The glare of headlights preceded the car around the bend. She gasped, fearing the man from town would accost her again. Tears stung her eyes at the hopelessness of her situation.

Seemingly at the last possible moment, Ezra tugged the reins right. The mare turned onto a narrow dirt lane that angled off the main road. A canopy of tree branches brushed against the buggy's roof.

Rosie glanced at the road just as a white sedan raced past. Instead of being seen, Ezra had maneuvered the buggy into a hiding place that protected them both.

She let out a ragged breath.

Ezra leaned close, his face mere inches from hers. Concern filled his gaze and his voice was tight with emotion.

"Who is he, Rosie?" Ezra demanded. "Who is after you and why?"

Chapter Two

"Take me home, Ezra."

"Who is after you, Rosie?" he again demanded.

"You have heard recently on the news of bikes being forced off the road and of Amish injured for no likely reason."

He nodded. "*Yah*, this I have heard. But those incidents were caused by unruly teenagers who wanted to make trouble. This white car was not driven by a teen."

"Did you see the driver?" Her tone was rife with defiance.

"Only from a distance when I first crested the hill. The windows of his car were tinted. With the failing light, I could see nothing when the vehicle passed by just now."

"Then you cannot say who was at the wheel."

He stared at her for a long moment. Rosie had been a determined young girl in school. She was even more so now. If only she would explain what had happened to her and why.

Ezra had no doubt that it involved Will MacIntosh, a known troublemaker who had convinced Rosie of his love. Will had gotten tied up in a number of schemes and died because of his involvement. Ezra had thought Rosie was an innocent bystander, but now he wondered if she knew more than she was willing to reveal.

She started to climb down from the buggy.

"Where are you going?" He grabbed her arm. "I will take you home."

"You do not have to do this."

"You are in danger, Rosie. Accept my help."

She hesitated for a moment, then with a stiff sigh, she scooted back onto the seat next to him. "You are a generous man, Ezra."

He almost laughed. His father had called him confused and misguided. Even now, many in the Amish community were less than cordial when they passed in their buggies. Ezra had spent too much time associating with the *Englisch*, trying to find his way in life.

With a flick of the reins, he turned Bessie onto the main road. The temperature had dropped, and although the rain had eased, the damp air was chilling. Ezra grabbed a blanket off the back seat and wrapped it around Rosie's slender shoulders.

"I am not cold," she insisted, yet her shivering body revealed the truth. He did not mention her pale skin or the fatigue that even the darkness could not hide.

Under other circumstances, he would have lit the lanterns at the sides and rear of the buggy, but tonight, caution was important in case they needed to hide in the underbrush again.

Someone wanted to do Rosie harm.

Do not get involved, Ezra's voice of reason warned. The advice came too late. Whether he liked it or not, he was already involved.

* * *

Rosie and Ezra traveled in silence as the buggy meandered along the narrow mountain road. The closer they drew to her house, the more concerned she became about facing her father and anticipated his caustic words and demeaning gaze. If not for Joseph, she would run immediately upstairs and hole up in her room. But her child was the only spark of joy in her life, and she would not reduce the limited time she had with him. If only she did not have to work and could be with him throughout the day. Her father had recently demanded payment from her to cover the cost of food and shelter, which had left Rosie with no choice but to take employment in town.

"Thank you," she said to Ezra as her parents' home came into view. "You were very kind to bring me home."

"I will fix your bike and return it to you. I have much to do tonight, but day after tomorrow, it should be ready."

"Danke."

"I must return to town in the morning, so I will drive you to work."

His offer bought tears to her eyes. She glanced away, thankful for the darkness so he could not see her reaction.

"I do not want to take advantage of your thoughtfulness," she said, her voice filled with emotion that even she recognized.

"It is no trouble. What time do you start work?"

"At seven. It is too early, *yah*?"

"I will be at your house by six fifteen."

"I will be ready." She started to climb down and then hesitated. "The man who came after me has brown hair with a patch of white at his temple. He thinks I have something that belongs to him."

She hopped to the ground and ran toward her house. The front door opened and her *datt* stepped onto the porch.

"You are late," he grumbled.

"An older patient named Mr. Calhoun was in pain and needed help." She lowered her eyes and hurried past him. Before stepping inside, she paused and gazed back at the roadway.

Ezra glanced over his shoulder. Even from this distance, she could see the smile that played over his full lips.

Her father scowled. "Why does Ezra Stoltz bring you home?"

"I fell from my bike. He was good enough to help me."

"He is not someone with whom I want you to associate."

Her heart sank. Why was anything she ever wanted to do forbidden by her father?

"You remember what happened to his parents."

Their buggy shop had been robbed and his mother and father had been murdered during the break-in, but their tragic deaths had nothing to do with Ezra.

Rosie's father scowled even more. "Ezra was drinking at a bar in town that day instead of helping his father in his shop."

Which probably saved Ezra's life. He might have been killed, along with his parents, if he had been home. Not that she was willing to voice her objection to her father. Some battles were not worth fighting.

"He has not courted or taken a wife," her father continued. "Nor has he joined the church. This is not a man with whom I wish my daughter to associate."

Her heart ached at her father's bigotry. Did he not see the plank in his own eye?

"I am not looking for a husband, *Datt*." Her voice was firm.

"Joseph needs a father."

Rosie could not argue. Her son needed a father, but that did not mean she needed a husband.

She stepped into the kitchen, smelling the homemade bread and hearty beef stew her mother had served for the evening meal. Her mouth watered and she realized she had been busy helping patients all day and had failed to take either her lunch or her evening break.

Food could wait. She quickly washed her hands at the sink and then hurried to where her son sat playing on the floor. She raised Joseph into her arms and smothered him with kisses until he giggled and nuzzled her neck. He was eight months old with a happy disposition and a laugh that drove away any thought of her problems.

Rosie's heart soared. Nothing mattered except her child.

"*Ach*, what has happened?" Her mother's eyes were wide as she pointed to the scrapes and scratches on Rosie's face and hands.

"I fell from my bike."

"You have a bad cut to your forehead. Sit." She pointed to the kitchen table. "I saved a bowl of stew. You are hungry, *yah*?"

Holding Joseph in her left arm, Rosie slipped onto the bench at the table, bowed her head and offered a prayer of thanks for her safe return home before she eagerly lifted a heaping spoonful of stew to her mouth.

"After you eat and prepare Joseph for bed, then you

will tell me what made you late coming home from work."

Her mother had a keen sixth sense. Rosie would be careful not to reveal what really had happened lest *Mamm* worry too much.

"The uneven pavement on the road caused me to fall, *Mamm*. I was not hurt."

"For this, I am glad, but the cut needs doctoring."

Her mother retrieved a first-aid kit from a kitchen cabinet and dampened a cloth that she wiped over Rosie's forehead. After cleaning the area, she applied ointment and covered the cut with a bandage.

"The town is decorated for Christmas, *yah*?" her mother asked as she returned the kit to the cabinet.

"Candy canes and snowmen hang from the street-lights." Rosie smiled. "Joseph would enjoy seeing the hanging lights and evergreen wreaths."

Although after what had happened today, Rosie did not want Joseph anywhere near town. She glanced at the end of the table, noting an envelope that had surely come in the mail.

In hopes of further distracting her mother from what had happened tonight, Rosie asked, "You received a Christmas card today?"

"From your cousin, Alice. She said baby Becca is growing and big sister Diane is almost as tall as their kitchen table."

"Diane is a sweet girl. I am glad you cared for her when Alice was on bed rest before Becca was born."

Mamm offered a weak smile. "She filled a void when you were gone."

The pain in her mother's eyes tore at Rosie's heart. She dropped her spoon into the bowl and scooted back from the table. *Mamm* rarely talked about that time when Rosie was held captive, for which she was grateful. Perhaps her mother's worry about Rosie arriving home late tonight had loosened her tongue.

"I will wash the dishes after I put Joseph to bed."

"No need to hurry, Rosie. There is only your bowl. I will have it washed and back in the cabinet before you return."

Rosie climbed the stairs with Joseph in her arms. She changed his diaper and dressed him in a fresh sleeper before they cuddled in the rocker. She crooned a lullaby as he nestled in her arms, her heart bursting with love for this sweet child.

His eyes drifted closed, but she continued to hold him, taking comfort from his precious closeness. His tiny hand clutched her finger, signaling their connection. Both of them had been through so much.

She thought back to Joseph's birth as she labored alone in the dark and damp root cellar. She had prayed her child would be born healthy and without complication. *Gott* had heard and answered her prayer. Somehow she had given birth to sweet Joseph, and for his first month of life, she had kept him warm and fed and secure in spite of their dire circumstances. Finally, they had been rescued and returned home.

The look on her father's face when he first saw them circled through her mind—it was one of relief, then shock when he noticed the baby in her arms. If not for her mother's heartfelt cries of joy and her warm embrace, Rosie might have run away again. The truth was she had no place to go and no one to give her and her son shelter.

She kissed Joseph's sweet cheek, laid him in his crib and covered him with a blanket.

Locking the door to the room they shared, she untucked the bottom edge of the quilt on her bed. Carefully, she worked her fingers along the stitched covering, and sighed when she felt the small toy and the money she had hidden there, both of which her father would not have approved. William had purchased the toy for their baby a few days after they learned Rosie was pregnant. She had secreted it away, knowing her father would not approve of anything William had given her.

Relieved that her secret hiding spot had not been discovered, Rosie slipped out of her torn dress and into her nightgown, but she was unwilling to go back downstairs. She did not have the energy to face her *datt's* questioning gaze or the concern she had seen earlier in her mother's eyes. Plus, she did not want to talk about her foolish mistake of falling for an *Englisch* man, which had caused her mother so much pain.

Rosie crawled into her narrow bed and extinguished the lamp. For these last seven months, since she and Joseph had been found, Rosie thought she had been safe, but the car tonight had run her off the road. The man demanded information Will had stolen.

Her stomach tightened. For her child's sake, she needed to find out what Will had done. When Joseph was older, he would want to know the truth about his father.

Her eyes had not fooled her today. The man with the streak of white hair was the same man she had seen at Will's trailer.

The man had killed the father of her child.

Now he was coming after her.

Chapter Three

Ezra woke with a start the next morning and blinked, trying to distance himself from the dreams that had circled through his mind. He had tossed and turned all night as visions of a young Amish woman with golden hair and blue eyes disturbed his usually placid slumber. What was it about Rosie Glick that put him in such a state of flux?

With a heavy sigh, he rose from the bed, feeling confused and frustrated by the way his mind continued to focus on her troubled gaze that tugged at his heart. He poured cold water from the pitcher into the ceramic basin and washed with a vengeance as if to cleanse himself of any residual influence she might have on his life.

His father had called Ezra a dreamer who allowed thoughts of what could be to interfere with the reality of the present moment. Since his father's death, Ezra worked to remain in the present, which did not include a pretty woman with a troubled past.

With two hours of chores awaiting him, he hurried to the barn and was soon joined by his brothers, fifteen-year-old Aaron and eight-year-old David. Working rapidly, the three of them milked the cows, then fed and watered the livestock.

Inside the house, his two eldest sisters, Susan, seventeen, and Belinda, three years her junior, prepared breakfast. When the chores were finished and after washing at the pump, Ezra climbed the porch steps and pushed open the kitchen door, breathing in the rich aroma of fresh brewed coffee and homemade biscuits hot from the oven.

Susan turned from the wood-burning stove and greeted him with a smile as he wiped his boots on the rug and hung his hat on the wall peg.

His oldest sister cared for the four younger siblings, for which Ezra was grateful. Susan was pragmatic and task-oriented, not a dreamer like her older brother.

Seven-year-old Mary, blonde and blue-eyed, had gathered eggs from the henhouse earlier and now brought the cool milk and butter inside from the bucket, where they had remained overnight. Aaron and David followed her into the kitchen.

At one time before his parents' deaths, Ezra had thought of ways to get out of work. Now he focused on the farm and what needed to be done. The responsibility to feed and care for his siblings had fallen hard on his shoulders. If he had been less of a dreamer and more attentive to his parents, they might still be alive.

His five siblings gathered at the table and followed Ezra's lead as he bowed his head to pray. The others were oblivious to the struggle that plagued him. His own inciting role in his parents' deaths weighed him down like a giant millstone, as the Bible said, so that he had trouble offering thanks. At least his youngest brothers and sisters had been at school that day and away from the house. Perhaps that fact was the blessing on which he needed to focus.

Aaron had been working in the fields, and Susan had been at a quilting. If only their mother had gone with her.

He raised his head and reached for his fork, needing to redirect his thoughts. "Tell me, David, what you are learning at school?"

The boy looked pensive as he spread apple butter on a biscuit. "We learn our sums."

"And you mind the teacher?"

"*Yah*. Why would I not?"

Thankfully, David had not followed in Ezra's footsteps.

"You are going to town again today?" Susan asked.

He nodded. "I must take the buggy to the blacksmith. Something is wrong with the springs."

"If you opened *Datt*'s buggy shop we could check the springs ourselves," Aaron said. "It has been a year and four months, Ezra."

"Someday, Aaron, but not now."

"There are buggies in the shop near ready for sale," his brother persisted. "You helped *Datt*. You could finish the projects he began."

Aaron gave Ezra more credit than he deserved. "Perhaps after Christmas and into the New Year."

His brother shook his head. "In January, we will be cutting ice for the icehouse. Come February, you will have another excuse."

"Whether we open the shop this winter or not, I am still going to town." He turned to Susan. "Is there something you need?"

"Susan would like to go with you." David smiled impishly and reached for another biscuit.

"Davey, eat your breakfast and mind your mouth," Susan admonished. "It should be filled with food and not words that make no sense."

Evidently, Ezra was not the only one aware of Susan's interest in John Keim, the blacksmith's son.

"Bishop Hochstetler's wife has need of a schoolteacher next year since Katie Gingrich and Benny Trotter are courting," Belinda explained, sounding older than her years. "She says they will surely be married by the time school starts again."

Knowing his sister's long held desire to teach, Ezra forced back a smile. "Have you forgotten your sums, Belinda? You are fourteen."

"I soon will be fifteen and sixteen the following year. I would make a good teacher."

"I believe you would."

"The bishop's wife will search to find someone within the community," Belinda insisted. "A teaching job would provide income. This would be a *gut* thing."

"*Yah*, bringing money into the house would be *gut*, yet you are needed here. When your sixteenth year approaches, we can discuss this again."

Her enthusiasm faltered. "Susan cares for the family."

Ezra nodded. "Susan is getting older. She must think of her own future."

"Not long ago, you said she is to think of the family first and her future second."

Ezra had said exactly that, but since then, his heart had mellowed. Perhaps he was yearning for his own freedom. He pushed aside the thought. Regrettably, he had turned his back on his family once. He would not make that mistake again.

He ruffled David's hair with one hand and squeezed Mary's chubby cheek with the other, wishing the twinkle would return to her pretty eyes. She was too young to grieve so long.

Ezra pushed back from the table. "Breakfast was *gut*. Thank you, Susan and Belinda."

He smiled at his youngest sister, hoping to bring a smile to her lips. "And *danke*, Mary, for gathering the eggs. You, too, are a help to your sisters."

Mary nodded but refused to smile, bringing sadness to his heart. If only he could change the past.

With a heavy sigh, he stepped to the door, grabbed his hat and then glanced back at Susan. "Shall I tell John Keim you have a lovely voice and might accept a ride to the next youth singing?"

Her cheeks pinkened. "Tell him I send my greetings."

Ezra hurried to the barn and harnessed Bessie to the buggy. He would visit the blacksmith and talk to the blacksmith's son to determine if John had the makings of a good husband for his sister. Ezra was not ready to lose Susan's help, but he would not stand in her way to have a family of her own.

He thought of Rosie, trying to raise her son. From what Ezra knew about her father, Rosie was not receiving the support she needed. All the more reason for Ezra to help her in whatever way he could.

The road to the Glick farm angled downhill. Bessie's gait was sprightly, and both he and the mare enjoyed the brisk morning trot. Ezra would give Rosie a ride to work today. Tonight, if he got home early enough, he would fix her bike and deliver it to her home tomorrow.

He did not want her on the road alone until he asked questions in town about the big man in the white sedan. Ezra had not seen him before, although these days he did not go to town often. Earlier, before his parents' deaths, he had run with some of the *Englischers*. He remembered most of the people, but not the older man with the splash of white hair.

He did remember Will MacIntosh, but he would not mention his name to Rosie. She had been swayed by Will's handsome looks and lavish spending. Ezra had been caught in the deception of the world as well and had yearned for material possessions and the money to buy them.

He did not blame Rosie for leaving the Amish way for a time, but he did blame Will for taking advantage of her innocence.

Rosie woke before dawn and prepared to leave her house earlier than usual. She worried Ezra would forget his offer to give her a ride. If so, she would be forced to walk to town.

"You should stay home," her mother insisted.

"I am scheduled to work. Plus, it is payday. I must get my check."

"And what will they say about the cuts and scrapes to your face and hands?"

"I will tell them I fell from my bike just as I told you."

"Your father could take you in the buggy," her mother suggested.

Rosie shook her head. *Datt* would not agree to making the trip to town just so his daughter—a daughter he still had trouble accepting back into the family—

could pick up her paycheck at an *Englisch* nursing home. Much as her father wanted Rosie to contribute to the financial needs of the family, he also struggled with her recent decision to seek employment in town.

"Another *Englischer* will catch her eye," her father had grumbled to her mother, and Rosie had overheard.

Forgiveness was the Amish way. Unfortunately, his daughter's mistakes were too hard to forgive.

She grabbed her black cape from the peg near the door, and after kissing Joseph, she hurried outside. Her father stood in the door of the barn and peered questioningly at her as she walked briskly toward the road.

Brave though she wanted to be, her heart pounded rapidly in her chest. If Ezra did not soon appear, she would have to make the trip on foot and would need to be on guard as she traveled along the roadway. Thankfully, the sound of horses' hooves alerted her to an approaching buggy. Her heart lurched. Not from fear but from a sense of thankfulness as she spied Bessie rounding the bend. Good to his word, Ezra had come to fetch her this morning.

Rosie stood at the edge of the pavement and waved as his buggy approached.

"Have you been waiting long?" he asked as he pulled the buggy to a stop.

"I just came from my house. Your timing is perfect."

Ezra reached for her hand and helped her into the seat next to him. The warmth from his body drove away the chill of the morning air.

"Your cape is not thick enough for such a cold day," he said.

Just as before, he reached for the blanket and wrapped it around her.

"Thank you, Ezra, for the blanket and for the ride, although I hate to take you from your farm."

"I need to be at the blacksmith's today and do some other errands in town. So you have not taken me from what I had already planned to do."

Rosie had half hoped he was making a special trip to see her, but that thought would be prideful and would play into the comments her father sometimes muttered about her haughty heart. *Datt* did not realize being locked in a root cellar had left her anything but proud.

"You did not see the man again?" Ezra flicked the reins and hurried his mare along the road. The sun was rising, and the morning light cast a surreal glow over the mountain.

"I pray I do not see him again," Rosie stated as she tucked the blanket around her waist.

"I will inquire about him in town."

"It is not your worry, Ezra. Please do not add this burden to your daily tasks. I am sure he left the area last night when we saw him drive past."

Ezra glanced at her for a long moment before he turned his gaze back to the road. "As focused as he seemed to be to do you harm, Rosie, I do not think he will disappear so easily. Perhaps there is something you are not telling me."

He glanced at her again and asked, "Are there secrets you must hide?"

Her cheeks burned, but she held his gaze. "You need not burden yourself with my mistakes, Ezra. You have your own past with which to struggle."

His brow furrowed and his lips drew tight. He glanced back at the road, making her believe the rumors she had heard about Ezra were true. For a period of time, he had forsaken the Amish way and had gotten caught up in the allure of the *Englisch*.

It was something they had in common.

Still she did not want to discuss her own past with a man who had only yesterday acknowledged her for the first time since she had returned home.

"Let's talk of something other than the past," she suggested with a defiant shake of her head.

"Two months ago, I applied for the job at the nursing home," she shared, needing a neutral topic to fill the silence.

Ezra kept his gaze on the road as she chatted. He did not speak for far too long, as if lost in his own thoughts. Thankfully, his interest seemed to pique when she started to discuss Mr. Calhoun, the delightful older gentleman with whom she had formed a special bond at the nursing home.

"Last night his rheumatoid arthritis was causing him undue pain," Rosie said. "He asked for medication but none was given. Finally, I went to Nan Smith, the new night nurse. She promised to straighten out the confusion. Mr. Calhoun does not have a family, but he is such a kind man and appreciates anything I do for him."

"I am sure you brighten his day with your pretty smile."

Her pulse quickened, and she wondered if she had heard Ezra correctly. No one had ever said she had a pretty smile. She did not need compliments or flattery, yet hearing Ezra's comment and seeing the sincerity in his gaze brought a smile to her lips.

"You are generous with your words, especially for an Amish man."

"Amish men speak the truth, Rosie."

Her heart fluttered with the speed of a hummingbird drawing nectar from a blossom. In an effort to calm the rapid rhythm, she focused on Mr. Calhoun and their special relationship.

"Hopefully, the night nurse cleared up the pain-medicine problem so he got the rest he needed," she said, as they entered town.

The Christmas decorations added a festive charm to the morning, and in spite of everything that had happened, Rosie's spirits lifted. Ezra turned onto a side street and pulled Bessie to a stop in front of the nursing home.

The double doors were adorned with two large wreaths tied with shiny red bows. Potted pines, decorated with sparkling white lights and red bows, sat on each side of the double doors.

He pointed to the parking lot.

Rosie pulled her eyes from the twinkling lights and followed his gaze. Her euphoria vanished, replaced with dread as she spied a white sedan identical to the one that had tried to run her off the road yesterday.

"Stay with me," Ezra insisted. "Do not go to work today."

"Surely the car belongs to someone else. I will be all right, Ezra. You need not worry."

"The blacksmith's shop is on Sycamore Street off the square. If there is a problem, you can find me there."

She hurried inside and passed the Christmas tree decorated with gold and red bulbs. Hurrying along the hallway to the left, she rounded an arrangement of poinsettias that surrounded a Norfolk Island pine and stopped short. A man stood in the doorway of the manager's office. Thankfully, his back was to her, but the streak of white hair confirmed he was the same man who had attacked her last night.

The manager's voice filtered into the hallway. "Come on in, Larry, and close the door."

At least now, she knew his first name.

Had he found out where she worked and followed her here? Or was his presence a coincidence that had nothing to do with Rosie or her job? She would not wait to find out.

Turning down a side hallway, she hurried to the kitchen, located on the far wing, where she would hide out this morning, preparing the patients' trays. By the time breakfast was served, the man would be gone.

At least that was her hope.

Ezra tied Bessie to the hitching rail and entered the nursing home. Whether Rosie wanted his help or not, he needed to ensure she was all right.

He walked past the Christmas tree and turned down a nearby corridor to the right, where he was greeted with a bevy of activity as aides dressed in pastel-colored scrubs hurried from room to room, waking patients and getting them ready for the new day. He headed down one hall after another, but he could not find Rosie.

Stopping in the middle of the hallway, he glanced into a patient's room.

Someone came up behind him. "May I help you?"

Ezra turned to stare into the face of a middle-aged man with dark eyes and a receding hairline. He was big and bulky and appeared in good physical shape.

"Do you have a reason to be in Shady Manor?" the man demanded.

Ezra glanced at the name tag hanging from a lanyard around the man's neck. Bruce O'Donnell, Shady Manor Manager.

At the end of the hallway, he spied another man. The guy with the patch of white hair stood staring at both of them.

Ezra needed a reason to be on the nursing-home premises, without making mention of Rosie. Her favorite patient came to mind.

"I know it is early," Ezra said. "But I came into town this morning and wanted to see how Mr. Calhoun is doing."

"Are you kin?"

Ezra shook his head. "No, but he is a nice man who enjoys company. Could you direct me to his room?"

"Visiting hours begin at nine, after the patients have eaten breakfast." The manager pointed him toward the nearest exit.

Ezra wanted to find Rosie, but not when the man with the streak of white hair was watching his every move. He headed outside and pulled his buggy around the side of the building, where it would be less noticeable. Ezra would stand guard at the nursing home for as long as Rosie's assailant remained inside.

In less than thirty minutes, the big man left the care facility through a side door. He walked quickly across the parking lot, climbed into his car and drove off.

Ezra let out a lungful of pent-up air. Minutes later, Rosie ran outside. Her face was pale. Tears streamed from her blue eyes.

He grabbed her hand. "Did someone hurt you?"

"Oh, Ezra!"

He wrapped his arm around her shoulders and hurried her to the protection of the buggy. "Tell me what happened?"

"Mr. O'Donnell called me to his office. He is the manager of the nursing home. He—he claimed—"

Ezra rubbed her arms and waited as she struggled to catch her breath.

"Someone told him I was snooping around in patient records last night."

"I do not understand."

"It probably had to do with Mr. Calhoun. I had talked to the night nurse. She planned to check his chart, but I never looked at any of his records."

"Did you tell Mr. O'Donnell?"

"He would not listen. He said medication had been stolen, and…"

She hung her head. "He accused me of being a thief."

"This does not make sense. Are you sure you heard him correctly?"

Rosie nodded. "He fired me, Ezra. He refused to give me my back pay and mentioned calling the police." Her eyes widened. "I am frightened."

He wrapped his arms around her. "Do not be afraid, Rosie. You are safe now."

Only she was not safe, and the danger seemed to be getting closer.

She laid her head on his shoulder as the tears fell.

"Shh," Ezra soothed. Rosie was soft and warm and smelled like lavender. Everything within Ezra wanted to take away her pain and protect her from anyone attempting to do her harm. He pulled her even closer, wishing he could wipe away her tears.

"I wanted to say goodbye to Mr. Calhoun," she whispered. "But when I went into his room—"

"What happened?"

"Mr. Calhoun—" She glanced up. Sorrow filled her eyes. "Oh, Ezra. Mr. Calhoun is dead."

Chapter Four

Rosie's head swirled with confusion. Seeing Mr. Calhoun's body with a sheet draped over it had startled her. Foolishly, she had thought he was asleep. When she pulled aside the cloth, she realized her mistake.

His frozen gaze and white pallor had broken her heart. Unwilling to believe what she saw, Rosie had run to the nurses' station only to be told what she knew to be true.

Tears came again. She leaned into Ezra's embrace, feeling the strength of him. He rubbed her hand over her shoulder and clutched her even closer.

"Last night, he was fine," she gasped between sobs. "He was in pain, but his vitals were good. I promised him help. Nan assured me she would track down the missing medication."

"The nurse you spoke to, do you trust her?" Ezra asked.

"Why would I not? She is new to the home and eager to make changes for the better." Rosie sniffed and swiped her hand over her cheeks, in an attempt to wipe away her tears. "This is all so frightening. First the man chases after me, and now a patient—a *gut* man—dies, and I am called a thief."

"Perhaps we need to talk to the nurse. She might provide information about Mr. Calhoun's physical condition, including any complications that may have occurred."

As much as Rosie wanted to remain in Ezra's arms, he was right. Nan could provide information about Mr. Calhoun's death.

"Nan left the nursing home shortly before I arrived this morning. She may have been with Mr. Calhoun when he died. That would bring me comfort if he had not suffered and slipped away peacefully."

"If that is indeed so."

Rosie stared at Ezra's questioning gaze. "You do not believe *Gott* called Mr. Calhoun home?"

"I am wondering if *Gott* had help."

Rosie widened her eyes. "You think foul play was involved?"

"I do not know, but one thing is certain, you need to talk to Nan. Do you know where she lives?"

"In a new area of homes on the far side of the mountain. She invited me to visit and gave me directions."

"I will take you there." Ezra glanced at the door to the nursing home. "We must hurry in case the manager has called the police, as he threatened to do."

Rosie's heart sank. If Mr. O'Donnell involved the police, she might be hauled in for questioning. Would they believe her or Mr. O'Donnell, a well-thought-of businessman within the community?

Surely Nan would provide information about Mr. Calhoun's death. Perhaps she would also shed light on why Rosie had been fired.

* * *

Ezra helped Rosie into the buggy and then climbed in next to her. He did not want to frighten her any more than she already was, but Rosie's world was spinning out of control. If Mr. O'Donnell filed criminal charges, she would have a hard time proving her innocence, especially if medication had, indeed, gone missing.

An innocent Amish woman was the perfect scapegoat. Rosie did not have the wherewithal to defend herself against slander. Plus, she had been involved with a man known to skirt the law when it served his advantage. The *Englisch* would never realize how a woman who longed for love could be blind to the truth about the man to whom she had given her heart.

To make matters worse, she had been kidnapped and held captive. A weaker woman never would have survived, but Rosie had endured the months of her pregnancy and had delivered her child in a root cellar all by herself. Ezra called that admirable and heroic, yet he doubted the local authorities would see her in a positive light.

Ezra encouraged his mare forward. Instead of taking the main road out of the nursing home, he circled to the rear of the parking lot and turned onto a backstreet.

"Does this lead to the mountain homes?" Rosie asked.

"*Yah*, it is a bit longer in distance, but it keeps us out of the downtown area. If the man with the streak of white hair is on the road, I do not want him to see you."

She lowered hear head and struggled to compose herself. He wrapped his arm around her shoulders and pulled her closer.

"After we talk to the nurse, I will take you home. We

Amish do not talk about stress, but it is true that anxiety builds and rips us apart. You need time to heal."

"I need to find out what happed to Mr. Calhoun," she insisted.

"You also need to find out why the man with the patch of white hair is out to do you harm."

"His name is Larry. I overheard the nursing-home manager talking to him." Rosie wiped her hand over her cheeks. "I have so many questions. Perhaps learning about Mr. Calhoun's death will provide a few answers."

The community of newly constructed homes appeared on the distant hillside. "I remember when the mountains were covered with trees," Ezra mused, thinking of the changes that came with the increase in population. "The town grows too fast."

"Nan worked in one of the big medical centers in Atlanta. She wanted to enjoy a more rural way of life and moved here after she got the job at the nursing home."

Ezra glanced around the side of the buggy and studied the road.

"Do you see something?" Rosie asked.

"No one in a white car, if that is your concern. I saw Larry in the nursing home earlier. I went inside to ensure you were all right, but the manager told me to leave. I mentioned wanting to visit Mr. Calhoun. Perhaps that is the reason the manager told me to leave. He knew Mr. Calhoun was dead."

Rosie shivered.

"You are cold?" Ezra asked.

"Not cold. Just worried, especially since Mr. O'Donnell said he might call the police. What would they do to me, Ezra?"

"You have done nothing wrong." He glanced at her, hoping to see more clearly into her heart.

Ezra considered himself a good judge of character, yet he had been wrong about people in the past. He did not want to make a mistake when it came to Rosie.

"You have done nothing wrong," he said again. "This is right?"

She bristled. "Of course I have done nothing wrong."

Could he believe her? Ezra hoped so.

Hearing the suspicion in Ezra's voice, Rosie steeled her shoulders and pursed her lips, not willing to be undermined by a man who seemed supportive one minute and suspicious the next. She had revealed too much.

Earlier, she had appreciated his concern and the way he had offered comfort with his strong arms and his gentle, soothing voice. Since he had found her at the foot of the ravine, Ezra had been a rock in the midst of her chaos. Now she felt the exact opposite about him.

Ever since she had met William, her life had been anything but peaceful. The Amish way that she had loved during her youth had become confining and restrictive in her teen years. Was it William, with his free spirit, who had swayed her away from that which she knew?

She had been young and foolish. Everything that had happened—her capture and confinement—had changed her outlook. Now she had Joseph, her precious child, who gave meaning to her life. She had gained maturity through all the strife. Not the easiest way to grow up, but *Gott* knew what she needed.

Although sitting next to Ezra in his buggy after the death of a delightful gentleman had her questioning everything. She clasped her hands and kept her gaze on the mountain homes, unwilling to allow her emotions free rein.

"Nan told me her street is the second turn to the left."

Ezra encouraged his mare onto the street. The steady pace of the horse's hooves sounded as they headed up the hill. The neighborhood sat quiet in the crisp morning air.

The stillness troubled Rosie.

"There is no activity," she said at last.

"The *Englisch* are at work, even the women," Ezra explained. "Children are at day care or in school."

"I hope Nan is home." Rosie noted the numbers on the mailboxes and pointed to a house on the left. "There. That is the house number she gave me."

Ezra turned his mare onto the driveway and got out of the buggy. He tied the reins to a tree and then helped Rosie climb down. All the while, he glanced around the area as if searching for anything suspect.

"You are worried?" Rosie asked.

"Not worried but cautious. As you mentioned, it is quiet here."

They hurried to the door. Rosie knocked then glanced down the street, following Ezra's lead. His concern added to Rosie's unrest. She rang the bell again.

Just before she was ready to return to the buggy, the door opened. A very sleepy Nan stood in the threshold, rubbing her eyes, her red hair disheveled. "Is everything all right, Rosie?"

"I am sorry to bother you. You were asleep?"

"Not yet. I was getting ready to go to bed." She glanced at Ezra and held out her hand. "I'm Nan Smith."

"Forgive me for not introducing you," Rosie said as

the two people shook hands. "This is Ezra Stoltz. He agreed to drive me here. I came to find out about Mr. Calhoun."

"Come in," Nan said, opening the door wide.

Rosie and Ezra entered the foyer.

"I talked to one of the other nurses last night about Mr. Calhoun's missing meds," Nan explained. "We couldn't find his OxyContin so I gave him a couple ibuprofen. I also called the pharmacy and left a message about the missing meds."

"Did the other nurse know what happened?" Rosie asked.

"She didn't seem concerned. I did a little investigating on my own and found Mr. Calhoun wasn't the only patient with missing medication."

"What do you mean?"

"What I mean is that Shady Manor has a problem. Many, if not most, of the patients had orders for strong opioid pain medication—hydrocodone or OxyContin—but when I searched the medication cart the meds were missing."

"Had they already been given out?"

"Not that I could tell. I didn't even know the opioids had been prescribed for many of the patients—patients who don't have significant pain. I left a memo for Mr. O'Donnell."

Nan's forthright sharing about what had transpired last night convinced Rosie the nurse had left work unaware of Mr. Calhoun's passing.

"Would either of you like coffee?" she asked as she ushered them into the living area. "I'll fix a fresh pot."

"Do not trouble yourself with coffee," Rosie insisted.

"It's no trouble." Nan pointed to the couch. An overstuffed chair sat nearby. "Sit here. The coffee will not take long to brew."

Rosie held up her hand in protest. "We can talk without coffee. There is something I must tell you."

Nan stepped closer. "Is something wrong?"

"Mr. Calhoun died this morning."

"Oh, no!" The nurse raised her hand to her throat. "I'm so sorry to hear that. He was in pain last night, but his symptoms weren't life-threatening."

"I went in his room to say goodbye—"

"Goodbye?" Nan narrowed her gaze. "Now I'm really confused. Are you leaving Shady Manor?"

"Mr. O'Donnell terminated my employment this morning. He said I had gotten involved in a situation beyond my job description. He also said I had tampered with patient medication and he threatened to notify the police."

"You're kidding."

"I wish I were. He told me to leave immediately. I could not leave without saying goodbye to Mr. Calhoun. When I entered his room, I knew something was wrong. The nurse said he had suffered a heart attack."

"Which may have occurred, although I don't recall any record of a heart condition." Nan shook her head. "He was such a nice man."

Rosie agreed. "He said I brightened his days, but the opposite was true. He was considerate of my situation and always encouraged me to work hard so I could someday become independent and take care of Joseph on my own. His words were always filled with kindness and concern. You know I would do nothing to cause him harm."

Nan rubbed Rosie's shoulder. "You were a friend he looked forward to seeing."

"But I do not understand what happened."

"I'm working later today, Rosie. I'll check his chart and see what it says. The coroner's report won't be back for days, but I'll talk to the staff and see if they know anything about his death."

"Will you be able to read the coroner's report?"

"Perhaps." She shrugged. "And I want to track down the reason his medication was missing as well as the pain meds for the other patients."

"Can you talk to the pharmacist and Mr. Calhoun's doctor?"

Nan nodded. "After I get some sleep. How will I let you know what I find out?"

Rosie glanced at Ezra.

"I will bring Rosie to your house in a day or two," he quickly suggested.

A warmth settled over Rosie. Once again, Ezra had come to her aid. "It will not be a problem?" she asked him.

He smiled. "Perhaps then we will be able to ease your concerns about Mr. Calhoun. It will not be a problem."

Rosie turned back to Nan. "We will see you either tomorrow or the day following to find out what you have learned."

She hesitated a moment as a thought surfaced. "Perhaps I am being foolish, yet I must say this anyway. If you would be so kind, do not mention my name to Mr. O'Donnell. He claimed I interfered with nursing duties last night. Perhaps he feels I was too demanding in my desire to help Mr. Calhoun. Keeping my name out of the situation might be a good idea."

Nan nodded. "You're probably being overly cautious, but I won't divulge your interest in Mr. Calhoun's death. Especially since Mr. O'Donnell accused you of wrongdoing." She patted Rosie's arm. "I do not want to get you in more trouble."

"Thank you, Nan."

The nurse glanced at the wall clock. "The pharmacy will open soon. I'll talk to the pharmacist before I get some sleep. I'm sure she can solve the problem about the missing meds. She may have information about Mr. Calhoun's other medical problems, too. Perhaps she'll let me know if he was prescribed any medication for his heart. I'll also mention my concern about the number of pain prescriptions that seem unnecessary."

Rosie was relieved, knowing Nan would get to the bottom of what was happening at Shady Manor. "By any chance, Nan, have you seen a middle-aged man with a streak of white hair at the home? His first name is Larry."

"That sounds like Larry Wagner. He was in Mr. O'Donnell's office the night before last. O'Donnell introduced us. Is he causing a problem?"

Rosie shrugged. "He thinks I have something that belongs to him, but he is mistaken."

"He seems harmless, Rosie. I wouldn't be too concerned."

But Rosie was concerned, although she would not burden Nan with details about who Larry Wagner really was. A friend of Mr. O'Donnell's who was out to do Rosie harm. She needed to be careful and cautious where Mr. Wagner was concerned.

Rosie squeezed the nurse's hand. "I appreciate your help."

"Like you, Rosie, I'll feel better once the mystery is solved."

After leaving the nurse's home, Rosie followed Ezra to the buggy. She stopped for a moment to peer down the mountain. Shady Manor was visible in the distance. What was happening there that had caused a sweet old man to die?

Nan had mentioned a mystery, which was exactly what Mr. Calhoun's death might prove to be. How did he die and why had his medication gone missing?

Chapter Five

As concerned as Ezra had been about Rosie at the nursing home, he was even more concerned now. Somehow by befriending Mr. Calhoun, she had gotten tangled up in a search for missing drugs.

The Amish tried to distance themselves from the *Englisch* world, but they read newspapers and stayed relatively current on issues that might have bearing on their own areas of the country. The drug epidemic that seemed rampant across the United States had touched the Amish community, leaving some of their youth addicted.

Will MacIntosh was involved with Larry Wagner. But what was the connection?

On the way home, Rosie kept her head turned away from Ezra. Was she weighing what Nan had said or was she thinking back to her time with Will?

"I keep wondering about the missing medication," Ezra said, finally voicing his concern. "We both know prescribed drugs can be illegally sold for profit. Larry Wagner shows up and drugs go missing. He believes you have information that Will took from him. If Larry is involved in a drug operation, could that mean Will was involved as well?"

Rosie straightened her spine. He could sense her displeasure even before she turned to stare at him, her eyes filled with accusation. "How can you think Will was involved with drugs?"

"I was merely asking a question."

She lowered her gaze and shook her head. "I do not know anything about what William did except that the man with the streak of white hair—"

Rosie hesitated. "Nan said his name was Larry Wagner."

Ezra nodded.

"Well, Mr. Wagner believes I have something that Will took from him."

"Drugs perhaps?"

She shrugged. "I had the feeling it was information."

"Something that would incriminate Wagner?"

"Maybe. That seems likely."

"Did Will give you any papers or files?"

She shook her head.

"What about pills? Or a wrapped container that could hold pills?"

"Nothing like that. He gave me a beaded necklace that broke the night he was killed."

"Did Wagner have something to do with your necklace breaking?"

She shook her head. "Mr. Wagner did not break the necklace."

Ezra waited for an explanation. Realizing she would provide no additional information, he turned his gaze back to the road. He did not want to unsettle Rosie more than she already was, but he needed to find out the truth about her relationship with Will.

"Did *he* break the necklace?" Ezra finally asked.

"He?"

"Will MacIntosh. Was he abusive?"

"No, of course not. It's just that…"

Again she hesitated.

"Just what, Rosie?"

"Ezra, please. Some things are not to be shared."

He pursed his lips and forced the frustration that welled within him to calm. Will was not the nicest of men and there was no telling what he had done to Rosie. A broken necklace could also symbolize a broken heart or a broken arm or a black eye. Had he been abusive that night, or told her to get out of his life even when she carried his child?

Ezra sighed. He was foolish to get involved with a woman who had given her heart to a dead man whose character could be embellished with time. Eventually, her memories of Will could become more grandiose than the reality of who he had been when alive.

Needing to focus on something more practical, Ezra clucked his tongue, encouraging his mare forward. He directed her along the back roads and away from town, but he was still worried about the man with the patch of white hair.

Ezra turned to glance back at the road they had just traveled. If they were followed, he had no idea where he and Rosie would hide. Last night, they had eluded Wagner by hiding in the woods. They were currently traveling on a road that butted up to fenced farm fields that offered no place to hide.

His chest constricted as he thought of the danger that

could overtake them both. Driving Rosie directly home this morning would have been smarter than going to the nurse's house.

"You are worried we will be seen?" Rosie asked, as if reading his thoughts.

He nodded. "*Yah*, it would be easy to spot us on the open road. The fallow fields offer no protection."

"I have placed you in danger," she said, her voice low.

"Danger does not worry me, Rosie, but I am concerned about your safety. Wagner was talking to the manager of the nursing home. What if O'Donnell gave out your address?"

"You mean the address to my father's house?"

"That is exactly what I mean. The man could track you down."

"My father will not let him into our house. *Datt* will protect me."

Ezra nodded. "This is something for which you are certain?"

"*Yah*. My father would not let anyone harm me or take me from my home."

"What about before?" Ezra asked.

"William MacIntosh did not kidnap me, Ezra. I went with him of my own accord."

Because she loved him. Ezra knew that, yet he had half hoped Rosie would deny her feelings for Will.

They rode in silence, which only made Ezra more unsettled. Rosie was probably thinking of Will and mourning his death. Ezra wanted her to explain how she really felt, in case he had it wrong.

"Thank you for taking me to town and to Nan's house," Rosie said. "Thank you, also, for bringing me home. I have occupied too much of your time and must apologize."

"There is nothing for which to apologize. I told you I had work to do in town."

"Which you were not able to complete after I was fired."

"Do not be concerned about me. You have enough to worry about with your own safety and that of your son's as well."

The Glick home appeared ahead. Ezra glanced around the property in search of Rosie's father but failed to spot the older man. Mrs. Glick came outside, the baby in her arm. Even from this distance, the child saw Rosie and waved his hands in the air.

Ezra pulled on the reins. Before he could help Rosie down from the buggy, she was on the ground and heading to her son. Ezra watched her hurry toward the porch, feeling a sense of loss he had not expected.

Rosie stopped at the steps and turned, as if realizing he was watching her.

"Have you met my son?"

What? He shook his head.

She took the baby from her mother, kissed his cheek and then carried him back to the buggy. "Ezra, this is Joseph. His father was William MacIntosh, as you know. I made a mistake once, but I did nothing that would cause a man to come after me now. I have asked forgiveness from the bishop for my fickle heart, but I was not involved in anything illegal."

"I never thought you were."

Her lips lifted into a weak smile. "I am grateful for your help yesterday and today. There are few people who have reached out to me since I have returned home."

"Are you sure it is the people who would not help or is it that you have holed up on this farm without returning to the community you knew?"

She hesitated. "What about you, Ezra? Do you join in the activities of the community or have you holed up on the mountain?"

"I have brothers and sisters who need my care."

"And I have a son who needs mine. Perhaps we are not that different. Again, thank you."

Before she could turn her back on him again, Ezra raised his hand. "I still have your bicycle."

"I will not return to town soon so do not worry yourself about something that would probably be an impossible task. Sometimes that which is broken cannot be fixed."

She hurried back to her house. Her mother had already gone inside. Rosie stopped on the porch and turned to watch him leave.

"Wave goodbye, Joseph." She took hold of the baby's hand and waved it in the air.

Ezra could not respond. Goodbye was not what he wanted to say. The word lodged in his throat and refused to be spoken. Instead he flipped the reins and encouraged his mare to turn back to the road that would take him away from Rosie Glick.

His leaving would be good for both of them. Rosie would remain with her troubled father and her mother, who always seemed fearful. The family would eke out an existence far from town and with only a few ways of interacting with the other Amish. They would remain distant, removed from the regular Amish community as if their daughter's mistake had taken away their de-

sire to live life to the fullest. Were they so guilt-ridden
by her mistake that they refused to enter back into life?

Ezra doubted their Amish neighbors would consider
the Glicks's problems any more challenging than the
problems other families had. Ezra could relate, as Rosie
had mentioned. He had lived reclusively on the mountain and been unwilling to be baptized or involved in
the social aspects of the Amish way. His sisters had
suffered because of his closed outlook, but now he realized his mistake—he would give them the freedom
they desired and needed.

Susan was of courting age. He would not stop her
from falling in love and marrying and from making her
own way in life. Belinda, when she was old enough,
would make an excellent teacher, of this he was sure.
He would not inhibit her desires any longer.

And the buggy shop? His brother would have to
wait. Ezra was not ready to step back into the workshop
where his parents had been murdered. Not yet. Perhaps
in the future, although today as he left the Glick farm
and traveled up the hill, he could not think of tomorrow, and it was too painful to think of the past, while
focusing on the present only brought visions of Rosie
to mind with her pretty blue eyes and blond hair.

He thought of her open expression and her willing-
ness to reach out to an old man in a nursing home, as
well as to give her heart to her son. But she had given
her heart to someone else. To an *Englischer*. She loved
him still, Ezra was sure.

Better that Ezra leave now before he think any more
about Rosie. He would push her out of his mind, although he knew it would take time—time and effort,

because saying goodbye to Rosie felt like a knife stabbing his heart.

Silly of him to have gotten invested so quickly, although looking back, Ezra realized Rosie had captured his interest years ago in school.

Now he feared if he stayed around her any longer, she might also capture his heart.

Chapter Six

Rosie woke to the sound of a car engine. Her heart jumped to her throat, and she instinctively reached out her hand and touched the crib to ensure Joseph was still there.

The rise and fall of his chest comforted her until the pounding at the front door had her racing to the window. Pulling back the curtain, she looked down to see a light-colored SUV.

Was it white?

She blinked and rubbed her hand over her eyes, trying to wipe away the sleep and the dream she had about a certain Amish man with understanding eyes and a square jaw. Ezra was not the one pounding on her door.

She heard her father's footsteps as he scurried downstairs. "What is it you want?" he asked, raising his voice.

Garbled sounds floated up to her, as if an argument ensued, then she heard footsteps on the porch. If only she could see what was happening.

It sounded like a scuffle. She strained to see through the darkness until two forms took shape.

She gasped as she saw a man throwing punches at

her father as he cowered in the cleared area at the front of the house. Heart in her throat, she turned again, to ensure Joseph was safe, then glanced back, seeing her father on the ground. The man towering over him was poised to strike again.

His fist pounded into her father's stomach. Even at this distance, she could hear *Datt* moan as he rolled into a ball, trying to protect himself.

"Don't tell me you forgot how to fight, Wayne?"

The assailant grabbed her father's shirt, yanked him to his feet and pummeled him again.

"No," her mother cried from below. *Mamm* ran to where her husband had dropped to the dirt again. "Leave him alone, Larry."

Larry? Larry Wagner? The man with the streak of white hair? How did *Mamm* know his name?

"Wayne tried to be tough in his youth, but deep down he was a coward then, and he still is a coward." Larry brushed his hands together before he looked at the house. His gaze fell on Rosie's bedroom window.

She stepped back, hoping he had not seen her.

"Where is she?" he demanded. "Where's Rosie?"

"She's gone, Larry. Now, leave us. You and your kind have caused us enough pain."

"You're lying, Emma."

She got into his face and pointed to his car. "Leave now and don't come back."

"I'll find her," he said as he brushed his pants legs and glanced at her father huddled on the ground. "If you weren't here, Emma, I'd finish him off. You know how I felt."

He looked at the house and shook his head. "Did

you get what you wanted? I could have given you so much more."

"Leave, Larry. And do not return."

He climbed into the car, turned out of the drive and headed back toward town.

Rosie flew down the stairs and out the door to where her mother kneeled, cradling her father.

"Help me get your *datt* to his feet," her mother said.

Rosie put her arm around her father's shoulders and helped him stand. He was woozy and wobbled on his feet, but with their encouragement, he slowly climbed the stairs and entered the house.

"We will take him to the bedroom," her mother said with no additional explanation of what had happened.

Rosie eased her father onto the bed and then hurried to draw water into a bowl and bring towels to clean his cuts and scrapes.

Her mother met her in the kitchen. "I will tend to your father. Go back to bed."

"I can help."

Her mother shook her head. "No. Return to your bed."

"But—"

"Do as I say, Rosie."

"It was my fault, *Mamm*. The man said he wanted me."

"And I told him you were gone. Do not go outside. He will not come into the house, and we must make sure he does not see you if he drives by again."

"I did this to you, and I am so sorry, but—"

She stared at her mother, knowing her own eyes were filled with question. "He called you Emma. How did he know your name?"

"Rosie, go to bed."

Her mother hurried back to the bedroom, closing the door behind her.

Rosie glanced out the window and looked at the spot where her father had been accosted by the same man who wanted to do her harm.

What was happening to her life? She had experienced a few months of peace after being released from captivity and had been raising her son and healing from her own ordeal, but everything was happening again, only now everything was so much worse.

Her parents were in danger, yet there was something her mother had not revealed. She knew the man who had come after her—Larry Wagner, the man with the streak of white hair. How could that be?

One thing was certain, Rosie could no longer stay and bring more danger to her parents. She had done enough to cause them problems. She needed to leave in the morning.

But a sinking feeling settled in her stomach. She needed to leave but where would she go?

Sleep eluded Ezra. Every time he closed his eyes, he saw Rosie, brow furrowed and fear reflecting from her eyes. With a sigh, he turned to his side and rolled out of bed. He would not stay put when so much awaited him.

He glanced again out the window, relieved to see the first hint of morning light on the horizon. He would get an early start on the day. Surely Rosie rose early, just as everyone did in every Amish home. He envisioned her mixing flour for the breakfast biscuits and could almost smell them baking.

Realizing he was smelling the biscuits his sister

Susan was making eased some of his angst. As always, he was grateful for her help and hurried downstairs.

"You are early for breakfast," Susan said.

Ezra reached around her and grabbed a warm biscuit from the baking sheet. "There is work to be done this morning."

"Yet, you were up late tinkering with a woman's bicycle. This belongs to someone you know?"

He bit into the biscuit and tasted its sweetness.

Susan turned from the stove and stared at him, her brow raised as if waiting for his reply.

He swallowed and smiled. "There is coffee?"

She took a cup from the cupboard and filled it with coffee from the pot. "I always have coffee ready in the morning. But you did not answer my question about the bike."

"It belongs to Rosie Glick."

His sister's eyes widened ever so slightly before she turned back to the stove. "The same Rosie Glick who was held captive for eight months?"

"I know of no other woman by that name in this area."

"I heard she works at the nursing home in town. This is who you have visited these last few days?"

"You are full of questions this morning, Susan."

"And you, my *bruder*, are hesitant to answer them." She broke two eggs into a skillet. The hot grease sizzled. "Do you wish ham to go with your eggs?"

"Not this morning. I must leave soon."

"Before chores?"

"The boys can handle them today. I will return in an hour or so."

"You are delivering the bike?"

"*Yah.*"

"*Datt* ran a buggy-making shop. Now you are working on bicycles. Is this a new venture?"

"I am helping a woman who has no one to help her. Surely this is something you can understand."

Once the eggs cooked, Susan used a spatula to lift them from the skillet. She arranged them on a plate, next to two more biscuits.

"You have a soft heart, Ezra, especially for those in need. This is a good attribute, *yah*? But you must use your head as well as your heart."

She smiled knowingly at him as she handed him the filled plate.

"I am not blind, Susan. I see clearly."

"Yet you still struggle to find your way and have not yet accepted baptism. Having this family to care for returned you to us, but I sense you do not know the direction with which you should walk into the future. We hold you back, perhaps. This woman might hold you back even more."

"I would think my staying here would be a good decision."

"*Yah*, in *my* mind it is the right decision. But we are talking about you, Ezra. You must decide what is best for you."

"Sometimes circumstances take that decision from a person. He no longer has the freedom to decide due to the responsibility placed on his shoulders."

"You are a strong man, Ezra. You can carry much weight, but you do not need added burdens that will weigh you down even more."

He scooped a forkful of eggs into his mouth and washed it down with coffee as she spoke.

"Rosie Glick is not a burden, Susan. I appreciate your concern for my well-being, but you need not worry. I know where I am going."

He hurriedly finished breakfast and headed to the barn to hitch Bessie to the buggy. The day was cold, but he appreciated the clearness of the air and welcomed the chance to leave his sister's watchful eye.

Susan was right. He did question his future, but his wanderlust had ebbed with the deaths of his parents. The Amish life that had initially held him back from experiencing the world now provided stability and a firm foundation on which to build his future, although he questioned where the future would take him.

He loved his brothers and sisters. He could not and would not abandon them again.

In spite of what Susan said, Ezra had his eyes wide open when it came to Rosie Glick. He would return the bike to her this morning and that would end their relationship. He had helped her to escape Larry Wagner. She had lost her job and planned to remain safely at home. Ezra no longer need worry about her.

But as the buggy left his house and headed down the mountain, Ezra knew the man with the patch of white hair was still a threat. He had come after Rosie once. He would surely come after her again.

Chapter Seven

Rosie left her house soon after the first light of the winter sun appeared over the horizon. She cradled Joseph close in her arms. On her back, she had tied a bundle of his clothing, extra blankets and diapers. She refused to disturb her parents, and instead of saying goodbye, she had left them a note on the kitchen table, explaining that she would contact them once she and Joseph were settled. Somewhere.

Today, she would walk to her Aunt Katherine's house. Katherine was her mother's sister, who lived higher up the mountain—her husband had died two years ago, and her daughter, Alice, had married and moved to Ohio a few years earlier. Katherine's son-in-law was a good carpenter, like her husband had been. Holmes County in Ohio was experiencing a tourist boom with much new construction. Hotels, shops and restaurants were springing up, bringing jobs that Alice's husband had quickly found in commercial construction. Perhaps Rosie could find a job there in one of the many stores or restaurants. But first, she needed to ensure she and Joseph were safe. If she holed up in her aunt's house for a day or two, the man after her might give up his search. Then she and Joseph could leave the North Georgia mountains and take a bus to Ohio without fear of being followed.

Rosie glanced down at her sleeping child, unwilling to think of what the future might hold. She needed to focus on today. Once they arrived at her aunt's house, Rosie could make plans for the next leg of their journey.

The air was cold to her cheeks. She pulled Joseph's blanket over his head to protect him from the morning chill. The temperature had dropped in the night and a shiver of concern traveled down her spine. She glanced back at her parents' home. A lump formed in her throat as she remembered when she had snuck out in the night to meet William. How naive she had been. And foolish.

At that time, she had been seeing life through the eyes of an immature girl, giddy with what she thought was love.

William had little love for her in his heart. He had more love for himself and his need to be the center of attention. Rosie doted over him like a fool, which somehow fed into his need to be accepted. His own father had been abusive and had little use for William.

They were alike in that way, a fact she had learned all too soon. Although she did not consider herself self-centered at the time. Looking back now, she saw the pain she had caused her parents because of her own desire to experience life beyond her small Amish world.

Now she was leaving home again, but this time to protect her parents, although she doubted they would consider her absence to be in consideration of their own well-being. Her mother doted over Joseph. Surely, *Mamm* would cry for his loss.

Rosie turned back to the road and walked with determined steps to the end of the driveway, holding her breath as if her parents could hear her in the still morning. Her heart was fragile, and with a little coaxing, she could easily be swayed to remain at home.

She shook her head, unwilling to acquiesce and wondered again about how Larry Wagner knew her parents. If he came to her home once, he could easily come again. She had to leave and find a safe haven for her child. Joseph did not need to be raised holed up in a farmhouse where love was hard to be found and an abusive man had beat up her father. The child deserved laughter and sunshine and friends with whom to romp over the grassy meadows. She would find a new home for them that was free from danger.

A sound echoed down the mountain, causing another chill to run down her spine. Not an automobile, for that she was thankful, but a steady rhythmic sound that made her pause and glance into the dense forest that edged the narrow roadway. The sound grew louder, yet was still unrecognizable. She shivered, knowing anyone or anything could be approaching.

Unwilling to remain in clear view, she pulled Joseph closer to her heart and skirted her way into the woods. Tree branches snagged her coat and scraped against her cheeks. She kept her hand protectively over Joseph, covering his precious face from the branches and bramble.

Once deep in the woods and protected by dense foliage, she stopped and turned to stare through the underbrush at the road. The sound intensified, causing her heart to pound harder in her chest.

The baby stirred in her arms. She patted Joseph and rocked the baby, hoping to soothe him back to sleep. His eyes opened as he stretched, his precious face wrinkled up like a prune. A very cute prune that would have made her smile if not for the seriousness of their situation.

She glanced at the road and the bend on the other side of the dense forest, hoping to spy whatever was approaching. Pulling in a deep breath, she waited and watched as a horse and buggy came into view. She almost laughed with relief.

A gasp escaped her lips when she recognized the very handsome man driving the buggy. Without forethought, she ran from the forest, arriving at the roadway as the buggy approached.

The driver pulled up sharply on the reins. The horse pranced to a stop.

"Ezra, what are you doing here?"

His gaze softened when he saw her. Then, as if fearing someone was following her, he glanced into the woods in the direction from which she had just come and again at the road in front of them.

"What's wrong, Rosie? Did something happen?"

She quickly filled him in as he climbed from the buggy and hurried to her side.

"You're running away from home?" he asked.

"I'm leaving to protect my parents. Larry Wagner came to our house last night. He beat up my father. Thankfully, Mr. Wagner left."

"He was looking for you?"

She nodded, ashamed of the danger she had brought to her parents. "But the strange thing is that he knew my parents' names. Even more confusing is that they knew his."

"You are sure it was Larry Wagner?"

She nodded.

"Did he see you?"

"No, but my mother forbid me to go outside lest he be spying as he drove by. She wants me to be a prisoner in my own house." Rosie shook her head. "I cannot do that, Ezra. It is not the way I choose to live."

"Where are you going?"

"To visit my aunt Katherine. She is a good woman. Her daughter, Alice, married and moved to Ohio. I am hoping Katherine will take Joseph and me into her house until I can find a way to get to Ohio."

"Are you talking about Katherine Runnals, who lives higher up the mountain?" Ezra asked.

Rosie nodded. "You know my aunt?"

"I do. The road uphill is steep in places. Carrying Joseph and the pack on your back would be difficult. Let me take you there in my buggy."

She nodded. "Again you have come to my aid at my moment of most need. *Yah*, I will gratefully accept your offer."

He helped her into the seat and climbed in next to her. He touched her hand. "You are cold. The morning air is damp."

He reached behind the seat and pulled out a blanket. He threw it around her legs and then pulled a smaller lap quilt out and wrapped it over her shoulders.

In the pale morning light, Rosie noticed the delicate stitches on the quilt, close and tight, and the straight rows that marked a steady hand well-accustomed to wielding a needle and thread.

"The covering is much too beautiful to be out in the elements, Ezra. This quilt deserves a special spot in your home."

"I have others in the house. This one was made for the buggy."

"Your mother did the stitching?"

He nodded. "My sisters helped cut the fabric and stitched the pieces together on the machine, but my mother did the quilting. She sat each night near the fire, the fabric stretched on a small free-standing frame my *datt* made for her. She would sit for hours with her needle going in and out of the fabric."

"Is that how you remember her?"

Ezra flicked the reins. The buggy jerked into motion. He scooted closer to her and glanced at Joseph, who had fallen back asleep. "He is a good baby?"

"*Yah*, he is a good baby."

She pulled him closer and turned her gaze to the road. Ezra had ignored her question about his mother. Rosie's comment had been too personal. She should not bring up topics that caused Ezra pain. Her own parents were very much alive, for that she was grateful, yet recalling the beating her father had taken last night convinced her all the more that leaving home was for the best no matter how much she would miss her mother.

Would she miss her father? She glanced down at Joseph, who looked like a mix of William and her own *datt*. The two men who had been in Rosie's life. Now one was dead and the other was bruised and battered because of her. She was a bad influence and brought trouble to those who knew her.

She flicked her gaze to Ezra. Her stomach tightened. She knew so little about the grown man sitting next to her, but she recalled all too well the handsome boy she had often peered at over the top of her schoolbooks. Ezra had seemed oblivious to Rosie's presence, yet she remembered the way he helped the younger children and ensured the wood-burning stove was stoked and the fire burning bright. The other boys paid it little notice unless the teacher called on them, yet Ezra was quick to add logs or rearrange the wood to enhance the output of heat.

He glanced at her and lifted his eyebrows. "Did you say something?"

"I did not speak my thoughts aloud, but I was recalling your last year at school. I had not seen you since then until you saved me after my tumble down the hill."

"I would call that more than a tumble." His smile warmed her. "Plus there were a number of times when I saw you, but you did not have eyes to see me."

She raised her brow and tilted her head. "Did I ignore you?"

"You were more interested in someone else."

Now she understood. Ezra had seen her with William. Her cheeks burned with embarrassment as she tried to recall any time she had ignored Ezra. "I apologize for being impolite."

He held up a hand. "Did I lead you to believe that you were less than polite?" He smiled. "Your attention was turned to someone else. I used to think William MacIntosh was a fortunate man."

Ezra's words took her aback. She did not know how to respond, and so she turned to gaze deeply into the forest, wishing she was witty and bright and could make conversation instead of wanting to crawl in the back of the buggy and hide.

Surely, Ezra was exaggerating to make her feel better. He was that kind of man, one that would do anything to help a woman in need.

Which she was.

Gratitude. Again, her heart filled as she thought of his timely intervention today and yesterday. She had thanked him more than once. She would not become a clanging gong, as scripture said. Better to seal her lips so she would not embarrass herself further.

Again she heard a sound that was hard to distinguish. This time, the sound came from farther below on the mountain.

Ezra must have noticed the sound as well. He tilted his ear and glanced around the side of the buggy.

"Someone comes."

"Another buggy?" she asked, suddenly not concerned with giving voice to her thoughts.

He listened more intently. "I do not hear horses' hooves on the pavement. I hear a motorized vehicle."

"A car?"

He nodded and glanced into the dense woods that skirted the roadway. "Surely there is a path we could take deeper into the forest."

Rosie followed his gaze, but she saw only the thick undergrowth that would catch on the buggy's wheels and prevent its progression.

"Stop and let me off."

"What?" His eyes widened.

"Joseph and I will hide in the woods. The buggy cannot go there, but we can."

"I won't let you go on your own."

She touched his hand. "Be practical. If it is the man with the patch of white hair—if it is Larry Wagner—we cannot let him find me. If I hide, you can remain in the buggy. It is doubtful that he would harm you. Once he has driven past, we will join you in the buggy again."

Ezra seemed hesitant, but as the sound of the engine grew louder, he nodded. "I will come to get you once he has passed. You will be all right?"

She nodded. "Joseph and I will be fine."

Ezra helped her down from the buggy and watched as she hurried into the woods. Then, he climbed back to his seat and encouraged Bessie forward just as a vehicle—a white SUV—rounded the bend.

The driver tooted his horn. Ezra steered his mare to the edge of the road and watched as the SUV, the same one that had run Rosie off the road, drove past.

Ezra glanced at the woods, wishing he could see Rosie, but then if he saw her, the man with the patch of white hair could as well.

The SUV braked to a stop and then backed up. The driver's door opened and Larry Wagner, tall and muscular with a streak of white hair, hurried toward the buggy. "I'm looking for the Runnals home. Can you give me directions?"

"Is that Majorie Runnals for whom you are looking?" Ezra asked.

"Not Marjorie. Her first name is Katherine. She lives around here, but I'm not sure where."

"There is someone by that name in town." Ezra scratched his jaw. "Although on second thought, that person's name might be Christine Reynolds. Could that be the woman for whom you are looking?"

The guy shook his head. "I told you I'm looking for Katherine Runnals's home. Don't you Amish stick together and know everyone in the area?"

"I do not know all the Amish in town. Perhaps that is where she lives."

"Thanks for your help," the man said, his tone sharp and laced with sarcasm. He hurried back to his car, made a U-turn and drove off.

As soon as the car disappeared from sight, Ezra climbed from the buggy and ran into the woods.

"Rosie?" He looked left and then right, trying to find her in the dense underbrush. "Where are you?"

Heart in his throat, he ran farther, calling her name over and over again. Why didn't she answer him?

He had been foolish to let her hide on her own. Although she was not alone. She had Joseph, a tiny baby who could not protect himself. Now both of them had disappeared, and Ezra was to blame. His parents were gone, now a beautiful woman. His sister had been right this morning. Ezra never should have gotten involved. He had tried to help Rosie, but he had caused her harm instead of making her life safer. If he had been a real man, he would have found an area to hide the buggy and would have stayed with her and her child.

"Rosie?" He was frantic. Fear for her well-being climbed his spine and made him want to scream with rage.

"Why, *Gott*?" he said aloud.

"Ezra?"

She was standing near a large pine tree, Joseph still in her arms. He ran to her, unable to voice his feelings. Instead he opened his arms and pulled her close.

"What happened?" she asked.

He shook his head, confused by the mix of emotions that had welled up within him.

"Was it Mr. Wagner?"

"Yah." Ezra nodded. "He wanted to know where your aunt lived."

She gasped. "You told him?"

"I would not do that. Come. We must hurry. You cannot go to Katherine's house."

"But I have nowhere else to go."

"*Yah*, you do." He grabbed her hand. "Hurry."

"Where are you taking me, Ezra?"

"I'm taking you to my house at the top of the mountain. We will be able to see the road and anyone who might approach the house. You will be safe there."

At least that was Ezra's hope.

Chapter Eight

Rosie feared not only for her parents' safety, but also for her aunt's. Suppose Larry Wagner found Katherine's house? He had physically attacked her father. Rosie cringed thinking of what he might do to her sweet aunt.

"I'm worried, Ezra," she said once they had returned to the buggy.

"I have five brothers and sisters who will keep watch on the road heading up the mountain, Rosie. No one arrives at our house without someone in the family seeing their approach. As I told you, you will be safe with us."

She stared into his eyes. "I know you will protect me as best you can, but right now, I am worried about Katherine. Even though you did not provide directions to her house, someone else might. There are so few families who live on this mountain, I doubt Katherine would be hard to find."

"Wagner turned around and was headed down the mountain, Rosie. More than likely, he was going back to town."

"He may be stopping at my parents' house again." She

shook her head. "I do not think they would have mentioned Katherine to him so how did he know about her?"

"If he knows your parents, he might also know your aunt."

Another thought crossed her mind, and she cringed. "My employment paperwork at the nursing home." She grabbed Ezra's hand. "It asked for information about my next of kin and had a space for another point of contact. I filled Katherine's name into that blank. A contact phone number was requested, which she does not have. Thankfully, the form did not ask for an address."

"So if O'Donnell shared your information with Wagner, he would know about Katherine. These two men must be working together, but you cannot blame yourself, Rosie. How would you have known that the information on your employment application could get into the wrong hands?"

"I have to see Katherine. I will not be at peace unless I make sure she is safe. Plus she needs to know about Larry Wagner. Perhaps she could leave the area and visit her daughter over Christmas to remain safe."

"How terrible that we would think someone would hurt a woman, yet after what Wagner did to you, there is no telling what might befall her. You are being prudent and wise to want to ensure Katherine remains safe."

Ezra grabbed the reins. "My father built buggies, as you probably know."

She nodded.

"When his work was done and he was ready to deliver a buggy to the buyer, *Datt* would do a test ride. He made a path around our farm. It runs above your aunt's home. We can look down on it and hopefully stay out of sight in case the man is there."

"We can do that now?" she asked.

Ezra nodded. "The turnoff that will take us to the path is not far. It would be a wise choice to keep you safe as well. If the man returns this way, you might have to hide in the woods again, which is not something I want to have happen. By taking the path, we will stay off the main road and out of sight."

He flicked the reins and pointed in the distance. "The turnoff is not far."

Joseph stirred in Rosie's arms. To quiet the baby, she softly crooned a lullaby and smiled when he fell back to sleep.

"You sing like a songbird," Ezra said.

Embarrassed by the compliment, she kept her eyes on Joseph.

"My words bother you?" Ezra asked.

"I could never be bothered by nice things you might tell me, but I do not wish to be prideful."

"I doubt you could be that, Rosie. Besides, it is important to recognize your own gifts from *Gott* and thank him for them."

"I do that, Ezra, but I do not recall anyone paying me compliments. My mother wanted me to be free of prideful thoughts. She thought compliments were frivolous. I was to accept who I was and not wish for more than what *Gott* had given me."

"And your father?"

"I am not sure how he felt. He was not one to express his feelings, except if I did something that brought his disapproval, which I hate to admit was more often than I would have liked."

She adjusted the blanket around her sleeping child. "Even his gaze was often filled with accusation, as if he was waiting for me to make a mistake. I tried to be a dutiful daughter, yet I failed frequently."

Ezra shook his head with regret. "Amish fathers are the heads of their families, and they usually take delight in their children. I am sorry you did not have a better life growing up."

"But it was the only life I knew, Ezra, so how could I say that it was bad? It was what it was."

"Yet you did not feel love."

She glanced away, trying to sort through the mix of feelings. Had she felt love from her parents?

"Perhaps that is what I was searching for all my life."

She had made the wrong decision concerning William, she refused to add. Humiliation washed over her as she thought of the extent of her mistakes and the errors of her ways. She had turned from all she had been taught and run after a man who had promised her so much. Truth be known, the pretty jewelry and things of the world were not what she had sought. Instead it had been love, only she had learned too late that what William wanted to give her was not love...anything but.

"Did you ever make a mistake that you wish you could change, Ezra, yet if you did, that which is most precious to you would have to be given away as well?"

She glanced down at her sleeping child, who had been the good brought from her foolishness. She would do nothing to change her life as his mother. Surely that would be hard for a practical man like Ezra to understand.

She sighed. "You have made me share more than you wanted or needed to hear. Have you this effect on other women who accept rides in your buggy?"

"If by other women, you mean my sisters, I would

say they are more than willing to share what is on their minds, even when I do not want to hear it all. They are strong women, perhaps too strong." He laughed. "I wonder if there will be any man determined enough to accept my fourteen-year-old sister into his heart. Belinda is forthright and speaks her mind whenever she chooses."

"An Amish wife should stand next to her husband but never in front of him." Rosie intoned the saying she had heard often within the Amish community.

Ezra smiled. "It was something my own mother said, along with the phrase 'equally yoked,' which she claimed referred to the balance between husband and wife, both working together and in step as they went through life and raised their family."

"My mother did not walk next to my father," Rosie said. "She walked behind him."

Glancing at the passing countryside, Rosie wondered why she was sharing so much with Ezra. She did not want to disrespect her mother, although she questioned how telling the truth could be disrespectful. Still, there was something about Ezra that made her lower the barriers she usually had in place. A mistake on her part, no doubt. She wanted to trust him, but she had trusted the wrong man before and did not want to make a similar mistake again.

"The turnoff is just ahead." Ezra glanced back, checking the road they had traveled. "Even though I am sure Larry Wagner is heading to town, taking the back path is still a wise choice. There is a northern access to the mountain, and he could come around that way, although it is doubtful."

"I am worried about Katherine."

"We will pass on the hill above your aunt's house and will be able to see if a car is in her driveway."

"And if the white SUV is there? What will we do then, Ezra?"

"We will decide what to do when and if we see his car."

"If I had gone to Katherine's house—" Rosie pulled in a deep breath and glanced down at Joseph.

"You are thinking of that which has not happened. Beside, you are not with Katherine." He smiled. "You are here in the buggy with me."

She adjusted the blanket around her baby and nodded. "Yes, I am with you."

Ezra chuckled. "From the struggle I hear in your voice, this is not a good thing?"

She glanced at him and laughed.

His heart leaped in his chest at the sound, then abruptly, he turned his gaze back to the path, startled by his reaction and unsure of the mix of emotions that were playing havoc with him. How could her laughter cause him such confusion?

Rosie seemed unaware of the effect she was having on him.

"The mountain is beautiful," she said, staring into the distance. "I have not taken the time to notice how tall the trees are here. Farther down the mountain, where I live, the land is more for farming. Trees have been removed and the ground cultivated for planting. I wish there were more rustic areas like this where I live."

Ezra looked anew at the forest that surrounded them. "My father, brothers and I would hunt near here and come home with fresh meat for my mother to cure and eventually serve. Our hunting trips were good memories I think too rarely about these days."

He smiled ruefully, recalling the jovial mood his father would be in whenever he and the boys hunted. "It is good for a man to be with nature. I must explore the forests more often myself."

Rosie pulled the blanket around Joseph.

"You are cold?" Ezra asked.

"A little."

"It is always cooler in the wooded areas. We are almost to the ridgeline, where we will leave the heavy tree cover and emerge into the sunlight."

"And will we see my aunt's house?"

"*Yah*, soon."

"I am worried, Ezra."

"But your worry does not change whether the man is with your aunt or not. My mother used to say that we will cross that bridge when we come to it."

"My mother said the same." She glanced down. "I will probably say it to Joseph, as well."

"We humans allow worry and fear to have dominance in our lives."

She tilted her head. "I would not think you worry about anything, Ezra. You seem assured of where you stand in life."

Rosie did not realize what he carried within his heart and the weight that had settled on his shoulders a year and four months ago, a weight that would stay with him throughout his life.

"There." He pointed to a small white house, nestled on the hillside. "That is the house for which the man was searching."

"Aunt Katherine's house." Rosie smiled. "We visited often when I was young."

"She is a good woman. Katherine and my mother were friends."

"Then go to her house, Ezra. Talk to her. Tell her to beware of the man with the streak of white hair."

He looked at Rosie for a long moment. "You could tell her yourself."

"And if Mr. Wagner comes to her house, what will she do? She would not want to lie and might reveal where I am. You go, but do not mention that I will be staying at your house." Rosie touched his arm. "Please. For me."

Her eyes were so blue, and her hand, gripping his arm, made his chest tighten. What was it about this woman that had such an effect on him?

He pulled the buggy into a cluster of pine trees situated near an abandoned barn. "I will do as you ask. Stay here, Rosie. No one can see you from the road."

"Be careful, Ezra."

"I will return soon." He jumped to the ground and started down the hill. Halfway to the house, he glanced back. Rosie had climbed from the buggy and was peering around the side of the old barn. His heart jolted as their eyes connected for one long moment before he turned back to the path and hurried toward the house.

Rosie was taking over his life. Too quickly. Two days ago he had been his own man, then he had seen her ride past the hardware store. Something had snapped in him, bringing back all the memories of their time together in the schoolhouse. Rosie had never shown interest in him and probably thought of Ezra as merely an older boy who struggled with being Amish.

What had been wrong with him then?

Something was wrong with him now, but it did not involve his upset with the Amish way. It had to do with a pretty girl with big eyes who was too serious. Why would Ezra be interested in such a woman?

He did not know why. All he knew was that he was interested—very interested—in Rosie.

Joseph's eyes blinked open. Rosie smiled at her baby and lifted the little one onto her shoulder. "Do not fuss, Joseph. We need to be quiet while we are close to Aunt Katherine's house. She could be in danger, and Ezra is warning her."

The baby cooed and chewed on his hand. Rosie rocked him back and forth to keep the baby happy, and all the while her gaze was on Ezra, now standing on Katherine's back porch.

He knocked on the door a number of times and then hurried around to the front of the house.

Was Katherine not home?

As Rosie waited for Ezra to reappear, she noticed movement on the road below. Her heart stopped. The white SUV was heading up the mountain.

She glanced at her aunt's house, searching for Ezra. He must be oblivious to the danger that approached.

Joseph whined. She patted and rocked and shushed the baby. "You need to be very quiet."

The little one tugged a strand of hair free from her bun and put it in his mouth. "Oh, sweet baby, that is not good for you to eat."

Rosie pulled her hair from his reach, hoping it would not cause an outburst from Joseph and somehow alert Wagner.

The car continued up the hill.

Where was Ezra?

The palms of her hands were wet. She wiped them on her skirt.

The baby started to fuss. "Shhh, Joseph."

Vulnerable and exposed, Rosie's pulse raced as she watched the SUV turn into Katherine's drive.

She had to do something to protect her baby, but where could she hide to keep Joseph safe?

Chapter Nine

Holding Joseph with one hand, Rosie grabbed the reins and guided the mare and buggy into the dilapidated barn. She pushed the door closed and peered through a crack in the wall of the old structure.

Mr. Wagner climbed from his SUV. He slammed the door, sending a jolt to her heart. With quick, determined steps, he walked to Katherine's back door and knocked. When no one answered, he put his hands on his hips and turned to stare at the hillside. He shrugged his broad shoulders, left the porch and climbed the hill, heading straight to where Rosie and Joseph were hiding.

Her heart pounded nearly out of her chest. She rocked the baby and held the reins with her other hand, needing both Joseph and Bessie to remain quiet. One cry from Joseph or a flick of Bessie's tail could alert Wagner to their whereabouts.

He approached the barn. Rosie held her breath. *Please, Gott, protect us.*

Joseph stretched his arms and sighed.

She froze, fearing Wagner had heard.

Rosie peered through the slats that covered the window. The man stood poised at the top of the hill, near the barn. He turned his ear, listening.

As she watched, he reached for the barn door.

Tears burned Rosie's eyes. In another second, he would find them.

"May I help you?"

Hearing Ezra's voice, Rosie shifted her gaze to where he stood near Katherine's house.

"You're the guy in the buggy," Wagner shouted back. "I thought you didn't know where Katherine Runnals lived."

Ezra ignored the comment. "What do you want?"

"I'm looking for a young Amish woman with blond hair. She worked at Shady Manor, the nursing home in town. She needs to pick up her paycheck."

"You work there?" Ezra asked.

"I know the manager and told him I would help locate his missing employee."

"Buses leave from town every day. Your missing Amish woman is probably on her way to another state. Florida is a favorite destination for many Amish in the area."

Wagner sniffed and shook his head with frustration. He glanced back at the barn and pulled in a deep breath before heading back to his car.

Rosie's knees went weak. She let out the breath she had been holding and cuddled Joseph closer to her heart.

"Thank You, *Gott*," she said. "Thank You for providing this barn in which to hide, and thank You for sending Ezra to distract Mr. Wagner just a second before he would have found us."

Once again, Ezra had come to their rescue.

As soon as the SUV turned out of the drive and headed back down the mountain, Ezra ran up the hill toward the cluster of pines. His heart stopped. The buggy was gone. So was Rosie.

Hearing a weak cry, Ezra hurried along the path, following the sound that grew stronger. The cry—a baby's cry—was coming from the dilapidated barn.

He threw open the door.

Rosie gasped with surprise.

Ezra ran to her, his heart nearly bursting with relief. "I feared Wagner would find you."

"He almost did. But *Gott* provided."

Ezra was not sure whether *Gott* had intervened, but he was overcome with gratitude that Rosie and Joseph were safe.

"What about my aunt?"

"No one answered the door so she must not be home." Ezra motioned Rosie toward the door. "We must leave the barn and go farther up the mountain. You will be safe at my house."

"Are you sure?" Her eyes were filled with questions.

"You can trust me," he said, hoping she believed him. After everything that had happened, he wondered if she trusted anyone.

"Perhaps we need to involve law enforcement, Rosie. The police in this area are not helpful. Some say they have their hand out and their eyes closed. It is different in Willkommen, some miles from here. The town has a sheriff who understands the Amish way. He was injured some time ago and is still recuperating, but an acting sheriff is filling his spot, and is well-thought-of by *Englisch* and Amish alike. We can talk to him if need be."

Rosie shook her head. "Not now. I do not want to involve anyone else at this time. Mr. Wagner will eventually give up his search for me, Ezra. If I can stay with you and your brothers and sisters for a short time, that will be a help. I must contact Katherine's daughter about a place to stay in Ohio. Perhaps she will take me in until I can find a job there."

"Ohio is a long way from Georgia."

Rosie nodded. "This is true, which means a long way from Larry Wagner."

And a long way from Ezra. He did not want to think about Rosie leaving the mountain. To go so far away would end any hope Ezra had of getting to know her better. Pretty and courageous, Rosie would find an Amish man in Ohio who would take interest in her. She would forget about all she left behind, including Ezra.

After the adrenaline rush of nearly being confronted by Larry Wagner, Rosie now sat in the buggy next to Ezra, feeling totally depleted. She also felt a bone-chilling cold that was due to the drop in temperature, and also to the realization of how twisted her life had become.

Joseph was awake but content and warm in her arms. Tears stung her eyes when she thought of what could have happened to her child.

"Ezra, you have done so much for me, but I have something to ask of you."

He must have heard the seriousness in her voice because he pulled up on the reins and stopped the buggy. Turning to her, he nodded as if encouraging her to continue.

"If—if something happens to me—"

"What are you talking about, Rosie?" His face was washed with a mix of worry and concern.

She raised her hand to stop him so she could explain what she needed.

"I am worried about Joseph. If something happens to me, will you ensure he is reunited with either my mother or Katherine?"

"Rosie, you and Joseph will both be safe at my house. Wagner thinks you have left the area. You do not need to worry."

"I fear you are too optimistic, Ezra. As much as I appreciate your help, and I do so much, I still must know that my son will not be abandoned. He is all I have, and I am all he has. To find peace, I must know he will be cared for."

Ezra nodded. He reached for her hand. His eyes were as blue as the nearby lake, flecked with gold and filled with tenderness that was like a balm to her troubled soul.

"Joseph will be well cared for, this I promise. We have a full house at the mountaintop, but we always have room for more. If your mother or aunt are not able to care for him, he will come into my family. You will see how quickly my brothers and sisters accept him."

He pointed ahead. "The house is not far. Shake off your concerns. My family will welcome you, Rosie. They will welcome little Joseph, too."

True to his word, Ezra guided the buggy around the bend in the path, where she caught sight of a rambling house that sat almost at the top of the mountain. An expansive yard surrounded the home and a drive led from the road to the wide back porch. A tin roof stretched over the rear of the house and the door that, she surmised, led to the kitchen.

"The two younger children are at school, but Susan, Aaron and Belinda should be at home." He pulled the horse to a stop, climbed from the buggy and hurried to the far side to help Rosie down.

Carrying Joseph in her arms, she glanced back at the panoramic view of the valley that spread out in front of the house. "It is so peaceful. The view reminds me of a painting of the Alps that hangs in Shady Manor."

"I have heard many things about these mountains, but never has anyone compared them to the Alps."

"The beauty, Ezra. It takes my breath way."

"Which is not good. I want you to keep breathing."

She laughed, seeing the seriousness he tried to exude while the joviality of his voice gave away his true feelings.

She glanced at the far side of the property to where a workshop stood. Stoltz Buggy Shop, the sign over the door read.

"Your father was well-known for his craftsmanship. I have heard my father mention his work. I am sorry about what happened."

Ezra nodded, his frivolity gone, replaced with a tightness that revealed the pain he still carried. His parents had been murdered sixteen months earlier, if Rose recalled clearly. Not long before Will was killed. Life had changed for both Rose and Ezra at that time. Darkness had overshadowed each of their lives. She still felt that darkness no matter how much she wanted to move into the light.

She glanced again at the road that twisted up the mountain. No matter what Ezra said, she was vulnerable even here.

"What will stop the man from finding me, Ezra?"

He pointed to the roadway that snaked up the mountain. "We will see his car, Rosie. He will not approach us without warning."

"And if he comes at night when we are sleeping?"

"Then I will ward him off and keep him away from you. You have my promise."

The door to the kitchen burst open and a pretty girl in her late teens stepped onto the porch. "You have brought company," she said, stretching out her hand to grip Rosie's. "Welcome. I am Susan, the oldest girl in the family."

"This is Rose Glick and her son, Joseph. They will be staying with us for a period of time."

A hint of confusion washed over the younger woman's face before she pointed to the kitchen. "It is cold. Let us enter the house. I have hot coffee and cinnamon rolls that have just come from the oven. You are hungry?"

Rosie had thought only of Joseph's hunger and not her own, but the mention of fresh-baked rolls made her realize how hungry she was.

"Both sound inviting, Susan. You are as generous as your brother."

She followed Susan into the house and was taken with the well-appointed kitchen, the quality of the oak table, sideboard and dry sink, as well as the furnishings in the main room, visible from where she stood near the door.

"Come in. The heat from the stove will warm you along with the coffee."

"Could I wash my hands first?"

"Of course." Susan stretched out her arms. "Let me hold your son while you remove your cape. You will find a basin and pitcher of water in the small room to the right."

"You've been so kind." As much as Rosie did not want to leave Joseph, she saw the eagerness and excitement in Susan's blue eyes as she held out her hands.

Joseph loved people and had never been shy around strangers, so Rosie felt sure he would go to Susan readily. And that was the case. "I shall be back momentarily."

Rosie washed and dried her hands and returned soon thereafter to retrieve her little one. She found Joseph sitting in a high chair that looked handcrafted. Seeing her as she entered the kitchen, he kicked his legs and his hands waved in the air. He laughed and his merriment filled the kitchen and brought a smile not only to her face, but also to her heart.

"You have a big boy chair," Rosie said to her son. She glanced at Susan. "The craftsmanship is lovely."

"Our father made the high chair for Ezra, but all of us used it. We keep it in the pantry for when friends visit with small children."

"Thank you for letting Joseph sit in such a special chair. You are both very thoughtful."

"I gave him a tiny morsel of roll," Susan admitted. "I hope you do not mind."

Rosie smiled at the powdered sugar icing that ringed his lips. She stepped closer and bent down to smile into his face. "You love Susan's rolls, I can tell." Taking a napkin from the table, she wiped his mouth. "Susan knows what you want before you even know yourself."

"She has a gift for hospitality," Ezra said. His love for his sister was evident, and that fact only made Rosie like him even more.

"I will pour coffee." Susan started to rise.

"Let me." Rosie headed to the stove and lifted the coffeepot from the rear burner. She filled one of the cups on the counter. "Coffee, Ezra?"

"Please, but you did not come here to work."

Rosie laughed. "Pouring coffee is hardly work, but work is good. I do not like to have idle hands."

"You sound like our mother," Susan reflected. "She did not want to rest until night came and it was time to sleep. She had more energy than all the rest of us together."

Rosie smiled at the shared memory. "I am sure you have inherited her appreciation for work. Your home is spotless. With such a large family, this is sometimes hard to do."

"We all work together," Susan said sweetly.

"Your parents would be proud of you." Rosie looked at Ezra. "It is hard to step into the parental role."

"No one can take their place," Susan said. Her focus was on Joseph, and she failed to see the look of knowing that passed between Ezra and Rosie.

"Ezra is a good older brother," Susan continued. "He runs the farm well. Aaron is a help. David as well, although David sometimes thinks he can do things by himself."

"He is wise beyond his years in many ways," Ezra acknowledged, "while still a boy at other times. I did not want the younger ones to lose their innocence. Life is hard. Losing parents is especially tragic, but they have handled the loss bravely." He glanced down at his coffee. "Sometimes I think they fared better than I have."

Susan patted his hand. "They feel secure with your guidance, Ezra. You have given up your freedom, the freedom you sought. This has been one of the many gifts you have given the family."

He drank deeply from his cup and then pushed back from the table. "I must unhitch the mare and get to the chores. The day will be gone if I do not start working."

He glanced at Susan. "You will show Rosie to the guest room."

"Yes, of course." She smiled at Rosie. "You might want to rest for a bit. Joseph can stay with me."

Much as Rosie did not want to be a burden to Ezra's family, she appreciated the offer, and from Joseph's laughter, it was evident Susan had stolen his heart.

"You do not mind?" Rosie asked.

"I would not offer if it was not something that I wanted to do."

"Perhaps resting for a few minutes would be good. But if Joseph becomes unsettled or too much for you, let me know."

"The guest room is at the top of the stairs to the left. The linens on the bed are fresh."

Rosie sipped the rest of her coffee and carried the cup to the sink. Looking out the window, she could see the road below. If what Ezra said was true, the family would know if anyone approached the mountaintop from the road. Larry Wagner would not surprise them. Tonight she would worry more about her safety, but now, in the light of day, she felt secure.

She turned and found Ezra staring at her. His gaze burned into her as if he wanted to tell her something more.

Her heart lurched in response, causing a wave of concern to wash over her. She might be secure from Larry Wagner today, but Ezra was another problem. The way she responded to his closeness and his concern for her well-being brought another fear to her heart. How could she leave the mountain and Ezra and head north, knowing she would never see his welcoming smile or understanding eyes again?

She had noticed him in school years earlier, although she had not, at the time, understood her own attraction to the handsome boy three years her senior. Now she realized the truth of those feelings. Ezra was a *gut* man. He would make some woman a fine husband, but that woman was not Rosie. She had to put Joseph's needs first, which meant leaving the mountain and everyone she knew to start a new life. A life without Ezra.

Chapter Ten

Ezra tackled the chores with a vengeance, as if wanting to fight off the feelings for Rosie that were taking hold inside him. He also wanted to crush Larry Wagner, who had caused her so much pain. He cleaned the stalls and the tack, rubbing the saddles with soap and wiping them clean until they glistened in the light from the window.

A fence needed mending on the distant pasture, but he did not want to stay away from the house for a long time, lest something happen while he was gone. He remembered too well the terrible tragedy that had befallen his parents.

A robbery gone wrong, the police had proclaimed. *Very wrong...* Ezra's stomach tightened. Their murder had been due to his own desire to live life to the fullest. Only he had brought pain and grief to himself and his family.

Foolish and stupid. He felt as slimy as the muck he raked from the stalls.

Worried that the cattle would find the hole in the fencing, he saddled one of the geldings and rode to the distant pasture. Working quickly, he fixed the fence temporarily to keep the animals contained.

As he galloped back to the house, his heart nearly stopped when he saw a car heading up the hill. White, but not a SUV. He breathed out the deep breath he had been holding, slipped from the saddle and guided the horse into the barn minutes before the car pulled to a stop.

A man dressed in a blue uniform stepped from the unmarked vehicle. He was in his early forties with a thick neck and deep-set eyes. He nodded to Ezra.

"I'm Officer Vincetti, and I'm trying to find a woman who worked in town at the Shady Manor nursing home. She's Amish with blond hair and blue eyes. Her name is Rosie Glick."

"This is the Stoltz farm. Perhaps you could check in town for the address of the Glick family."

The officer nodded. "I am aware of who you are, but I hoped you would have information about Ms. Glick."

"She has done something wrong?"

"That's what I need to find out."

Ezra said nothing and hoped his silence might encourage the officer to provide more information. Thankfully his plan brought success.

"Ms. Glick has been accused of breaking into a secured area of patient records," the officer volunteered. "Some drugs have also gone missing, which is why I need to talk to her."

"Has she been accused of taking the medication?"

"The manager of the nursing home has mentioned her possible involvement."

"And this man is to be trusted or is he overlooking his own mishandling of medication?" Ezra asked.

The cop raised an eyebrow. "The manager is well-thought-of in town, Mr. Stoltz. Is there something you would like to share with me?"

"Only that the Amish make easy targets. We keep to ourselves, and our ways are sometimes hard for the *Englisch* to understand. Integrity is the hallmark of an Amish man or woman. I wonder if you are looking in the wrong community for the thief."

"Do you know anything about Rosie Glick?" the officer persisted.

"I know that if she is Amish, she can be trusted."

"If you see Rosie Glick, let me know." The officer handed him a business card.

"I do not have a phone on which to call you."

Vincetti nodded. "I know many of the Amish have cell phones or telephone booths near their property. You should be able to contact me."

"I appreciate your attempt to rid the town of crime, but this time of year, many Amish visit family or go on vacations. Pinecraft, Florida, is a well-known destination. Perhaps you should search there."

The officer glanced at the house and honed in on the guest-room window, which made Ezra uneasy. Hopefully, Rosie was asleep and not peering from the window.

The door to the kitchen opened. Ezra swallowed hard. He wanted to warn Rosie to stay inside, but instead of Rosie, Susan appeared.

"Is something wrong, Ezra?" she asked.

"Nothing, Susan. It is cold out here. Go into the house."

The policeman watched her go back inside. Then he rubbed his chin. "As I recall, you ran with a bunch of bad boys in town. People say you changed after your parents died, but I'm not so sure. If there's something you're not telling me, I'll find out. Do you understand?"

Ezra continued to stare at Vincetti until he climbed into his sedan and drove back down the hill.

Ezra let out a deep sigh of relief and glanced at the guest-room window, where Rosie stood staring down at him, her gaze filled with questions.

Ezra had told her she did not need to worry, but he was wrong. A case of tampering with records and stealing drugs was being made against her. A very strong case.

What have I done bringing her here?

He turned and walked into the barn, trying to sort through the mystery that was Rosie Glick. Surely, she was not guilty of criminal activity. But one thing was certain—Rosie Glick was keeping secrets.

Rosie's stomach churned. She rubbed her hand across her midsection, hoping to quell her upset. She had awakened to the sound of an automobile pulling into the drive. Fearing it was a white SUV driven by the man who kept coming after her, she had thrown back the quilt, climbed from the bed and hurried to the window.

Relieved not to see an SUV, she soon realized the visitor was anything but friendly, yet Ezra seemed to chat with him as if they were buddies. Were they? If so, had he told the policeman about the woman hiding out in his guest room? A woman suspected of tampering with patient records and stealing patient medication? Drugs that could be sold on the street?

She raked her hand through her hair, unfazed when her bun came loose and her hair fell askew over her shoulders. How foolish of her to place her trust in Ezra. The boy she remembered had a sharp edge at times, in spite of the help he gave the teacher with the stove and other chores. He never seemed totally happy and would often stare out the window as if willing himself to be anywhere but school.

Like Rosie, he had run with a bunch of *Englisch-ers*. She understood that wanderlust that made everything outside the Amish way look inviting. How quickly she had succumbed to its lure. But she had even more quickly realized her mistake.

Now she embraced the Amish way and wanted nothing to do with anything of the world. She was not sure where Ezra stood. He had come home to care for his siblings, and that was admirable. But where was his heart? Was it still on the other side of the divide between the *plain* life and that which was *fancy*?

Plus, she feared he had contacted the police, although she did not know how. Did he have a cell phone?

Her hands trembled as she tried to redo her hair, bemoaning the strands that refused to comply. They were as she had been in her younger years, rebellious and hard to handle. No wonder her father had not welcomed her back into their home. Although even if Joseph did something to upset her, she could never turn her back on her own child.

She hurried all the more to tidy her hair, before she slipped the *kapp* over her bun and scurried out of the room, needing to see her baby and hold him in her arms. Joseph was the only one she trusted. He gave meaning to her life. She would do anything for her child, yet she had left him with a stranger, nice though Susan was. Tears burned Rosie's eyes. How weak she had been, choosing sleep over the security of her little one.

Rosie ran down the stairs, nearly tripping over her

feet, which would not move fast enough. Breathless, she bounded into the kitchen, almost ready to cry.

Ezra pushed open the door and stepped inside, bringing with him the clean, sweet-smelling fresh air of the outdoors. His gaze caught hers, questions filling his eyes, but she saw something else that tangled around her spine and made her stop short. Not fear, not worry, but attraction that was raw and uninvited. His look made her heart lurch and her chest tighten and a delicious warmth spread over her.

"You are in a hurry?" he asked.

She glanced around the kitchen. "Where is Joseph?"

"In here, Rosie." Susan's voice sounded from the living area.

Rosie rounded the corner and laughed when she saw Joseph standing up, holding onto Susan's hands and taking feeble steps forward. His giggles made her fear flee. Still awash with the warmth from Ezra's glance, Rosie felt weak yet also confused about being in this strange man's house.

"Joseph is walking," Susan said with joy. "He is so proud of his accomplishments."

Unable to contain her relief, Rosie clapped her hands and reached for her baby boy, drawing him close before she twirled him around the room. "You are so adventurous, trying to walk with Susan. I was worried *Mamm* had slept too long. In fact if I had slept longer you would probably be running around the downstairs without me being able to catch you."

Joseph giggled and wrapped his arms though her unkempt hair. Then he placed his wet mouth against her cheek in the sweetest kiss she had ever received.

Laughing with contentment, she stopped to enjoy

the moment and then glanced up to see Ezra staring at both of them. The pain on his face confused her. Was he jealous of her son or upset that she was having fun with her baby?

She hugged Joseph closer, unwilling to let her moment of happiness be spoiled by a man she did not understand.

She and Joseph would leave the mountain as soon as possible. First, she must talk to Katherine and find information about Alice. Then she and Joseph would take the next bus to Ohio. They would make their new home there, far from the man in the SUV and far from Ezra and the confusion he made her feel.

Ezra stomped across the kitchen, ready to go outside again and head for the pasture. He had been foolish to think Rosie needed twenty-four-hour protection. A policeman had come to the house, but he had not found her. Hopefully, Ezra's hinting that she was headed to Florida would make them look south and not at the top of the mountain.

When he reached for the kitchen door, it flew open and David and Mary hurried inside with books in their arms. Both of them had rosy cheeks and windblown hair.

"Ezra," they both squealed, throwing themselves into his arms. Their warm welcome pushed away the sorrow he had felt seeing Rosie embrace her little Joseph. Sorrow had welled up within him thinking of his own parents, who had encircled him with their arms when he was young. The parents who had been murdered because of him so that none of the children would know the care and concern that came from a loving *mamm* and *datt*.

He dropped to his knees and drew his siblings closer.

"We both did well on our math tests," David boasted. "Mary made one mistake, and I made none."

"You are star students." Ezra felt a swell of pride, as if he was their father.

"Teacher says we must be working hard at home to learn our lessons so well," Mary said, her eyes wide.

"Your teacher is right," Ezra agreed, knowing both children took their studies seriously.

"Can Miss Gingrich come for dinner sometime, Ezra? She is very pretty." His little sister's eyes widened, and she nodded as she spoke as if to underscore the validity of what she said.

"Miss Gingrich is a pretty lady," Ezra replied, "but we will wait for a bit before we invite her."

"Why?"

He smiled at Mary's upset. "Because we have visitors."

"Where are they?" She pushed past him and stopped at the threshold to the main room. No doubt, she had expected a familiar face and was taken aback seeing Rosie and Joseph.

"My name is Mary." She introduced herself to Rosie. "I am seven years old."

"It is nice to meet you. I am Rosie and this is Joseph. He is eight months old. Your sister Susan has been teaching him to walk."

Mary stepped closer. "Will you let him walk so I can see?"

Joseph cooed at Mary and reached for her as if an instant connection had been made between them. As Ezra watched, Rosie placed Joseph on the floor and then encouraged him to stand while she held his hands.

He took two steps forward, giggled at Mary and then dropped to the floor and crawled toward her.

"Looks like he prefers his old mode of transportation," Rosie laughed.

Mary sat on the floor and held out her arms. Joseph crawled into her lap, looking proud of himself as he smiled first at Rosie and then at Mary.

"He likes me." The little girl laughed.

"He does," Rosie agreed.

David was more unassuming than his sister. He glanced at Ezra as if for support and then turned his gaze to Rosie.

She motioned him forward. "You must have a name."

"His name is David," Mary volunteered.

"Joseph would like to play with you, too, David," Rosie declared.

The boy ran to the corner and grabbed a few wooden blocks. "We can build a tower." He dumped the scraps of wood on the floor and started to stack them. Joseph grabbed a piece and waved it in the air before he dropped it on top of the other blocks.

As the children laughed, Rosie joined Ezra in the kitchen. "You have a lovely family," she told him.

"You have yet to meet Aaron and Belinda," he said. "They will be home soon."

"I am sure they are as enchanting as the others."

"*Enchanting* is not how I think of my family."

"Perhaps because you are so close to them and do not see the specialness of each of them. You are a fortunate man, Ezra."

Although he knew that to be true, at times he would not accept the goodness that surrounded him and made him feel even worse for the pain he had caused his family.

"I appreciate your comment, Rosie."

She rubbed her arm as if feeling ill at ease. Glancing again at the children, she smiled before turning back to him. "I saw you talking to the police officer. Did you call him?"

Ezra heard accusation in her voice. "Why would I do that?" he asked.

"To find out more about me perhaps?"

"I know all I need to know about you, Rosie, and I believe everything you have told me. The policeman stopped here on his own."

"Was he looking for me?"

Ezra could not hide the truth from her. "He was looking for you, *yah*."

"What did you tell him?"

"That you were probably on a bus heading south."

"Did he believe you?"

"I do not know. The manager of the nursing home told him you broke into patient records and that medication was stolen."

"He will arrest me if he finds me."

"The police want to question you, but as I told you before, the Amish do not trust the local police. If we go to Willkommen—"

She shook her head. "I want nothing to do with the police."

"I am not sure how long it will be before someone sees you, Rosie."

She bit her lip. "Earlier you assured me of my safety if I came here to stay with your family. Now you realize I am placing all of you in danger."

"I did not say that. I am worried about you. Would it not be better to involve law enforcement we could trust?"

She nodded. "If we could trust them. I am not willing to put my life and my child's life in the hands of someone I do not know."

"The police took you home after you were freed from the root cellar."

"You know the story?"

"Only the part I read in the papers."

"My memory is not always good," she admitted. "So much happened. Yes, an officer took me home, but my father was not happy about my homecoming or what the officer said to him. I do not want any involvement with them again. If this is something you cannot condone, Ezra, then I am ready to go elsewhere."

He almost laughed at her sincerity, knowing she had nowhere to go except her aunt's house, where she would be even more vulnerable.

"You can stay here, Rosie, for as long as you need to. As I said earlier, I will do everything I can to keep you safe. I did not call the police, nor will I involve any law enforcement unless you request that I do so."

He grabbed his hat from the peg by the door. "You may question my integrity, but I will not cause you pain, at least if I can help it. I have made mistakes, *yah*. But I feel you know about mistakes, Rosie, and carry a similar pain. Nothing will make me disparage you or undermine your trust."

Chapter Eleven

The smells of bacon, sizzling in a skillet, and fresh-baked biscuits hot from the oven woke Rosie with a start the next morning.

She rubbed her eyes and pulled herself from bed, realizing she had slept more soundly than she had in months.

Peering into the portable crib Sandra had found in the basement, Rosie smiled, seeing Joseph's sweet face. His mouth opened and closed as if searching for food. He would wake soon, ready for breakfast.

She dressed and got Joseph ready for the new day before heading downstairs. Susan greeted her with a big smile before her attention turned to Joseph. "How is that big boy who wants to walk?"

He giggled in reply and kicked his feet.

"Let me get him settled in the high chair, Susan. He needs to eat to get energy for his walking exercise today."

"You are too precious," Susan said, bending over him, making him laugh even more. "There is a sippy cup in the cabinet, if you want him to use it. I have a pot of oatmeal on the stove."

Rosie appreciated the offers. "He would love oatmeal. I will cut up a portion of a biscuit into little bites and fill the sippy cup with water."

"Bananas are in the pantry, if he likes fruit."

"What does he not like?" Rosie laughed.

"He is a big boy. Does he take after his father?"

Rosie hesitated, then shook off her uneasiness. "He looks like both sides of the family. Speaking of family, where are the children?"

"Tending to their chores. They will come inside soon."

"Shall I pour milk for David and Mary?"

"Please, I appreciate the help. Belinda is checking the henhouse for more eggs. She should be here soon."

"I enjoyed talking with her and Aaron over dinner last night. They both seem to know what they want for the future and are committed to staying in town and staying Amish."

"That is due to Ezra. He has worked hard to make sure they understand everything that is good about the Amish way."

"It is what Ezra believes?" Rosie asked.

Susan glanced at her for a long moment. "I am not sure for himself, but for them, it is the best path."

"I know he got involved with the *Englisch*."

Susan nodded. "In his *rumspringa*, only it lasted longer than anyone expected. He stayed away from home and rarely returned to see *Mamm* and *Datt*. They did not expect such actions from their firstborn son, but Ezra needed to do what was right for himself."

"And now?"

"You will have to ask him."

Something Rosie would not do. "Will you be at home today?"

Susan nodded. "*Yah*. There is something you need?"

"I need to talk to a nurse with whom I worked. But I do not want to take Joseph. I need someone to watch him. Would you be interested?"

"Of course, I would love to take care of him. He is so sweet. He has his mother's disposition."

Rosie smiled, appreciating Susan's statement.

"Will you ring the dinner bell?" Susan asked. "It will call the family. I do not want the breakfast to get cold."

Rosie stepped onto the porch and found the metal gong hanging near the large, steel triangle. She hit the gong against the triangle, enjoying the mellow sound of metal on metal. For a fleeting moment, she thought of calling her own family to breakfast.

Ezra hurried from the barn and stopped when he saw her. His face broke into a wide grin. "I feared something was wrong."

"Nothing is wrong except your breakfast is getting cold."

"I will gather the children."

She liked the sound of the comment, thinking of her own children hurrying inside after doing the chores with their father.

But when she stepped inside, Joseph was crying. The sound tore into her heart.

"Something is wrong?" She glanced at Susan.

"He took a drink from the cup and started to cry. I wonder if he hurt himself."

Rosie lifted his upper lip and felt his gums. She nodded knowingly. "His gums are swollen and red. I believe he is getting a tooth. He may have clamped down on the sippy cup and hurt his gums.

"Shh," she soothed.

His crying waned when Mary stepped into the kitchen. In an instant, he was kicking his feet in happiness, tears forgotten.

Rosie wiped his nose with a tissue and then washed her hands before the rest of the children raced inside, bringing in the cool morning air and the freshness of a new day.

Ezra was the last to enter, his eyes twinkling, his cheeks ruddy. Rosie was hard-pressed to keep her eyes averted, and she caught herself turning to stare at him. He patted Joseph's head, making the baby laugh all the more, and then held a chair away from the table for Rosie.

She did not know what to say and so she said nothing.

David chuckled.

Ezra gave him a stern glare. "Young man, you can help your sister with her chair."

"What?" David looked aghast.

"First Belinda and then Mary."

The boy rolled his eyes but dutifully held his older sister's chair.

"Thank you, David," Belinda said, her smile proof she appreciated the gesture.

Mary pulled out her own chair. "I can seat myself all by myself."

Ezra laughed. "Someday, Miss Mary, you will enjoy a man's help."

"I would let Joseph help me with my chair," she said, waving to the baby, who waved back, his hand slapping the air with enthusiasm.

"Why were you crying?" she asked him.

"Joseph is getting a tooth," Rosie explained. "His gums hurt when he bit down on the cup as he tried to take a drink of water."

Mary pointed to the cup. "Take small sips, Joseph, and be careful not to spill your water or hurt your mouth."

"You are a good teacher, Mary." Rosie appreciated the children, who made her feel so welcome and seemed to enjoy having Joseph with them. In her parents' house, she had felt like a stranger who was not welcome. Here was just the opposite.

Ezra glanced at her and smiled. Silly of her to have gotten upset with him yesterday. He was a *gut* man and a loving brother who was putting his family before his own needs.

After Mary and David left for school, Rosie helped Susan with the dishes while Ezra worked on a broken fence. He had cautioned the women to keep watch on the roadway and to ring the dinner bell if they saw a car approaching.

Today, the fear Rosie had felt seemed distant. She had slept well and laughed with the children and everything that had happened seemed as if it was at another time or had happened to another person.

Then she thought of Mr. Calhoun, who had died, and the missing medication.

Ezra returned to the house and smiled as he entered the kitchen, filling her with gratitude for his help. "I know you have much work to do," she said, "but I wondered if we could talk to Nan today about her visit to the pharmacist and what she learned about Mr. Calhoun's death."

"You and I are thinking similar thoughts. Although I do not want you on the road until more time has passed. I will go alone."

"Susan said she can watch Joseph, and I would like to go with you, although I agree about the main roads. What about the back trails we were on yesterday?"

"This would work although some are narrow that weave toward town, especially around the mountain area where Nan lives."

"Can you ride?" Susan asked. "Belinda and I ride our horses to town sometimes. The riding paths are shorter than the paved roads, and if we do not have a lot of groceries to carry, we can do our errands and get home in a much shorter time."

Rosie looked down at her dress. "I ride, but this is all I have to wear."

Susan laughed. "Which is not a problem. My sister and I wear pants under our skirts. You are more slender than I am, but we can pin the waist. Today is warmer than yesterday. I have a wool sweater you can wear under your cape."

"Then it is decided," Rosie said with a nod. "We will ride to Nan's house and find out what she learned about Mr. Calhoun's death and the missing medication."

Ezra saddled the horses—Duke and Duchess—and brought them to the back of the house. Rosie hugged Joseph and thanked Susan again for staying with her baby.

Wearing the pants under her skirt and the heavy sweater along with her cape, Rosie was comfortable. "I used to ride when I was a girl," she told Ezra as he held the stirrup and helped her into the saddle. She took the reins. "This is like going back in time."

"To a good place, I hope," he said.

She nodded. "Yes, a good time and place. When I was young, my father was a caring man who I knew loved me. He changed over time."

"Perhaps he did not want his daughter to grow up. Can you pinpoint something that happened when he started to change?"

She shook her head. "The only thing I remember is that we went to town when I was thirteen. A man standing on the street corner said I was a pretty girl and asked my father if he could take my photograph."

"I do not think this would be something your father would want for his young daughter."

"He did not answer the man, but he grabbed my hand and jerked me into the nearest store. Then he kept watch at the store window until the man left the street and drove away. From that time on, my father acted as if I had done something wrong, as if I had encouraged the man in some way."

"You are beautiful, Rosie. Your father must have realized his little girl was growing up."

She shook her head, not willing to accept his statement. She was not beautiful. She was headstrong and self-centered, and she had brought too much pain to her family. She did not deserve their love or attention, and her father was probably correct in realizing what would happen, as if the man's attention had been a prophetic warning about her wayward future.

She grabbed the reins from Ezra and held the horse back until he had climbed on Duke, then she encouraged Duchess forward and headed for the front gate.

"Rosie, wait. You and Duchess are going in the wrong direction."

She pulled up on the reins and glanced over her

shoulder at Ezra. He pointed to a trail near the one that had brought them to the house yesterday.

"We will ride this way unless you have changed your mind about wanting to take the back trails."

She had almost left Ezra. She was too focused on herself instead of others, just as her father had told her on more than one occasion.

"I will follow your lead," she said, feeling a bit ashamed of her impetuousness. Amish women were to be subdued and subordinate. Would she never learn her place in the Amish world?

Chapter Twelve

Ezra was impressed with Rosie's riding ability and enjoyed the sunshine and crisp morning air. The temperature seemed mild after the recent cold spell. Rosie's cheeks were pink with exertion, and her laughter floated across the fields, filling him with happiness. If only life could be this freeing. Both Ezra and Rosie needed time away from the worries and cares that had surrounded them since he had followed her out of town just a few days ago.

At the top of a rise, he pulled up on the reins and waited for Rosie to join him.

"It's beautiful here," she said as her horse sidled next to his. "I had forgotten how much I enjoy riding. It takes me back to my youth. To a better time."

He understood. "As a boy, I rode all over the mountain. Often my mother would send me on an errand to town, but other times when my chores were done, I would come up here to dream of what my future would be."

"You dreamed of what, Ezra?"

He shrugged. "Adventure. Travel. Being famous.

Foolish dreams, my father told me when I tried to share my thoughts with him."

"And your mother?"

"She would listen and smile without finding fault." He smiled at Rosie. "Mothers are like that, *yah*. They allow their children to dream."

"Did she worry about you leaving the faith?"

"She said I would find my way." He stared into the horizon, thinking of the painful journey he had traveled in order to find the way his mother had mentioned. Even now, he was not sure what the future would hold or where he would be years from now.

"My father always admonished me to never stray from being Amish," Rosie said. "Yet too often, he stayed away from church and refused to visit relatives and friends on the other Sundays."

"Was he a recluse or just shy?"

"Perhaps an unhappy man who never fit in."

"You left home because of him."

She jerked her head to stare at Ezra. "What did you say?"

"He is the reason you fell in love with Will MacIntosh."

"I fell in love with William because I was foolish, naive and wanted much more than the Amish way would provide. I wanted worldly happiness."

"You wanted love, the love your father should have given you, Rosie. When you did not find it within the family, you looked for it elsewhere."

She sighed. "You are passing the responsibility of my actions onto my father. They were my sins."

"Think what you like, Rosie Glick, but the need to be loved is man's most important need. Everything hinges around whether we feel loved and lovable. The love we long for most deeply within our hearts, within our beings, is our love for *Gott*. Yet He is not visible to us so we must find earthly love that teaches us what true love, the love that comes from *Gott*, is about. The father is the most important person in a girl's life as far as her feelings of acceptance and self-worth. If a father shirks his responsibility and does not adequately love his daughter, she will always search for that love, but as I mentioned, in the wrong places or with the wrong people."

"You sound like a philosopher. How did you get so knowledgeable?"

"I went to the library after my parents were murdered. I needed to decide how I could best help my siblings heal. I read over and over about a father's love. I had taken my father from his daughters so I had a responsibility to bridge that gap and fill in the void I had created."

"You talk as if you were responsible for your parents' deaths."

"I was." With a slap of the reins against his horse's rump, Ezra rode off, leaving Rosie to stare after him.

He had said too much just as he was wont to do around her. He had never told anyone about the guilt he carried. He did not need to share his own pain, but somehow Rosie made him want to bare his soul and let her see the core of who he was—a man who had caused such pain. No one would ever be able to love him when they learned the truth. A self-fulfilling prophecy, the psychology books had said.

He was getting close to Rosie, too close. He needed to let her know who he really was lest she think him something he was not. Rosie deserved a good man with

an unscarred past, a man who could love her uncondi-
tionally and without hesitation. Ezra was not that man.

He looked back, watching her encourage her horse
forward. She had taken off her *kapp* and her hair had
pulled free from its bun and billowed around her face
and into the air as she rode. He had never seen anyone
more beautiful or anyone whom he needed to avoid
at all costs. He could not be attracted to Rosie or he
would bring pain to her as well as to his own already
broken heart.

Rosie did not understand Ezra. He shared so deeply
yet when she wanted to tell him how good he really was,
he rode off, not wanting praise or her words of encouragement. Perhaps he enjoyed hiding behind whatever
guilt he thought he carried. Some people needed to be
a victim, although Ezra did not seem like a victim. He
took full responsibility for his actions and would not
listen if she tried to tell him otherwise.

Ezra had not killed his parents. He had been in town,
hanging out in a bar with his *Englisch* friends when
his parents had been murdered. Perhaps that was his
guilt. That he had not been home when he could have
protected them, although he probably would have been
killed as well.

He had poor hindsight, but she would not tell him
that, lest he ride off again and leave her on the mountain. She needed to get to the nurse and find out what
the pharmacy had said. She also hoped Nan would have
news about Mr. Calhoun's death.

How could anyone think Rosie was involved in a
drug racket?

Her heart skipped a beat. *William!*

Ezra had made reference to William's possible involvement, and she saw it all more clearly now. His frequent visits to a cabin in the woods, where he picked up packages wrapped like small boxes to be mailed. Only William did not go to the post office. Instead he would drive to distant towns to deliver the goods, as he called them.

Had the packages been filled with drugs?

She shivered with the realization. No wonder the nursing-home manager suspected her. Will's involvement was probably common knowledge around town or with law enforcement. She had been right not to go to the police. They would arrest her and throw her into jail.

Ezra pulled his horse to a stop and waited for Rosie.

"Nan's home is over that rise," he said. "The police want to question you, Rosie. We do not want anyone calling law enforcement about two Amish people on horseback in the area. We might be smart to weave our way through the dense wooded area and leave our horses behind the house, then we could cross Nan's backyard and arrive, hopefully unnoticed, at her house."

"That is a good plan, Ezra. I will follow you."

He guided his horse along a narrow path that led to the bottom of the incline. Rosie stayed close behind him. Once at the bottom of the hill, Ezra encouraged Duke into the wooded area.

"We are probably being overly cautious," Rosie whispered, although she appreciated Ezra's desire to keep her safe. Seeing Nan's house, she pulled up on the reins and slipped from the saddle.

"What are you doing?" Ezra asked.

"I am heading to my friend's house, knocking on the door and staying long enough to learn what she has uncovered. I do not like being a sly cat who sneaks around."

Ezra climbed down from his horse and tied the reins to a nearby tree. He looked at her and held out his hand. "We will go together."

She slipped her hand into his, feeling the strength of his grip. They stepped into the cleared area behind Nan's house and hurried toward her back door. The bell worked but no one answered.

"Perhaps she is still at work," Rosie said.

"We are a little later than we were before," Ezra said. "She might be asleep."

Rosie rapped again on the door, and when no one answered, she pointed to the side of the house. "Nan said she can see the town lights from her bedroom window, which means it is located on that side of the house."

Together, they rounded the corner. Holding her hands around her eyes to cut down on the glare, Rosie peered through the window, grateful the blinds were partially open.

Her heart lurched. Nan lay strewn over the bed, her arms splayed, her red hair disheveled.

Rosie pounded on the window. "Nan, it is Rosie. Wake up."

Ezra stepped closer and looked through the glass.

"Something is wrong." He pulled Rosie to the back of the house. "I will ask the neighbor to call an ambulance."

Tears stung Rosie eyes. "I fear something terrible has happened. Along with the ambulance, they need to call the police."

Sirens sounded in the distance. Ezra turned to glance into the underbrush, where Rosie waited with the horses. The neighbor stood on the street to flag down the ambulance.

Ezra did not have a good feeling about what the EMTs would find. Nan had not moved since he and Rosie had first looked through the window.

Again, he glanced at the wooded area, relieved Rosie was hidden from view. The police did not need anything additional to cause them to question her involvement in what now looked like a death investigation.

The shrill squeal of the siren neared. A police sedan turned the corner, followed by an ambulance. Both braked to a stop in front of the house.

Ezra hurried back to the wooded area where Rosie waited. Her face was pale, her mouth drawn. He squeezed her hand, hoping to provide support.

Two policemen sprang from the car. They spoke briefly to the woman on the sidewalk and then hurried to the front door. Finding it locked, they rounded to the rear, tried that door and then broke one of the side windowpanes and unlocked the door through the opening.

The police disappeared inside. Some moments later the front door opened and they beckoned to the EMTs.

Rosie stepped closer to Ezra, as if needing his reassurance. He put his arm around her shoulders. "I fear the outcome will not be good."

"They killed her, Ezra, because she was asking questions about the missing drugs. They probably killed Mr. Calhoun, too, although I do not know what he did to them. Maybe he questioned the missing medication and why he was not getting anything for his pain."

"Who are you including in the guilty?"

"The manager of the nursing home must be involved, and I saw Larry Wagner in his office the day I was fired. They fired me, thinking I was snooping around too much."

"Yet the manager let you go home."

"Mr. Wagner came to my house that night, but my parents stopped him."

"Wagner planned to apprehend you on the road, Rosie. He had damaged your bike and thought you would travel to town on foot."

"If only we knew what William was supposed to have given me."

The EMTs emerged from the house, pushing a stretcher. Nan's body was covered with a blanket.

Ezra wrapped his arm around Rosie's shoulders and felt her flinch. She turned away, no doubt, unwilling to watch her friend being placed in the ambulance.

The police questioned the neighbor and then stretched yellow police tape around Nan's house before they went to the other houses on the street gathering information.

"They are talking to the neighbors in case anyone heard or saw anything," Ezra said.

He ushered Rosie closer to Duchess. "You need to go back to my house. Wait there. I will try to find out more information."

She grabbed his hand. "You cannot stay, Ezra. They will suspect you. The neighbor has probably already told them about the Amish man who knocked on Nan's door."

"I told her that the nurse had hired me to build bookshelves for her living area. It is not unusual for Amish craftsmen to take jobs with the *Englisch*."

"But the police will take you to their headquarters for questioning."

"I will wait until the police leave. Go now, Rosie. Joseph needs you. Tell Susan I will be home later."

"Oh, Ezra—"

He placed the reins in her hand and hoisted her onto the saddle.

"I do not want to leave you," she said reluctantly before she encouraged Duchess forward through the thicket.

"Keep Rosie safe, *Gott*," Ezra murmured as he watched her find the path and head toward the mountain. She was well-protected within the forested area, and he doubted the police would notice the slight movement he saw as the horse hurried over the crest of the hill.

Turning his gaze to the street, he watched the police head back to Nan's house. One of the officers remained stationed at the front door. The other drove away in the squad car.

The neighbor with whom Ezra had spoken earlier stepped onto her back patio carrying a broom and started sweeping.

Ezra approached her, hat in hand. "Ma'am, I had to tend to my horse, but I saw you talking to the police. Do you know anything about Ms. Smith?"

"The EMTs said she overdosed. They found pills at her bedside." The woman shook her head as if unable to understand what had happened. "The pills were from the nursing home where she worked. Evidently she had been stealing drugs from the patients."

She glanced again at Ezra. "Perhaps you should talk to the police. One of them is still at the house. Do you want me to call him?"

Ezra held up his hand. "That will not be necessary. I

will stop at the police station in town and talk to them there."

She nodded, as if satisfied. "It's terrible. Such a shame. You just never know about your neighbors."

The woman turned back to her house, and Ezra slipped into the woods and quickly rode up the hill.

The mountain used to be a peaceful place without crime. Once he started to associate with the *Englisch* everything changed.

He should have warned Rosie about Will MacIntosh, when he first saw them together. Had it been his pride or his upset that she was interested in another man when she had paid so little attention to him?

Perhaps he *had* been upset with her, but he should also have been upset with himself. They had both made mistakes, but neither of them were murderers or involved in a drug racket. Yet they were both being pulled into the corruption that was happening in the area.

Neither of them knew anyone who could help change this terrible situation. Not the police, not the Amish community and not the townspeople who thought the nursing-home manager was an upstanding citizen. No one would believe the Amish if they accused the good citizens of wrongdoing.

Ezra and Rosie needed to find evidence they could take to the sheriff in Willkommen to solve this tangled case involving prescription drugs. If only Will had given Rosie information, they could use that now to substantiate what they had learned.

If only, Ezra thought again.

Chapter Thirteen

Rosie could hardly see the path as the tears fell. She was responsible for Nan's death. The nurse had always reached out to her with kindness, yet Rosie had alerted Nan to Mr. Calhoun's pain the night he had died and had asked Nan to give him the needed pain medication. The medication, Nan all too soon realized, was missing.

Rosie tried to put the pieces together, but none of them fit. It was all so confusing. Why was she in the middle of the problem? Had Will, in some way, set her up to be a target? Did it involve whatever he was supposed to have given her? All that was wrong about their relationship was coming back to haunt her now.

If she was in danger, Joseph was as well.

She thought of Ezra's family and the innocent children. What would happen to them if the man in the white SUV stopped at their house? Would little Mary with her wide eyes and forthright nature divulge that a woman and baby were staying at their house, which would put all of them in danger? Rosie's heart ached for what could happen.

She had to leave to ensure the children were kept

safe. She would take the Amish taxi to the bus station once she learned where Katherine's daughter lived.

Money would be a problem. She had saved a little from her paychecks and had hidden it in the quilt, along with the toy Will had given her for their baby. Hopefully the cash would be enough for a bus ticket, but she would arrive in Ohio with nothing extra.

A fork in the path appeared in the distance. To the right would take her to Ezra's house. If she went left, surely it would lead to her aunt's home.

Stopping at Katherine's house would not take long. Susan had assured Rosie that she would take care of Joseph. Ezra would be at Nan's house for some time.

She tapped her heels against the horse's flank and turned him onto the other path, the one that headed, hopefully, to Katherine's house.

Rosie would be careful and watchful. She did not want another encounter with the man in the white SUV.

The trail meandered downhill. Duchess picked her way along the rocky path. Something slithered out from under a boulder. Rosie's heart lurched when she saw the snake.

The mare spooked and increased her speed. Rosie tried to hold Duchess back, but the mare refused to respond to the tug on the reins.

Duchess's trot turned to a gallop. The wind whipped at Rosie's cape and pulled at her bun.

"Oh," she groaned as the path became steeper. The horse was galloping far too fast for the treacherous terrain. Rosie should have taken the other path, the one she knew.

Once she had made sure Joseph was all right, she could have walked to Katherine's house. It would have taken more time, but at least she would not be hurling down a hillside so fast…too fast.

She pulled on the reins, hard. The mare eased up a bit and then increased her pace again.

"Oh, please," Rosie called out, not knowing what to do.

A slight rise appeared on the path ahead. The house would not be far. In the distance, Rosie saw the barn where she had hidden with the buggy yesterday and felt a swell of relief. Surely the mare would come to a stop near the structure. But the horse continued at break-neck speed. A fence appeared ahead. Instead of going around the obstacle, Duchess headed straight for it, and at the last possible moment, jumped over the barrier.

Rosie screamed. The reins slipped from her hands. She reached for the saddle horn but ended up grabbing air. The mare came down hard. Rosie slipped right. Her leg left the stirrup and without anything to hold her back, she fell.

"Oof!" Rosie landed on her side, her hand thankfully breaking her fall. Her hip ached. Dazed, she watched the mare gallop off.

So much for riding back to Ezra's house. She rubbed her head and pulled herself upright. A wave of vertigo fluttered over her. She felt her arms and legs, ensuring nothing was broken. Relieved that her limbs were intact, she tried to stand. The path swirled in front of her. She regained her balance, stepped gingerly forward with one foot and moaned. Sharp pain radiated from her ankle.

Katherine's house was not far. If she could hobble there, then perhaps she could take her aunt's buggy to Ezra's house. She felt sure he would return the buggy later in the day.

She exhaled with frustration, imagining his upset when he found out she had taken the other path, the one that led away from his house. Once again her own stubbornness had caused problems. For herself and for Ezra.

A dull ache started in her head. She rubbed her forehead, hoping to relieve the pressure that had built up there, and limped past the old, dilapidated barn to the newer one located near the house. The barn doors were open. Rosie peered inside as she passed, thinking her aunt might be working there, but the barn was empty and the buggy was gone.

Her heart plummeted. Katherine must have taken the buggy to town or she might be spending the day with friends. She could be anywhere instead of where Rosie had hoped she would be.

Standing just outside the barn, Rosie glanced down the valley, knowing she would have to walk back to Ezra's house. The trip would not be pleasant or speedy with her aching leg.

So much for her good idea. Another mistake that she could add to the list, if she was making a list. Although she would rather not put anything in writing that would show her ineptitude.

She placed her hands on her hips and sighed. A stiff wind blew her long hair into her face. Plus, she had lost her *kapp*.

Totally flummoxed and upset, she swallowed down the lump in her throat and brushed away the new rush of tears. She was becoming much too emotional.

Limping along the path, she heard a sound from the road below and turned. She blinked away the tears as her heart pounded a warning. A car was coming up the hill. A white SUV.

The man with the swatch of white hair. Larry Wagner.

Her blood chilled. She looked at the steep incline she would have to navigate to get to the path and how much farther it was to the wooded area, where she could hide.

Surely Katherine had locked her door. A few years back that was not the case and the Amish would not have secured their homes, but recently, as Rosie was all too aware, crime had come to the mountain and the Amish had started to secure their homes and their property. Except the barn was open.

Rosie headed there. She stepped inside and closed the large door behind her just as the sound of the engine announced the man had turned into the drive.

Where could she hide?

She blinked, getting used to the darkness, and headed to the stalls in the rear. Where would he first look, if he entered?

She shook her head, confused as to what to do.

Outside a car door slammed. She envisioned Wagner climbing Katherine's porch steps and heard a distant knock on the door.

A ladder led to the hayloft above. Climbing would be difficult with a twisted ankle, but she would be able to hide there out of sight. At least that was her hope.

She started up the ladder and groaned. Her leg throbbed when she put weight on it. Hiding in one of the stalls might have been a better choice.

The door to the barn started to open, sending daylight into the darkness. Ignoring the pain, she scurried up the final rungs and scooted behind the bales of hay just as Wagner stepped into the barn.

From her lofty perch, she could see him. He stepped

toward the first stall and peered inside, then went to the next one and the next.

Perhaps she had made a good decision after all to hide in the loft. Just as long as he did not look up. Fearing she might be visible, she scooted back farther, causing a bale of hay to wobble and a hen roosting there to squawk.

The hen flapped her wings and flew to the ground below.

Rosie's heart nearly leaped from her chest. She gripped her hands together as if in prayer, only words would not come. The only thing she could think of was "save me."

While *Gott* was silent, her heart was not. It pounded like a freight train.

Larry Wagner sighed. Grabbing the ladder, he climbed one rung after the other, coming closer and closer. She looked around for another exit but found none. The only thing she could do was jump down, but with her bum leg, he would surely get to her before she could escape.

Her hands were wet with sweat, her throat was dry and her pulse raged like a river down a mountain gorge. Her ears roared, yet she could hear his footfalls on each rung as he climbed.

Almost to the top, he stopped. Laughter filled the barn. His laughter.

What was so funny?

A meowing sound, followed by more laughter.

"Well, aren't you the cutest kitten ever?"

She peered from her hiding spot. A tiny kitten was perched on the edge of the loft. Wagner lifted the ball of fluff into his arms.

"What are you doing up here, scaring that ol' hen?

You made me think someone was hiding from me."
He laughed again. "You haven't seen a little Amish gal
with blond hair, now have you, kitty? She's got something that could cause me a lot of problems if it got in
the wrong hands."

The cat mewed.

"I'll come back to talk to Katherine. Maybe she'd
want to give you away. I'd like a little fellow like you
around." With the cat in his arms, Wagner climbed
down the ladder.

Rosie rested her head against the bale of hay. The
sound of his car backing out of the drive brought tears
to her eyes again. She had eluded detection thanks to a
small kitten. Then she realized who had protected her. She
closed her eyes through the tears and gave thanks to *Gott*.

Ezra returned home and hurried into the house, expecting to find Rosie. Susan looked up from the rocking chair. Joseph was asleep in her arms.

"Where's Rosie?" his sister asked.

His heart stuttered. "She has not returned?"

"I thought she was with you."

Ezra did not wait to hear anything else Susan said.
He ran to the barn, threw open the door and peered into
Duchess's empty stall. Climbing back on his horse, he
glanced at the trail he had just taken. The only turnoff
was the path that led to Katherine's house.

Surely Rosie had not ventured there without him.

He slapped the reins and guided Duke forward
along the trail Ezra and Rosie had traveled yesterday.
He shook his head, mentally chastising himself. Why
had he sent Rosie off alone? He could have taken the
buggy to town later and made inquiries to find out what

the police suspected concerning Nan's death. Instead he had allowed Rosie to travel across the countryside unprotected.

His heart ached and he wanted to scream with concern and worry and, yes, even rage, which was not the Amish way.

He had lost his parents. Would he lose another person he cared for as well?

He scanned the wooded area at the side of the paths, hoping to see some sign of her. Perhaps she had fallen off the mare and was lying at the bottom of a ravine, like when he had first found her.

Suppose the man in the SUV had her? He could have captured her and taken her—

Ezra could not think of such things or he would not be able to go on.

Katherine's house was not far ahead. Perhaps she was there, sipping tea with her aunt and sharing recipes.

If only that could be, but when he turned the bend and came out from the wooden area, he saw the barn door open and the buggy gone.

To ensure he was right, he searched the barn and knocked on the front and back doors.

"Rosie, where are you?"

The dilapidated barn sat on the rise. The old building had provided protection before. Could she have gone there again?

He stumbled over the rocks as he took a shortcut up the steep incline, needing to find her. Now. Before his heart stopped.

He pulled open the door and stepped into the dark interior, smelling the mix of hay and dung. A dove cooed from the rafters.

"Rosie?"

His heart crashed. He dropped his head into his hands. Where was she?

"Ezra?" A whisper, but her whisper, her voice, soft as silk.

"Rosie, where are you?"

"In the rear—"

Before she could finish, he was at her side, kneeling in the hay, pulling her into his arms. "Oh, Rosie, I was so worried. I thought—I thought…"

He could not say the terrible things that had run through his mind. All he could do was pull her even closer. He wove his fingers through her hair and smelled the sweet scent of her shampoo and felt the softness of her skin and the way she molded to him as if she was drowning in an ocean and he had saved her. Only he had not saved her or protected her. He had sent her away from him. Alone.

"I am so sorry and ask your forgiveness."

She did not respond, but tears fell from her eyes, wetting his shirt and making his heart break all the more.

"I am sorry," he said again, his voice little more than a whisper.

"Oh, Ezra, I am the one at fault. I took the path to Katherine's house and put myself in danger. When the man came—"

"Larry? Did he hurt you?"

She shook her head. "A kitten saved me." She smiled through her tears. "Along with help from *Gott*."

"I should have been here with you." He glanced down and saw scratches on her arms. "You are hurt."

"I fell from the horse and twisted my ankle. It will heal."

"Can you walk?"

"Not easily."

"Let me help you up." He wrapped his arms around her shoulders and guided her to her feet.

One of her legs buckled. Without effort, he lifted her into his arms. "We must hurry back to the house before Wagner returns."

Holding Rosie in his arms made Ezra's chest swell and his ears ring and his heart pound, not from fear, but from her closeness. All he wanted to do was continue to hold her. But danger was circling too close and he would not make the same mistake again.

He carried her to the door of the barn and looked outside to ensure they were alone, then he brushed his lips over her forehead, feeling like his heart would surely explode within his chest. All he had ever wanted was to hold Rosie, only not under these circumstances, not when a man who wanted to do her harm was prowling the mountain, coming closer and closer.

Ezra needed to find out the truth about what was happening at the nursing home and with the patients' drugs. Then he would make the trip to Willkommen and give the information to the sheriff or acting sheriff there. With the right evidence, they would not be able to ignore his suspicions or what he said. Ezra could not bear to have anything happen to Rosie, and right now, everyone was after her.

She was suspected of stealing drugs. For all he knew, she could also be suspected of murder, and although he had acted foolishly today, he would not let her stray from his sight until everything was out in the open and her name was cleared and the man in the SUV and the manager of the nursing home and everyone else involved in this corruption were under arrest.

Chapter Fourteen

Rosie did not want to put Joseph down that night. After dinner, he fell asleep in her arms. She cuddled him close as Ezra said good-night to the young children. Mary ran back to wrap her arms around Rosie's neck, and then slyly, she kissed her cheek and kissed Joseph's as well. The baby's lips twitched into a smile as if he knew sweet Mary had kissed him.

"You have been a good friend to Joseph," Rosie told the girl. "Thank you for playing with him."

"I wish he was more than a friend," Mary said as he patted his head and smiled at the sleeping child.

"More than a friend?" Rosie asked, not understanding.

The girl shrugged. "*Mamm* and *Datt* have gone to heaven so there will be no more children in our family. I do not want to be the youngest. I want a brother or sister." She looked at Rosie with big eyes. "Could Joseph be my brother?"

Rosie glanced up to see Ezra standing in the kitchen. He had, no doubt, overheard the girl's comment, but the look on his face was hard to read. Was he angry that

Mary had mentioned their parents' deaths, or was he upset that she wanted Joseph to be part of the family?

Rosie lowered her gaze, suddenly unsure of her place here. After Ezra had found her in the barn, she had never wanted to leave his arms. Undoubtedly she was dazed from everything that had happened, but she thought she had felt Ezra's lips brush against her forehead. Wishful thinking, probably, like a young schoolgirl who flirted with boys. Not that Rosie had done anything like that. She had focused on her studies, wanting to make her *datt* proud of her—something she never succeeded in doing.

Ezra had wrapped her ankle, his touch gentle, his concern sincere, which only enhanced her feelings for him. Thankfully, Duchess had returned to the barn no worse for her escapade. Rosie kept reflecting on all that had happened. Without doubt, something special had passed between them today in the barn, but now, after hearing Mary's innocent comment, Ezra seemed to stiffen and be aloof again.

She pulled Joseph closer and touched Mary's cheek with her free hand. "It is getting late. You rise early in the morning, Mary, and need your sleep. You had best go to bed."

"I will see you and Joseph tomorrow?" It was a question, as if the child was afraid they would leave, which they would do soon. But Rosie could not think of leaving sweet Mary and David, who was always so logical and tried to be grown up. Belinda, at fourteen, was blossoming into a lovely young woman ready to take on more responsibility within the family, especially if Susan had eyes on a young man in town, which is what she had surmised from some of the comments the children had made in passing.

Rosie rubbed her hand across Mary's shoulder. "Joseph will see you at breakfast." Seemingly reassured, Mary nodded and followed David upstairs.

Susan was mending a torn shirt of Aaron's, while he worked on a small propane motor that needed fixing. A knock sounded at the door. Rosie's heart raced. Ezra's face revealed the concern he felt.

Although she had not heard a car, Rosie rose and searched for a place to hide. Ezra pointed her to an alcove off the kitchen. The small area was covered by a curtain.

"Wait in there until I see who is at the door."

"Do you think—" The words would not form.

He shook his head. "I did not hear a car."

Still—

Ezra was gone, walking back through the main room toward the door. Another rap sounded.

"Who is it?" Ezra's voice was sharp and demanding.

Rosie scurried into the hiding spot, bit her lip and turned her eyes to the ceiling, trying to hear something—anything—that would give her a clue as to who had come pounding at the door.

The sound of the door opening and heavy footsteps coming to where she hid made her heart lurch.

She held her breath.

The curtain pulled back and Ezra peered in, smiling. "You can come out." His voice was low, his eyes twinkling with mirth.

"There is someone here?" she asked.

He nodded. "John Keim, from town. He is the blacksmith's son. He came to ask if Susan could accompany him to youth singing this weekend. The group will also do some caroling."

Rosie smiled. Her heart soared with joy for Susan, whose cheeks turned pink and eyes took on a softness whenever John's name was mentioned. "How does her big brother feel about someone courting his younger sister?"

"I feel like a father who does not know if he wants her daughter to grow up or stay young."

They laughed together. She glanced down at Joseph, feeling stronger. "I must put him to bed, plus it would be better if John did not see me."

"He and Susan are taking a short walk. I told them they can talk on the front porch."

"They would probably prefer the front room, although…" She smiled. "They would be alone on the porch and could huddle together to keep warm."

He laughed again, causing Joseph to startle.

"Put Joseph to bed and then come downstairs," Ezra suggested. "We can have a second cup of coffee. I do not think John will stay long."

"That sounds *gut*."

Leaving Ezra in the kitchen waiting for her and carrying her baby upstairs felt so natural and so normal—exactly what Rosie wanted for her life. After she covered Joseph with another blanket, she went to the window and looked down at the young couple walking in the moonlight, their heads close together, their hands entwined.

Rosie thought of what she had done and wondered how any good Amish man would be interested in a woman who had given herself to the wrong man and in the wrong way. Ezra deserved better. He deserved an Amish woman who would be a support and stand at his side, a helpmate through life of whom he could be proud.

She turned to go downstairs, heavyhearted, knowing she was not that woman.

Maybe it was seeing John at the door, acting nervous and embarrassed as he asked to take Susan to the singing that softened Ezra's heart. Or perhaps it was his sister's look of concern, as if she thought Ezra would not agree to let her go, that made him review the last sixteen months since their parents had died. He had been too hard on all of them in the beginning. He had been even harder on himself.

Thankfully, he was beginning to realize that Susan needed to be free to find her way in life. She was a beautiful woman, strong in her faith and committed to the Amish way. She would not wander off, seeking the world, as her brother had done.

And Rosie. His heart ached. All Rosie had wanted was to be loved. Anger swelled within him toward her father, who had not provided the positive role model she had needed. If he had been a better father, Rosie would have been content with her life and would have found love the normal Amish way.

Ezra would have continued to watch from a distance as a good Amish man courted her and the banns of marriage were read and the ceremony performed on a Tuesday or Thursday after fall harvest.

Perhaps things happened for a reason, even difficult things that caused pain. The journey to this moment for both of them had been filled with twists and turns that neither of them would have expected, yet they were together now, and if he could judge by what had happened in the barn and the feelings that had passed between them, something good was drawing them together.

Light footfalls on the stairs signaled Rosie was returning to the first floor. He stood, wanting to welcome her, if not into his arms, at least into the kitchen, where they would share coffee and spend time alone together.

He had not expected to be so overwhelmed with her beauty as she came into view. She had lost her *kapp* on the path, and her hair fell softly over her shoulders, encircling her pretty face and big blue eyes, which stared at him full of questions. Did he notice a hint of longing in her gaze, as if she was feeling the churn of confusion just as he was?

He took her hand and drew her next to him. She looked up expectantly.

The guilt lifted from his shoulders. He forgot children were sleeping upstairs, and his sister was saying goodbye to John outside. All he could think about was Rosie and the way she had felt earlier in his arms. Her soft skin, her sweet smell, the way his body responded to her nearness.

He stepped closer and put his hand around her slender waist. The warmth of her touched a place of pain that he had carried too long. He saw her face. Her lips lifted up to his and the world stopped. Time stood still and she was the only thing his eyes could see or ever wanted to see as he lowered his lips and—

"Ezra?" Susan's voice called as she shut the front door behind her and ran to the kitchen. "Did you tell John to ask me to the singing?"

She stopped short when she entered the kitchen. Rosie had a look of shock on her face and he felt equally as surprised. Susan appeared confused as she glanced at both of them.

"Is something wrong?" she asked.

"No, everything is fine," Rosie soothed, stepping farther away from him. "I was just saying good-night."

All too abruptly, she turned and fled up the stairs, leaving him with a jumble of emotions and a yearning so strong it was painful. He had almost kissed her. Their lips had almost touched before Susan, his sweet unsuspecting sister, had interrupted their moment together.

He tried to smile, but he kept thinking of Rosie, who once again was running away from him.

She deserved better than a man with a past, a man who had made too many mistakes to count and who continued to fall short of the mark.

Love was not in Ezra's future. Not now. Not ever.

Chapter Fifteen

Rosie woke early the next morning. She dressed quickly and got Joseph ready for breakfast. Once downstairs, she placed him in the high chair and cut up small portions of a banana for him to eat as she helped Susan with the breakfast.

Mary ran in with a basket of fresh eggs from the henhouse. She squealed when she saw Joseph and dropped a kiss on his cheek.

"Can I stay and feed Joseph this morning?"

Susan raised her eyebrows. "You know Ezra needs you in the barn."

"Oh, Susan, tell him I am growing so big and am needed in the kitchen."

Rosie smiled and waited until Susan nodded her agreement. "Perhaps Rosie will tell him."

She detected a sly smile on Susan's face as Rosie grabbed her cape. "I will let your brother know that I need your help, Mary. But I think Joseph is too interested in his new friend to feel like eating. Offer him the cup, Mary. He may want a drink of water."

The girl slid into the chair next to him and began to

explain everything that was happening in the barn as she lifted the sippy cup to his lips. "When you grow to be a big boy you will help in the barn, too, and you will be able to milk the cows and feed the chickens."

Rosie laughed as she hurried from the house and searched for Ezra. He was standing near the fence, filling one of the troughs with feed.

He looked up, his face full of longing. Her heart nearly broke through her ribs. His look took her back to last night and their almost-kiss. Was Susan's interruption a blessing or not?

Rosie did not know her own heart, and she was totally confused by the mixed messages she kept getting from Ezra.

"Mary would like to help in the kitchen this morning," she told him. "If you can spare her."

Ezra laughed. "She wants to be with her buddy Joseph. He is all she has talked about since she woke this morning. Yes, of course, she can remain in the kitchen."

"I am sorry that we are taking her from her chores."

"But she will help you with Joseph and that is how girls learn to be good wives and mothers. It is not a problem, Rosie."

She nodded, wishing he would say something else, but he turned back to the feed as if he had nothing more to say to her. Nothing about last night or the moments in the barn or whether his lips had touched her forehead.

There she was again, totally confused and not able to decide what he thought of her or if he even thought of her at all.

She turned to go inside, but he called her name.

She stopped and glanced back, not knowing what to expect.

"Your ankle is better?" he asked.

She nodded. "Much better. Thank you."

Rosie hurried inside and was welcomed by Joseph's laughter and Mary's giggles.

Susan smiled. "I am not sure if breakfast is being eaten or played with."

"He certainly is taken with Mary." Seeing the basket of eggs Mary had brought from the chicken coop, Rosie offered, "If you are scrambling eggs, I could break them and get them ready."

"I would appreciate your help."

Working quickly, Rosie broke the eggs into a bowl, added salt and pepper, stirred them with a fork and added a dollop of milk.

Susan stepped closer. "I do not add milk."

"I am sorry. I should have asked before I added it."

"Oh, no, I am glad to learn something new. I cook like my *mamm,* but that does not mean there are no other things to learn."

"According to my mother, adding milk made the eggs smoother." She took the bowl to the stove. "Shall I use the big iron skillet?"

"Yes, please, but let me add butter first."

Once the butter had melted, Rosie poured in the eggs and stirred them as they cooked.

Oatmeal simmered on a back burner, and biscuits baked in the oven. When Susan pulled them out, the rich smell filled the kitchen. "It is good to have a warm breakfast on a cold December morning."

"Christmas will be soon," Mary said from the table. "After school, can we make a pretty chain with colored paper?"

"May we," Susan said, correcting her.

"*Yah*, may we?"

"I am not certain Ezra wants any Christmas decorations in the house this year."

"But we have the paper, and I can make the glue with flour and water."

"I will talk to your brother. Now run to the door and ring the bell." Susan glanced at the skillet. "The eggs are almost ready, and the biscuits are hot. Everyone must eat before school."

"I will return in a minute," the girl told Joseph. "Listen for the bell."

The baby's eyes widened as if he understood Mary's comment. When the bell rang, he kicked his feet and laughed. Mary hurried back to sit at the table next to him.

"Wash your hands, Miss Mary, and pour milk for you and David."

The child complied with what her sister had requested.

Rosie watched Ezra through the window as he added fresh water to the troughs before washing his hands at the pump. The other children did likewise and then followed him inside.

The fresh morning air circled around them, their cheeks ruddy from the cold. As Ezra shrugged out of his coat, she could not help but notice how his shirt pulled over his muscular chest, which brought more thoughts of being in his arms.

Rosie's cheeks warmed and she lowered her gaze, hoping to free her mind of anything except the breakfast needing to be served.

Once the eggs were plated and the plates and bowls of oatmeal placed in front of each hungry person at the table, she slipped into the chair next to Joseph and across from Ezra. With a downcast gaze, she silently gave thanks for this family and for the welcome and love she felt here.

She glanced up and found Ezra starting at her as if he had read her mind when she had focused on love. They both reached for their coffee cups and sipped simultaneously. Again, their eyes met.

Rosie no longer wanted to eat. She took a spoonful of oatmeal and offered it to Joseph, who gobbled it down, followed by another and another after that.

He glanced at Mary between bites. She smiled at him and then at Rosie as she ate. "I like your eggs," she said sweetly.

Susan nodded in agreement. "Rosie's eggs taste *gut* to me as well, Mary. It is the milk she adds. When you help me fix breakfast, we will try her breakfast tip, *yah*?"

"Yah." Mary nodded. "I want Rosie to stay and fix eggs for us every day." She patted the baby's chubby hand. "I want Joseph to stay, too."

"You have all been very thoughtful and have made us feel welcome," Rosie said, carefully choosing her words. "Joseph and I thank you for this."

"It sounds as if you plan to leave us," Ezra said, his brow raised.

She did not understand his comment. Did he think they would stay forever? *"Yah*, we must leave soon."

"How soon?" Belinda asked.

"I am not sure." Rosie fed more oatmeal to the baby.

"You mentioned a cabin," Ezra said from across the table. "There are fishing cabins around the lake area. Perhaps we could go there today."

"Is this wise?" Both of them were cautious of what they said around the children, but there was no doubt that Ezra was talking about the cabin Rosie had visited with William.

"A number of cabins are located on this side of the lake," Aaron said. "Caleb, my friend who likes to fish, goes there often. He noticed a cabin in the woods that had shipping carts piled up on the street for the garbage man to take. The boxes were addressed to the pharmacy in town so he told Peter."

"Peter Overholt?" Ezra asked.

"*Yah.* You know Peter. He lives on the farm at the outskirts of town. You went to school with his brother, Jonas."

Ezra nodded. "What does Peter have to do with the pharmacy?"

"He works there. At least he did. Rayleen is the new pharmacist in town. She bought Mountain Pharmacy a few months ago and hired him shortly after that, but now she told him not to come to work. Peter does not know when he will be needed again."

Ezra glanced at Rosie, and from the look of concern on his face, she felt sure his thoughts were not on their near-kiss or being in each other's arms. The thought that came to her was why Peter was not wanted at the pharmacy. Did the pharmacist have something she wanted kept secret from the teen?

Ezra looked at the wall clock. "David, you and Mary need to leave for school. Finish your milk and take your dishes to the sink."

Both children did as their brother requested. Mary rinsed the plates and stacked them on the counter.

"It is my turn to wash the breakfast dishes," she announced.

"Go on, Mary," Susan insisted. "Ezra is right, we

stayed too long at breakfast. You and David must get on your outerwear. Your lunches are on the counter. Tell your teacher you are sorry if you arrive late."

"I will tell her we have company."

Mary's comment troubled Rosie. "It might be better to not mention that we are staying here."

"Is it a secret?" the little girl asked.

Rosie nodded.

With a knowing smile, Mary brushed Joseph's hair back from his forehead and kissed his check. "It will be our Christmas secret."

After the youngest two children left the house, Aaron and Belinda went outside to complete their morning chores while Susan busied herself at the sink and Rosie washed Joseph's hands and face with a warm washrag.

Ezra finished the last of his coffee and then pushed back from the table. "Come with me to the lake, Rosie. We will try to find the cabin you visited as well as the cabin Caleb told Peter about. Like Caleb, I question why the shipping boxes would be at an isolated cabin. Perhaps it is the same cabin you visited."

"It would be hard to know where to look, Ezra. Plus, I do not want to see Larry Wagner again."

"This is not who I want to see, either. We will take the bigger buggy with three rows of seats. You can sit in the rear. With your black bonnet, he will not notice you."

Rosie hoped Ezra was right because deep down she wanted to go with him. Not only to find the cabin that might have clues as to what was happening in town but also to determine if William had been involved in the drug operation. She had been so wrong about him.

Rosie glanced again at Ezra, a *gut* man who needed a *gut* woman in his life.

Perhaps it was fortunate Susan had interrupted them before they kissed. Rosie did not deserve Ezra, yet she had wanted him to kiss her yesterday. She wanted Ezra to kiss her today as well.

"We will take another back road," Ezra said as he helped Rosie climb into the rear of the buggy.

"You have many back roads on this mountain."

He laughed. "A man likes to have various ways to travel. This road will take us over the mountain instead of heading back down to the valley, the way we normally go to town. Eventually we will arrive at the lake."

"I do not recall seeing a lake when I went to the cabin with Will."

"Did you see anyone else when you were there?"

She thought for a moment. "I went with William only twice and each time I remained in his truck and saw no one. Will said he had to pick up a package, although both times he returned from the cabin with more than one box in hand."

"Cardboard boxes?"

"*Yah*, each box was marked with a name and address."

"Did you go with him when he made the deliveries?"

"Only once when he made a delivery to Atlanta."

"Do you remember the address?"

She shook her head. "The house was north of the city. That is all I remember."

"What about the cabin, Rosie? Was there anything to help identify it?"

"It was an A-frame and had a screened-in side porch."

"We will search for just such a place."

Rosie pulled her cape tight around her neck. The sun was shining, but the day was cold. Ezra wrapped a heavy blanket around her legs before he climbed into the front seat.

"If a car passes, duck down so they will not know you are there."

"I am not worried," she assured him.

Ezra was. Not overly, but he was concerned and hoping the man in the SUV would remain in town or wherever he lived and not venture to the lake.

Susan stepped onto the porch, carrying Joseph in her arms.

"Keep watch," Ezra told her. "Lock the door while you are home alone and do not let the children linger outside when they come home from school. I have already warned Belinda and Aaron."

"You are worried for our safety?"

"I am worried someone may come here looking for Rosie. Do not open the door to anyone except our family. The man who drives a white SUV is not to be trusted."

"Joseph and I will stay inside with the doors locked."

"That is *gut*."

Ezra nodded farewell and then flicked the reins. The mare snorted as she turned onto the paved roadway.

"You are warm enough?" Ezra asked, glancing back to where Rosie sat bundled under the heavy covering.

"*Yah*, I am fine."

The clip-clop of the horse's hooves and the rumble of the buggy wheels over the pavement made conversation difficult. Ezra wished Rosie was sitting next to him so he could put his arm around her to keep her warm.

The turnoff to the lake appeared. He pulled on the reins. The mare stepped into the turn and increased her pace to a sprightly trot.

"The lake is in the distance. Thankfully we have the road to ourselves." Ezra glanced back.

Rosie smiled. He wanted her to sit next to him even more.

The road ambled downward toward the water, where ducks floated and geese honked as they flew overhead. Today, the lake was devoid of boats and fishermen on the shore, and in spite of the cold temperature, Ezra appreciated the beauty of the rolling hills surrounding the shimmering water.

He stopped the buggy to admire the setting and heard Rosie stir. She climbed from the rear, scooted next to him and inhaled the mountain air.

"It is beautiful here," she said. "I do not remember seeing anything this serene when I was with William. Although perhaps I was not looking at the surrounding scenery."

Ezra's heart faltered. Rosie's attention had, no doubt, been on Will. Tall and muscular and with his wavy hair and thick neck, he'd attracted women, and Rosie in particular. All Ezra could remember was the anger that flashed from Will's eyes and the smirk on his full lips.

"When in love, we do not always see clearly," Ezra said.

She angled her head and looked quizzically at him as if she did not understand the comment. Perhaps she thought he was revealing his own heart. If so, the frown she wore was message enough that she was not interested in Ezra.

Chapter Sixteen

"A road angles away from the lake," Ezra said as he and Rosie sat on the side of the road in the buggy. "And another road beyond that."

Rosie followed his gaze. "I wish I could remember some landmark that would make it easier to find the cabin."

"Perhaps you should sit in the second seat, directly behind me, instead of all the way in the back. You will be better able to see the landscape and any buildings we pass."

"And if a car approaches, I will hide in the rear."

Once Rosie was settled, Ezra flicked the reins. They turned onto the first road and paused momentarily at each cottage and cabin to give Rosie time to determine if anything looked familiar.

"Do not get discouraged," he said when the road came to a dead end. Ezra guided Bessie to an adjoining side street. At the next intersection, they turned right, heading back to the lake on the second road.

Rosie placed her hand on Ezra's shoulders and leaned forward. "We both hope the cabin will provide information about the drug operation. But what if we do not find the cabin?"

"We will keep looking until we do find it."

His optimism plummeted as their search stretched on. Rosie mentioned never having noticed the lake when she and Will had stopped at the cabin. Perhaps Ezra was wasting his time and hers, looking for something that could not be found. At least not around the lake.

"Aaron's friend saw shipping boxes outside the cabin addressed to the pharmacy," Ezra mused aloud. "Does that mean the pharmacist is involved?"

"She would have to be suspicious with so many patients being prescribed pain medication," Rosie said. "What about Dr. Manny, who treats the nursing-home patients? Would he not be involved since he writes the prescriptions?"

"Perhaps he gets a bonus for the number of prescriptions he writes. Surely some state-wide agency monitors drug prescriptions, yet with so many pharmacies, it might take time to identify abuse."

"Ezra, stop the buggy." Rosie pointed to the right. "There. That is the cabin."

Just as she had mentioned earlier, the small, single story structure was an A-frame with a screened side porch.

"I do not want the buggy to be seen in front of the cabin," Ezra cautioned. "We will look farther for a back path where we can tie Bessie."

"Then we will peer through the windows?" she asked.

"*Yah.* If we want Wagner arrested, we need evidence of wrongdoing. As we both know, the police are often not interested in what the Amish have to say. We will ensure they are interested by providing evidence they cannot ignore."

They rode past the cabin and soon found a path that angled into the woods. The dirt road was narrow and the buggy bounced over the rough terrain. When they were a far enough distance from the road so they could not be seen, Ezra pulled up on the reins. He hopped down and hitched Bessie to a nearby tree, then he helped Rosie to the ground.

"We must be careful," Ezra insisted. "The cabin appears empty, but this might not be the case. Perhaps you should stay here while I look around."

She shook her head. "I will go with you. I need to ensure it is the same cabin I remember."

"Then we will go together, but if we see anything suspect, we will turn around and come back to the buggy. On this we can agree?" he asked.

"*Yah*, cross my heart."

He wanted to laugh at the expression Mary sometimes used, but they did not have time for frivolity or lightheartedness.

If there was trouble, Rosie needed to flee as quickly as possible. The fact that she would be vulnerable worried Ezra. What they might find worried him even more.

They started to walk, pushing back the long branches and prickly vines. Both of them were silent as they made their way through the underbrush until they arrived at the wooded area behind the cabin.

Ezra watched for movement, then slowly edged toward the cabin. Rosie followed close behind him.

They climbed the steps to the back porch. Ezra held his finger to his lips and stepped to the window. He placed his hands around his eyes and peered inside, grateful that the blind was only partially closed. He could make out a large worktable and folding chairs.

"Boxes are strewn in the far corner, overflowing from a trash container," Ezra said as he continued to stare through the window.

"Did you try the door?" Rosie stepped closer and grabbed the knob. The door pushed open.

She raised her brow. "For criminals, they are not very smart to leave a door unlocked."

He glanced behind them and to the right and left. "Stay here, Rosie. I will look inside."

Ignoring his warning, she entered the cabin.

His pulse raced. "Someone could be sleeping."

She shook her head. "I can see into the bedroom. The bed is unoccupied."

Ezra followed her. Once inside, he hurried to the table littered with bubble-wrapped pill containers and prescription bottles, and read the names on the labels. "Tom Rogers. Brian Holmes. Annalise Carter."

"Annalise lives at Shady Manor. The pill holders are called blister packs, according to what Nan told me."

Rosie peered at the blister packs in the trash can. "I recognize a number of patients' names."

A car sounded outside. Ezra glanced through the front window. A white SUV turned into the drive. A second car parked directly behind the SUV.

"That is O'Donnell, the manager of Shady Manor," Rosie whispered as her former boss stepped from his car.

Ezra grabbed her arm. "Come. We must leave now."

They hurried to the back door, pulled it open and closed it quietly behind them just as the front door opened.

Heart pounding and with a warning voice chastising him for putting Rosie in danger again, Ezra ushered her across the clearing and back to the wooded area. He glanced over his shoulder, fearing they were being followed.

"Do not stop, Ezra, or they might see us."

He grabbed Rosie's hand, and together they made their way to the buggy. She hid in the rear and Ezra climbed onto the front seat. He slapped the reins and turned the mare toward the road, only this time they headed for the lake, never passing the house again. Ezra needed to get away from the cabin, away from the lake and especially away from the two men involved in the drug racket.

They had found the cabin but had failed to retrieve evidence that would bring Wagner and O'Donnell to justice.

Rosie nudged Ezra's shoulder with something she was holding in her outstretched hand.

"I took one of the blister packs labeled for a Shady Manor patient," she said when he glanced back. "Perhaps it will convince law enforcement to investigate."

As enthused as Rosie seemed, Ezra was less confident. Pill packages would do little to prove what was really happening, even if it had been retrieved from an isolated cabin in the woods.

Without hard evidence to incriminate O'Donnell and Wagner, Rosie would remain one of law enforcement's prime suspects, especially if she was caught with one of the empty pill packs on her person.

Perhaps Peter could provide information about the pharmacist. Was Rayleen involved? If only Peter would be able to tell them.

"Where does Peter live?" Rosie asked after Ezra told her his plan.

"Just outside town. Remember Aaron mentioned his older brother. Did you know Jonas?"

Rosie shook her head. "If he was a few years older than you, he would have been five or six years older than me. I was a quiet child that stayed to myself."

"I remember you as having your hand in the air, always ready to answer questions and always having the right answer."

She smiled. "Perhaps your memory is mistaken."

"If Wagner and O'Donnell remain at the cabin sorting through their pills, we can drive to Peter's house and talk to him, if he is home. Then we can return to the mountain without running into anyone who could do us harm."

They rode in silence until the town appeared in the distance. Ezra pulled onto a small farm and stopped near the two-story Amish house. He waved to Peter, who peered from the barn.

Ezra met him there. Rosie stayed in the buggy. She needed to remain out of sight, plus, Peter might be more apt to talk to Ezra without her standing close by.

The conversation did not take long. Ezra returned to the buggy and hurried the mare onto the roadway. "We'll take the back way as soon as we come to the turnoff."

Once they were on the mountain path and hidden from view by the dense wooden area that flanked the road, Rosie climbed to the front and slipped onto the seat next to Ezra.

"What did Peter say?" she asked.

"He does not know why Rayleen told him she did not need him at work. Peter said a big shipment had just arrived from one of the pharmaceutical companies. Usually Rayleen has Peter unload the medication while she organizes it on the shelves in the pharmacy."

"What about the opioid drugs that could be sold for profit?" she asked.

"Many of those are kept locked up. Peter does not have access."

"But he sees the meds?"

"He knows where they are kept, but he has no idea how many are in stock. He did check the computer inventory. The pills that came in one morning were disbursed by afternoon."

"To the various nursing homes in the area?"

"Or somewhere else. He saw pills for one of the patients that had not been packaged along with the other medication going to the nursing home."

"What happened?"

"Peter pointed out the problem to Rayleen, but she did not seem concerned."

"What about Nan? Did he see her at the pharmacy?"

"A woman with red hair stopped in two days ago. Rayleen told Peter to go the deli and order his lunch. When he said it was too early in the day, Rayleen gave him twenty dollars for a pizza and told him to keep the change."

"Did he go?"

"He did and when he finished the pizza and returned to the pharmacy, the red-haired woman was gone and Rayleen was on the phone. He heard her say something about a nurse from Shady Manor, but he could not make out what else was being said. Later that day, Rayleen said she no longer needed his help."

Rosie was the reason Nan had visited the pharmacist. Once Rayleen realized the nurse was onto her or onto the nursing-home racket, she must have warned Larry

Wagner and the nursing home manager. Had they killed Nan, making it seem like an overdose?

The nurse's death was Rosie's fault. Another mistake she had made that had led to pain and suffering and murder.

Rosie had to leave the mountain. She had to leave so no more people would die. She glanced at the Amish man who had done so much to ensure she remained safe.

More than anything she wanted Ezra to remain safe. She had to leave the mountain not only for her own good and the good of her child, but also for Ezra. No matter how much she wanted to stay.

Chapter Seventeen

Mary ran into the house when she came home from school, her face flushed and eyes wide. She stopped in the kitchen and peered into the living area. "Where is Joseph?"

"Upstairs. He is taking a long nap today." Ezra looked out the kitchen window. "Where is your brother?"

"Davey is walking slowly. I ran home because I have to tell Rosie the news."

"Here I am." Rosie came down the stairs carrying Joseph, who rubbed his eyes and looked like he wanted to go back to sleep. When he spied Mary, he started to laugh.

"I need to tell you about the Christmas pageant at school."

Rosie nodded to encourage the girl to continue.

"Mrs. Trochman's baby was to be the infant Jesus, but the family is going to Pennsylvania to visit relatives. Now they must leave early so that means we need a new baby."

She stopped and looked from Rosie to Ezra.

Ezra smiled. "A new baby?"

"A real live baby," Mary explained. "Our teacher said for us to go home and think of a baby we can borrow."

"You are going to borrow a baby?" he teased.

Mary put her hand on her hip and rolled her blue eyes. "We will *not* borrow a baby because we have Joseph."

"Joseph?" Rosie stepped closer. "Tell me what you are thinking, Mary."

"That Joseph could be our infant Jesus."

Rosie glanced at Ezra as she touched Mary's shoulder. "That is nice of you to consider Joseph for your pageant. You and your family have been so generous to have us in your home, but Joseph and I must leave soon."

Tears swarmed the young girl's eyes. "You cannot leave. Joseph is going to be my brother. I am a good big sister. You said how much he loves me."

Rosie leaned down and rubbed her hand over the girl's cheek. "He does love you very much, Mary. You see how he laughs and waves and kicks his feet when you are close by. He does that because he wants to be your friend."

"Does he want to be my brother?"

"I am sure he would want that, as well, if he could talk, but Joseph and I must move to another area. Perhaps someday we will come back here or you will come to where we live and you will be able to see each other again."

"But I told my teacher that I know a baby who could be the infant Jesus."

"What have I said about making promises you cannot keep, Mary?" Ezra cautioned.

She pouted her lips. "But you promised that we would be happy again and that *Mamm* and *Datt* would be watching out for us and that I would feel their love, but all I feel is sadness. When Rosie and Joseph came here, I thought we could forget what happened and start a new family."

Ezra reached for the child and pulled her into his arms, his own heart feeling the pain she expressed. "We are a family, Mary, and always will be a family. You are a wonderful child and *Mamm* and *Datt* are still in our hearts. That will never change."

"But once Rosie came into our house, you became happier, Ezra. Everything changed for the better. I do not want to go back to the way it was."

He closed his eyes, wishing they could all go back to before the robbery, when his parents were still alive. He would be a different son. He would not make the careless comments that set everything into motion.

Ezra was to blame for his parents' deaths and his sister's pain. Yet they could not go back, and if even if they did, that meant leaving Rosie out of the moment and more than anything he wanted her here, standing in the kitchen, her eyes filled with understanding. Perhaps she, more than anyone else, knew about mistakes.

"Ask Rosie to stay, Ezra." Mary burrowed her face into his shoulder. "Tell her she can join our family."

Ezra wanted to do that, but when he looked at Rosie she turned away from him and walked into the living area with Joseph and stood at the window, staring into the distance. She planned to leave the mountain and leave all of them to make her new life in another place. She did not need a man who had thought only of himself and who could not provide the love and acceptance his family needed.

Rosie helped Susan prepare the evening meal while Joseph sat on the floor. The wooden toys Mary had given him to play with surrounded him, but he seemed less than interested.

"Joseph is not his joyful self," Susan noted as she peeled potatoes.

"He slept a long time today, perhaps it is the tooth." Although Rosie worried it could be something more.

She glanced outside to where the children were working with Ezra. "I thought Mary might come inside to play with Joseph, but she is helping Ezra."

"He has been a good leader for our family," Susan pointed out. "And he showers attention on the younger children. I believe Mary's outburst today was more about her own grief rather than his lack of concern. Plus, she has given her heart to Joseph."

Susan reached for another potato. "Joseph is an adorable baby, and your presence in the house has brought a warmth we have not felt in all this time without our parents."

As much as she appreciated Susan's comment, Rosie knew she and Joseph had done nothing to add to the family unity. Instead, they had brought strife.

"Perhaps it is the time of year," Rosie mused. "Christmas is for family gatherings and celebrations. Those not with us are more deeply missed."

She thought of her own parents. Her *mamm* would cook a plump chicken, prepare stuffing, mashed potatoes and gravy for the meal. Her *datt* would eat silently, hardly noticing *Mamm's* efforts to make the day meaningful.

"When I was young, my father would read from scripture the story of Jesus's birth to begin the day," Rosie continued. "It was a joyous time and a holy day."

"You said in your childhood. Did that change?"

"Everything changed as I grew older. My *datt* turned inward. He would spend all morning on the chores, and he ignored the scripture. I always felt I had hurt him in some way, yet I did not know how. I tried to earn his love and drive away the darkness that had settled over our house."

"Your parents had no more children?"

She shook her head. "A sweet niece lived with us for a while when her mother had a difficult pregnancy and needed bed rest. The little one brought joy to my heart, but even she could not change the pall that seemed to hang over our family."

"The child has returned to her parents?"

Rosie nodded. "The family lives in Ohio. I am hoping they might have room for Joseph and me, at least until I can find my way."

Susan raised an eyebrow. "Would that be Katherine's daughter?"

Rosie nodded. "Do you know Alice?"

"I knew her years ago but have not seen her for some time. Ohio is a long way from Georgia."

"But it is time we leave. All of you have been so kind to take Joseph and me into your home."

"And into our family," Susan added. "Mary is right, you have brought a lightness of heart to Ezra and a joy to all of us. We have the room if you wish to stay."

If only Ezra felt the same.

"All of you need to go on with your lives," Rosie insisted.

"I do not think Ezra feels that way."

"He must look for a wife within the community. With me here, he is not free to make that next step."

Susan placed the pot of peeled potatoes on the stove. "I do not think he needs to search farther."

Her words touched Rosie. If only they were true, but Susan saw through her own eyes and did not realize all that Rosie sensed when she was with Ezra. Plus, Susan had a false picture of Rosie. She did not realize what she had allowed to happen and the pain she had caused her family.

The smell of roasting meat filled the kitchen when Susan opened the oven and placed the large pan of meat on the back of the stove. "The broth from the roast will make good gravy. Thick and rich."

Rosie washed her hands and then picked up Joseph. His forehead felt warm when she tucked him close to her cheek. He laid his head on her shoulder and cuddled closer.

"His tooth must hurt," Susan said.

"He feels like he has a temperature. I will rock him by the fire if you do not need my help."

"Take care of Joseph. Will you have something to eat with us?"

Rosie shook her head. "Maybe later, once the baby is feeling better."

She slipped into the rocker and sat close to the wood-burning stove. The warmth was inviting, and she cuddled Joseph in her arms and softly sang a lullaby he liked.

The children and Ezra came inside and peered at them from the kitchen. They talked amongst themselves in hushed tones as if they, too, were concerned about her child.

Ezra washed his hands, then entered the living area

and peered down at the baby. "Susan said Joseph has a fever."

Rosie nodded. "He feels warm. I was hoping he would fall asleep, but his eyes remain open."

"You must eat."

She shook her head. "Not now. Not until he is better."

"We have medication for fever, but it is not for babies."

"I would fear doing more harm since he is so young."

Ezra nodded. "Do as you think best. I will have Susan save a plate for you."

"Thank you, Ezra." The man was thoughtful and considerate, for which she was grateful. If only he could find a good woman to help him take care of the children and be his partner for life.

Rosie glanced at where he stood in the kitchen. Their eyes met and a warmth settled over her. She looked away, forcing herself to ignore any response on her part to his understanding gaze.

The family spoke little during dinner, and Rosie caught the boys glancing with concern to where she sat. They all appeared worried, just as she was.

Ezra encouraged the four younger children to go to bed early. "With sickness in the house, you all need to get a good night's sleep to ward off the germs."

If one of them got sick because of Joseph, she would be even more upset. *Gott, keep them safe and healthy.*

The house sat quiet as she rocked her baby. Joseph's eyes eventually closed and hers did as well.

Sometime later, she woke with a start. Ezra was sitting in a rocker, staring at her. She adjusted in the seat, feeling embarrassed.

Looking down at Joseph's flushed face and feeling the heat radiating from his little body filled her with fear.

She brought his face up to her cheek, the heat nearly burning her. "His fever is too high"

Ezra rose from the chair. "What can I do?"

"Get a washcloth and towel and a basin of tepid water."

"In here." He motioned her to the bedroom where he slept. "There is a clean towel and cloth on the stand. I'll fill the basin with water."

Rosie laid Joseph on Ezra's bed and removed the blankets from around his hot body. Her hands trembled as she unsnapped his sleeper and pulled his hands and legs free.

Ezra returned with the bowl. He dipped the washcloth in the water, rang it out and handed it to her. She wiped the baby's arms and legs and patted Joseph dry with a towel. Then she repeated the process, wiping his face and stomach. Turning him over, she rubbed the cloth gently over his back.

"This should lower his temperature and cool his body a bit, but I am worried, Ezra."

"There is an urgent-care clinic in town that is open until midnight. We should take him there."

Rosie did not want her baby out in the cold with so high a fever, but he needed medical help. If anything happened to him—

She slipped Joseph back into his sleeper, refusing to dwell on "what if."

"I can hold him while you get what you need for the trip to town," Ezra offered.

Much as she did not want Joseph out of her arms,

she needed to get blankets and diapers and a bottle with water for the trip.

Ezra took the baby and instead of being stiff, he cuddled Joseph close and peered down at him with love in his eyes. Rosie's heart almost broke at what she wanted for her child—a good father to shower him with love, to teach him the ways of the farm and of life, to counsel and encourage him as he grew.

She turned and ran upstairs to fetch the items for the trip to town.

Soon ready, she took the baby from Ezra's arms, their hands touching, their eyes meeting, both of them struggling with worry about Joseph's condition.

"I will hitch the buggy," Ezra said. "We need to tell Susan."

"I already did. She is praying."

"I am as well," Ezra said with a nod before he hurried from the house.

Alone in the kitchen, Rosie's heart nearly broke as she glanced down at her precious child, sick with a raging fever. She was helpless to care for him.

Please, Gott, do not take him from me. I could not bear to go on. I promise to leave this area and this wonderful family so they can continue with their lives without my interference.

She sighed. Leaving would be hard, especially leaving Ezra.

Chapter Eighteen

The night was pitch-black as Ezra hurried Bessie down the mountain toward town. Rosie sat in the rear, cradling Joseph. Ezra glanced back, seeing only her big eyes wide with worry. He knew her face was pale as death, just as it had been in the kitchen.

He wanted to reach out and touch her hand and offer support, but she did not need his touch when her baby was in her arms. Her only thought was Joseph.

Hopefully, a good doctor would be on duty, one who could examine a small infant and diagnose what was wrong. Ezra shivered thinking of what could happen.

He knew too well that everything could change in the blink of an eye. A robbery, a murder, five children orphaned with only a big brother to care for them.

He shook his head, recalling all the mistakes he had made and regretting each of them. If only *Gott* could forgive him. If only he could forgive himself.

Headlights from farther down the mountain appeared in the distance. Usually the road was void of traffic except an occasional Amish buggy with teens coming home from a singing.

Why would a car be on the road this late at night?

He stomach twisted. He had not seen the man with the streak of white hair since the cabin. Hopefully Wagner was still there counting his illegal pills and the money he had to be raking in, as plentiful as a good fall harvest.

Ezra hated to worry Rosie even more, but she needed to be warned. "A car is coming up the mountain. Surely it will pass by, but be prepared to duck down if the driver pulls to a stop."

"Can you tell if it is an SUV?"

"All I see are the headlights." They were positioned higher than on a sedan, which meant it could be an all-terrain vehicle. Not that he would share the information with Rosie.

He braced himself as the auto drew closer. The headlights blinded him for a moment and spooked Bessie. He steadied the reins to keep the mare in line.

Without warning, the SUV swerved in front of the buggy and screeched to a stop.

Bessie balked but stopped just in time.

The driver rolled down the passenger window and leaned across the console. He raised his voice and shouted to Ezra. "Strange to see an Amish man on the road this late."

Grateful that Wagner had failed to recognize him, Ezra said nothing and hoped Rosie and the baby were out of sight.

"I'm looking for an Amish gal with a baby." The man slurred his words as if he had been drinking.

"I have not seen anyone on the road. You should head back to town. A bear is said to prowl the mountain at night. I have heard stories of him crashing through windshields and causing damage even to the biggest cars."

"You're making that up."

"Am I?"

The man pursed his lips as if considering Ezra's warning before he slipped back to the driver's seat and, using the master controls, rolled up the passenger window. He reversed direction and drove off.

Ezra let out a sigh of relief. He turned to the rear, but saw no one. Where was Rosie?

She climbed out from under the blanket, still holding Joseph. "He will not give up looking for me, Ezra. He thinks I have information that I will turn over to the police. If only I did. We must find a way to stop him."

"He will go home now, Rosie. We will worry about him in the morning. Right now, we need to head for the clinic before it closes."

Ezra turned his gaze back to the road and flicked the reins, hurrying the mare to town, to the doctor and to help for Joseph.

Do not let another person die, Gott, especially a precious baby who has found a place in my heart.

Ezra realized someone else had taken hold of his heart.

Rosie.

The urgent-care clinic was ready to lock its doors for the night when Rosie and Ezra arrived with Joseph. They were quickly ushered into an exam room.

"Do you mind if I stay with you?" Ezra asked after the nurse had left.

"Of course not. I appreciate your support."

She cradled Joseph in her arms. He was still so hot.

A nurse knocked on the partially closed door and pushed it open. "I need to get some information." She pulled up a stool to the laptop computer that sat on a small side table. After punching a few keys, she started to fill in information.

"Do you have access to a phone?" the nurse asked.

"No."

"Address?"

Rosie glanced at Ezra. "We are between homes at the moment."

"Some type of contact information is necessary in case the doctor wants to get in touch with you, ma'am."

"Three fourteen Mountain Road," Ezra volunteered his address.

"Thank you, sir. And the baby's name is Joseph Glick?"

"Yes," Rosie responded.

"When did you or your husband notice the baby not feeling well?" the nurse asked.

Rosie held up her hand. "He is not—"

Ezra's gaze met hers.

Flustered, she ignored the nurse's comment. "Joseph took a longer-than-usual nap this afternoon. Later in the evening, he started to develop a fever and refused to eat. He had no interest in toys or—"

She glanced again at Ezra. "Or his seven-year-old sister, who loves him so much."

"Did you take his temperature?"

"I do not have a thermometer."

The nurse raised her eyebrows. Her questioning gaze made Rosie feel like an irresponsible mother.

"Mrs. Glick, did you give him anything to take down the fever?"

"We had nothing in the house for an eight-month-old."

The nurse clipped a device to Joseph's toe and watched as a number appeared on a small digital screen.

"His oxygen saturation level is 98." She placed a digital thermometer under his arm until it beeped and recorded both results in the computer.

"Axillary temp 103," she said.

The words burned a hole in Rosie's heart. "His temperature is so high. What about his oxygen level?"

"His pulse ox is normal. I'll let the doctor know about his temp." She left the room.

Rosie wiped her hand over Joseph's hot brow. "Surely they will give him something to take down the fever," she whispered to Ezra.

"The doctor will order it, Rosie. A little longer and he will be with us."

The doctor pushed into the room without knocking. "I'm Dr. Philips." His name was embroidered on the pocket of the lab coat, which he wore over scrubs.

"Tell me about your son's symptoms."

Rosie repeated what she had told the nurse. "Usually he is happy and playful. Today, he was too tired to interact with anyone."

The doctor felt Joseph's neck, pressed on his stomach, tested his reflexes and looked into his ears and his throat.

"His throat is red. Some spotting. Could be strep. We'll draw blood for lab work and take a urine specimen. The results will be back tomorrow. One of our nurses will contact you."

He checked the computer. "You folks don't have access to a phone?"

"I can return tomorrow," Ezra volunteered.

"The labs should be back by early morning. We'll give you a copy of the results for the child's medical records."

"What do you think he has?" Rosie asked.

"Looks like strep throat to me. We could do a rapid strep test, but I'll just go ahead and prescribe an antibiotic. We'll swab his throat. Something might grow out in the next twenty-four to forty-eight hours. The nurse will give him Tylenol to take down that fever and start an IV. Joseph is dehydrated. Fluids will help. We'll read his blood smear here and do the preliminary urinalysis before you leave."

Rosie glanced at the wall clock. "I am sure the pharmacy is closed at this time of night. Where can we get the prescription filled?"

"We can fill it here and send you home with the meds. Joseph should be feeling better and no longer contagious in twenty-four hours."

The doctor shook their hands before he left the room. The nurse entered soon thereafter, administered the medication and started the IV.

"You folks make yourselves comfortable." She glanced around the room. "I can bring in another chair."

"That won't be necessary," Ezra assured her. "I can use the computer stool."

Rosie pulled her chair closer to the exam table where Joseph was lying. "You'll feel better as soon as your temperature drops," she said, smiling at her little one.

He reached for the IV tubing. She blocked his hand and then dug in the tote where she had tucked an extra blanket and diapers. She had also brought a toy.

"What is that?" Ezra asked.

"A finger puppet Will gave me soon after I learned I was pregnant. He wanted me to keep it for the baby."

Joseph grabbed the toy and waved it in the air. Distracted when the nurse came back into the room to check the IV, he opened his hand and the toy dropped through his fingers.

Ezra picked it up and studied it more closely once they were alone again. "There's something hard inside the puppet."

"Probably a weight," Rosie mused.

"Which seems strange for a baby's toy. You would not want anything hazardous to hurt Joseph."

Ezra turned over the toy and drew out a small metal object. "This is not a toy, Rosie. It is the cover for a flash drive."

She leaned forward. "I do not understand."

"A flash drive stores information that can be saved from or downloaded to a computer."

He scooted next to the laptop. "Let me show you."

"Why would William want his child to have a flash drive?" Rosie asked.

"We will know more when we determine what the drive contains."

Ezra inserted the flash drive into the USB port, tapped the keyboard and watched as information unfurled across the monitor.

"What do you see?" she asked.

"Records. Names and shipments to various addresses in the surrounding area." He scrolled down further. "Looks like as far away as Atlanta."

"Names and addresses? You mean delivery information? Could it be where Will took the packages?"

"More than likely. Patient names are also listed and

the number of pills received from each prescription."
Ezra turned to Rosie, his brow raised. "The records are
quite thorough."

"Will was worried about someone coming after him.
He often told me that he needed protection."

Ezra opened another file. Pictures appeared. "Here
is a photograph of the nursing-home manager. Another
shows Larry Wagner, the man with the patch of white
hair."

Ezra clicked on another file. He pointed to the screen.
"Look at this photo."

Two young men, probably in their early twenties,
who looked alike and had the same swatch of premature white hair. They stood behind a table loaded with
prescription drugs.

Rosie leaned closer. "The men resemble Mr. Wagner."

"They could be his sons. Another person stands behind them."

Ezra enlarged the screen and moved the curser so
the man came into view.

Rosie's stomach tightened.

The third man in the photo was someone she knew
too well.

The man was Will MacIntosh.

Ezra kept thinking about the pictures on the flash
drive. The two men in the photo with the swatches of
white hair kept playing through his mind. From their
close resemblance, they could be twins.

After his parents' deaths, Ezra had worked hard to
keep from thinking about that terrible day, yet tonight,
everything kept flooding back to him. He heard the si-

rens in his head and the words of the person who had come to find him at the bar. "Your parents were shot," the man had said.

Bessie had never traveled so fast. Ezra had taken the back road and had arrived home moments after the ambulance to find both his parents, lying in pools of blood on the floor of the workshop. His father had been pronounced dead, but his mother was still responsive.

He had pushed past the EMTs, dropped to his knees and reached for her hand. "Forgive me, *Mamm*." He had cried like a child who had gone against his mother's instructions, but his guilt involved more than a child's disrespect. Ezra had led the killers to his parents.

The guilt still hung heavy on his shoulders.

Ezra sighed with regret as they approached the top of the mountain. He glanced back at Rosie, holding Joseph, and then tugged on the reins, guiding Bessie through the gate and past the workshop to the house.

Once the buggy came to a stop, he hurried Rosie inside and helped her settle Joseph in the crib. The baby was less feverish and Rosie's relief was evident, although she appeared exhausted and ready to collapse.

"Rest now," he told her. "We can talk in the morning."

"Sleep can wait, Ezra. There are some things I must explain."

She followed him downstairs to the kitchen and beckoned him to sit while she stood by the table. Once he was seated, she began to speak.

"My father made me feel like I was always doing something for which he was not pleased. William made me feel pretty and smart and nice, at least in the beginning. Only Will's type of love was flawed. He was more interested in himself, which I realized too late."

"This is all in the past, Rosie. You do not need to open old wounds."

"I want you to know what happened, Ezra." She glanced down and clasped her hands together as if in prayer. "We drove all the way to Dahlonega to buy a pregnancy test kit. I did not want anyone here in the Amish community to suspect what I feared was true. A few days later, Will gave me the toy for the baby. By then, I had realized my mistake."

Her eyes were filled with pain when she looked at Ezra. His heart broke for the suffering she had endured.

"Will did not love me," she continued. "He loved the control he had over me. A man with a streak of white hair came after him and killed him. I am certain it was Larry Wagner."

"I am sorry, Rosie." Ezra started to stand. He wanted to go to her and hold her close, but she held up her hand to stop him.

"Someday I will tell Joseph about his father, although I do not know how much I will reveal. But that is in the future and right now, I am concerned about the present. I have brought danger to you and your family and maybe my aunt Katherine, as well as being responsible for Nan's death."

"Rosie, you are innocent of any wrongdoing except of loving the wrong person."

"You are right." She nodded. "William *was* the wrong person. When I saw his picture this evening, I knew I had to tell you."

Ezra stood and took her hand. "The picture explained much to me, as well. My mother was still alive when I arrived home that day. As I kneeled beside her, she clutched my hand, her eyes starting to glaze over. 'Doppelgänger,' she tried to say. '*Weisses haar.*'"

Ezra's heart ached, recalling how she had struggled to make him understand. "The EMTs administered oxygen, but she pushed the mask aside. Raising up ever so slightly, she repeated, 'Doppelgänger, *weisses haar.*' Tonight, when I saw the picture, I understood what she was trying to say. Doppelgänger. Two people who look similar, like twins."

"And white hair?" Rosie asked. "You think she was talking about the men in the picture?"

He nodded. "Twins, each with a streak of white hair."

"Your mother was revealing information about the killers." Rosie's eyes widened. "The day we found out I was pregnant, Will told me he would soon have money so we could leave town and start a new life together."

Tears filled her eyes. "Oh, Ezra, I'm so sorry." She turned toward the stairs.

He grabbed her arm. "Rosie, talk to me."

"Do you not realize what that picture tells me? A third man was involved. That man was Will." She pulled her arm from his hold and ran up the stairs.

Ezra stared after her. Will MacIntosh had killed his parents? Could that be so? A chill settled over him.

He walked outside, needing fresh air and a moment to think about what Rosie had said. He stared into the night, then turned his gaze to his father's workshop. Ezra had locked the door that day and had never gone into it after the police investigation.

Needing to face the past, he retrieved the key. Stepping inside, his gut tightened as he saw the blood stains on the floor. He fisted his hands, then stepped toward the row of buggies. With a little work, a few of them would soon be ready for sale. Aaron was right. Stoltz Buggies could flourish again.

He ran his hand over his father's workbench. His tools—saws and plains, drills and bits, hammers and screws and nails—all neatly in their places, just as they had been the day his parents died.

He peered into the "hole," as he and his father called the propane-run hydraulic lift that lowered buggies from the main floor down to the basement below. A buggy sat on the lower level, partially framed—it was the buggy Ezra was supposed to have been working on that fateful day. Instead, he had been with his so-called friends.

Shame covered him. He had not been able to protect his parents because he was carousing in town. Wanting to gain respect among the *Englischers* who frequented the bar, he had bragged about his father's business and the money it earned.

His gut tightened. The day before the murders, Ezra had mentioned the cash his father kept in his workshop, money the twins had come looking for. Had Will come with them?

Ezra thought again of that day at the bar. He could see the profile of a man sitting near him, who had turned to listen—his eyes sparked with interest—when Ezra talked about the money his father kept on hand. That one statement had led to his parents' deaths.

Realization hit Ezra hard.

The man at the bar had been Will MacIntosh.

Chapter Nineteen

That night, sleep eluded Ezra. Instead, thoughts of Rosie circled through his mind. Not only her internal beauty, but also her pretty face and expressive eyes and the way his heart pounded faster whenever she was near. He thought of her in his arms, their lips almost touching.

He ached thinking of what would never be.

She did not need a man who had bragged about his parents and caused their deaths. Whether Will MacIntosh was a killer made no difference. Ezra's parents would not come back to life, and their wayward eldest child would forever carry the guilt for that terrible day that had changed his life forever.

He rose earlier than usual the next morning, needing to leave the comfort of his bed in order to help Rosie. The least he could do would be to pick up the lab results from the clinic in town.

With quick, sure moves, he saddled Duke and took the back path to town. The air was cold, but Ezra did not concern himself about his own comfort. He thought only of Rosie and her baby.

Once in town, Ezra guided Duke past the nursing

home. He glanced at the sign in front of the manor. Dr. Manny, MD. The physician who ordered all the pain pills and extra medication for the patients. Manny had to be involved.

More than likely there were other criminals stealing drugs from the infirmed who ran larger operations with greater profit. However, for a mountain town with a small population, the doctor and nursing-home manager, along with the man with the streak of white hair, were doing well financially with their simple racket. Prescribe drugs, steal them from the patients and sell them to buyers in distant towns.

The local pharmacist was probably handsomely rewarded for her participation and for turning a blind eye to the illegalities of overprescribing highly addictive opioids. She was being bribed to keep her mouth shut and not alert the authorities.

The operation could have continued indefinitely except for an Amish woman who wanted to ensure her favorite patient had medication he needed for pain. Along with Rosie, thanks needed to be given to a nurse who had uncovered incongruences that did not add up. Nan had died because of what she had found.

Ezra's veins chilled. They had killed Nan. They would kill Rosie too. As soon as he had the lab results and any new medication the doctor ordered for Joseph, Ezra would return home and pack up the entire family for a Christmas holiday visit. His mother's family lived in Tennessee. Surely they would open their homes to them.

From there Ezra would notify the Tennessee authorities, who would pass the information on to the sheriff in Willkommen. Once the guilty were behind bars, Ezra and his family could return to the mountain, along with Rosie and Joseph.

Ezra turned at the third intersection and hurried toward the door of the clinic. Hours of operation—6:00 a.m. until midnight. Ezra had arrived just as it was opening.

After tying his horse to the hitching rail, he hurried inside and stopped at the receptionist's desk.

A woman wearing pink scrubs glanced up. "May I help you?"

"I need to pick up lab results for Joseph Glick."

"Dr. Philips will not be in today, but Dr. Manny is available."

"The doctor from the nursing home?"

She nodded. "That's right. Dr. Manny and Dr. Philips own the urgent-care clinic and share responsibilities. A number of other doctors fill in as well." She glanced down the hall and smiled. "There's Dr. Manny now."

The receptionist explained what Ezra needed and handed the lab results to the doctor. He glanced over the forms.

"The preliminary throat culture shows gram-positive cocci," he explained. "No doubt group-A strep. Ensure the baby takes all the antibiotic. A slightly elevated white count, but nothing to be alarmed about. If anything changes, have the mother bring him back. She and her child are staying with you?"

Ezra did not want the doctor who worked at the nursing home to know Rosie and Joseph's whereabouts. "I can contact the mother and give her the information," Ezra assured the doctor.

Once he had the lab results in hand, he hurried to his horse and headed out of town. At the turnoff to the back road, he glanced over his shoulder. His chest clenched as he spied a dark sedan. The car accelerated.

Ezra clucked his tongue and encouraged Duke, but before they could make the turn, the car swerved, cutting them off and forcing Duke into the ditch. The horse lost his footing on the embankment and fell on his side, hooves flailing in the air.

Ezra was thrown to the ground. Air whooshed from his lungs. He gasped, worried about his horse, but equally worried about the manager of the nursing home, who stepped from his car, gun in hand.

"You've caused enough problems, Stoltz. I'll take care of you. Wagner will take care of your girlfriend."

Rosie jerked awake. Jumping from the bed, she hurried to the crib and touched Joseph's forehead. He was warm, but the fever had dropped significantly.

She would let him sleep while she helped Susan with breakfast, but when she went downstairs the kitchen was empty. Rosie added logs to the kitchen stove and arranged the wood so it caught.

Once the fire took hold, she boiled water for coffee, poured it over the grounds in the aluminum drip coffeemaker and moved the pot to the warming area at the back of the stove.

The smell of the hearty coffee filled the kitchen. She opened a number of drawers, searching for a bus brochure. Finding it in the hutch, she pulled it out and read the schedule.

A bus traveled to Cincinnati, Columbus and Berlin, Ohio, weekly. She ran her fingers along the page, needing to find the departure information.

"Today at 2:00 p.m.," she said to herself. The bus

would leave some hours from now. She would need to arrive early to buy her ticket. Joseph could sit on her lap.

She would ask Aaron to drive her to town in the buggy. Not Ezra. Knowing Will could have been involved in his parents' deaths made her too upset to talk to Ezra face-to-face. Instead, she would leave a note, expressing her gratitude for all he had done.

She pulled paper and a pen from the drawer, but tears blurred her eyes as she wrote. Her heart nearly broke as she thought about leaving.

Susan's footsteps overhead signaled the girl was up and would soon be downstairs. Rosie sealed the note in an envelope and wrote Ezra's name on the outside, then placed it on the bookcase in the living area. He would find it tonight when he reached for his Bible before going to bed.

Her hands were shaking as she wiped the tears and focused on pouring a cup of coffee when Susan hurried downstairs, apologizing as she entered the kitchen.

"I must have overslept, which is not something I usually do." Susan tucked a stray strand of hair behind her ear. "How is Joseph?" she asked.

"His temperature is not so high. The antibiotic the doctor gave him must be working."

"I am glad." Susan poured coffee for herself. "I heard Ezra earlier and asked if he wanted breakfast, but he declined the offer. I laid my head down for a few more minutes and just awoke."

"Ezra was up early?" Rosie asked.

Susan nodded. "He wanted to go to town. Something about lab results for Joseph and medicine if the doctor ordered anything new."

Rosie glanced at the barn. The buggy was visible

through the open door. "He must have saddled Duke and ridden over the mountain."

"That is the fastest route. Hopefully, he will be back before breakfast is ready."

"The children are doing chores?"

"I am sure they are eager to get everything done. Mary mentioned a final pageant practice this morning before school starts. I think she wants to go early and talk to the teacher."

"Probably about Joseph not being able to participate."

"Perhaps. Last night, she confided that the teacher changed the date of the performance because so many families were leaving to visit relatives. The pageant will be held this evening."

"Tonight?"

"With the concern about Joseph being sick, she and Davey failed to share the change in plans."

Rosie's heart ached, knowing she and Joseph would be on a bus this evening, heading to Ohio.

As if aware of Rosie's upset, Susan paused from cutting slices of ham for breakfast. "Are you worried about the baby's safety?"

Rosie shook her head. "No, but it is time for us to leave the mountain and travel someplace new."

"Then you were serious about leaving, as you mentioned yesterday?" Susan asked.

"It is what I must do."

"And what of us, Rosie? Have you thought how your leaving will hurt the children? It will also hurt Ezra."

"You are a dutiful sister, Susan, who loves her brother, but his interests would be better served by me leaving. As I have mentioned before, Ezra needs to focus on his own life and his own future."

"I agree, but that is why you should stay."

Rosie wrinkled her brow. "What do you mean?"

"I mean that Ezra needs time to determine the direction he should take in the future."

"Exactly. Which is why I need to leave so he has time to decide for himself. Right now, he is worried about my safety and Joseph's. That occupies his thoughts. He needs to be free of us."

"I think more than your safety is playing through his mind."

Susan placed a skillet on the stove and added the ham. She scooped a large wedge of butter into a second skillet and sighed with frustration when she reached for the basket of eggs and found it empty.

"I will gather the eggs," Rosie said.

"It is Mary's job."

"*Yah*, and Mary is helping in other ways. Joseph is still sleeping. If you hear him cry, call me."

Rosie hurried outside. She peered into the barn as she passed, seeing the mare she had ridden to Katherine's house. She still needed to talk to her aunt.

The hens clucked as she entered the chicken house and searched the nests. "We need your eggs for breakfast, you sweet ladies," she cooed. "Your eggs are making the children strong and smart and ready for the new day."

Mary joined her there. "I was going to get the eggs soon, but I had to clean one of the stalls. Thank you for helping me with my chores."

"It is no problem. You have been such a help to me with Joseph."

"Is he still sick?""

"His temperature is down a little, which means he

feels better. I am sure he would like to see you once the sleepyhead gets up."

"I will come inside soon."

Rosie took the eggs to the kitchen and stopped short, hearing Joseph's cry.

"He just started," Susan assured her. "Bring him down for breakfast. The food is almost ready."

Rosie washed her hands and then hurried upstairs, relieved to see Joseph's cheeks were not as flushed as last night and his eyes were brighter.

"You are feeling better today," she said, clapping her hands. "*Mamm's* big boy is ready to get up?"

Rosie carried him downstairs.

Susan's glanced up from the stove and smiled. "You look better this morning, Joseph. Perhaps you will have something to eat."

"Let me put him in the high chair. A portion of biscuit and a little water might be a good start. If he is interested in food, I will give him more to eat."

As soon as she placed the food in front of him, the baby reached for the biscuit and cup and could not eat and drink fast enough.

Grateful that he was feeling better, Rosie turned to Susan. "I hate to ask again, but would you mind watching Joseph for a short time this morning? I need to talk to Katherine. I was there the other day, but she was not home."

"You will take the buggy?"

Rosie shook her head. "I would like to saddle Duchess instead. The back path will get me there more quickly. I hope to return before the children leave for school."

"Your leg is better?" Susan asked.

"Much better."

"Of course I will watch Joseph. He is such an easy baby and is so full of love." Susan began to plate the food. "Do not forget the riding pants that are on the dresser in my room."

"You do not mind?" Rosie asked.

"Of course not."

After donning the leggings, Rosie grabbed her cape and hurried outside. Aaron helped her saddle Duchess.

"You will be back soon?" he asked, giving her a hoist onto the mare.

"Before you finish breakfast."

At least she hoped that would prove true.

Chapter Twenty

Ezra fought against the rope wrapped around his hands and legs. The manager of the nursing home had brought him to the cabin and tied him up. Now O'Donnell was frantically gathering pills off the table and shoving them into a suitcase.

"I know about your drug operation," Ezra taunted, hoping to unsettle O'Donnell. "The police have been alerted."

The manager laughed nervously. "Some of the police have known the entire time. They enjoy the extra money they receive by looking in the other direction."

"The pharmacist is onto you."

O'Donnell chuckled again. "You Amish are so unworldly. We couldn't do this without the pharmacist."

"She does not want to be involved with anything illegal. Can you tell from the questions she asks and her concern about how much the operation has grown?"

Ezra hoped a portion of what he said sounded plausible. According to Peter, the pharmacist seemed upset. Surely that had to do with what was occurring and her involvement. Providing just a little doubt could be enough to unnerve O'Donnell completely.

"You didn't talk to Rayleen," he insisted.

"Why do you say that? She fills prescriptions for many of the Amish. We are not blind to what is going on. The nurse, Nan Smith, died because she demanded information, but before you killed her, she had called the police and told them her concerns."

"I don't believe you. I told you the police are in favor of our operation. It serves them well."

"I am not talking about the local police. You are right. Most of them are corrupt. But the sheriff in Willkommen. Do you know him? He is hard-working and honest. He listens to the truth."

"You're lying, Stoltz. You don't remember the day you were in that bar talking about your parents and the money they kept in your father's workshop. I was there. I heard you. You were boasting about how wealthy you were and how special your father was." He laughed. "Only you made everyone there take note."

"Especially the Wagner twins, who killed my parents?" O'Donnell raised his brow. "You know that to be true?"

"So does the sheriff. Tell your friend Larry who works with you that his sons should enjoy their last days before they end up in jail."

"You do not have proof."

"Do I not?"

The manager slammed his fist against the table. "So Will *did* steal information."

"You are jumping to the wrong conclusions." Ezra tried to back step. The last thing he wanted was for O'Donnell to go after Rosie. He glanced at the clock. "The sheriff and his deputies will be here soon."

"Your girlfriend, Rosie, must have the information."

"She received nothing from William. You do not have to worry about her. Worry more about yourself and what you will tell the authorities when they arrive."

"You Amish were never good at lying." O'Donnell pulled out his phone, tapped in a number and lifted the cell to his ear. "Larry…"

He glanced at Ezra.

"The woman's probably hiding at the Stoltz's house. Manny gave me the address. Three fourteen Mountain Road. You were right all along. If Will stole information, she's got to have it. Don't let her get away." O'Donnell smirked. "After you take care of her, come to the cabin and get rid of her new boyfriend."

He disconnected and pushed another button. "Rayleen, it's Bruce. I've got the pills and the money. Meet me at the interstate. A buyer's waiting for us at the airport in Atlanta. Once we leave the country, the authorities won't be able to touch us."

Ezra's blood chilled. He wanted to scream with rage. His plan to outsmart the criminals had backfired. They knew about the evidence and, even worse, they believed Rosie had it in her keeping.

The thought of what could happen if Wagner found her was too much for Ezra to bear. He had made another mistake, and this time it would cost Rosie her life.

"What will I tell Ezra when he returns home?" Aaron asked Rosie after she had mounted Duchess and grabbed the reins.

"Tell him I needed to warn my aunt about Larry Wagner."

"The man with the white streak of hair?"

She nodded. "When I come back from seeing Katherine, I want you to drive Joseph and me to the bus station."

"You are leaving?"

"*Yah.* While you are in town, you must find Peter. Tell him to contact law enforcement and share what he knows about the pharmacy. Wagner and the manager of Shady Manor are stealing drugs from the patients. Rayleen and Dr. Manny are probably involved."

"The local police will not listen," Aaron said. "They did not help after our parents were killed. Ezra calls them corrupt."

"That is why Peter needs to call the sheriff in Willkommen. He will listen and act on what he hears."

Rosie nudged the horse's flank. "Let's go, girl."

Duchess headed down the hill at a good clip. Thankfully, this time, there were no snakes. The mare remained on the path and Rosie stayed in the saddle.

Nearing Katherine's house, she pulled on the reins. "Whoa, girl."

Rosie slipped to the ground and tied the horse to a tree branch near the old, dilapidated barn, all the while watching for anything that looked suspicious.

The door to the new barn near the house hung open. Rosie peered inside, relieved to see her aunt. Katherine was petite and well-rounded with rosy cheeks and expressive eyes that now looked worried as she hurried to greet Rosie.

"I did not expect your visit, child. Is everything all right?"

"I wish it were. I have been staying with the Stoltz family. There is a vile man with a streak of white hair who seeks to do me harm. I fear he might hurt you, Katherine."

"You must be talking about Larry Wagner."

"You know him?"

Katherine nodded. "*Yah*, but I have not seen him for years."

The look on her aunt's face made Rosie step closer. "Is there something you need to tell me?"

"Why do you mean, dear?"

"Larry knows my parents."

Katherine's eyes widened ever so slightly. "Why, yes, he does."

"How could they get involved with someone like him?"

"You should ask your father."

"*Datt* would never tell me anything about his past. Nor would *Mamm*. Therefore you must tell me."

Katherine nodded knowingly, her eyes filled with understanding. "Your father should have told you long ago, dear, about his past. He left the Amish life in his youth and ran with some wild boys in town. Larry Wagner was one of them."

"And my mother?"

"She was a pretty girl and liked the things Larry bought her."

Confused, Rosie stepped closer. "My mother was involved with Mr. Wagner?"

"Only for a brief time. She eventually came to her senses and realized she did not want to leave the Amish community. Your father was interested in her as well. He and Larry sparred often, each trying to earn your mother's love. When your *datt* promised to remain Amish, your mother made her choice."

"And Larry?"

"Supposedly, he left town heartbroken. He reappeared some years ago. You must have been twelve or thirteen. You and your *datt* were shopping in town. From what I heard, Larry said something to you that bothered your father."

The man on the street who had wanted to take Rosie's picture.

"You look so much like your mother, I think your father worried that Larry would take you from him."

"That is foolish talk, Katherine."

"Of course it is, but your father always sees himself as the victim. He is right, and everyone else is wrong."

"I was wrong to get involved with Will MacIntosh."

"Do not be so hard on yourself." Katherine touched Rosie's shoulder. "Mistakes happens. We know that. So does your father."

"Perhaps, although *Datt* has not been able to forgive my transgressions."

"Shame on him after all the problems he caused in his youth. Your father has always been quick to point his finger at others, yet he ignores the three fingers pointed back at him. That is why he was always so strict with you, child. He did not want you to make the same mistakes he did. What he did not realize was that by being hard on you, he was forcing you out of the family. You did not find love at home. Of course you would look for it somewhere else."

Katherine's words touched a hole in Rosie's heart. "I take responsibility for my own actions."

"*Yah*, but knowing the reason behind the actions allows us to forgive ourselves as well as those whose lack of compassion set us up to make those mistakes."

"I cannot blame my father."

"Perhaps not, child. But I can. Why do you think he isolates himself from the church? He knows he was at fault, yet he is not willing to admit his failings as a father. The pain he carries forces him to distance himself from his family and from his community. I worry about your mother. She is a *gut* woman to put up with your father."

"Perhaps when I leave the mountain, he will come back to the church."

Katherine's eyes narrowed. "You are leaving?"

"To make a new start for myself and my son. I had hoped Alice would have room for us at least until I can get a job and find a place to stay."

"I am sure my daughter would love to have you visit, but go only for a short time until Larry Wagner, who seeks to do you harm, is stopped. Then come back, Rosie. There is a *gut* man here who could use a strong, sensible woman like you."

Rosie did not understand.

Katherine took her hand. "You are staying at the Stoltz home, *yah*? Ezra carries much of the burden for his parents' deaths. It is time for him to move beyond the past and embrace the present."

"I did not come here to talk about Ezra. I came to warn you about Mr. Wagner."

"If Larry stops to visit or to create mischief, he will not find me at home. Just now, I was hitching my buggy to visit my husband's sister. She has invited me for Christmas. I have locked the house and am ready to go. But first, let me give you my daughter's address. She and her husband are well-known in Holmes County."

Katherine drew paper and pen from her bag and jotted down the address. "Tell Alice I will visit soon. You being there gives me another reason to make the long trip. Perhaps your mother will come with me."

"That would be wonderful." Rosie hugged her aunt. "Enjoy Christmas, Katherine, and be safe."

She glanced at the valley and her heart lurched, seeing a vehicle on the road below.

"Someone comes." She narrowed her gaze. "It is a white SUV."

Katherine steeled her spine and shoved her chin out with defiance. "I am not afraid of Larry Wagner."

"He will stop at nothing to find me, including hurting you." Rosie grabbed her aunt's arm. "Come with me. You can help with the children."

Katherine hesitated for only a moment and then hurried up the hill with Rosie. She untied Duchess and, using a large boulder as a step stool, hoisted Katherine into the saddle and climbed behind her aunt.

Heart in her throat, Rosie spurred Duchess on. She had to alert the children and get them to safety.

Where was Ezra? Rosie had hoped he would be home by now. But his horse was not in his stall as she jumped to the ground and called to Aaron, who was working in the barn.

"Help Katherine from the saddle, then hitch Bessie to the buggy. You and the children have to leave. Katherine is going with you."

Rosie raced into the house. "Hurry, you must leave now," she called to the children. "Grab your coats and capes."

She lifted Joseph from his high chair and wrapped

him in two heavy blankets. "Susan, take him. Take my baby and keep him safe."

Rosie glanced around. "Where is Mary?"

"She is making something for you and Joseph. Aaron said you planned to leave soon."

Rosie raced up the stairs, taking them two at a time. "Mary?"

She found the little girl sitting on the floor of her room, coloring a picture. Her face was blotched as if she had been crying, which broke Rosie's heart.

"You must go with Susan and the others, Mary. It is not safe here."

The girl did not understand. Instead she handed Rosie the picture. It was a drawing of her family with each person's name written under the various figures.

Ezra was the tallest. Mary had made him stand above the others, looking strong, with a wide smile on his face. His arms were wrapped around an Amish woman holding a baby.

"That is you and that is Joseph," the child said, pointing to the woman nestled in Ezra's embrace. "I made you part of our family."

"Oh, Mary, if only that could be, but right now you need to hurry."

She ushered the girl down the stairs, wrapped her in her cape and hurried her outside to climb into the buggy. She sat next to Katherine.

"Rosie, come with us," Mary begged, scooting over to make room on the seat.

"I must stay here."

"But the man is looking for you," Susan warned.

"And if he finds me it will give you more time to get away." She hugged Joseph and kissed his forehead.

"*Gott* protect you all. Now hurry. Head north and then take the turnoff for town."

Her heart nearly broke with fear that the children and Aunt Katherine would not be able to escape in time.

Rosie would be the decoy. Her own well-being did not matter if the children and her aunt were kept safe.

Ezra! Her heart lurched. *Dear Gott, keep him safe as well!*

Chapter Twenty-One

Rosie ran to the edge of the property, where she could
see the car below. Wagner was driving like a maniac,
coming much too fast up the mountain road. She could
make out his face behind the wheel. If she could see
him, he could see her.

His eyes widened. He accelerated even more.

She needed to hide. But where? She ran along the
drive and stopped at the entrance to the workshop.
Something prompted her to reach for the knob. The
door opened. Relieved, she stepped inside, then gasped,
seeing the stains on the cement floor that surely marked
where the Stoltzes had died.

She closed the door behind her and ran to a row of
buggies in various stages of completion. Ezra had probably helped his father build the buggies, yet after his
death, the work had never been finished.

Seeing a large, open hole in the flooring, she stepped
forward and peered down to where a partially framed
buggy sat on a wooden platform. The platform, attached
to a hydraulic lift, looked like an elevator of sorts that
moved equipment from one floor to another.

Rosie backed away from the steep drop-off, thinking again of the fall she had taken, days earlier. Wagner had shoved her down the ravine; she would not let him shove her down the opening today.

The sound of the car turning onto the drive made her heart pound. Her mouth went dry. She grabbed a wooden mallet off the nearby workbench. The heft of it brought a sense of security—a false sense of security she soon realized. Even with the mallet, she would be no match against Larry Wagner.

Gott, help me.

Needing to hide, she climbed into a buggy that looked ready to sell. The upholstery smelled new. An extra piece of the heavy fabric lay behind the second seat. She crawled under the swatch, just as the workshop door opened and Wagner stepped inside.

Rosie tucked herself into a ball and thought of Ezra. Where was he? Wherever he was, she prayed he was safe.

O'Donnell had tied Ezra's hands and feet, but he had not bound them to the chair. As soon as the nursing-home manager left the cabin and drove off, Ezra rocked forward and stood, balancing on his tied legs. He hopped toward the worktable, his gaze focused on a utility knife with a razor-sharp blade.

Leaning forward, Ezra stretched out his hands until he made contact with the knife and nudged it closer. Once within reach, he grabbed the handle and carefully positioned the blade against the rope wrapped around his wrists. With short strokes, he sawed back and forth through the thick hemp.

He glanced at the wall clock, his heart sinking. Time

was passing too quickly. His hands cramped from the awkward position, but he would not give up. Rosie was in danger, and he needed to protect her.

He kept slicing the knife against the rope until, finally, with one last forceful thrust, the binding broke free. Relief swept over him. He bent over, freed his legs and raced for the door. He had to get to Rosie before it was too late.

Chapter Twenty-Two

Hunkered down in the back of the buggy, Rosie was too scared to cry and terrified that Mr. Wagner would see the buggy shake with her trembling. Thoughts of all the struggle he had caused flooded over her, bringing an unexpected swell of determination to outsmart this man who had brought so much pain to so many.

She gripped the mallet, ready to strike if she was discovered. Violence was not the Amish way but neither was quiet acquiescence in the face of evil. She needed to protect the children and stop this heinous creature who would, most surely, do them harm. The longer he remained in the workshop, intent on finding her, the more time they would have to get away.

Please, Gott, she silently prayed.

Wagner's footsteps sounded on the cement floor. Slowly, steadily, he moved closer. She imagined him peering into each buggy, trying to find her.

"Rosie?" he called, his voice low. "Can you hear me?"

He knew she was in the workshop. Did he hear her heart pounding and her pulse thumping all too loudly?

She refused to think of what he would do to her. She only knew what would happen to the children if he found them. She had to distract Wagner until the children could get to safety.

"Rosie?" He stepped closer.

She bit down on her lip, trying to focus on that discomfort instead of his nearness.

"Ezra's hurt and calling for you," the man taunted. "He needs you, Rosie. I'll take you to him."

Lies!

"You know Ezra is a handsome man," Wagner continued. "He likes you, Rosie. He wants to be with you."

She longed to cover her ears and drown out his voice.

"You're hiding from me, only I don't know why. Surely you're not afraid of me."

He stepped closer, then closer still.

The slightest movement would—

In one fell swoop, he threw back the covering and grabbed her arm.

Rosie screamed.

Wagner tightened his hold. "I've got you now."

The mallet dropped from her hands. Unable to pull free, she kicked and gouged her short fingernails into the palm of his hand.

Rage flared his nostrils. "Where's the information Will gave you?" he demanded. "I need it. Now."

She shook her head and continued to thrash her free hand against his face. Her feet pummeled his chest.

He yanked her from the buggy. She fell onto the cement floor, landing on her side. "Aagh!"

Pain ricocheted across her shoulder and down her spine. She clawed at the cement to get away. He kicked her side. Air whooshed from her lungs. She rolled to her stomach, drew up her legs and started to crawl.

He grabbed her hair and pulled back her head. She screamed with pain. He loosened his hold, then kicked her again. She collapsed, unable to breathe.

"Where is it? Where's the information?" His face was next to hers. His rancid breath fanned her neck.

"Tell me," he threatened.

"I have…nothing."

He slapped her face. "Don't lie to me."

She rolled against the buggy. "A toy…for the baby. That is all Will gave me."

"Where is it?"

"In the house."

"Take me there."

She tried to stand. Her legs buckled.

He kicked her again.

"No!" she cried.

"Stand up," he demanded.

Glancing down into the nearby hole, she felt her stomach roil. She grabbed the spokes of the buggy wheel and pulled herself upright.

He laughed at her struggle.

Through matted hair, she stared at the evil flashing from his eyes. "You killed Ezra's parents."

He shook his head. "You've got that wrong. My boys killed them. They needed money and wanted to earn it on their own."

"You call murder a way to earn money? You are despicable."

"I told them no one would track them down and no one has. Not until you. Did Will tell you what happened?"

"Was he involved?"

Wagner laughed. "What do you think?"

"Tell me!"

"First, give me the information Will provided, then you can learn the truth about your boyfriend."

"You killed William because he knew too much. He wanted to leave town, to get away from you, but he needed evidence. Did he blackmail you?"

"He thought he was smart, but Will was stupid and easy to kill."

"You have no goodness within you."

He tipped back his head and laughed.

The door at the far end of the shop opened.

Ezra!

Rosie's heart stopped. He had come to save her, but saving her meant putting himself in danger. Tears burned her eyes. She blinked them back, needing a way to distract her assailant.

"You loved my mother," she said, baiting him. "But she wanted nothing to do with you."

"What are you talking about?" Wagner snarled and stepped closer to the drop off. "If Emma had married me, you could have been *my* daughter."

"I thank *Gott* for the father I have," Rosie responded.

He raised up, ready to lunge at her.

"Wagner." Ezra's voice sounded loud and menacing.

Larry startled and turned too quickly. His foot slipped over the edge of the drop off. He flailed his arms, trying to gain his balance, and toppled backward into the pit, his hands thrashing the air, his scream echoing in the workshop. He landed with a thump.

Nausea swept over Rosie, followed by vertigo. She clutched the wheel of the buggy, ready to collapse, but before her legs gave way, Ezra was there, wrapping her in his arms.

"Are you all right?"

She nodded.

"Wait here." He glanced into the pit and hit a large button on a sturdy pipe attached to the floor. Slowly, the dropped platform, carrying Larry Wagner, rose to the first floor and came to a stop.

Ezra grabbed rope and tied Wagner's hands and legs to the nearby support column before hurrying back to Rosie.

"Wagner's alive, and he will come to soon. Where are the children?"

"In the buggy, headed to Peter's house. He will notify the Willkommen sheriff."

"We need to join them there." Ezra wrapped his arm around her shoulder and ushered her out of the workshop and toward the barn.

"Are you sure you are okay?" He touched her hands, her arms. He ran his fingers over her back.

Tears streamed from her eyes.

"Talk to me, Rosie. Where are you hurt?"

She was in shock, and suddenly unable to speak. All she could do was step into Ezra's embrace. He held her tight as she cried. Her tears were for all that had happened since she had first fallen in love with Will. For her mistake that caused so much pain to her parents and to Will and to Ezra's parents.

"Rosie, it is over. Larry Wagner will not hurt you again. The manager of the nursing home is on his way out of town with the pharmacist, but they will be found."

"Too much has happened, Ezra."

"What do you mean?"

"I cannot stay," she gasped, knowing they had no future.

"You have to, Rosie. You and Joseph."

"Every time you look at my son you will think of his father, one of the men who killed your parents."

"My mother said, 'Doppelgänger,' that means two people."

"But there could have been someone else, namely Will."

"He may have overheard me bragging about the money my father kept in his shop, but other people were within earshot that day, including your boss at the nursing home. O'Donnell could have shared the information with the twins."

"You are trying to make me feel better."

"I want you to stay, Rosie. My parents died sixteen months ago." He provided the exact date. "My life changed that day, but when you—"

Rosie gulped in a deep breath. "Are you sure of the date?"

"*Yah*, of course, I am sure of this."

"That was the day Will drove me to Dahlonega. We found a drug store and I bought the pregnancy kit."

She grabbed his arms. "It was the day I found out I was pregnant. We had a leisurely lunch in town and did not get home until late that evening. That means Will was not involved with the robbery or the murders."

"Rosie, even if he had been involved, that would not have changed the way I feel about you or Joseph."

The sound of an automobile caused them to glance down the hill. Ezra let out a sigh of relief and motioned the car forward. Rosie wiped the tears from her cheeks as the vehicle pull into the driveway.

Willkommen Sheriff's Department was stenciled on

the side of the car. Aaron and his friend Peter sat in the passenger seat next to a big guy in uniform behind the wheel.

Ezra squeezed her hand. "Looks like law enforcement has finally arrived."

that night. She sat up, as she read the words. Corrupt. Beloved town. She loved the village. How could it be corrupt and cursed if she did not get outside before the clock struck twelve... "Did you put this away?" he asked.

Chapter Twenty-Three

Rosie sat in the living area of the Stoltz house later that same day, holding Joseph in her lap, relieved that all the children were home and unharmed. The EMTs had bandaged the cut on her forehead and a bad scrape on her arm. She was sore and bruised, but thankful to be alive.

"We went as fast as we could," David said, his eyes wide, his words tripping one over the other, as he explained the children's escape down the back of the mountain. "Mary was crying, but Katherine told her *Gott* would provide."

"I was scared," the little girl said truthfully. She slipped her hand into Rosie's. "I did not want anything to happen to you."

"You were brave, Mary." Rosie looked at all of them. "You were all very brave."

"We went to Peter's house," Belinda explained. "And stayed with his *mamm* while Aaron and Peter hurried to the grocery and called the Willkommen sheriff's department."

"The pharmacist had already notified them," Aaron added. "Rayleen had let Mr. O'Donnell think she liked him, but all the time she had been gathering evidence on the drug operation. She knew the police in town were corrupt and feared if she did not get outside help, she might end up dead, like the nurse."

"But how did you boys meet up with the sheriff?" Ezra asked.

"We saw his car parked in front of the pharmacy and ran to tell him what was happening on the mountain. He wanted us to show him the way, although he planned to drop us at a neighbor's house. When you waved us forward, Ezra, we knew we would be safe."

"The sheriff's timing was perfect," Ezra said. "And the local police and ambulance arrived soon after the sheriff."

"Did they catch the manager of the nursing home?" Belinda asked.

Ezra nodded. "*Yah*, Mr. O'Donnell was apprehended with a suitcase filled with patient drugs from the nursing home. The staff is being questioned and the FBI has been called in to determine if any drugs crossed state lines. The Wagner twins and Dr. Manny were also arrested, and law enforcement is studying the information Rosie was able to provide on a flash drive."

"What about Mr. Wagner?" David asked.

"He is in the hospital now and expected to recover." Rosie patted the boy's shoulder. "Why do you ask, Davey?"

"Before we dropped your aunt Katherine off at her house, she said she knew him when he was a young man. He made mistakes and did not try to be a good person. She said we should always try to do our best."

Rosie nodded. "Katherine is right. I wish she could have been with us this evening, but she is leaving in the morning to visit her sister and will stay for Christmas."

The children sat in silence for a long moment, each one, no doubt, reflecting on what had happened.

"I give thanks to *Gott* that we are all together." Ezra shared what Rosie was thinking.

Suddenly, he glanced at the wall clock and smiled. "Get your coats and capes, children. We must hurry to the schoolhouse."

Mary looked confused, then her face widened into an excited smile. "The Christmas pageant."

She placed her hand on Joseph's forehead. "He feels cool, Rosie. We still need a baby Jesus."

Rosie laughed. "I think Joseph would like to be in the pageant as long as you will be near him, Mary."

"Did I not tell you?" Her face beamed. "Because my name is Mary, I get to hold Joseph while the angels sing and the shepherds visit the manger scene."

David stuck out his chest. "I am a wise man."

Ezra laughed and ruffled David's hair. "You are wise beyond your years. Now hurry, children, so we can get to school on time."

The schoolhouse was abuzz with activity when Rosie and Ezra found seats. Mary held Joseph and stood near the front of the classroom with a blue veil draped over her blond hair. Joseph was wrapped in a blanket, looking sweet and innocent. David stood to the side with the other two wise men.

Susan had found John Keim in the crowd and was sitting next to him. Belinda was chatting with a girlfriend and Aaron and Peter were surrounded by friends, who probably wanted to hear more about riding in the sheriff's car.

Rosie sighed, relieved that she knew a little more

about Will's involvement with the drug racket. He had attempted to gather evidence to incriminate the guilty, although whether he planned to give the evidence to the authorities or use it as leverage to be free of the operation, she would never know. At least he had not been involved in the robbery and murders.

Ezra placed his hand on her shoulder. She smiled at the warmth of his gaze and the strength of him as his arm touched hers. The teacher snapped her fingers to get the children's attention. The room started to quiet.

"Mary kept her secret about being the star of the pageant," Rosie whispered.

Ezra nodded. "Usually she tells everything, but she kept this a surprise. No wonder she wanted Joseph to be in the pageant."

He leaned closer and winked playfully. "There is a secret I have not told you yet."

Her cheeks warmed. She tilted her head. "Is it a Christmas secret?"

"Hmm. I guess it is."

"Are you going to tell me?"

"Not now." He glanced at the front of the classroom. "The pageant is starting. I will tell you later."

Chapter Twenty-Four

That night, after the evening meal had been eaten and the dishes washed and put away, the children went upstairs as if they knew Ezra and Rosie needed time alone.

Susan offered to put Joseph to bed and Rosie appreciated her thoughtfulness.

Ezra took Rosie's hand once they were alone. "Remember the night John Keim came to the door to talk to Susan and you said they would huddle in the cold just to be together?"

She nodded. "I remember."

"If you do not mind, I would prefer we stay inside to talk."

Rosie laughed. "Otherwise the children would be watching us through their bedroom windows."

He squeezed her hand. "I wanted to tell you how much you mean to me, Rosie, and how I need you in my life. So much has happened recently and some people would think that more time would be needed, but I have loved you my whole life."

Her heart nearly burst at his words, the feeling of being loved and accepted filling her to overflowing.

"I love you," he said again. "I have always loved you since I first noticed you in school, only you never had an interest in me, and I never thought I had a chance to win your heart. If not for the mistakes we both made, if not for the pain of losing my parents, I might never have had the courage to tell you how I feel."

"Oh, Ezra, you don't know what you are saying."

"But I do know—I know I love you, and just as Mary said, I want you and Joseph to be part of our family. I want to be Joseph's father and help you raise him. He is wonderful baby, and he will grow into a *gut* man. But I want more children, and we will add onto our house. Aaron and I will run the buggy shop and make good buggies for the community that will bring honor to my father's name. He was not proud of my actions before his death, but he always knew that with *Gott*'s help, I could turn my life around. First, I must be baptized, then…"

"It is too soon for us, Ezra. You do not know what you are saying."

"Rosie, you are a beautiful woman. You make me a better man. I want to spend my life with you forever, if you will have me."

"You are you asking me to marry you?" she asked, unwilling to believe her ears.

He nodded. "If you say no, I will not be able to—"

Raising on tiptoe, she captured his lips with hers, and cuddled more closely against him, both of them melding together. When she finally pulled back, she smiled sweetly.

"My answer is yes." She laughed. "Yes, Ezra Stoltz, I will marry you."

"On Christmas?"

She shook her head. "You know the banns must be

announced in church for three weeks. We must prepare the house. The children will help. I will ask Susan to be my attendant. Dresses need to be stitched. I must buy a new *kapp*. Food must be cooked so that everyone will be able to join in our celebration."

"Your parents?"

"*Yah*, I will talk to my *datt* and tell him I understand why he was hard on me. I must forgive him. Then perhaps he will be able to forgive me."

"And I will talk to the bishop about accepting baptism." Ezra pulled her closer. "For so long, I struggled with anger and guilt, but now my heart holds only joy."

His eyes twinkled as he gazed down at her. "We will tell the children after we read the Nativity story on Christmas morn. Until then it will be our Christmas secret."

"I like secrets," she sighed, "when I share them with you."

She turned her face to his. Her heart soared as they kissed, sealing the promise of their future together.

"Merry Christmas, Rosie."

"Merry Christmas, Ezra. You have given me the best gifts of all—the gift of family, the gift of a future walking at your side and, most important, the gift of love."

He brushed his lips against her forehead. "*Gott* rescued us from a place of darkness and brought us into His light."

She nodded. "He has blessed both of us by bringing us together. Forever."

"Which is how long I want to keep kissing you." Ezra's voice was low and husky with emotion as he lowered his lips to hers.

Forever, she thought, was not nearly long enough.

* * * * *

"You don't ever complain. You take care of someone
else's *kinder* without hesitation, and you're giving them a
home they haven't had in who knows how long."

"Trust me. There was plenty of hesitation on my part."

"I do trust you."

Beth Ann's breath caught at the undercurrent of
emotion in his simple answer. "I'm glad to hear that. I got
a message from their social worker this afternoon. She
was supposed to come tomorrow, which is why I stayed
home today to make sure everything was as perfect as
possible before her visit."

"I wondered why you didn't come to the project house
today."

"That's why, but now her visit is going to be the day after tomorrow. What if she decides to take the children and place them in other homes? What if they can't be together?"

Robert paused and faced her. "Why are you looking for trouble? God brought you to the *kinder*. He knows what lies before them and before you. Trust *Him*."

"I try to." She gave him a wry grin. "It's just…just…"

"They've become important to you?"

She nodded, not trusting her voice to speak. The idea of the three youngsters being separated in the foster care system frightened her, because she wasn't sure what they might do to get back together.

"Don't forget," Robert murmured, "as important as they are to you, they're even more important to God." His smile returned. "How about getting some Christmas pie before we have to fish three *kinder* out of the brook?"

With a yelp, she rushed forward to keep Crystal from hoisting Tommy to see over the rail. Robert was right. She needed to enjoy the children while she could.

Don't miss
An Amish Holiday Family *by Jo Ann Brown,*
available November 2020 wherever
Love Inspired books and ebooks are sold.

LoveInspired.com

HARLEQUIN

Heartfelt or suspenseful, inspiring or passionate, Harlequin has your happily-ever-after.

With new books published
every month, you are sure to find the
satisfying escape you know you deserve.

HNEWS2020